REALMS OF EDENOCHT

The War Wizard

Realms of Edenocht

D.S. JOHNSON

The War Wizard
A Young Adult Fantasy Fiction Action Adventure Novel

DS JOHNSON
2020

First Printing: 2020

ISBN 978-1-7339333-4-6

Illustrator -DS Johnson

Rosecrest printing
Herriman, Utah 84096
www.dsjohnsonbooks.com

Dedication

To my son's Joshua and Ryan who always wanted a bedtime story. To my husband Don who patiently waited for me to do the dishes while I was engrossed in learning how to write a novel for the kids. To my sister Hannah who helped brainstorm plot and characters on so many occasions.

To all my readers young and old, thank you for giving me a chance to take you on an MMORPG book experience.

Contents

Realms of Edenocht

Prologue-Destruction of Srinna Vossa

The Rise and Fall of The Necromancer- the end of the Realms

She's... Sinking... The... City!

Bright-white flashes burst from their fingertips, and hues of an electric blue shot across the rotunda with a deafening crack. The once impeccable crystal stone cracked like a twig. Half-crouched and slightly leaned back, he stretched out his hand and slipped under the downward slash of a long blade already dripping. He leaped into the air and flipped over the concourses of the sky-blue robes of the Commission.

Gavin Rhill's treacherous needs exempted him from feeling and his conscience was now void. Eyes bloodshot with fury, he sank into the depths of his insanity. The popping cracks of the fire and ice elements against each other reverberated across the slick floor, tousling him about and jarring him from his thoughts. Dust plumes erupted from pockets of crumbling walls, and he gripped his shaking head as he pleaded to be released from his harrowing prison. But it was too late, he belonged to the Shadow now.

The hairs on the back of his neck stood out straight, and a rippling effect crawled up and down his skin. An electrifying-bolt of unyielding energy surged past his ear. He flipped his long black hair from his flat-gray eyes, which sunk deep into the pallid hollow of his face. The pungent odor of singed hair and flesh stifled his nose and wreaked havoc on his focus. Anger and hate surged from his bosom.

Sweat dripped onto his sliver-thin black eyebrows and down his face and landed at the corner of his mouth. He glowered over the madness and zeroed in on the door at the end of the mysterious hall and searched for an acceptable route to his destination. Gavin seized his opportunity and flung himself into the air. He rolled over an on-coming deluge of potent magic, but the heat burst his blood-red cloak into flames.

Gavin slipped his arms out of his battle robe and twisted away from the engulfing barrage. He rolled into the fall and jumped to his feet and shut the roaring shrieks from his ears. The pounding of his heart as he flipped over a spear beat heavily in his head. He thrust his hands out and released his newly acquired powers. Rock fragments pierced the air like speeding razors and struck several of the newly arrived armored men. Cursed with unrelenting pain, it paralyzed them from the inside, and they crumpled to the floor. He dug his toes into the floor and boosted himself with a blast of air, and whizzed past so fast, the soldiers spun in their boots.

"Gavin, stop!" Castos yelled.

Castos, the leader of Queen Ambrosia's United Forces, stood erect.

"You can't stop me," Gavin's voice was high, and his words dripped off his lips like thick syrup. The thought welled up inside his chest like a smoldering flame, and he could taste it, smell it, and see his destiny. "I have destroyed your beautiful Srinna Vossa," he said.

Gavin's hissy tone and cynical smile bit at Castos' nerves. Castos anger surged, and he slammed his long gold-entwined staff on the ground.

"We will rebuild it. You can't stop goodness. How many people have to die?" Castos said.

"You're worse off than I thought," Gavin said.

Gavin threw his head back and laughed a humorless vicious sound. Castos crossed the staff in front of his broad-carved expression and lifted his palm face up and conjured the elements he controlled. A crackling fire burst into existence and danced on his flesh.

"Time to put an end to this senseless bloodshed," Castos said.

Castos lifted his staff high and with the fire particles of the universe, he sent the ravaged energy directly at Gavin. Gavin sucked in his belly, pulled in his arms and legs, and transformed into an invisible shriek of air. He rushed over Castos and fed the inferno with life breathing oxygen. The air pulled the fire back toward Castos and unleashed it onto its own master. The fire didn't care what it consumed, simply that it feasted on life's sustenance. Absolute horror hit a split-second before Castos was annihilated by his own power.

Gavin sailed through the air with exhilarated weightlessness. His thunderous laughter rattled the windows until they shattered and sent glass shards careening to the ground. Gavin Rhill soared down the long corridors, disarming enchantments along the paths. When he reached the door, he hovered momentarily, then unraveled the misty tendrils of the air element and transformed back into his human form. His skinny, almost malnourished figure emerged.

The towering solid wood door was intricately carved with ancient symbols and runes. Gavin's long thin fingers manipulated the old puzzle which had taken him over a year to figure out. With the last knot pushed, the door opened with a gasp. A small puff of wind bathed his face with the odor of musky dust. An aroma he quite enjoyed. He heaved the heavy obstacle open and slipped inside. Gavin waved his hand across the smooth orderly lines on the inside of the door and several clicks and a few slides of unseen latches echoed against the hollow roundness of the room as it sealed shut.

Gavin's bones ached from the cold darkness. His shadow ran across the tiles and his heart jumped. A lump formed in his throat until he realized it was *his* shadow and not *the* Shadow. He searched the circular room and found a large, majestic desk on the far side. Heavy weaved curtains framed tall windows, and he found a slight beauty in the carved vaults. Every wall was covered top to bottom with shelves of scrolls and books that were so jammed pack they overflowed.

"You must not fail," a deep echoey voice said.

The Shadow's voice ripped through his mind and the horrifying image of the shadow sent shivers down his spine. He shook it off and picked up the first parchment on top of the desk, read the heading and tossed it on the floor. He picked up another, then another. His intrigue half stopped him, but he knew he had but a few moments until the Council would know where he was. He put his thoughts aside and hastily rummaged through the scrolls and parchments that sat barren and lonely.

"Where is it?" he snarled.

He ravaged the last few particles of writings as the persistent gnawing in his navel grew. With one foul sweep of his arms, he sent the rest flying to the floor. He slammed his fits on the table, his knuckles pure white. A bead of sweat dripped from his drooped-head and splashed onto the marble surface. He stared into the backs of his eyelids and tried to think where the Binding of the Crypt spell would be hidden.

Then it came to him. *How have I forgotten the search spell?* He thought. Gavin closed his eyes and focused, and a dusting of rusty orange sparkles danced into existence and floated about the room. His heart skipped a beat as the magic was sucked into a book, but then shoved back out. Over and over, the magic came up empty. His emotions couldn't take anymore, and his fear of failure, and what the Shadow would do to him, threw him into a rage. Gavin's tantrum sent books, scrolls, and reading implements flying around the room. Loud booms and cracks echoed against the outer walls of the secret vault of Srinna Vossa, and shrieks of agony crested the horizon.

****

"Queen Ambrosia, what do you want us to do?" Aarin asked.

"We wait until the Commission gets here," Queen Ambrosia said.

Queen Ambrosia's soul was plagued with pain and sorrow as she gazed down from her sixty-level skyscraper. Her beloved Srinna Vossa was under attack, and she knew her time was limited. The peaks of the circling spires that surrounded the main building barely passed her flat. The three moons reflected brilliant strings of haze and illuminated the night. Srinna Vossa was a group of islands that floated on the Teorran Belt, which was raw magic that sprung into the sky like a fountain.

"Our magic defenses are about to fall, and if the Velshari breakthrough, it will be all over," Aarin said.

Arron's once bright eyes were now pained and wounded.

"They will have to hold. We can't let them into the city," Ambrosia said.

"Do you not care? Your people will die, *all* of them. The Velshari has the comet at their disposal. Never in history has anything been able to break our defenses," Aarin said.

Ambrosia turned on her heel and shot him a penetrating glare, and he found her eyes were red and puffy from crying.

"Do *not* proceed to lecture *me* on caring for *my* people. I will lay down my life for them. I will take the scrolls of the most importance with me to my death. How dare you accuse me?"

Ambrosia's small slender frame shook with fury, her knuckles clenched white at her sides. The pressures she held as Queen of the most powerful city on Edenocht all but overcame her. Aarin stood at attention. His face shadowed from a lack of sleep.

"I'm sorr-"

"You are not permitted to speak," Ambrosia said.

Ambrosia threw her hand across her body in a downward strike. Her cheeks burned dark pink and her long, pale blue robe blew slightly in the wind that came in from the open balcony. Ambrosia's soft slipper shoes kicked her gown into a rhythmic billowing pattern as she paced the floor.

"How dare he," Ambrosia said.

Her words were barely audible, and her breath steamed in the coolness of the night. Aarin's chest tightened, and he struggled to breathe, and he went weak in the knees. Sweat crested his shoulder-length brown hair, and he feared he was about to be sent to his death for questioning her. A brisk wind coursed around the room and a flicker of light cast a shadow as a forest-green wyvern landed on the balcony. The rider dismounted and tossed the reins over its neck, and the wyvern pulled in her massive wings tightly to her side and pawed the smooth surface. The rider pulled off his black leather riding gloves and slipped them under his belt. His chain armor under his obsidian body armor clinked as he moved toward the queen. His square and handsome face framed his deep green eyes. Tears escaped as Ambrosia ran into his arms.

"Jerim, what are we going to do?" Ambrosia asked.

She buried her tear-stained cheeks into the crease of his shoulder, and he wrapped his arms around her and pulled her tight.

"I'm here now with the Rangers, and the commission has dispatched their troops. I've stationed six battalions at each corner of the island and more on the smaller islands. Medrith and I will take you and Serin to safety," Jerim said.

Ambrosia swallowed the lump in her throat.

"No, I must stay here," Ambrosia said.

"But Ambrosia," Jerim objected.

Jerim pulled back from her and rested his warm hands on her bare shoulders. The cool of her skin felt good under the heat of his.

"No, you must take Serin to the Wyvern realm where she will be safe," the queen wiped her eyes with a handkerchief, "You must promise me you will take care of her. Promise," she demanded.

Realization overcame his mind, and his worst fear was now coming true. He was going to lose her forever, and all he could do was nod and whisper.

"I will," Jerim said.

"Good, then I will send for the inner circle to secure the scrolls," Ambrosia said, "Aarin, send for the mages."

"Yes, your highness," Aarin said.

"Oh, and Aarin," the hairs on the back of his neck stood as the chills ran down his spine, "I'm sorry for losing my temper."

Aarin nodded and left the room. Ambrosia bit her lip to keep it from quivering and wrung her hands tightly.

"Ambrosia, tell me, what happened," Jerim said.

Jerim moved to the long meeting table and pulled out a soft velvet tall-back chair and motioned for her to sit. Ambrosia sat down eloquently, resting her intertwined fingers in her lap. She explained that the day had started out quiet and non-eventful, but by mid-morning, the alarms had sounded and Gavin Rhill's airships had surrounded the horizon and the Velshari attacked the magical barriers around the city.

"Wait, you said they arrived mid-morning, and the shield dropped fifty percent power by early afternoon? Why did you wait so long to notify me?" Jerim asked.

Ambrosia's eyes widened as the realization stabbed at her heart.

"I thought the mages could handle it," Ambrosia said.

He gave her hand a gentle squeeze.

"Go on," Jerim said.

Jerim sat back in his chair with his arms crossed and his brows scrunched together in the middle of his face as she recited the rest of the events.

"They haven't broken the shields yet and now that you're here everything will be alight," Ambrosia said.

Ambrosia's words were more to convince herself than Jerim. She stood and slowly returned to the soft flowing pale-blue drapes that danced in the night breeze of the open arched doorway of her balcony. Jerim wanted to grab her and Serin and throw them onto his wyvern's back and race into the wyvern's realms and never come back. Jerim grappled at his emotions and his love for her, and his heart sank. He had known her since they were children and were supposed to get married, but the universe had other plans, and he was forced to love her from a distance. He swallowed the lump in his throat, and he scooted his chair out and placed it back under the table. Jerim came up behind her and wrapped his arms around her waist. He leaned into her and kissed the top of her head.

"I must tend to the ranks, but I will return soon," Jerim said.

Ambrosia gripped his arm and squeezed tightly.

"Be careful, you made a promise to me," Ambrosia said softly.

She turned in his embrace, and her eyes locked onto his. Her eyes were filled with fear, duty, and pain, and he leaned in and kissed her. The sensations coursed through their bodies, and they relished in a moment that might never happen again. Jerim didn't want to release her, and he pulled her tighter. Ambrosia sank into his passion and struggled with her own thoughts of escape. Jerim pulled away and wiped a tear from her pale cheek. She was most exquisite, even after hours of crying, and he wanted to remember absolutely every detail of her face.

"I will. I love you Ambrosia Svirtari of the Travelers," Jerim said.

Ambrosia's heart leaped, Svirtari was the sir name they would have had if they had married and Jerim was her one and *only* love. He released her and forced himself to step back and pulled his gloves out of his belt and slipped them on. The wyvern lowered her body to the ground, and he grabbed the reins. Ambrosia flicked her finger and sent a tuft of air to boost him up. He swung his leg over the mighty beast and tightened the reins. The deep green colors of the Forest Wyvern glinted in the glows of the night as she stretched out her wings and shoved off with her thick hind legs. Jerim soared into the sky, and they met the captain of the Air Wyverns on the southern edge of the island.

"How is the Queen doing?" Eliot asked.

"She's holding up," Jerim searched the night sky. "What are the damages?" Jerim asked.

Eliot could tell Jerim's heart was broken. Eliot was his clan brother and understood the love they had had since they were children. Jerim rested one hand over the other on the horn of his saddle and the chinking of metal straps and belts the wyverns wore, clashed against the motion their wings made as they hovered in the night sky.

"We counted sixty fully-loaded airships near the borders. The scouts have reported three fleets making good time from the north. There are four fleets coming in from the south." Eliot said.

Eliot shifted his metal helmet and tried to keep the bile from escaping his esophagus.

"We need to take this battle away from the city. Send your fleet south and Oscar's north," Jerim said.

"Sir, when are the Earth Wyverns coming?" Eliot asked.

"I'm not sure they are," Jerim said.

"Why not?" Eliot asked.

"Torn bridges, I guess, now, get going," Jerim said.

Eliot saluted and yanked the reins. The mighty creature swooped toward his command, and he motioned to his battalion. Hundreds of crystal-white wyverns leaped into the sky. The sheer size of these magnificent creatures was breathtaking. Even more so, as their scales reflected and shimmered in the twinkling of the lights. Medrith and Jerim swooped in the opposite direction and over the island's lush green jungle. Homes and buildings lived in and under the protection of the jungle floor, along with the glorious white stone of the crystal city walls. The city's force fields were harnessed in large crystals at the top of evenly spaced spires that stood several hundred lengths tall and circled the outer rim of the city.

"Take down these airships," Jerim yelled.

Jerim hovered over the leader of the dark- blue Water Wyverns.

"Yes, sir," Greston grunted.

A sea of blue took to the sky and divided into groups and swarmed the airships. They pulled the elements of water and began flooding the ships. Plumes of steam filled the night sky, as the Velshari blocked with counterspells of fire to evaporate the water. The water wyverns, however, were stronger, and one by one the ships began to sink. It didn't seem to make much difference, as there were so many that when one ship fell, another took its place. Jerim flew back toward the city center, making his way to the Fire Wyverns. The deep-red and charcoal-black wyverns waited near the city's main port. Medrith's sharp claws gripped the treetops as she landed.

"What are your orders?" Ada asked.

Ada's long copper red hair flowed off the back of her head and her oval face was delicately pointed and garnished with a dusting of ginger freckles on her high cheeks.

"Keep your forces here on Srinna Vossa," Jerim said.

Ada nodded and shot into the sky. Her platoon had more experience in battle and riding, but they found it hard to keep up with her ferocity. She had more to prove than just being able to lead her people. Gavin Rhill murdered her father trying to find the scroll, and she was just plain angry.

Medrith released the branches, and the treetops flicked back and forth, but before Jerim could make it more than a hundred lengths, a deafening crack scorched the night sky, leaving a scar of brilliant opal light. Shattered crystals tumble to the ground and the barrier into the city fell, releasing a flood of red-robed Velshari into the main port. Medrith stopped dead in her tracks, rolled her head, flipped upside down, and barreled back toward the open gate. When Jerim reached the north side of the island, he saw Ada's forces engaged with the oncoming attackers.

Shrieks of agony cried out as massive blasts of fire billowed from the guts of the fire wyverns. The sky lit up as though it were noonday, and everything nearby melted and withered. Another deafening crack reverberated across the sky as another crystal shattered. Small bursts of icy white lighting strikes tangled with bursts of bright blood-red bolts sprinkled the horizon. A small ball of flaming gas in the distant horizon appeared to grow a little bigger, and Jerim tried to deny the pulsing knot growing in his stomach.

"The Comet of Sariandi, the Goddess of Destruction," Medrith said.

"I guess it's true then," Jerim said.

"The Commission is here on the eastern shores," Medrith said.

Medrith stretched out her long neck and Jerim laid close to her as she beat her wings toward the eastern shore. When they reached the shore, they descended like a falling stone. Medrith pulled up at the last second and set down without even a thud. Jerim dismounted and ran through the sand and waited as the enormous airships slipped up onto the fading sandy shores. Half-lowered planks plunged into the soft moist grit upon reaching the shore. A stalky brute of a man scaled the long plank and made his way to Jerim.

"Jerim, what are the damages?" Trendell barked.

"We have lost two of the towers," he gripped the short, stalky, brute of a man, tightly at the forearm, "We need to evacuate the city and secure the inner buildings," Jerim said.

The clanking and banging of swords, spears, and armor overpowered the distant sounds of agony. Hordes of men in rows of fours rushed from the ship's cargo bays and filled the shores with men standing at attention awaiting orders.

"Yes, Sir," Trendell said.

Trendell banged his hand against his chest and turned, leading with his head, and briskly reached the front line. The Commission was divided into ranks of archers, spear and swordsmen, and elemental mages. Trendell barked out his orders and with an enormous shout, the Commission broke up, each group making their way to their destinations.

"Jerim, we saw a battle already in action. Why are we just now evacuating the city? Shouldn't we have done that sooner?" Trendell asked.

His voice was confused and hurt.

"The Rangers arrived not long ago, the mages thought they could handle it," Jerim said.

"I see," Trendell said.

"This is going to be a very difficult battle," Jerim said.

"What do you say by that?" Trendell asked.

"The Sariandi Comet is coming," Jerim said.

Trendell's head lowered.

"Well, then we fight to the death," Trendell said.

"With honor, brother," Jerim said.

"With honor," Trendell repeated.

Trendell gripped Jerim's forearm tightly, then joined his men in the barrage of oncoming Velshari. Ada moved to the sky as the Commission took over the land battle. She turned her attention to the oncoming airships and joined her second battalion. A group of Velshari yelped, as large vines wrapped around their bodies, and swallowed them into the ground. Jerim had commanded the foliage around the inner buildings to devour the Velshari. The sun's first rays broke through and danced on the heavy smoke that filled the sky. Bursts of flames erupted around the island, and rain and windstorms chased fiery lighting strikes into the sky.

The outer perimeter sections of brilliant-white stone walls now sat in rubble. Storms of arrows went buzzing and fizzing into the sky, and metal boots slogged between the slippery sludge of fallen comrades. Swords swooshed and clanked as they met other swords. The closer the comet came, the stronger the Velshari became, making it harder for the Commission. Chaos and confusion surged the city. A sea of red cloaks engulfed every road and alleyway, throwing magic and swinging swords at everything that moved. The white stone was now stained red and smeared with black shadows of what used to be men.

"Fall back and send a squad to the city center. Set up blockades," Trendell called.

Amid the clouds that hung over the island, Trendell saw the comet barreling toward them with a shield of fiery damnation. His heart sank into his stomach and a tightening in his chest practically took his breath. He swooped his sword upward and blocked a dart of lightning aimed directly at his chest.

****

Ambrosia gritted her teeth.

"There's more than one person that can use the power of the comet," Ambrosia said.

"What are you going to do?" Aarin asked.

"Sink the island and destroy Srinna Vossa," Ambrosia said.

Ambrosia walked sternly toward her deep-oak desk, and Aarin's stomach lurched inside him as the words hit his mind.

"How? Why?!" Aarin asked.

"With this," Ambrosia pulled out a long parchment that was rolled tightly, "The Incantation of Undin," she said, fingering the edge.

"And how will sinking the island stop Gavin Rhill?" Aarin asked.

"It's the only way to destroy the Teorran Belt," she said, dropping one end.

"But that would kill everyone on the islands, and the earth below?" Aarin plead.

"Yes, and that is the tragedy that Gavin Rhill has brought upon us," Ambrosia said.

She slammed her fist into the hardened wood of her desk, and Aarin stifled the shock that was surpassing his emotions.

"Trust me, I have racked my brain for rotations for another way, but there isn't. I don't want to do this anymore than you or anyone else," Ambrosia said.

Her voice was shaky, and she trembled with the daunting task before her.

"What if we-" Aarin started.

"Aarin, there is no other way. Besides, even if there was, Gavin will torture every living thing until he finds it. This way he will believe it is buried in the center of the planet," Ambrosia said.

Her tone was full of defeat, and he understood that she indeed had been searching for another way, and he could now see the despair in her eyes. Ambrosia had not quite accepted her fate, and the understanding of not being able to raise her child and see her grow into a woman, to never be with Jerim again and her wonderful council and all her loved ones ate at her emotions. It was almost too much for her to bear.

"What shall I tell the armies?" Aarin asked.

"That its time and send Jerim," Ambrosia whispered.

Aarin bowed. His once childlike eyes were now eyes glazed over. Ambrosia studied the scroll once more and sat it on the desk and walked to the edge of the balcony. One hand on the cold stone and the other gripped her blue sapphire stone necklace. Her gold and teal blue robe draped gently over her tired body and her delicately woven crown sat on her pounding head. The anguished cries of her people now sat on numb ears. A small pink hand gripped the lower half of her robes. With the innocence of young age, a small girl gazed up.

"Mommy, what's happening?" Serin asked.

"Oh, my dear little one," the Queen picked up her little girl and buried her little girl's teary face into her shoulder, "Shhh shhhh shhh," Ambrosia whispered.

Ambrosia didn't see Jerim walked briskly up behind her. His clashing and clanking were hidden under the booms and crashes from the distance.

"Ambrosia, you sent for me?" Jerim asked.

Jerim found the little princess in her arms and his heart pounded against his ribs. He swallowed hard, shoving the bile back into his stomach.

"It's time," she whispered.

She could hardly see his bruised face amidst the heavy shield of her own tears.

"Is there any other way?" he asked.

"There is no other way,"

Jerim didn't want to accept the answer but had no choice.

"Alright," Jerim said.

Jerim slipped his arm around her waist and pulled her into his embrace. Her long blonde hair tickled his skin. He put his hand on the side of her face and leaned in. He stared into her eyes and slowly and thoughtfully he kissed her.

"I love you. I always have, and I always will," Jerim said.

"I love you too. I have to tell you something," she looked at Serin, then back to Jerim, "Serin is yours, not Mikal's," Jerim pulled back and studied Ambrosia's soft blue eyes. His heart swelled, and he smiled his intoxicating grin, "You're not mad?" she asked, "I'm sorry I never told you."

"Nor should you have. You were about to become Queen, and that would have complicated things," Jerim said.

"Mommy, I'm scared," the Princess said.

The tiny voice was shaky, and she played nervously with her mother's hair. Ambrosia studied her daughter's face one last time.

"You go with your father," Ambrosia said.

"Where?"

"Into the sky with the flyers, alright?"

Ambrosia's cool lips touched Serin's warm cheek as she gave her the last kiss she would ever give her.

"But when will I see you again?"

The queen gave Serin to Jerim, and he wrapped her in her blanket. Sobs escaped as Ambrosia's resolve was falling apart.

"Go... take her to the wyverns and never come back," Ambrosia managed.

With tears streaming down his face, Jerim bowed and leaped off the stone-carved terrace, and onto Medrith's back. Ambrosia sent a furling burst of air under the wyvern, throwing them into the sky above. Medrith pulled in her wings and shot into the sky like an arrow. To fight a war was one thing, but to give up one's own flesh and blood, is another, and she gripped the handrail for support. She watched the green dot disappear, then threw up her arms. Ambrosia called upon the powers of the Teorran Belt and began to recite the incantation.

****

Gavin's calculated plan turned to a frenzy of rash thoughts and feelings. Everywhere he searched, he couldn't find the scroll. Even with his search spell, it continued to elude him. He pulled and shoved every book and piece of parchment out of his way, and he hurled a massive spell around the room. Glittering strands of text danced and swayed around him, and one by one disappeared. The words he longed for were not found. The only words present were those left by the Grand Cleric.

Gavin Rhill,

You will never have this scroll as I have destroyed it once and for all.

If you continue your quest, you will be met with certain death. FOREVER!

Did you think that you were the only one that could use the comet's power?

Grand Cleric Mathieu

Gavin was shocked out of his delirium with the sudden shift and sensation of falling, and he ran to the window. Clouds of dust and smoke began to rise, and he slammed his fists on the stone wall.

"She's... sinking... the... city," he yelled.

He threw out his arms and sucked himself into the air. The sudden force blew out all the light in the room as he vanished. Gavin conjured a windstorm that careened through the city and wiped out everything in its path. Debris floated upward as the ground fell out from under it. The comet's power helped Queen Ambrosia stand perfectly still while chanting. Even as the island fell, she was as firm as she had been at first. The last words she uttered were that only a blood heir could enter the secrets of the forgotten city.

The Teorran fountain fell into the center of the ground below, and the islands plummeted into a new existence. Enormous rock walls encompassed the fallen earth, covering everything under hundreds of lengths of the ground. It left but a few of the spires that were still intact, standing as a reminder of what the glorious city once was.

1-What Funny Business Are You Up To

300 Years Since The End Of The Realms

Seconds before a deafening crack of thunder echoed, a flash of lightning crossed the darkened skies that frequent the isolated island. The ever-persistent clouds never gave much warning before unleashing their wrath, making this part of the sea barren of much life.

"Let's get a drink before we ship off. We're only halfway around the Turbulent Reef," Merrick said.

Merrick fought the howling wind and lashed the mooring line to the dock, and Shaz scaled the plank. Shaz pulled his tunic tight around his neck, and they walked briskly toward The Screaming Siren Tavern. They trudged up the hill and shielded their eyes from the wind and dirt. The dark clouds opened and dumped the heavy rain, and the soft dirt rapidly turned to mud. Merrick gripped the heavy latch and flung the door open, which smacked against the stone wall with a BANG.

A pitch-black jaguar prowled in behind the men like a shadow. No one noticed her until her bright yellow-orange eyes cautiously scanned the room. The black jaguar followed Shaz around a man that was half-slumped in a chair. The tavern was hardly quaint, but it was warm and designated as neutral territory and sailors, deckhands, and the occasional outlaw stopped here for a quick reprieve. Small wooden tables strewn about the tavern in no particular order, and large silver platters of meats and bread covered the tables. The pungent odor of alcohol mixed with sweat and tobacco filled the air. Each time the heavy wooden door swung open, eddies of cold air wafted throughout the room. Half-burned candles in sconces let off as much feeble light as they could. Long wooden planks hung over large tables acting as crude chandeliers were covered in spent wax.

The massive, ornately carved fireplace filled one full wall and the waring fire warmed the tavern with its simmering, crackling embers. The floor-length colorful skirts of the serving ladies brushed and swooshed as they busily moved from table to table helping hungry, thirsty and the occasional rude and grabby, customers.

"Quickly Shaz, before Yerild sails off without us," Merrick grumbled.

Merrick pulled off his wet cloak and tucked it into the crook of his elbow. His broad width navigated the crowded room toward the bar.

'Do you think Captain Yerild is crazy enough to set sail in this storm?' Shaz asked.

'Yerild is a wild card. I wouldn't put it past him, son," Merrick said.

Shaz ran his fingers through his long pale blonde hair and pulled the soaking wet locks from his handsome face. He slipped off his cloak, revealing a slender, but muscular build. Several patrons mumbled to each other as he and Jagwynn worked their way through the smoke-filled room. Shaz was used to being gawked at. His entire life he'd been the only one he'd ever seen with blonde hair.

"One laager, and one miote, please," Merrick said.

Merrick slapped a copper on the counter. A sudden chill ran down Shaz's back as the hairs stood out straight. Shaz scanned the tavern and found a dark hooded figure with large beady-gray eyes and a nose that resembled a beak sitting in a corner. Its hands appeared crippled, and its frame was bent almost in half. It was as if he was half-man and half-crow. Jagwynn arched her back as a low rumbling growl broke her lips. The bird creature withdrew into its hood and hissed at the jaguar. Shaz had gotten the chills before, but this was different, and he wasn't sure why. Shaz sidled up next to Merrick at the bar, and he saw a second hooded figure in the opposite corner of the room. The man sat up and stared in his direction. His hood covered most of his face, which made Shaz uneasy.

The barkeeper set two tankers on the counter, and Shaz took the fruity beverage and gulped it down. The second hooded man stood and began making his way toward them. He was tall and strong with an air of authority about him. The man pulled back his hood and opened his robe and put his hands on his hips. Bright colored cloth draped and encircled his stately frame, starting at his forehead and ended at the floor. His dark eyes were kind against his black skin, and the colorful swaths around his head gave him a unique appearance.

"I would like to introduce myself," he stated. He bowed to each of them, "My name is Ceros, I am a representative of the Sun Goddess. It is imperative that I talk with you both, at this moment, privately," he indicated to his booth.

"Um..." Shaz said.

Shaz looked at his father, who held up his hand.

"Please Shazmpt, may we talk?" Ceros asked. Shaz raised his brow and sized the man, noting his curved sword and its size. "It is imperative that we talk at this instant. Merrick, I'm sure you appreciate the magnitude of this moment," Ceros said.

"What is he talking about?" Shaz asked.

Merrick stared at the stranger. He knew Shaz was not a boy anymore and sighed.

"I guess Yerild's going to have to wait after all," Merrick said.

Ceros motioned for them to move to his table in the corner and then followed them. The hair on the back of Shaz's neck stood out and a pit in his stomach formed. He wasn't sure what was going on, but this was the second time since they came into the tavern. He turned to the corner of the room and the beaked figure was no longer there. A prickle sat at the back of his mind and he was sure the creature was still in the tavern. Shaz casually glanced around and found it skirting around a table of outlaws pretending to talk to them.

"Let me first tell you how pleased I am to finally meet you," Ceros said. His lips half-bent into a well-groomed grin under a dark beard. Shaz's mind circled back to the man sitting in front of him, "Obviously you've not been made aware of your unique situation," Ceros said.

Ceros gave Merrick a 'you're-in-trouble' look, and Merrick rolled his eyes.

"Mathieu has his reasons, and you are certainly not the one who makes the decisions around here. Neither is that ridiculous council you call yourself a part of," Merrick said.

Merrick's brows tightened, and his jaw clenched. Shaz's heart jumped and his blood quickened under his skin. Shaz tried to figure out what the connection between the two men was, and his alert level soared. A rapid heat lit in the center of his chest under his sternum, a feeling he had never felt before.

"Not tell me what?" Shaz asked.

Ceros dismissed Merrick's threat and smiled at Shaz.

"Shazmpt,"

"It's just Shaz," Shaz said.

"Shaz, you were born for a purpose and it is time you become the force you were meant to be," Ceros said.

"That is what you believe, but I am going to let Shaz decide for himself what he becomes," Merrick said.

"I don't think it's up to any of us, Merrick," Ceros said.

The heat in Shaz's chest was growing and a bit of panic tingled his arms.

"What are you talking about," Shaz asked.

"You possess special abilities that can assist the Dodjen in their fight against the rising evil in our land, and I have come to seek your help," Ceros said.

"Why here? Why now? Aren't you supposed to be corresponding with Mathieu?" Merrick asked.

"Mathieu had stopped his communication with the council, and we are in great need. If he is not going to honor his commitments, then we will take matters into our own hands," Ceros said.

Shaz's uneasiness crept into his throat and his mind raced around the details of what was happening.

"We are a secret society commissioned by the Sun Goddess. We've been around since the dawn of time. The scales have been tipping ever so slowly towards the darkness, since the rise of the wicked necromancer, Gavin Rhill. He leads a large and powerful army called the Velshari," Ceros said.

"You have to be soooo dramatic," Merrick said.

Merrick crossed his arms over his chest and glared at the dark-skinned man. Shaz found himself nodding and remembered the stories his Grandfather Mathieu told him. Ceros sat forward in his seat and gave Merrick a steely glare.

"You are a literal descendant of The Tooatha De Danann, an ancient people blessed with extraordinary gifts."

"I know that, so what is it you want," Shaz said.

The creature was now standing a few feet away, and Shaz wondered why Merrick and Ceros didn't show concern. The pit in his stomach continued to grow, *could they even see it,* he wondered.

"Merrick isn't your blood father. He raised you as his own, but Reinholt O'Connon is your blood father and you are the heir to *his* kingdom," Ceros said.

The words hit Shaz with a heat of irritation, and his nerves were about shot. Merrick's heart sank, and Shaz could somehow tell Ceros' words had hit a soft spot.

"But I love you as my own son, Shaz, believe me," Merrick said. He squeezed his son's shoulder.

"I know father, I have always known,"

Shaz paused a moment, listening to the heavy rain against the small window above him. His thoughts continued to race around, and he reached out with his mind to find the creepy figure. Ceros interpreted his hesitation for his pondering the truth of his heritage.

"I know this is a lot to take in, but I still need to tell you about the Sev-Rin-Ac-Lavah."

"The secret artifacts that are powerful and everyone wants them, yeah I know," Shaz said.

Shaz was getting annoyed at the blabber of the person, and Merrick snickered. He wasn't sure how long it was going to take before Shaz's snarky sarcasm was going to show up, and it just did.

"Yes, the Sev-Rin-Ac-Lavah, are four separate and ancient artifacts that hold tremendous powers. The legend says, when these four items are united, they evoke the powers of the universe," Ceros's eyes glossed over as though he were looking into the future. Merrick rolled his eyes and Ceros shook his head clear and said, "Gavin Rhill is obsessed with finding the Sev-Rin-Ac-Lavah. He desires to use its powers to become as the God's."

"So, that is what the legend says, and what's it to me?" Shaz asked.

"Only a war wizard can do it. *You*, Shaz, are the *war wizard* and the only one that can join the Sev-Rin-Ac-Lavah together. But you mustn't join the Sev-Rin-Ac-Lavah, you *must* destroy them, *and* Gavin Rhill," Ceros' words all but cracked under their own pressure.

Shaz endured a long silence. Merrick's heart rate slowed and Ceros's quickened. The figure was a few booths behind him, Jagwynn was gripping the floor with her claws and the pit in his stomach sank even lower.

"So, become a war wizard, kill a man with a funny name, and find and destroy legendary artifacts, got it," Shaz said.

Merrick blurted a guffaw and Ceros slammed his fist on the table.

"This is serious, Shaz. This is real. You'll find out all too soon and you must be ready for it. But since you don't think this important, I will give you this and be on my way," Ceros said.

He pulled out a small blue stone.

"What's this?" Shaz asked.

Ceros whispered to the stone in an unfamiliar language, and the stone glowed.

"This is your birthstone. It allows you to inherit the sword, a small part of the Sev-Rin-Ac-Lavah," he handed it to Shaz.

As the stone touched Shaz's skin, a loud crack erupted from the sky, shaking the tavern. Jagwynn scurried from under the table as Shaz and Merrick leaped to their feet and drew their swords in one fluid motion. They stood with their backs to each other's and surveyed the room.

"What funny business are you up to?" Merrick growled.

Some patrons covered their heads while others hid under tables. The constant tingle on the back of Shaz's neck was gone. Shaz scanned the tavern and the beaked figure was gone too.

"Ah, now he knows," Ceros said.

"Who?" Shaz asked.

"Gavin Rhill," Ceros said.

"What does he know?" Merrick asked.

"Better yet, how?" Shaz asked. *The birdman?* he thought.

"Now do you believe me?" Ceros asked.

Merrick glared and Shaz put his sword away.

"I assume Mathieu has the box and satchel entrusted him?" Ceros asked.

"Yes, I will tell him you came by," Merrick said, "Come on, let's go."

2-You Have Been Chosen To Hold The Honor Blade

In the secret depths of the forest, enormous, intertwined trees sat at the foot of a rocky mountain. Outlines of the forest were so rich and fleecy that an opening could hardly be detected. Hidden by shadows over a melodic hush of forest noise, six hunters blended into the shrubs and underbrush. Shaz stood in the thickest part and breathed in the aroma of ripe raspberry bushes, which sprung up in clumps. They climbed around the trees, springing bright-red luscious berries that dangled from long spindly vines.

Small rodents scurried about bristling leaves and twigs which disguised the sounds of their feet. The richly saturated sun hung high in the sky, and soothing sprigs of amber light glistened off the interwoven hues of green. Gloomy vaults high in the trees secured a scattering of immense ferns. Shaz spotted the Nukpana, a two-headed stag with short fawn-colored hair and dark spots on its back under a large shag tree. Shaz was always the lead hunter, as he could see further than anyone else on the island.

Shaz held up a clenched fist and pursed his lips. He made a combination of bird calls and clicks and five calls returned giving him their locations. Shaz slowly took the bow off his back and latched the string. Understanding wind speed, warmth or coolness, the distance rise and fall of the aimed arrow, all determined the accuracy of its placement. Shaz made several hand gestures to indicate to the others where the beast was and where to aim.

With two heads the Nukpana can hear and sense twice that of a regular stag and were exceptionally fast. The beasts' foul breath stung his nose and its breathing echoed in his ears, even though he was a good fifty lengths away. The Nukpana was said to be a myth, but Shaz had seen it many times and had convinced his hunting party to help him hunt the beast. Riddick, Shaz's best friend, was the first to join the mission, and they would have gone it alone, but they convinced the other hunters, who understood Shaz, had exceptional skills, and they finally agreed.

Riddick was covered with dusty chalk, which disguised his bright red hair and freckles. He was lying on a large boulder at the far end of the clearing, and his bow and arrow were all that stuck out. Another hunter positioned himself lying on his belly with his legs gripping a high tree limb. The other men positioned themselves to the rear and sides of the beast and stood against tree trunks or under large bushes. The wind brought a coolness as it picked up specks of mist from the rushing falls nearby and carried it toward the hunters.

Shaz breathed in and focused on his heart rate. Ever since he returned from the Turbulent Reef, he couldn't get Ceros and the beaked figure out of his mind. He tried to listen to the blood beating in his ear until it was the speed he wanted, but it was accompanied by thoughts of the Sev-Rin-Ac-Lavah. He licked his lips and puckered. Shaz blew through his curled tongue and whistled a familiar animal noise, and each hunter took aim. Shaz slipped an arrow into the grove and settled his bow into his arm. His fingers gripped the taut cord, and he pulled the arrow against the string. Sweat ran down his temples and onto his brow. He narrowed his vision, and the forest blurred away, leaving a narrow tunnel of white.

He made the call again, this time with two calls. In unison, the whipping sound of six arrows hummed through the air. The Nukpana jolted and shot out from the trees and shrieked by with lightning speed. The hunters all sprang from their hiding places, and they started after the beast. The hunters found the Nukpana near a large cove of pine trees and shrubs, on the other side of a small clearing, that was surrounded by raspberry bushes. Shaz's chest burned with heat the closer they came to the beast.

"Look, over there," said Riddick.

Riddick pointed at the large fallen body half under a bush. Shaz tried to keep his focus, but the air thickened, and a strange light filled the surrounding space and Shaz's head wobble and swayed. His knees became loose, and he struggled to stay standing. Several shades of purples and grays swirled around in confusing patterns, and it rose and fell in intervals. The nearby sounds of the men rushing to their kill faded away and an intense humming vibrated the air. Shaz's chest constricted and his lungs tightened. The overwhelming pain, anguish, and fear surged into his limbs, leaving them numb and tingling at the same time. It filled him with exhausted frustration. A strong but faint voice gnawed at the back of his mind, but he couldn't understand it. A soft cool breeze blew in with diligence, clearing the insanity from his mind. Relief settled his limbs and chest palpitations, and he became calm.

"I am Drafang," a strong but gentle voice said.

The flowing purple streams of silken mist molded together in a bright light and grew with intensity. Shaz peered with half-open eyelids. His arm over his face shielded the light from a glimmering white form that floated toward him. The tall liquid form of the two-headed Nukpana emerged from the light.

"I am Drafang, an Ambassador to magical creatures. I wish to aid you on your journey," said each head, taking a turn.

The Nukpana bent one knee and knelt. The purple hues of color changed to oranges, reds, yellows, and topaz. Cool misting strands of silky tendrils wrapped in and around Shaz's legs and swirled around his chest and ruffled his hair. The strange sensations of cold and hot that surged through his body exhilarated his sense, and he struggled to make words.

"I don't understand. What are you? What is happening?" Shaz asked.

"You have freed me from this worldly form. I have waited many long rotations to offer my magic to you," Drafang said.

"Your magic?" Shaz asked.

"My magic interprets the languages of the animals and creatures. I can be a powerful aid to you," the heads said.

"Why would you do that?" Shaz asked.

"To bring balance back to the world, humankind are not the only ones that have suffered the tragedy of the End of The Realms and Gavin Rhill's evil. Animals and creatures of every kind need you, and I am the only link they will have with you," Drafang said.

"But what can I do, I'm nothing special," Shaz said.

"That is not true, honored one. It is you, the sign, the omen. We have been waiting many lifetimes for this day. I understand you have not yet found your way and are at the beginning of your journey, but there is an enormous wealth of knowledge to gain from the animal kingdom. Will you accept me as your companion?" Drafang asked.

The two-headed stag bowed deeply.

"I would be honored, Drafang, but I don't know what I am supposed to do exactly?" Shaz said.

"I understood Ceros had instructed you," Drafang said.

"Well, yes, sort of. Grandfather has taught me much, but I don't understand what it all means," Shaz said.

"I trust you will figure it out. I will leave you my worldly fang to prove to you I am real and that our connection is real. Creatures of all kinds will recognize it and will know you are the chosen one, and a friend," Drafang said.

"I just don't know what if I fail?" Shaz asked.

"Trust yourself, you are better than you think," Drafang said.

Shaz sank under the weight of his self-doubt. He didn't want to do any of this. He wanted to believe Ceros was a figment of his weeks at sea and it hadn't happened, but now with Drafang standing in front of him, how could he pass this off as unreal. His heart pounded against his chest and the truth sank into his soul.

"Thank you, Drafang," Shaz said.

Shaz bowed to the Nukpana, and it reared up on its hind legs. The massive hooves of the beast brought up spiraling drifts of silky mists from the cloudy bottom surface. They floated around, then lowered to the ground and took Drafang with them. The faded light whirled around, leaving Shaz unsteady and shaking in the cool rapture of the evening forest. He fell to the earth panting and once again heard the other hunters and forest life around him. His chest tingled with electric energy, and he found the cold fang that hung at the center of his chest under his tunic. He reached inside his shirt and pulled out the fang already tethered. The fang tickled with a kind of heat that was also cold on his fingertips.

"Are you alright?" Riddick asked.

"I'm fine, just give me a few moments," Shaz said.

Shaz covered his face and blinked several times. His eyes burned while hot tears filled the now bloodshot surface.

"Alright mate, but you are officially twigging me out."

Riddick towered over him, casting a shadow on his friend.

"Did you see it?" asked Shaz.

"See what?" Riddick asked.

Riddick hated it when others found things he didn't. He paid special attention to scrutinizing detail, even to compulsion.

"No, no, nothing. I thought I saw something. I guess it's just these blasted headaches," Shaz said.

Riddick relaxed a little but kept his alert level on high. Shaz and Riddick stayed out of the way for a few more minutes until Shaz's eyes cleared and the color in his face returned, and then they joined the others. The hunters were dutifully setting up camp and making tools to transport the animal back to the village. Shaz's thoughts now swirled around the Nukpana, Ceros, and the beaked figure. He was sad for killing the beast now that he knew what it was. Now that he knew *who* it was.

In a way, he was glad to have the companionship of Drafang, but Shaz still didn't understand completely. Grandfather had taught him who he was and the legends that surrounded him, but Shaz always thought he was making it up and dismissed it. Shaz's thoughts occupied his mind the rest of the night and the next day as they returned to the village. Riddick wasn't sure what was going on and had never seen Shaz so quiet. He tried a few times but didn't push for an explanation. In his guts, Riddick had a feeling the legends of their fathers were playing a role, and he found his own thoughts set in.

Shaz turned the excitement of the hunting details over to the other hunters and decided to go home. Shaz turned the corner and saw his grandfather standing near the largest tree fortress. Grandfather was handsome for his age, with long silver hair and eyebrows. His sky-blue eyes twinkled in the sunlight, and he had fair skin which was uncommon in the island's humidity. Grandfather stood with his back straight, holding onto his staff majestically. Shaz understood Grandfather was different because out of all the people that ever came to the island, no one resembled him. It made him feel good that he wasn't the only one that looked different, but come to think of it, so did Riddick. Shaz sensed his urgency and shook off his thoughts and made his way through a crowded corner of the village, and over to the fragile man.

Many people walked by and bowed to grandfather who returned the gesture with a slight nod. After one of the most severe storms handicapped the island, Grandfather was instrumental in rebuilding the village. Most of the village respected him some, however, were afraid of him. As one of the village healers, he often used strange words and potions to cure difficult ailments. Many people thought he used unknown powers, which frightens them. Shaz bent slightly at the waist and put his forefinger to his lips, then in an arch-like motion he placed his finger on the tip of his forehead and stood back up.

"Apong lalaki," Grandfather said in Denasian, which Shaz understood to mean 'grandson', "Why have you taken so long?"

"I am sorry, Grandfather. I didn't know you were expecting me. I just returned. I haven't been home yet," Shaz said.

Shaz shifted his weight from one foot to the other and shoved his hands in his pockets.

"I have a matter of business to attend to in town. Will you accompany me, please?"

"Of course," Shaz said.

Shaz's mind returned to the events of the last few weeks as he followed Grandfather through the crowded village. He questioned all the games he used to play with him. The kinds of games that made him have to think and the older he became, the harder the riddles became, and the longer he would have to spend figuring them out. The realization of the care Grandfather took to instruct Shaz in as many customs and tales of other creatures and beings weighed heavily, and his shoulders sagged. Shaz never thought it for important, until now, and now he regretted not paying more attention to the details.

Shaz waited for the baker and his wife to carry out large bundles of hot bread. His favorite was the long skinny kind, with a crunchy outside, and a soft fluffy inside. Women in brightly colored dresses with their hair pulled up with fancy clips went from one shop to the next, carrying baskets full of market items. Shaz heard goats, sheep, and other live stalk in the outer areas of the village.

Short and squat buildings with round tops, made of mineral-like clay tiles, speckled the ground floor in and between large Waslick and Pine trees. The officers' buildings, however, were in the extra-large trees on the edge of the village. The bark on the outsides of the trunks intertwined with ivy and raspberry vines, already ripe from the summer heat. The trees held ancient rooms and structures that had been carved out and stood several stories high.

"Apong lalaki, don't your ears work? I said let's go," Grandfather said sternly.

"Oh, sorry grandfather, I was just-"

Grandfather started into one of the large tree structures.

"Yes, yes, now let's go."

Shaz climbed the large spiral staircase in the center of the hollowed-out tree. He had been in the structures many times before accompanying his father on official warden business, but Shaz always found it remarkable, with all the carvings, engravings, rooms, and out coves on the inside of a tree. Small holes strategically placed around the circumference allowed for daylight to enter. Chandeliers with candles hung from various places for light during the dark hours. Along the outside edges of the structure, doors hung from spindly remains of the inner tree. Soft thatching made from tall grasses and soft cloth created ceilings over the rooms.

Each room rotated around the tree in an upward spiral. Planks from the staircase bridged the rooms with tall banisters made of wood and shiny metals that edged the planks. It took time for Grandfather to maneuver the stairs and Shaz patiently waited behind him. Shiny black and grayish-green carvings stood on wooden pillars and hung from corded ropes. They gave a sense of history and bounty, but most of the stories were long forgotten and the symbols too. A short pudgy lady wearing a bright rust-colored dress and a hat with feathers wrapped around the brim barreled out of the room on the upper level and Shaz stepped aside to let her pass.

"Wait here. I'll only be a minute," Grandfather said.

Shaz slumped against the center post that held the staircase. He was certain that when adults said they would be just a few minutes, it was usually much longer. A sudden tingle in his chest startled him, and he stood up. He wondered who would call his magic, and he guessed it was Grandfather, but for what? Several minutes later, Grandfather returned carrying a long satchel strapped over his shoulder and a box wrapped in cloth and descended the staircase. Shaz was certain this is what Ceros talked about, but didn't know what it was. At the bottom of the stairs, Shaz held the solid wood door open.

"Meet me at the family prayer hut after sunset."

"Aye," Shaz said.

Shaz squinted from the sun hitting his face. He shielded his eyes and when he could see he searched for Grandfather. Shaz was always amazed at how he was there one minute and gone the next. Shaz started back home and maneuvered slowly around the forest as the daylight broke into twilight. He wondered why he needed to accompany Grandfather because he did nothing, and he knew Grandfather could go up the stairs on his own. He considered every conclusion he came up with and finally decided it must have been that Grandfather needed Shaz's magic to get the satchel.

Shaz climbed the rope ladder and made his way around the slender rounded walkway around his treehouse. The inside was dim as the heavy leafed canopy shielded the light from the structure. He paused in the center of the large room and a sudden sadness filled his chest. He would soon have to leave this place, and he ran his finger along the small sofa on his way to his room. Jagwynn caressed the floor as he entered. Shaz plopped onto his bed and Jagwynn laid her massive head on his lap.

"It's going to be alright, Jagwynn. Things will be different, but we will always be together," Shaz said. His tone was gentle but had a hint of dread in it. He rubbed her between her eyes, "Come on let's go meet grandfather."

The prayer hut was a small round structure which surrounded a narrow tree about twenty lengths from the main house and was attached by a long rope-bridge that hung suspended in the air. Shaz left the house and made his way over the swaying bridge, with Jagwynn following behind. Her tail swished back and forth to steady herself as her weight made the bridge droop and sway. A tall wooden door sat ajar slightly as Shaz and Jagwynn approached. Shaz opened the door and found Grandfather sitting on a soft pillow with his legs folded and his hands resting on his knees. The pitch from the burning candles tickled Shaz's nose and gave a gentle hint of light. Shaz came up next to grandfather and sat with his legs crossed on another pillow. Jagwynn lay down on the floor and stretched out on her side. Grandfather opened his eyes.

"The time has come for you to receive the items Ceros told you about. But first, you must tell me about your dream," Grandfather said.

Grandfather peered into Shaz's eyes, his jaw tight and his brows firm on his wrinkled face, and Shaz shifted with the uneasiness that sank into his being.

"How do you know about my dreams?" Shaz asked.

"I am your Grandfather, I know things," Mathieu's eyes softened, and his jaw relaxed.

Mathieu had taught Shaz that he was a war wizard and that he had the ability to control the elements. He also knew he could use the shadow magic and that he wasn't ever under any circumstance to use it. Shaz could tell that Grandfather also had magic, but he never asked him about it and was content until now. Now he wanted to ask him a million questions.

"Alright, all I see is a large city. I've never seen such a place. It's all white and sits on the ocean shore. There are many people there," Shaz said.

Grandfather rubbed his long finger on his chin.

"Ebassia," Grandfather said.

"The city from your stories?" Shaz asked.

"Yes."

Shaz rubbed his face and combed through his hair.

"What does it mean?" Shaz asked.

"It means that is your first assignment. After the moon's alignment, when the tide is high, you must travel through the barrier. You must be ready. It is imperative you understand these things as best you can," Grandfather said.

Grandfather's voice was full of anxiousness, and Shaz peered into his eyes to find an explanation. The dread that the barrier was real sank into his awareness, and he figured that meant *every* story Grandfather had ever told was also true.

"What am I do to there?" Shaz asked.

"That I do not know, that is for you to figure out," Grandfather said.

Shaz sucked in a deep breath and ran his hands through his hair. Grandfather reached out a took Shaz's hand, then gripped it tightly.

"Close your eyes and clear your mind," Grandfather said. Shaz closed his eyes and focused on the sounds of the night. Soft chirps and clicks from beetles and crickets and the rustling sounds of the leaf people filled his mind. He took in a deep breath and filled his senses with the fresh night dew, which had settled on lush greenery. "Now open your eyes," Grandfather reached in front of him and removed the satchel, revealing a beautifully carved sword sitting in a dark leather scabbard. Grandfather stood slowly, and Shaz could see the age weighing heavily on his body. "Kneel," Grandfather said and handed him the sword.

Shaz knelt in front of grandfather and took the sword. The hilt was solid steel and wrapped with leather strapping, and the crossguard was thick and rounded down with sharp edges, giving it a fine but rugged feel. A small oval crevice sat in the shoulder of the blade under the crossguard. Shaz recognized this was where he was to put the sapphire he received from the Dodjen. He pulled the stone from his pocket and placed it in the opening.

"Now speak the ancient language and bind the sword to you," Grandfather said.

"Ma'rray machina ma no ha. Notenta ray mevina ano te, tay're nar'rah shento stay na marri she'late nochari," Shaz said.

Shaz watched the magical symbols etched in the blade glimmer a deep-blue and radiate the rays of the three moons. The sapphire sank into the blade and melded into one. The colors glowed brightly for a few moments, then settled on a dim undertone of a silvery-blue.

"Apong lalaki, you have been chosen to hold the Honor Blade, sword of the Bairr Tiornecht and part of the Sev-Rin-Ac-Lavah. It is your destiny to fulfill this calling and return the world to balance," Grandfather said. Grandfather held his hands out in front of him with his palms facing the ceiling. He whispered in his native tongue and his frame shook and his hands glowed. "Put your hands on mine," Grandfather said.

Shaz put his hand on grandfather's, and the energy surged into his being. Shaz breathed through the sting of the energy that was being tugged at from his core, and he tried to relax. Shaz closed his eyes and allowed the bright colors of his magic to surge to the surface, and Grandfather gasped.

The candles in the room grew bigger and brighter, even as the wind and air swirled around the room. It brought the scent of the fresh ocean breeze, grass, and berries. A small silver-strand of misty thread appeared above Shaz. The strand danced about and became a bundle of interwoven threads, lengthening and stretching until it surrounded them.

Shaz tried to stifle the powers like he had always done, but he couldn't stop the conduit that was now being shared with Mathieu. A chilly mist ran through Shaz's bones, and he shivered from the icy-hot silver and red-orange flames that now danced around them. New faces loomed in and out of the haze, and voices filled the air. Memories, visions, and knowledge filled his mind, and he swayed with dizziness. The icy hot mist turned to red-hot searing pain and burst up his core, and he grappled for air. Shaz couldn't yell out, his chest was so tight, and he couldn't move. Panic filled his awareness, and he was about to be overcome with total fear. A tingling of magic relieved the pain and the tightness around his chest and Shaz realized it was Grandfather's magic soothing him. The images faded away and Shaz felt the energy release his mind. He closed the magical conduit they shared and sweat rolled down his face and back, and he sagged onto his heels and breathed heavily.

The wind swirled several more times, then evaporated into the darkness. Grandfather's eyes glazed over, making them virtually invisible. Grandfather stared another moment, and with a slight shake, he blinked.

"What just happened," Shaz asked.

"The powers of the Sev-Rin-Ac-Lavah are now with you, and I have removed my shield from you," Grandfather said.

"Shield, from what?" Shaz asked.

"I have been shielding you from Gavin Rhill and yourself," Grandfather said.

"Myself?" Shaz asked.

Grandfather shooshed him and motioned for him to take the sword. Shaz rose and gripped the hilt, the tingle of the sword's magic surged through his body. Eyes wide and heart-pounding, Shaz studied the sword and its markings. He had access to untold knowledge but didn't know how to use it. Shaz tried to put the thoughts in order as the influx pummeled his attention. Grandfather clasped his shaking hands together and exhaled a long, steady breath.

"In the field of observation, chance favors only the prepared mind," Grandfather said.

Grandfather tapped Shaz's temple with a long, skinny finger. Shaz slid the sword into the scabbard and fastened it to his gold braided belt. Grandfather turned to Jagwynn and held out the box. With sweat glinting on the soft curves of his face, he removed the cloth and opened the box. He pulled out a thick braided collar studded with the same blue sapphires and placed it around her neck. Grandfather turned to Shaz.

"I will make the necessary arrangements to take you to Ebassia," his throat tightened as he tried to hold back the tears, "I am proud of you, my Apong lalaki. Go now, be strong, hold true, and come back to me."

With a tear in their eyes, Shaz embraced Grandfather tightly. Grandfather left the hut leaving Shaz and Jagwynn alone in the cold night.

3-Tie These Around Your Waist

Shaz stood on the dock staring into the deep blue expanse of the ocean, Jagwynn sat next to him with her back straight and searched the sea. Small sailing vessels scurried about the shoreline, coming and going in and out of the fleet of large trading ships which had arrived earlier in the day and were making port. Sailors from the many islands of the Turbulent Reef were crawling around their ships like fire ants protecting their hill. Shouts filled the air as the captains barked orders loudly.

Riddick slung his pack over his shoulder and headed down the pier. His large boots clunked down the dock and he stopped next to Shaz.

"Hey, there you are, lets' get on board, yah?" Riddick said.

The sun's mid-day heat bounced off the water and left a humid odor of seaweed and moss, and Shaz shook his head from his thoughts.

"Yup, let's go," Shaz said.

Shaz slapped Riddick's shoulder, and they dodged an on-slaught of fowl, as they made their way around the many docks and piers until they located the Mirabella. The captain of the Mirabella was a short, stout man with a long burly beard and large belly. Covered in salty sweat, Captain Yerild clamored across the pier barking orders. Grandfather told Shaz that Captain Yerild was a Dodjen, and would be the one to take him through the barrier.

Jagwynn followed behind Shaz and ignored the stares of the sailors. The three maneuvered the ship's cargo and climbed up the steep boardwalk and boarded the ship. Large precisely wrapped piles of ropes lay about the pristine deck which reflected the sun's rays. All sizes of ropes tied to the masts and bulkheads weaved back and forth here and there in a delicate spiders' web.

Strong bronzed men in tattered dirty tunics pulled and wrapped the heavy ropes and secured the sails to the masts. With square knots, they tied and checked all the assembly's making ready to set sail. The Mirabella was a barkentine square-rigged on the fore and fore-and-aft rigged on the main and mizzen masts. The shorter mast behind the mainmast was on a ketch which aided in the ship's steering. The crew of about fifty seemed too small for her size.

"Good to see you again," Captain Yerild said as he wiped his palms on his pants and gripped their forearms. "Batovi, take our guests to their cabins. Show them around, then report on deck."

A thin, scrawny sailor hurried over and guided them around the ship. They climbed down the ladder into the hull, and both Shaz and Riddick had to duck. He moved so quickly through the dimly lit corridors that Riddick had a hard time seeing where he'd gone and blinked several times to adjust to the darkness. Even with the dimmed light, Shaz could still make out all the details. Rows of ropes hung on the sidewall and long bulky wooden poles, the length of the ship, rested in the hooks that were secured to the sides of the hull. Shaz noted the rows of cannons that lined near the edge on the opposite side. They passed the ship's galley and the lower bay-hold which held the cargo.

Batovi stopped and opened the oval door of the bunkrooms and motioned to them that this was their quarters. Shaz stepped into the room which had two hanging bunks, a washbasin, two trunks, and a small mirror. Batovi bowed and hurried back down the passageway. A small port window rested high on the wall, letting in a bit of daylight, and the bunks had heavy woolen blankets and small pillows tucked in neatly.

"Home sweet home for the next week, yah?" Riddick said.

"It's not pristine, that's for sure, but she's tidy," said a small lanky boy.

The boy lifted his cap and stared at Jagwynn with enormous eyes. He hesitated and took a small step toward her.

"What's your name, lad?" asked Shaz.

"William," the boy said.

"This is Jagwynn," Shaz said. Shaz knelt and scratched her belly. He motioned to the boy. "Would you like to pet her?" he asked.

"Yes, sir!" the boy stammered.

"Jagwynn, will you let this lad pet you? His name is William," Jagwynn yawned and showed every one of her needlepoint sharp teeth and laid down on the wooden floor, "I think that's a yes," Shaz said.

The young boy touched her and Jagwynn leaned into his touch. Shaz showed him how to rub her ears and scratch her belly, and William enjoyed every minute and so did Jagwynn.

"Hey, the lower bunk is mine," Shaz said.

"Why? I'm taller than you," Riddick said.

"Because I am better than you, and because I said so," Shaz said.

"I'll wrestle ya for it," Riddick said.

"You're on," Shaz said.

But before they could start a brawl, Jagwynn bared her teeth and a low growl escaped her throat. William leaped up and scurried out of the room. An old man with greasy black hair disheveled about his head and hanging over one eye stood in the doorway. With the other beady eye and half his teeth, he stared at them. Shaz and Riddick turned and put away their packs. Shaz threw his pack on the top bunk and Riddick took the bottom. After they managed their things, they went to leave the cabin they turned to find the man still there.

"Hello, is there something we can do for you?" Riddick asked.

Shaz tried to hold back a laugh and coughed to clear his throat, seeing Riddick so proper, and Riddick shot him an icy glare. The man's deep charcoal eye penetrated them, and they felt uncomfortable.

"What can we do for you?" Riddick asked.

The old man only stared. They squeezed by him and hurried down the passageways back toward the top deck.

"Wow, that old man is creepy," Riddick said with a shudder.

"Yeah, no kidding. I didn't know what to do," Shaz said.

"So, you met Ole'Baggins did you," a sailor said with a chuckle. "He's harmless. He lost the sight of one eye in a fight against a white shark years ago, and the other one is failing because of old age. He's as good as deaf, so he just stares all the time. His nose still works well, though, he's the best cook around," the sailor said.

The sailor pushed a few bags into place on top of a pile of sacks.

"Well, he's still creepy," Riddick said.

The sailor laughed.

"My name is Sebastian, welcome aboard," Sebastian said.

Sebastian offered his weathered hand, and Shaz and Riddick shook it and climbed the ladder. Topside several men released the towropes and mooring lines and took the long beefy poles and pushed the massive ship off the soft silken bottom of the docks. The tide rippled against the pier, rocking the ship gently out to sea. A crew of men released the lines that dropped the sails and caused the sails to puff out with a POP and a loud gasp, and the ship lurched forward. The typical sending off crowd had gathered on the piers waving to their loved ones. Shaz searched for his Grandfather which he found in the back of the crowd resting on his cane and his father was behind him in the shadows. Shaz's stomach sunk and he shoved the knot in his throat. The realization that he might never be with them again ate at his heart, and he struggled to keep his emotions under control.

Captain Yerild set a course to the north-west of their island. Sailors ran around the ship, climbing rope ladders and scaling the masts to position the sails. Within a few hours, the ship was well underway, letting out a deep spray off the front bow as she cut through the choppy sea at a constant rate. The air was fresh, clean, and salty. The spray of cool seawater caressed their skin in the hot late afternoon sun.

"I love being at sea," Riddick said.

"Aye," Shaz said.

Shaz admired the clear blue sky and the rays of sun that danced on the surface of the sea. Jagwynn quietly stalked the cargo when she wasn't watching the men.

"Secure those lines," yelled a sailor.

He pointed to a mass of tangled ropes.

"Aye," the sailor said.

The sailor scurried to the pile and began untangling the ropes, and Shaz and Riddick helped. Captain Yerild kept a tight ship and rotated the crew between day and night shifts so that they could keep sailing with the wind. As they made their way further out to sea, the wind would often diminish in the late afternoon in which the crew took advantage to rest and tell stories. Shaz wondered how many tales were actually stories, and how many were true. It made his stomach lurch thinking about the fact that everything his Grandfather had told him *was* probably true. Which meant that he would someday meet giants and shadow creatures.

As the days passed Shaz, Riddick, and the crew went about their regular routines swabbing decks and positioning sails. Even though there was plenty to do, Shaz found it hard to keep his attention on his new duties. It wasn't like him to shirk his focus, but with all the voices in his head and the sword constantly humming at his side, he was disorganized and scattered.

By early afternoon on the fifth day, a heavy gale came on in an adverse direction and pushed the light fluffy clouds from the sky. Captain Yerild had the top-gallant masts and yards struck to make the ship ride more easily, but as the day advanced the violence of the wind increased. The men worked hard having to draft off one another in order to move about the ship. Much to their dismay, every effort to manage the ship was in vain. The clouds increased and darkened from every corner of the sky. The winds continued to blow harshly, tearing at the sails and spewed sprawling bursts of waves.

"Shaz, Riddick, get below deck now," Captain Yerild yelled, his voice boomed over the waves.

"But we can help," Riddick said.

"Not on my ship. I won't be losing passengers."

Captain Yerild slammed his foot against the ship and braced his body as his white knuckles gripped the helm.

"Let's go," Shaz said.

It surprised Riddick at first, but agreed when he understood the expression on Shaz's face. They managed the wind and the tossing of the ship to the hatch.

"It's not fair," Riddick said as they reached the galley.

He slumped into a booth and threw his arms across his chest.

"I don't like it either, but he's the captain," Shaz said.

As the storm increased, the ship swayed and jolted from side to side. Ole'Baggins and a few other sailors secured the stove and cooking tools. Jagwynn whined and gripped the wood floor with her claws. Riddick became seasick from all the jostling about and concentrated hard on not retching. Shaz tried to comfort Jagwynn and Riddick, but found it hard not to become sick himself. Blasts of torrential wind and rain scourged the ship, and it wasn't long until it was a perfect hurricane. Shouts of panic echoed amongst the ship, and Riddick and Shaz sat suffering from the persistent nauseousness, and uncertainty clouded their judgment. Fifty and sixty-foot waves crashed all around and a loud crack rippled the ship's bow, leaving an eerie echo in its wake.

"I can't take it anymore," Shaz jumped from his seat and toward the hatch. Riddick leaped from his seat right behind him, "Riddick, we've got to get to the surface. Help me with this hatch."

Riddick leaped onto the ladder behind Shaz and they heaved and pulled and twisted the crank just enough to squeeze their hands into the opening. After several long pulls and shoves, the hatch buckled, and the wood shot out in all directions. A blast of cold, wet air hit them in the face. They hurried out of the lower hold and onto the deck.

A sudden chill ran deep into their bones as the wind whipped around them in a cacophony of twists and gusts. The rain thrust around so hard that it stung their skin like needles. Shattered wood from casks and crates was strewn about in a tangled mess of ropes and flung around. They grabbed hold of the bulwark rails and leaned into the wind and struggled toward the helm. They were about parallel to the ship as the waves brought the ship up in a sideways tilt. William scurried out from the bollard pole with two ropes.

"Tie these around your waist," he yelled over the wind.

"What? I can't hear you." Riddick yelled back.

William mimicked tying the rope around his waist and handed them the ropes. They fastened them around their waists. Another loud crack echoed around the ship and sent a shivering wave through the floor. An immense wave raised from the starboard side several fathoms into the air and gained speed as it rushed toward the ship. Men yelled, trying to warn each other. Shaz and Riddick leaped toward the mainmast to grab onto whatever they could. The wave crashed into the ship, twisting and gnawing at the already stressed planks. The wave disappeared back into the sea, taking several men with it. A dreadful sadness filled the air.

William clung to the bulwark, which now hung off the ship's side and dangled over the water. The ship swayed side to side as the wind blew the starboard side into the ravaging waves. Shaz ran as fast as he could, seeing that William was going to be swallowed up in the sea. He slid into the bulwark pole and wrapped one leg around it. He reached William seconds before another wave toppled over the edge. Shaz gripped him tightly, and both gasped for breath as another mountain high wave crashed onto the ship. A rush of searing pain coursed into Shaz's body from all angles as the icy cold water tried to strangle the breath out of him. Shaz clung to William's limp body and a sharp pain stabbed his chest. The iron rod that circled the boom had sheared off and became tangled in the ropes and sliced Shaz's flesh, sending bright red blood into the water.

The ship popped back into the air barely before Shaz couldn't hold his breath any longer. He gasped and slid onto the deck. The sting of salt-water eased into his chest, replacing the icy dread. Riddick held onto the mainmast as the ship corrected herself. He let go and slid over to the edge and slipped his arm around William and pulled him from Shaz. Williams' lips were purple, and Riddick checked for breathing. He rolled him onto his side and banged on his back to force the water out of his lungs. A moment later, Williams' lungs sprang to life and spewed the water out. He coughed and gasped as he struggled to breathe.

Another loud crack sounded in the center of the ship, and what sailors were left scurried about to keep the ship from capsizing and taking the rest of them to a watery grave. Shaz gasped and wheezed from the sharp sting the salt-water left on his wound. The wound was deep and about a hand and a half in length. Riddick ripped Shaz's blood-soaked shirt into strips and dressed the wound as best he could.

Shaz slowed his breathing to a steady rhythm and tried to push the pain from his mind, but his head swayed, and his vision turned black.

"Take them both to Ole'Baggins, he'll know what to do," Sebastian said.

Riddick untied the ropes from around their waists and tried to shield his long locks from whipping him in the face. He helped Shaz below deck to the small galley room and onto a table, then ran to find Ole'Baggins.

"How in the world can that old man do anything? He's deaf, blind and *old*," Riddick muttered.

Riddick found him at the aft part of the cargo bay, and he grabbed his arm and led him to where he left Shaz. It was difficult to walk about the debris of the ship, let alone with a blind man. Jagwynn found a small cubbyhole in the middle of wooden crates until she saw Riddick. They reached the galley and Riddick led him to the table. Ole'Baggins put his hands on Shaz's chest and removed the soiled cloth. Jagwynn nuzzled Shaz's leg and whined.

"Go get the boy," the old man said.

"What, you speak? I'm not leaving Shaz," Riddick said.

"Go fetch William. He will die if you don't bring him to me. Besides, Jagwynn's here, and she won't let anything happen to your friend."

Riddick hesitated, then dashed out of the room. He skidded and slid while dodging holes in the floorboards. He swooped William into his arms and ran back to the porthole. Riddick dodged cross pieces of timber that stuck out of the interior walls and scattered about the passageways. Drenched with seawater, Riddick clamored into the room holding William.

"Lay him over there and fetch me some blankets from the cabins," the old man said.

Riddick put the boy on the table and ran out in search of the blankets. When he returned the old man was bent over Shaz whispering words Riddick didn't understand. Ole'Baggins held his hands above the wound with his palms face down and gently glided above the surface. The blood dried and formed a long scab-like covering with a light rust-colored glow around the edges.

Riddick wrapped the blankets around William, who was freezing cold, and pulled him tight. He cradled the boy and swayed with the rocking and tossing of the ship. Shouts from above mingled with cries of pain and anguish and several loud shudders rippled the hull. With a horrendous crack, the heavy main mast shattered into thousands of wooden shards and sprayed across the deck. It took three more crew members into the sea and their cries faded into the dark sky. The raging winds and torrents of rain slammed into the battered wood, leaving an eerie echo throughout the ship. Riddick's pale freckled face reflected a tint of green, and he tried not to wretch.

"Are you doing some kind of magic?" Riddick asked.

"No, not magic. Healing of the soul. I see with my heart, not my eyes. When the beast took my sight, I turned to my heart for healing and when I saw again, it was with different eyes. I see the souls of people now and their courage and strengths. You, for instance, are a noble leader with a great capacity to love. You are destined for important things and are this one's soul brother," Riddick knew he was right about being connected to Shaz like that, but for the rest, he thought the old man was just being nice. Ole'Baggins continued his whisperings and checked Shaz's forehead. Shaz was sweating heavily, his breathing irregular and strained. "This one," said the old man, "is an important one and the spirits are with him now."

After several more minutes, Shaz's breathing began to even out and the color in his face returned. Ole'Baggins made his way to William, balancing with the rocking and swaying of the waves. The old man held his hand on William's forehead and whispered the same strange words.

4-Maybe Now Is Time For A New Leader

Azrack kicked a stone as he padded over the harsh desert floor. Trenches that were carved into the landscape, made for excellent vantage points, but he was not on familiar ground. He was in the Ebon Hoards' territory who was a ferocious clan of gryphtons with little regard for life. The sun was blistering, and he licked his beak, trying to ease it of the dryness. Azrack slowed his pace and sniffed the breeze. He detected a hoard of gryphton soldiers several lengths ahead and crept close to the hot sandy ground. Azrack searched the surroundings and when he determined the size of the hoard, he rose onto his hind legs and reached his full height. Azrack's shadow formed over the warriors who squirmed.

"What are you doing, Kosaf? You *will* obey my orders," Azrack said.

"I obey no one," growled Kosaf.

"You think that taking orders from the shadow is better than taking orders from me?" Azrack said.

"Maybe now is time for a new leader," Kosaf sneered.

A low growl escaped Azrack's throat.

"So, you think you're a better leader than me? How long do you think you will last under the protection of the shadow? The shadow doesn't care about you. It will leave you for dead the moment you are of no use, and for what a trinket of gold or silver?" Azrack said.

"You offer nothing but a lifetime of servitude under a weak and dying king. The shadow offers a good price for my loyalty," Kosaf said.

Kosaf banged on his chest with tight fists. The gryphtons roared and cheered as they banged on their chests in agreement.

"You have led a raid against the Ebon Hoards and have angered them needlessly. They will attack our prides for revenge," Azrack said.

The soldiers looked from Azrack to Kosaf and back. Their confused looks gave Azrack hope he could persuade them to return to the Armada.

"The raid is past and gone and cannot be changed. Why should we care about the Ebon Hoards? They are no match for the shadow," Kosaf turned to the soldiers and puffed out his chest, slammed his battle-ax against his armor and shouted, "Warriors hear my voice!"

The hoard grunted and growled, and some jumped, and some raised their weapons high above their heads.

"We are hunters and warriors, not thieves and murderers. Kosaf would have you become slaves to the shadow. I know his heart," Azrack said.

"So, you say," sneered Kosaf.

"Brothers, hear my voice, for honor," Azrack said.

Azrack leaped into the trench and lifted his chin high and walked into the crowd of gryphton warriors. The soldiers were garbed in battle armor and heavy traveling cloaks. Majestic and colorful wings set deep into their backs lifted slightly and ruffled in the breeze. Azrack stopped at Kosaf and peered into the black eyes of his hoard leader. The renegade gryphton stared back. Azrack moved into Kosaf's space and sniffed around him and tasted the air. The stink of betrayal sank into his nostrils, and he was certain Kosaf now chose to serve the shadow. Kosaf rose to his full stature threatening Azrack who then rose to his.

"The few answers your call Azrack, the many follow me now," Kosaf said.

The soldiers grunted and snarled, and Azrack realized he was in the middle of a hoard of warriors who no longer answered to him. His dark brown eyes shifted rapidly, and he searched their energy. The warrior helmets covered their eagle heads and heavy leather, and steel armor covered their half-human-half-lion bodies. For an instant, Azrack's heart raced with fear, but then sadness. The warriors he once commanded now succumbed to the greed of their kind, and the empty promises of evil.

"This is not many, but a few misguided cubs. I still command the Armada of the king," Azrack said.

"This hoard is mine," Kosaf snarled. He banged his paw against his chest and ruffled his feathers. The hoard echoed back with grunting and growling salutes, "All mine! Try to take them from me."

It was against their laws for Kosaf to challenge his leader, but as the evil crept in, the once held with honor rules now held no importance.

"Whoever is loyal to me, follow me," Azrack snarled.

Not one warrior moved, and Azrack's heart sank. He backed out of the swarm of soldiers but kept his chest out and constant eye contact with Kosaf until he was where he could open his wings and leaped into the sky before Kosaf could launch an attack. The hoard reacted with shouts of victory that echoed through the trenches.

****

Azrack hunched over several maps scattered over a large table.

"If we move our forces here, we can secure the eastern borders," Ralti said.

"Kosaf took a hoard and now serves the shadow," Azrack said.

"What? That low life sc-"

"It is what it is, but we must guard against him taking anymore. Tell the Armada that his hoards are now dissenters and that if found they are to be killed on sight," Azrack said.

"Azrack, are you sure? That's not our way," Ralti said.

"We can't afford to go easy. The shadow is growing more and more powerful. It already possesses a hold of the Ebon Hoards and Kronos Hoards," Azrack said.

"Yes, sir," Ralti said.

Ralti gripped the edge of the table tightly and gritted his beak. Ralti didn't doubt it was true and understood why the punishment needed to be so tough, but he didn't like it. He knew Azrack didn't either. Azrack wouldn't reach that extreme if there wasn't anything he hadn't already tried. Azrack rolled up the map and patted Ralti on the shoulder as he left the tent. The dampness from the persistent rain that hung heavily in the air wreaked havoc on his lungs as he made his way to the king's quarters. This part of the land was once fields of grasses where wild steer and elk roamed. Now it was covered with battle barracks and trodden down by the constant trudging of soldiers. He moved briskly through the soldiers and into the King's tent.

"Sir, sorry to interrupt, but I have an urgent matter," Azrack said.

"What is it?" The King asked.

Azrack couldn't help hearing the old and feeble gryphton king let out an irritated growl.

"Kosaf attacked the Ebon Hoards and I fear he will make alliances with Kronos," Azrack said.

"Why is this pressing?" The King asked.

The King barely glanced up from his parchments.

"Because sir, didn't you put him in charge of the prisoner exchange?" Azrack asked.

The King's face drained of color and his knees wobbled. His head swayed, and he ran his paw over his face and sucked in a deep breath.

"Azrack, we need to mobilize forces toward the southern border to be ready to withstand Kronos," the King said.

"Sir, what about the peace talks?" Azrack asked.

"I fear there won't be any now," the king said.

Azrack's stomach turned.

"Yes, sir,"

Azrack left the barracks with urgency and almost forgot to close the flap behind him. The King turned to his trusted servant, who sat on his haunches in the corner of the room.

"Lahonti, take a letter," the king said.

The king climbed onto his nest-like bed and pawed at the loose straw. Lahonti crawled over to the writing desk and pulled out a parchment and ink and sat on a small stool next to a table. Lahonti was a smaller gryphton with a leaner mass than the soldiers. His long beak and sharp-pointed eyes hovered over the parchment, waiting for the king.

Kronos,

I write unto you concerning this war, which your brother has waged against my nation, in which you are still determined to carry on, even after his death. If you do not withdraw your armies back into your own lands, which are the land we are willing to let you keep, you will draw our full wrath upon you. We will not show mercy unto those who surrender. We will wipe you off the face of this land. I would offer you quarter if it were at all possible that you would live by our law, but as you are so past feeling, I fear you would be incapable. I will not honor any deals made by Kosaf on my behalf, for he dissented to the shadow. I will not exchange prisoners, save it be on conditions that you deliver up a gryphton and his wife and his children, for one prisoner. If you agree, I will exchange. If you do not agree it shall be blood for blood, life for life, and I will give you battle until you are destroyed off the face of this land.

For I am King Ruadan

Lahonti finished the last of the script, blew on the ink, rolled it up, and dripped hot wax on the edge. He centered the King's stamp and held it until the wax cooled. He slipped out of the tent and made his way to the currier's tent. Lahonti gave the messenger the note and returned to the king.

Ralti, Brigdon, and Helios mingled in the war room discussing possible moves when Azrack returned.

"The king stopped all peace talks with Kronos, and we must be prepared to take the southern borders," Azrack said.

Azrack rested his paws on the table and hung his head slightly. Ralti, Helios, and Brigdon stared at Azrack. Helios searched for a logical reason but came up empty.

"Why did the peace talks end? That was clearly the logical thing to do," Helios asked while rubbing his thick feathered chin.

"Logical, yes, but nothing about this senseless war is logical," Ralti said.

"Sir, what happened to Kosaf?" Helios asked.

"The shadow," Azrack said. "There will be no prisoner exchange either."

Helios sank onto his haunches and ruffled his feathers as a chill ran down his back. Brigdon grunted. Helios opened his mouth but then shut it. Azrack turned and paced the long skinny war tent.

"That leaves us at a sizable disadvantage," Helios said.

Azrack nodded and unrolled his map onto the table.

"Now that Kosaf has joined with Kronos, we need to change our strategies," Azrack said.

"I don't think it will do much good it's as if they already know what we are going to do anyway," Ralti said.

"That's true for the last several skirmishes we have been out-smarted and that was even *before* Kronos left. There must be something else at play that we aren't aware of," Helios said.

Helios ruffled his jade-green feathers and rummaged through his side satchel.

"We have a traitor?" Ralti asked.

"Let's hope not, but for now everything is on a need-to-know basis, and no one besides who is in this room needs to know," Azrack said.

Brigdon grunted, Helios nodded, and Ralti put his tightened fist on his heart.

"What are your orders?" Ralti asked.

"Brigdon, take your forces here," Azrack pointed to the pass on the southern border, "Helios, you take yours here," and pointed to the peaks, "Ralti, yours go here," he pointed to the grasslands on the farthest side.

5-He Is No Ruler

The sun was now far from the world and left the sting of winter hanging over the once bright and delightful land.

"Lahonti, send in my son," King Ruadan said.

Lahonti's heart sank as his leader's feeble voice barely overpowered the commotion of the soldiers nearby.

"Yes, my sire," Lahonti replied.

Lahonti pulled his wings in tightly, so he could pass the narrow opening of the king's tent, and hopped a few feet, then leaped into the air. His large golden-yellow-colored wings thrust against the ground, which allowed him to fly swiftly over the embattled tents and worn-out warriors. The conflict took many years to escalate, but as of late the reckless Kronos made their objection to the king's rule manifest. The letter sent by the king a rotation earlier added heat to the contention and Kronos retaliated fiercely, reducing the king's forces significantly.

Much of the king's land had become sparse of the needed resources because the Kronos had taken over the High Peaks where the water flows into the valleys. Kronos fortified the peaks heavily, and

Azrack found it impossible to retake them. King Ruadan fell wounded during the last battle and Lahonti spent most of his time caring for him, but his health was not improving, which left an uneasiness linger over the Armada.

"Groargoth, your father the King wishes to speak to you," Lahonti declared.

Groargoth peered down his beak over his plate of roasted meat.

"I know my father is the King, stupid," Groargoth snarled.

Groargoth's shiny-black eyes penetrated Lahonti's, and he bowed deeply and backed away. Groargoth put his plate down on the stool next to him and stood slowly. Long black feathers ruffled at the back of his head and down his neck. Instead of flying, Groargoth strode through the camp, trying to make sure every warrior noticed his presence.

The gryphton warriors, however, tried not to make eye contact with him. One choked on his ale and another stumbled as he passed their camp. Groargoth was an accomplished warrior, but he lacked the greatest skill to lead a troop of his own compassion. Groargoth struck his chest-plate with his fist as he walked by, which some returned with half effort, but most ignored him which angered Groargoth.

Groargoth approached the king's tent and gazed into the night sky. The heat of his breath penetrated the cold as it left his lungs. A star ripped across the three purple moons, and he took that as an omen. He threw out his chest, pulled his wings in tightly and entered the tent.

"Father, you sent for me?"

"Son, I have a special mission for you, come," King Ruadan said.

Groargoth bowed and knelt before his father's nest. His heart pounded. He was certain the time had come that his father saw him for what he was.

"Yes, father."

"Kronos is moving his hoards to the southlands. Take a small hoard and intercept their communication. Find out what he is planning," the king said.

"But father, that's a task for a recruit. Surely you need me for more important matters," Groargoth said.

"I have Azrack and his command for that. This is a task befitting to you."

Groargoth lowered his head. The words sank deep into his heart and sliced the last thread of desire he had for his father's acceptance. His mind raced through the years of disappointments from his father. The countless times he favored Azrack over him and his anger deepened in his soul and red-hot fury raged.

"Yes, father."

The King rested with his eyes closed on the large, padded headboard of his nest-like bed and for an instant, the thought crept into his mind that this would be so easy to kill the old gryphton. Groargoth jumped as Lahonti nudged through the opening. Groargoth stood and turned slowly, scanning the contents of his father's tent. He needed to find a way to secure his father's crown. He spotted the dagger Azrack gave his father on a side table as he moved toward the door. Lahonti observed Groargoth's eyes spy the blade and stepped in front of him. Groargoth glared at him and left the tent in a hurry, huffing and pouting as he threw the flap open. He kicked a pot of grub over as he stormed by. The warrior jumped in his face but Groargoth roared at him and when the warrior realized who it was, he glared at him instead.

"Lahonti, send Azrack in," the King said.

"Yes, sire," Lahonti replied.

Lahonti skirted around several soldiers and tents until he found Azrack tending his supper toward the back of the encampment. Lahonti wasn't surprised to find Azrack the General near the least of the soldiers.

"Azrack, the King requests your company," Lahonti said.

Lahonti's brilliant sun-like yellow feathers reflected the fire-light as he bowed deeply. Azrack turned and put down his large spoon.

"You don't need to bow to me, Lahonti," Azrack said, picking up his helmet and tucking it under his arm.

"Yes, sir," Lahonti replied again, still in a bow.

Azrack knew Lahonti would never stop being a servant. That is his nature. Azrack walked through the camp of battered, bleeding, and broken warriors. The events of the last few days plagued Azrack's thoughts, and he maneuvered through the soldier's camps. They'd attempted to take the northern border against the Ebon Hoards. Azrack led his team among the tall grasses. Jaxton and Pontos swarmed in from the eastern side but didn't expect the Ebon Hoards to have large weapons that flung fireballs long distances. Helios remembered them from an ancient text but had never seen them in real life. The launchers shot fire toward Azrack and his men and engulfed the trees that they were hiding in and covered the land with smoke.

Azrack's men struggled to breathe, and they tried to fly over the smoke, but the Ebon Hoards had strung woven twine together, making a barrier over them. Azrack sent warriors to cut the twine but had to fight the oncoming soldiers first. Helios studied the launchers and about mid-day he understood how they worked and what it would take to bring them down. Helios took a small group of soldiers and made their way close enough to take out the launchers with their slings.

They aimed with their sharpened rocks at the line that was strung into the center pole and attached to the bucket. The rocks sliced the rope, causing it to give way halfway through the next swing. The bucket of flaming tar plummeted to the ground, engulfing the Ebon Hoards instead. Screeches and yells rang out as the Ebon Hoard soldiers flailed about under the scorching heat. Azrack instructed his armies to flap their wings and make wind to feed the fire. The fire, however, didn't seem to take hold and died down to a smolder. Helios spotted a human figure wearing a bright- red cloak in the back of the camp, standing on a tall platform.

Azrack scrutinized the figure and understood it to be an elemental mage of the humankind. He had learned about the mages from legend but had never seen one until today. Azrack sent Brigdon down the center straight for the mage. Azrack and his soldiers slipped between the burning trees along the outer edges of the valley. Brigdon covered his beak with a cloth as he made his way through the fallen Ebon soldiers and behind the stand. Brigdon pulled his sling from his belt and loaded a polished and sharpened rock. He swung with one fast flick and released the stone. It hit the mage in the middle of his back and the mage crumpled to the ground.

The smoke and fire around the perimeters died quickly. Azrack scanned the damages and could see more Ebon Hoards crowning the far hill and was certain his small brigade was no match for their new hoards, so he signaled a retreat. Helios snagged the satchel the mage wore on his way out. Azrack was angry that they hadn't gained any ground and suffered so much. He was certain it was because of the human that was on their side, but wasn't sure what to do about it.

Warriors bowed or nodded and ruffled their feathers as Azrack made his way to the king's tent. His stern command lent for obedient warriors, but his compassion for them evoked their devotion to him. Groargoth turned and peered at Azrack. His jealousy sat deep in his core from the many years he spent under Azrack's shadow. Groargoth slipped into the shadows and followed Azrack to his father's tent and went around to the back. Groargoth put his ear on the rear tent wall to listen, and Azrack pulled open the tent and slipped inside.

"I am here, sire," Azrack said, bowing to one knee.

"Come," the King whispered.

Azrack stood and walked to the side of his nest. The king lifted his shaky paw and Azrack took it in his.

"It is soon that I must die," the King said softly. Azrack interrupted but silenced himself, "Azrack, you are the only one I trust with my kingdom. We must not let our kind fall into destruction," he said with labored breaths, "I will declare you are to become my successor, but I must ask you one more mission."

"No, sire, not me," Azrack paused, "What about your son?"

"He is no ruler. He is selfish and cruel. He is greedy and is no different from the lesser hoards seeking absolute riches. He will destroy our kind," the king said.

Groargoth stood back with hot anger in his chest, then put his ear back to the canvas wall.

"Perhaps a competition like when there is no heir to select from," Azrack plead.

"I will think about it, but for now I need you to take your best men and go into the valley of Baymoor. You must find an orb at the Ruins of Basete. It will help us defeat the mages the Ebon Hoards now have," Azrack furrowed his brows wondering how the king was already aware of the mages, he hadn't made his report yet, "I know I can trust only you," the king said slowly, coughing weakly.

"How did you know about the mages? What makes you think this vessel will defeat them?" Azrack asked.

A green glimmer in the King's eyes gave Azrack a sickening ripple of dread that crawled up his spine. He turned and found a round mirror he'd never seen before, which now hung on the wall. He wondered why the human mages would care to involve themselves in their battle unless there was something the humans wanted from their world. It had been centuries since the last rumors of human intervention surfaced. In fact, Azrack hadn't believed they existed, even when Helios swore they did, until he saw them for himself.

"You are not well. I must stay with you to take care of you," Azrack said.

Azrack sensed an eerie energy from the mirror and wanted a chance to figure out what it was about.

"No, Lahonti can do that. I need you to return with this vessel as soon as you can. You must hurry," the King said and closed his eyes.

"As you wish, sire. I will leave in the morning."

"No, you must leave now. Take your soldiers and make haste."

"Tonight? But we've just returned. The troops are tired and battered and need rest," Azrack said.

"I know you will be able to succeed, now go."

The mirror's irritating glow fizzled, and Azrack's heart thudded in his chest.

"Yes, sire," Azrack bowed.

Azrack ruffled the feathers at the top of his head and stood up tall and secured his helmet.

Groargoth stood at the back of the tent seething. *How could my father cheat me out of my inheritance? It's just as Kronos said it would be.* Groargoth kept to the shadows of the large trees that protected the tent and spied Azrack return to the weary warriors. The corner of Groargoth's mouth lifted into a sneer and a drop of drool fell from the corner as he wet his beak with the sting of vengeance. A soft growling gurgle came from the back of his throat and Groargoth summoned two soldiers who slipped into the shadows.

"Gather a hoard, we must find out what the humans want in our land," Groargoth said.

The soldiers bowed and left quickly. *Maybe if I can find out what they want, I can stop them and gain my father's favor.* Groargoth found Lahonti over at the supply tent and wondered if he would be able to make him talk. Lahonti grabbed a basket of dried meat, then pulled open the tent flap and backed out. Hot breath trickled down his back and he carefully turned around. Lahonti fiddled with the basket for a better grip as he stared blankly at Groargoth, who was now standing in front of him.

"Yes, sire, is there something I can do for you?" Lahonti asked.

Groargoth searched Lahonti, shifting from one eye to the other.

"You're useless and pathetic," Groargoth said.

Groargoth puffed air into Lahonti's face, and with a scowl stormed off. Lahonti sighed and continued back to the king's tent. He tended to the king's supper and helped him dress for the night, then sat on a bench in the corner of the room thinking.

"What is it, Lahonti?" the king asked.

"Sire, I think maybe you should write a declaration that you desire Azrack to become king," he paused to wait for the king's reaction, "So, that if there is not a suitable contender found it will default back to Azrack and not your son," Lahonti said.

"Very well," the king said, "Bring me some parchment."

Lahonti pulled a piece of parchment from an old wooden box. The lid was worn at the sides by years of wear from being secured to traveling wagons. The king felt as old as the box looked. It was the first gift he received from his father when he became the King.

Lahonti placed the parchment on the king's lapboard and gave him a quill and an ink jar. The king barely picked up the quill and dipped it into the ink and made several marks on the parchment, resting every so often to gather his thoughts. Lahonti picked out the official stamp from the box and set it on the board, seeing the king was close to finished.

"Perhaps you should make a duplicate, sire," Lahonti said.

"You make the duplicate, and I will sign it, but I'm tired," the king replied.

"Yes, Sire."

Lahonti had scripted many documents for the king in the past and was quite good at mimicking his marks. He took the parchment and blew on it then pulled another parchment from the box and scripted a copy. When the ink was dry on the second, Lahonti gave it to the king to sign. He rolled it up and tucked it into the inside pocket of his satchel. It was common for servants to carry things for their masters and usually wore larger satchels than other gryphton's.

Lahonti returned the quill and ink and stood and stretched his back. He tucked the large blankets in around the sleeping gryphton king and squeezed out of the tent and into the late night. The frosty night air seeped a faint tint of pitch from the many smoldering campfires throughout the Armada of gryphton warriors. The stars had long been twinkling in the night sky but seemed extra far away. Lahonti needed to find a place to hide the copy of the declaration. He was positive that if Groargoth found out, he would be killed for treason, and he had no doubt that Groargoth would search his satchel and tent. Nightbirds hooted in the distance while the soft clicks and chirps of the nocturnal insects softened the chilly breeze coming in from the north.

Lahonti scaled a few branches and leaped down and wove between large sticker bushes. He sniffed the breeze categorizing the scents and after an hour of searching for somewhere to hide the scroll, Lahonti was about to return to camp when he spotted a hole in a tree several lengths away. He stretched his wings and with a flap lifted into the air. He landed on the branch in front of the hole and sniffed the air for signs of life, and finding none, he reached his paw into the hole and found a small ledge inside. As he searched around, he came across something cold.

He brought it eye level and opened his paw. A gold ring reflected the little bit of starlight. *I wonder who put this here, and why*? Lahonti turned it in his paw. He couldn't help wondering if he was going to get caught by its owner, who somehow perceived it was missing. *It's very shiny*, he thought. He tried it on one of his toes and admired it. He put the parchment on the ledge and leaped out of the tree and returned to his tent.

6-Aye, Fits Just Like A Finger In The Nose

Late into the night, the ship slowed its rocking and swaying. Ole'Baggins dressed and washed Shaz's wound several more times with a mixture of saltwater and ale from an unbroken cask. There had been no noise from above in hours, and Riddick wondered if any men were left onboard. Riddick laid the boy on a bench and stretched.

"I'm going to check on what's happened. The winds are calm, and the waves have settled," Riddick said to Shaz.

He hoped Shaz heard him, but he was skeptical. He traversed the broken beams and spikes of sheared wood until he came to the hatch. Riddick climbed out onto the deck and his heart sank deep into his stomach as he avoided the body of a sailor pinned under the aft mast. The sails had long since torn away and there was nothing left of the main or forward masts. He combed the wreckage, searching for anyone. The Mirabella, once a beautiful vessel, was ripped to shreds and sat silently in the sea. Riddick found Batovi near the ballast, bleeding from a head wound and Sebastian opposite him with a broken leg. The sound of large boots clunked across the deck. The captain, who was worn and haggard, carried a sailor over his shoulder. He set him down next to the others.

"How's Shaz and William?" the Captain asked, choking back the lump forming in his throat.

"Shaz has a major gash across his chest, but Ole'Baggins stopped the bleeding, and he has no more fever. William will be alright too, I think," Riddick said.

"William made it?" Captain Yerild asked.

A small smile crested his lips.

"Aye, Shaz saved him from going overboard, but an iron rod tangled in the ropes sliced his chest," Riddick said.

The wind slowed, but rain still fell on the ship. The freshwater soothed their salty sun-beat skin. Riddick tasted the salt as it rushed from his hair and over his face.

"What are we going to do now that the sails are gone?" Riddick asked.

"I have no idea. I guess we wait until another ship comes and maybe they'll find us," Sebastian said.

"Does that happen?" Riddick asked.

"Not likely, but it's all we got," Yerild replied.

Riddick and the captain helped the wounded men down into the galley, where Ole'Baggins tended to them. They cleared away the debris by tossing it into the ocean to make the ship as light as possible. They went through the hull and moved wrecked pieces of the ship out of passageways and took an inventory of the cargo that was now ruined.

"We have but a few days' rations left, I reckon," said the Captain.

"Any guesses as to where we are?" Riddick asked.

"I can't tell yet. I figure I'll be able to tell when the stars are out, if the clouds clear up," Captain Yerild said.

"I am going to go check on Shaz," Riddick said. He climbed up the stairs and passageways into the galley. Shaz was gone when he came into the dimly lit room. "Where's Shaz?" he asked through a stifled yawn.

"I moved him to your cabin where he will be more comfortable, along with William," replied Ole'Baggins combing back his greasy black hair. Riddick was taken back when he saw that his eye socket was sunken into his skull. A long red jagged scar ran across his eye from his cheek all the way into his hairline, "Sure, aint pretty is it?"

Riddick nodded with a new respect and went to the cabin where he found Shaz covered with blankets. Jagwynn was on the floor under his bed and William in the upper bunk. He knelt next to the bunk and sobbed tears of sadness and joy. His body pulsed and swayed as the terrorizing events unfolded in his mind, and he feared he wouldn't be able to rid the images from his head. Jagwynn rested her head on his lap and whined.

Late into the night, the clouds parted. The derelict ship sat still in the wave-less sea, and they had no wind, not even a breeze. The three moons staggered the night sky and speckles of bright shiny stars gleamed through the spotty clouds, giving a soft purple hazy light to the Mirabella.

Riddick lay on the cabin floor and wondered if he would ever make it home. What might happen to Shaz and even himself? What could he do? How would they make it back to the island? The better half of the night passed, and Riddick hadn't slept at all. He climbed onto the deck and found the captain standing at the helm. The captain was as still as a stone statue, and Riddick wondered if he was sleeping standing up. Riddick made his way over to him.

"How bad is it?" he asked.

"Aye, it's bad," the Captain said.

"How far-off course are we? Do you think we could build a raft to make it to the mainland?"

Riddick searched the open sea for signs of land.

"We're about a hundred and ten leagues out to sea. There is nothing out here, not even a rogue ship would be out this far. They say it's haunted by sea serpents," the Captain said.

"How far back to the island?"

"Much further than that, I'm afraid. We are totally helpless."

"Hmm, well, there's got to be a way. We have some sails down below, will they work?"

"Aye, but we have nothing to hoist them on."

"Well, we will see about that," Riddick said and returned to his bunk.

Early the next morning, Riddick searched for tools, ropes, and any sturdy wood he could use to rig a sail. Batovi helped, and together they managed several large beams and the sails. Tying them together as tightly as possible, they set the makeshift pole in the leftover casing of the forward mast. The large pole sank into the crevasse and seated into place. The pole was much smaller than the original mast, so they shoved broken wood into the casing between the pole and the edges.

"See, fits just like a finger in the nose," Batovi said.

Riddick blurted a loud laugh. Batovi let out a gleeful snicker, pleased that his wit and humor hadn't been sucked out to sea.

"Aye, fits just like a finger in the nose it does," said the Captain coming around the helm.

The three men laughed so hard they turned red.

"What's all the ruckus about?" Shaz asked.

They turned toward Shaz, Jagwynn, and William and Riddick ran over to them.

"Hey, you're awake, I'm so glad," Riddick said.

"Yes, but I feel like a Nukpana rammed right into me," Shaz said gently rubbing his bandaged chest.

Riddick was about to ask how he would know what that felt like but left that for another day and said, "I bet. Ole'Baggins did some kind of magic on you. He said you will heal fine, and you William, you are lucky to be alive too," Riddick said.

Riddick ruffled his hair.

"Yes, sir," William said.

"Will she sail?" Shaz asked.

"Well, we have rigged a makeshift sail and hoping for a good breeze we may be able to get some distance behind us. We are about a hundred and ten leagues east of where we need to be, and vessels don't come out this far," Captain Yerild said.

The meager crew tried to make themselves busy until late evening when the sail picked up a slight wind and gently moved the ship in a northwesterly direction. The rudder was severed so it would be up to the position of the sail to guide the ship. After eating a measly dinner and checking on Sebastian, Riddick, and Batovi manned the sail once more. It was hard work holding onto the rope and pulling the heavy poles back and forth. It soon became very taxing, but the breeze was constant and considering they had one small sail, they made good time. Riddick and Batovi slept in times of little or no wind and let Ole'Baggins work his magic on their blistered and raw hands. Shaz grumbled from a makeshift chair, wishing he could help.

"We need to talk," the captain said, jarring Shaz from his thoughts.

"Alright," Shaz shifted in his chair so that he would be sitting up more.

"The storm has moved us into the barrier," Captain Yerild said.

"We're in the barrier?"

"Aye, that's why the storm was so heavy. We crossed where the barrier is still strong. I didn't realize it at first, but now, seeing the stars, we are sitting in the center. We need to get the ship further north, and then we can go west through the portal," Captain Yerild stroked his bearded chin, "The others don't know anything about the other worlds. I lost the few crew members that did. What do we tell them?"

Shaz forgot the others were supposed to stay on the mainland. "I have no clue," he said, looking into the sky.

"We best figure out something, at this rate it's going to take a full moons cycle to get to the barrier, and what if we run into the sea beasts, we'll have to tell them at some point," The Captain stood, placing one hand on his knee and pushed while pulling on a broken pole with the other.

Shaz found it hard to sleep that night. Images of sea-beasts from Grandfather's stories consumed his thoughts. And the tightness of the bandages made it difficult to move into a comfortable position. Since he wasn't sleeping, he decided to try to manage his way topside for some fresh air. He glanced over the deck and there was only one barrel of fresh water. His heart sank and his stomach ached. He hadn't eaten much because their rations were going fast. He sucked in a deep breath and closed his eyes. Drafang came to mind, and he pulled the fang from his tunic and twisted it between his fingers. He usually felt the tingle on his chest, but with all the bandages he hadn't felt it in days. It had a familiar and comfortable feeling rather than at first; it was almost painful. A small tingle of magic surge through his fingertips.

He rolled it around in his fingers and tried to think of a way to fix the problem, after all, they were in this mess because of him in the first place. Random images of birds and the sea creatures surfaced, and he tried to shake the thoughts from his mind. Sleep gradually overcame him and he returned to his cabin.

Early the next morning screeching sounds of a flock of pelicans cascaded through the ship. Riddick, Batovi, and William scrambled on deck and found a flock of white pelicans with their large beaks swaging in the air. The birds swooped down in a twirling motion and dropped several sizable fish onto the deck. Shaz climbed the ladder and made his way to the deck to find the birds swooping back into the sky and circle the ship. Shaz squeezed through the men and saw the fish lying on the deck. Shaz moved to the fish and picked one up. A hefty, full-bellied bird swooped down in a spiral and landed in front of Shaz. The bird lowered its head and then stretched his magnificent wings and hopped back into the air and joined the rest of the birds and they flew off the same way they came.

"Wow, did you see that?" William asked.

"Yes, how remarkable," said Shaz.

"Aye, I have never seen that before in all my life at sea," said the captain, scratching his hair covered chin.

Shaz thought about the night before and the images in his mind and remembered what Drafang had told him. He smiled and gave a silent nod of thanks to the animal kingdom. Riddick inspected Shaz and knew something was up. It wasn't just Shaz's mysterious behavior either. He couldn't place it yet, but when he was working with the wooden masts, it was almost like the grain of the wood was talking to him and now this. The men gathered the fish and hauled it below deck. Ole'Baggins threw one log into the stove and started preparing the fish. They all ate until they were full and there were still fish left. Shaz's chest was aching, and he excused himself and made his way back to his cabin.

Jagwynn followed him into the little room, and he pulled off his shirt. The bandage was snug, which helped with the oozing, but it made it hard to move around. Too much moving around pulled at the newly forming scabs and he tried to be careful as he removed the bandages. He winced when he got to a point that the bandage had stuck to the scab. He dipped the clean cloth in a bowl of water and refastened the new wrap. Shaz returned to the deck where he tried to help the crew keep the sails moving the ship forward.

"Captain, we are running out of fresh water, even with the birds bringing fish, we won't last long without it," Batovi said.

"Aye, well then lets' just hope for rain," the captain said.

Shaz whispered into the breeze.

"My bird friends, we need fresh water."

Riddick eyed him and scrunched his brows. Riddick kept Shaz where he could always see him and scrutinized his every action. Shaz pretended not to know, but he could sense Riddick's intentions. The day passed again, and Riddick gave up and went to bed. Shaz couldn't sleep again. His mind wouldn't rest. It was filled with thoughts from the sword, memories of the last several days, questions as to what Grandfather and his father were doing, and Drafang and the birds. Shaz brushed the morning fog from his mind and heard the pelicans arrive again.

7-Are You Responsible For This

The next morning the birds arrived as usual, except this time, there were more birds, each with their beaks full. Half the birds swooped down and dropped the fish, and the other half swooped down and emptied their full beaks into the water barrel. Everyone stood there dumbfounded at the marvelous sight, and Shaz had a smile on his face. The same rotund bird lowered his head in a bow and jumped into the sky. Riddick saw the smile on Shaz's face and was certain he had something to do with it. He came up to him and blocked him from going anywhere.

"Are you responsible for this?" Riddick asked.

"I don't know what you are talking about," Shaz said.

Riddick glared with that 'don't give me that' look and Shaz replied with that 'who me?' look.

"I mean it Shaz, what is going on?" Riddick asked.

Shaz looked around and then turned toward the open horizon.

"Do you remember the stories Grandfather used to tell us? The ones about the war wizard and the elemental sages?" Shaz asked.

"Aye, but what does that have to do with anything?" Riddick asked.

"Well, I am the war wizard," Shaz said.

Riddick stared at him for a minute then blurted a guffaw. Shaz stared at the horizon and waited for Riddick to compose himself. Riddick cleared his throat and looked at Shaz, who didn't have an amused look.

"You're not kidding, are you?" Riddick asked. Shaz shook his head. "I don't understand, how, if you're the war wizard, then why haven't you used all that magic stuff before?" Riddick asked.

"Because Grandfather was keeping me from it, to protect me from the Necromancer," Shaz said.

"So, now you're not being protected?" Riddick half-asked-half-stated.

Shaz nodded.

"I don't know what is going to happen, and I have no idea how to use magic. I haven't a clue on anything and I can't sleep, I can barely eat, and we're stranded in the middle of the barrier without a single option," Shaz said.

Riddick lowered his eyes and stared at his boots. A familiar sensation crept into the back of his mind, and he was certain of the truth of Shaz's words. Riddick opened his mouth to say something but shut it. He didn't know what to say. Shaz and Riddick stood there looking out to sea while Jagwynn lay on the deck soaking in the warm sun. The sun beat down on the sailors as they tried to catch every pocket of wind they could. In the last half-a-dozen days they made a fathom or two, but most of the time they sat adrift.

Late in the afternoon clouds began to fill in the sky. Out in the distance, Shaz could see a whirlwind picking up water and turning it around in the air. Soon two and three waterspouts sprung up, rolling and twisting across the sea. The closer they came, Shaz could see large billowing clouds above the waterspouts and the sea beneath, rippled and churned under the stress of the wind currents fighting for control.

The tube-like shapes had a glass-like appearance and seemed to be hollow inside.

"Sebastian, do we have a working canon?" called out the captain from the helm.

"Aye, I believe so captain, why?"

Captain Yerild pointed out to sea.

"Waterspouts," called the captain.

Shaz had only seen a waterspout once before, but they were able to steer around the pressure system that caused them without incident, but this time, with no way to move around them, they were sitting ducks. Batovi, with his bandaged forehead and Sebastian, who was now operating on a make-shift crutch, worked their way into the lower hull where the canons were kept. They checked for the steel ball and the flint. Batovi packed the fire powder and charges and using a long ramrod, he packed the explosives tight against the back of the chamber and then heaved the ball and dropped into the open shaft of the cannon and then positioned it out a nearby port hole.

Sebastian fashioned the wick in the hole at the other end, and stayed at the canon, while Batovi ran back to the hatch. He climbed half-way up the ladder and called out for the coordinates of the waterspouts. The captain took out his looking glass and searched the sky and called out some numbers, which then Batovi relayed them to Sebastian, who then scooted the canon into place and lit the wick.

A moment later, an ear-piercing blast of the canon-fire echoed into the empty sky. A sizable ball struck one waterspout dead on, and the disrupted spout released the seawater into a cascading waterfall. The crew cheered, but three more spouts sprung up in its place.

"Blasted all," cursed the captain. "Load up another shot."

"Load it up," Batovi called to Sebastian.

Sebastian loaded up another pack of fire powder and charges and using the ramrod he packed the explosives tight against the back of the chamber and heaved the heavy ball into the hole. Using the coordinates called out to him, Sebastian moved the canon and then lit the wick. Another deafening blow screeched through the air and the ball was propelled into the sky. The waterspout dispersed as the ball rammed through the crystal glass column. Waterspout after waterspout, the small derelict crew eliminated the oncoming threat.

"We only have one more ball left," Sebastian shouted to Batovi and then Batovi to the captain.

Shaz and William were standing on deck while Riddick went to search for more balls. Much of the cargo had been shifted around so badly or dropped into the sea that nothing was easily found. Riddick lunged over a high pile of debris and landed in water on the other side. The hull had been taking on water for the last few days and no one had noticed. Riddick caught himself on the swollen bags of beans that were no longer piled neatly. He swallowed hard as the pit in his stomach lurched and he raced topside.

"Captain, the ship is taking on water, in the aft hull about knee high," Riddick said.

"Get the siphon and see if you can get the water out, we may be able to patch the hole if we can find it," the captain said.

"Right," Riddick turned on his heel and ran back below deck.

He searched for the siphon, but it was nowhere to be found. With obvious frustration, he pounded the sidewall. The old man came out of the galley and handed him a long tube with an apparatus attached. Sebastian made his way over the pile of bags and helped Riddick pull the plunger in and out to create a suction. The siphon slurped and sputtered but caught hold of the liquid and started shoving it out the long tube on the other end. Riddick waded through the cold water until he found a crack in the timbers above the waterline. The hole wasn't big enough, and he slammed his fist on the plank. The hole widened suddenly, and Riddick stepped back with wide eyes. Riddick turned to see if Sebastian had notice and was relieved to see him fighting with the suction part. He shoved the tube through the hole and the water gushed back into the sea. At first it wasn't going very fast and seemed that it wasn't even working at all. But Riddick examined the waterline and was reassured when it didn't rise.

"At least we won't take on more water; if we can keep it from filling up, then the ship will stay afloat," Riddick said.

"Let's hope this works then," Sebastian said.

"Aye," Riddick said.

Riddick moved through the water and climbed over the pile of rubble and stayed to make sure things were going to keep working. The image of the hole widening in front of his eyes sat in his brain, and he ran every scenario he could think of. A thought kept coming back, that he was the earth sage from Grandfather's stories, but he shoved it out as soon as it entered and tried to stay focused on his tasks. A stiff breeze shifted in the air, which tasseled the men's hair and stung their noses. Riddick and Sebastian ran to the ropes that were tied to the makeshift mast and began maneuvering the sail once again. With renewed vigor they steered the boat past the last few waterspouts, but they didn't make it very far until the wind died down again. The crew struggled with the sails and became discouraged as the late day turned to night. They had decided that there was no use standing at the sails without wind and turned in for the night.

Shaz enjoyed his time at night alone, but wondered why he had a hard time sleeping. He was thankful, however, that he hadn't had a headache in days. The three moons slowly crept across the star speckled sky and Shaz found himself rehearsing the stories from his childhood. He let his imagination carry the stories to new levels and new events, and a few times a feeling in his chest would signal that he had hit on a solid truth. An unfamiliar tingle rippled down Shaz's back, which brought him from his thoughts, and he studied the surface of the water but found nothing. He examined the water for a time and finally decided he might be able to fall asleep and retired to his cabin.

After only a few hours, the rest of the crew stirred. Ole' Baggins made breakfast, and Riddick and Batovi dutifully tended the sail.

Yerild searched the sky with his looking glass and the day moved on. The sun beat down on the cold ocean, which made the air thick and humid. Small clouds speckled the sky, and the small crew tried in vain to urge wind into the sail.

Captain Yerild checked the compass and tinkered with the instruments on the helm, hoping that they would somehow tell him something different. The atmosphere rapidly shifted, and the captain stood stoically at the helm and began to whistle. The two sailors whistled with the captain in unison, as if trying to call up a breeze from the Dead Calm. Shaz hadn't believed in the superstitious belief's the sailors did, but now he was certain there was an element of truth to most, if not all of it.

The ship jolted up about five lengths and smacked into the water, throwing everyone about. They struggled to their feet and ran to the edges of the ship. An enormous silver and black tail, that resembled a snake, slithered just under the surface of the water for a few leagues then dipped back into the deep.

"What in the world was that?" said Sebastian as he searched the ocean.

"I have never seen such a thing. Captain?" Batovi said.

"Aye, I've heard rumors of a great serpent in the sea," Yerild said.

The ship bounced out of the water again and smacked back into the sea with a splash of water onto the deck. The crew dove and ducked for cover as the serpent's tail whipped out of the water, and with a lightning shriek it slipped back under the surface.

"Make ready the cannon," shouted Captain Yerild.

Shaz jumped with the pain and covered his ears as Yerild barked the order in his ear.

"Captain, we only have three balls left," shouted Sebastian.

"Aye, then we'll have to be a good aim."

"Aye, aye sir," Sebastian said.

Sebastian hobbled on his makeshift crutch down to the lower deck.

"Riddick, you help too," Captain Yerild ordered.

"Aye, aye captain."

Before he got to the ladder, the ship was again tossed back and forth. As he raised his arms to catch himself, Riddick slipped and fell into a glass lantern and bright red blood surged from his slashed skin. The stinging pain throbbed up his arms, and he tucked them under his armpits and held them tight. The sea creature emerged a few lengths under the surface and the captain hollered the coordinates.

"Fire," commanded the Captain.

"Fire," yelled Riddick.

The cannon ignited before Sebastian expected, and the recoil slammed him into an empty crate. He slouched to the floor, holding his chest. The ship rocked back and forth, and Sebastian's head spun from the blast and his face turned green. He threw himself forward as he vomited. He wiped his mouth and staggered back topside.

"What are you doing here?" a deep raspy voice echoed.

Shaz thought a moment, pulled the fang out from under his shirt and rubbed it between his fingers. The fang heated up and tingled his fingertips as he touched it.

"There it is. There's the blasted monster," cried Sebastian.

He pointed from the starboard side and started back to the cannon, but slipped on the sea-soaked deck.

"No," Shaz raced to the starboard side of the ship, "Wait, I don't think it wants to hurt us."

"What are you talking about? It's a blasted sea monster. Of course, it wants to hurt us," Sebastian yelled.

"No, I don't think it does," Shaz said calmly.

Sebastian struggled to his feet and stared wide-eyed at Shaz, then looked out into the deep alongside him.

"Who are you?" Shaz asked.

"I asked you what you are doing here?" said the creature.

"The storm pushed us here. We need to pass through the barrier," Shaz said.

The serpent rose from the deep-blue sea. Water came crashing down from off its back and head as it rose several lengths in the air. His enormous black eyes sat high on his head and underneath a sharp horn on top of its forehead. A lower clear eyelid flicked up and giant flexing nostrils snorted sprays of water as it breathed the dry air. The beast was covered with a variegated array of different colors of blue scales and gills, which created a camouflage under the water. In full daylight, however, the coarse scales reflected the sunlight and made all the men on the ship squint and cover their eyes. Long sharp curved fangs crested under the pucker of its lips and it flicked a snake-like tongue into the air. Riddick, Sebastian, Captain, and William all stood paralyzed and Jagwynn crept across the deck from the cargo hold with long, strong and steady stride.

"Who are you?" the sea creature asked.

"I am Shazmpt," Shaz said.

Stunned that it was talking, each man's mouth dropped, and their knees weakened.

"The barrier is the border of time. Once you cross, you will no longer be in our protection," the water serpent replied.

"Yes, I understand," Shaz said.

Shaz tried to calculate what the creature was thinking. The serpent's voice rumbled deep.

"You cannot pass,"

The serpent crossed his webbed wings behind his back. The sword hummed in its scabbard. Shaz instinctively pulled it from its sheath, revealing the first few symbols engraved on its solid form. The serpent spied the ancient marking and reared backward and bowed in reverence.

"My many pardons, I didn't know who you were. How can I help?"

"You must take us to Ebassia," Shaz said.

Shaz slipped the sword back into the scabbard.

"I can take you through the barrier of the Teorran of Time and then to the current that will take you to Ebassia, but that is as far as I can go," the water wyvern said.

He bowed and raised his wings, slapped the water's surface and grabbed a surge of air. He leaped out of the water and thrust high into the sky and flipped over, and head-first he dove back into the sea. Before anyone could speak, the ship bumped again and lurched forward with a start and slowly began to move.

The creature below the ship swam just underneath the water's surface and everyone hung over the edge, trying to take in as many details as they could. For a time, they moved north, then the ship turned tightly to the west. Shaz could make out a large hole in the sky, and a faint shimmer of blues encircled the oval shape. Thousands of tiny water particles danced on the surface of the oval, creating a mirror-like effect just before the ship launched into it.

Once passed the misty wall, it turned into a tunnel of water and sky. Magic soared into Shaz's body, leaving his mind exhilarated and full of radiant heat. The further in they went, a raining sensation under his skin, left him weak in the knees. He wondered what the tunnel was doing and determined it was taking magic from him. The ship gained speed and water sprayed from the front bow. The light-blue sky turned dark and specks of light whizzed by for a moment. It faded steadily into a deep shade of mid-night blue, and Shaz could tell they were now on the other side of the barrier. Shaz regained his strength as the magic returned to his body.

The ship slowed rapidly, leaving them unsteady on their feet. Shaz's eyes moved around the horizon and he knew he was now in a completely different world. He walked over to where Riddick was staring out at the sky, watching the moons glimmer above them. Small mountain peaks in the distance glowed against the purple hazy illumination of the three moons. *At least the moons are the same*, he thought.

The breeze flowed through their hair and they were thankful for the current that was pulling them toward the distant mountains.

"I wonder how long it will take to make it to the mainland?" asked Shaz.

"I didn't even know anything else, other than our own islands existed," Sebastian said, shaking his head at the thought.

"Me either," said Batovi.

Riddick shared the thoughts, but he now understood that there was a very big world out there, and his journey has just started. He shared a look with Shaz, and they breathed in a heavy breath. Shaz and Riddick turned to the captain, who seemed to have a little more gray in his beard.

"We are in the main current now. It won't be long until another ship finds us," Captain Yerild said.

Shaz turned to Riddick and motioned for him to walk with him. They moved around the water barrel and started toward the aft part of the ship.

"So, what's the plan now? Riddick asked.

"I have to go to Ebassia, it's my first task, whatever that means, and I think you need to return to Turob. My gut says that something there will be your first task," Shaz said.

"Aye, I've been feeling the same thing," Riddick said.

"Are you alright with that?" Shaz asked.

"Aye, wait, my first task?" Riddick asked.

"I tried to fight it too, but we both know who you are and how this is going to play out," Shaz said.

Riddick stared into Shaz's deep blue eyes and nodded. He *did*, in fact, know who *he* was, and he *was* trying to fight it.

"Be careful how you use your magic, remember what Grandfather used to tell us, that our magic can be tracked," Shaz said.

"Aye," Riddick said.

Shaz could tell a sudden weight encompassed his being, and he felt the same way.

"We'll see each other soon, that I'm sure of," Shaz said.

Riddick nodded, and they embraced each other in a tight squeeze.

8-Sounding Like An Idiot, That's What

Shaz stood on the pier and waved at the crew of the vessel that was going to take Riddick and the others back through the barrier. Riddick waved and Shaz swallowed the lump in his throat. Even though Captain Yerild had promised Shaz that Mrs. Bailey made the best roast on this side of the barrier, the sting of being on his own in a foreign land left a mark on his nerves. Shaz waited until the ship was out of sight and turned toward the city. Ebassia was nothing like Shaz had ever seen before. Large buildings stretched into the sky and disappeared into the atmosphere. Some buildings had square hand-honed stones and narrow arched triangular windows. The tops had several crenellations, as if they'd been perches in a time of war. Other buildings peaked at the tops with highly polished stonework and intricately carved details above the windows and doors. Waterways were lifted high to allow for ships to pass freely underneath.

"Excuse me," Shaz said.

Shaz maneuvered around the people that were now starting to fill the boardwalk.

"Watch it," said an old man, hobbling with a cane.

His bald scalp glistened in the bright morning sun.

"Sorry."

Shaz skidded around several small children as they raced passed the entrance to the working district. The fresh sea breeze became tainted with a hint of smoke as he approached the outer ring of the city. A stench of melted ore filled his nose and a small fire burned in a steel barrel next to him. The little warmth it gave was nonexistent, and he wondered why it was even there. The sun didn't yet reach the high-point in the sky, which left long shadows from the lifted aqueducts and outer buildings looming over the city floor.

"Over here," a young man called.

He was standing on the back of a long narrow passenger boat in a waterway several feet below the cobblestone path.

"Me?" Shaz asked, pointing his finger at himself.

"Yes, you," the young man said.

The young man wore shiny black shoes and dark, pleated trousers and his long dark hair pulled back, making his eyes bigger on his face. Shaz situated his pack on his shoulder and took the steps two at a time. "Do you need a ride?" the young man asked.

"Sure," Shaz said.

Shaz hopped into the watercraft and settled into the middle seat. The boat had three rows with two seats, each leaving a platform in the back, presumably for luggage.

"Where you headed?" the gondola driver asked.

"Umm?" Shaz said.

Shaz pulled out the small, crinkled paper and repeated the address. The boat boy took the long pole from the side and pushed against the moldy moss-covered stone. Shaz's nose wrinkled with the dank odor of the musky combination but settled into his seat.

"I could tell you needed a ride because you aren't from around here," the young man said, "Where are you from?" he asked.

Shaz wasn't exactly sure what to say. He was sure that no one would understand where he was from and decided it wouldn't hurt telling him.

"I come from Turob," Shaz said.

"Hum, I'm not familiar with that one, and I've heard and seen a lot," he said.

On the other side of the waterway, in a small shopping plaza, a young woman wearing a deep purple cloak caught Shaz's eye. Her hood slipped off the back of her head exposing long wavy brown hair and soft creamy skin. A small bag with green leafy things inside hung from the crook of her elbow, and she was inspecting a bundle of herbs. Shaz turned in his seat, so he could see her better and his chest pounded.

"It's far to the east," Shaz said.

His energy shifted, and he tried to figure out why there was something about her that made him feel this way. The girl too stood up straight and turned to scan the distance. She searched around, but when she didn't find anything; she returned to her herbs. The boat continued to move in the opposite direction over the calm flowing water, and Shaz stretched to keep his attention on the girl.

"Something you like?" the boat boy asked.

"Uh, No, it's just-" Shaz said.

"Uh huh," the boat boy said.

Shaz looked over his shoulder and realized how that must have appeared. A warm sensation crept up under his cheeks, and he thanked the coolness of the shade from an overhead stone bridge. It wasn't so much that he thought she was pretty, although, thinking about it, she definitely was. There was something different about her, something he couldn't explain.

"My name is Deagan," the young man said.

"I'm Shaz," Shaz said.

Shaz didn't really want to talk but figured it he would be rude if he didn't.

"So, tell me about Turob?" Deagan asked, pushing the stick into the soft murky bottom.

"Well, Turob is an island far from here and small, one could walk around it in a few days, but it has lots of tall trees and inlets," Shaz said.

"Sounds nice," Deagan said.

Everyone knew there were no islands in the east. In fact, there was nothing to the east or the west. Come to think of it, the north as well. Shaz held onto the side as Deagan turned a corner sharply and the little boat moved briskly. The old run-down doors and shops were now replaced with neatly put together storefronts. Fruit and vegetable stands speckled the walkway and freshly baked breads, pastries, and roasted meats now replaced the musky stink of the working district.

"We're now in the Commerce District," Deagan announced.

He shifted the pole to the other side and slipped the boat into a narrow waterway. Shaz couldn't get the girl out of his mind and stared at the people who were coming and going. He noted the alleys and passageways that gave a maze-like feel to the city. He glanced down a dimly lit passage and found the young woman. Her long brown hair glimmered in the new rays of the sun, and he stood up to get a better look. Deagan shimmied to rebalance the boat and stuck the pole into the murky bottom to slow it down.

The girl handed a big red apple to a rugged street boy. He thanked her, and she smiled at him. Her smile took Shaz's breath away and his chest heaved. The girl looked around again, and this time their eyes met. Shaz was instantly drawn to her in a way he couldn't explain, and he wondered if he was going to lose his mind. Their eyes locked onto each other, but Deagan couldn't keep the boat in one place and she slipped behind a wall as they moved on. Shaz felt a sudden loss and cursed. What he didn't understand was why his intrigue with her was so immediate and intense. He rarely thought of girls, why now? Why did she flex emotions he had never had before? When Deagan looked at Shaz's expression, he could tell she held more than just a pretty face.

"Do you know her?" Deagan asked.

"Hum? Uh no," Shaz said.

"You seem intent on that one," Deagan said.

"She's familiar to me somehow, but I've never seen her before," Shaz said. The boat bobbed around another bend and Shaz put his chin in his hand. "How much further?"

"We're here," Deagan said.

"Oh, sorry," Shaz said.

Shaz stood and grabbed his pack and threw it over his shoulder. He pulled some coins Grandfather had given him and handed a few to Deagan.

"Thank you, sir," Deagan said.

"Thank you for the ride," Shaz said.

Shaz slapped him on the back as he climbed out of the boat, and Deagan smiled at the coins.

"My pleasure, sir," Deagan said.

Deagan shoved the coins into his pocket and pushed off. Shaz didn't have any clue where he was or where to go.

"Hey, where do I go from here?"

"Twenty blocks through there," Deagan shouted, pointing to a narrow alley.

Shaz made his way between a group of people and was going to keep heading down the alley, but a prick at the back of his mind made him turn and look down a crossing pathway. Shaz spotted the young woman from the corner of his eye. He turned quickly and moved steadily toward the other side of the plaza. The crowds inten-sified, and he got stuck in a throng of school-aged children and he waited for them to pass. By the time the path was clear enough for him to make his way; she was gone.

"Blast," Shaz said.

As a hunter, he hated it when he lost what he was stalking, and this wasn't just another hunt. This girl meant a great deal to him, and he had no idea why.

"Did you want to buy some fresh fruit?" asked a friendly voice from behind the cart.

"Do you know that girl that was just here, the one with the purple cloak?" Shaz asked.

The woman shook her head. It kind of bothered him he spent so much time thinking of someone he'd never met and probably never would. He realized the time was getting late and he better keep going. The alley was close and tight and had lanterns which hung on the walls slightly higher than the doors, and there was little light shining on the shaded corridor. House numbers were etched into long skinny stones in the exterior of the house fronts, and small windows sat next to the doors. Stairways led up to houses sitting on top of the ones on the ground-level. Shaz's alert level intensified with so many people and homes that fit into the small area. As he examined the new kind of buildings, he decided he would rather live in one on top like his treehouse back home.

The door of 'sixty-two' had been decorated with a small flow-erpot with a bright pink flower. It was sitting half wilted on a stool next to the door, and a light-pink lace covered a window in the center of the door. Shaz knocked using the little knocker and stepped back. A little round woman opened the door with a big smile.

"Ah, you must be Shaz," she said, her red cheeks getting a little redder, "My you're a handsome one you are," Shaz shifted his pack but nodded, "Come in, come in," she said.

The house was warm with soft pastel colors that decorated the rooms. The aroma was delicious but seemed to have an off flavor hanging in the air.

"Thank yo-" Shaz began.

Mrs. Bailey dismissed him and smiled.

"Oh, no trouble. My brother speaks highly of you. This is an honor really," she said, between breaths, "Here, come let me show you to your room." Shaz followed her up a flight of stairs to a small room. The room had a decent sized bed, a side table, and an armoire. Quaint and comfortable, just the way he liked it. "Now, dinner won't be long, so go clean up,"

She motioned to a washroom across the hall and shut the door. Shaz put his pack on the bed and pulled out an extra tunic and a pair of trousers he received from the rescue crew. The trousers were a little short, but they were clean. He took them across the hall and poured water from a pitcher into a bowl that was sitting on a wooden table. To his surprise, it was warm. He wondered how Mrs. Bailey knew when he would arrive. He took the cloth hanging on the rod and washed and dressed, then went downstairs.

"Shhhh child, don't go getting all worked up, you should think of this as an honor to help, and besides he's an attractive young man," Mrs. Bailey said.

"Fine," a young woman said.

Shaz rounded the corner, and his blood raced through his body at lightning speed.

"You?" Shaz blurted.

"You?" the young woman blurted.

Shaz stared into her deep green eyes. The young woman returned the gaze and smiled. Shaz felt Mrs. Bailey's penetrating glare and cleared his throat.

"I saw you from the boat today."

"I know," she said.

"I'm Shaz."

"I'm Serin."

"Pleasure to meet you," Shaz said.

Shaz didn't want to stop looking at her, but he felt awkward because Mrs. Bailey was staring between them.

"You too. I hear you are going to stay here with Mrs. Bailey for a little while?" Serin said.

Serin pulled the hair at the side of her face and tucked it behind her ear, and Shaz's knees went weak. He chided himself for feeling so giddy about this girl and shoved his hands in his pockets.

"Yes, for a short time," Shaz said.

"Wonderful, now that you two have met, I'll finish in the kitchen while you two talk," Mrs. Bailey said.

Serin frowned at her. She knew what Mrs. Bailey was up to, and she didn't like it one bit, but she didn't want to make a scene, so she sat in the chair that was at an angle from the couch.

"So, Mrs. Bailey says you are from far away," Serin said.

She rested her hands softly on her lap and her legs crossed at the ankles under the chair. She hated making small chat and was going to let Mrs. Bailey have it at her earliest convenience, but there was something about him she couldn't explain. His blue eyes captivated her, and she wanted to stare into them.

"Yes, from across the sea," Shaz said.

"I didn't know anything was across the sea."

Shaz shifted in his seat and thought he better come up with something else to tell people. Grandfather told him that only a select few were aware of the barrier.

"Well, far away anyway," Shaz said.

Serin didn't want to give him any idea that Mrs. Bailey's attempt at matchmaking was going to work. Even though there was something about him she couldn't place, he was probably just like all the other good-looking but self-absorbed guys she'd met.

"I guess I'll have to take your word on that," Serin said.

"So, do you live here too?" Shaz asked.

"Oh no, I live on the outskirts of town. I just study the art of healing from Mrs. Bailey."

"The art of healing?" Shaz asked.

"Herbs, plants, things like that. I'm sorry, but I better go before it gets too late," Serin said.

"You have to leave already?" Shaz asked. *You derp, what are you doing? Sounding like an idiot, that's what* he thought. "Well, it was a pleasure to meet you."

"You too," she said.

Serin stepped into the kitchen and said goodbye to Mrs. Bailey, but gave her a glare and Mrs. Bailey snickered, and then started toward the door. Shaz walked with her and opened the door for her.

"Would you like some company, I could escort you home," Shaz said.

Serin hesitated and touched his arm and gave him a gentle smile. Shaz's skin soaked in her energy and Serin looked at him with a hint of puzzle in her eye.

"Thank you, but I'll be fine," Serin said.

****

Shaz sat straight up and his heart pounded against his ribs. He gasped for air, but the tightness constricted his efforts. His hair hung in his face and sweat dripped down his back. The small room was bright as the sun shone in, giving off warmth and comfort, but he found it hard to keep his eyes open. He sagged back into the mattress and pulled the sheets over his face. The pain in his head pounded against his skull and he was certain his head was going to explode.

"Not again," he muttered.

He put his arm over his eyes and tried to think of anything other than the pain, but all that came to his mind were the images from the nightmare. Shaz stirred at the soft knock on the door and he mumbled for them to come in.

"Mrs. Bailey asked me to bring you some new things," Serin said.

She put the clothes on the side table and a tug from her core gave her the impression there was something wrong and she hesitated.

"Thank you," he mumbled.

"Mrs. Bailey insisted," she said.

Shaz pulled the blanket off his face and labored to sit up. The pounding in his head made it almost unbearable to open his eyes, and his head weighed the same as an iron anvil. Serin's heart skipped a beat seeing him without his shirt on. His strong muscular frame quivered, and he managed to blink a few times through bloodshot eyes. Serin came to the side of the bed and sat down next to him.

"Lay down," she said softly.

Shaz laid back down and put his arm over his eyes.

"I'm sorry, I'm not trying to be rude," he managed.

"No, I'm sorry," Serin said.

For an instant, she perceived his pain and shuddered.

"I get these awful headaches," he said, with a shaky voice.

"I have something for that. I'll be right back," she said.

A few moments later, she returned and put a bowl of cold water on the side table and sat on the bed. She dipped a cloth into the water and a soft blue hue of mist encompassed the cloth and she wrung it out.

"Here, put this on your forehead," she moved his arm out of the way "Does the light make the pain worse?" Shaz nodded. She went over to the window and pulled the heavy curtains shut. "There, that should help," Serin said.

Shaz blinked a few times and opened his eyes slightly.

"Thanks," Serin pulled out the stopper of a blue glass bottle. "What's that?"

The odor of the potent concoction rippled through his nose.

"This will help with the pain and let you sleep."

She tipped the bottle onto her finger and rubbed the oily substance under his nose. The sweet earthy aroma surprised him, he actually liked it. Most medicines didn't taste or smell good. A cooling sensation started in his nose and went to his chest and moved all over his body.

"You don't have to do this," Shaz said.

He didn't want her to see him like this, and he afraid she would see him as weak and broken. Serin tipped the oil again and wiped the medicine on his forehead and around his eyes, then down his neck to his collarbone, arms, and wrists. Her cool skin was comfortable on his warm skin and he relaxed into the mattress and sighed.

"Better?" she asked.

"Yes, thank you," he said.

Serin returned the stopper and was about to put it on the table when she saw the long-jagged scar across his chest.

"That must have been horrible," she said.

"It doesn't hurt anymore, it's just not pretty," he said.

"Can I ask you what happened?"

"That's a long story. You probably don't want to hear it," Shaz said.

"Actually, I do," Serin said.

"Alright, I saved a young sailor from going overboard. A steel bar sheared off the main ballast during the storm and tangled in his ropes, and while underwater, the edge sliced my chest."

"Oh my, how terrible, did the boy live?" she asked.

"Yes, but barely."

"How brave of you," Serin said.

Serin softly rested her hand on his arm, and Shaz hoped she would stay.

"I guess. My best mate told me I was stupid, so I'll take brave over stupid," he said with a small grin.

9-Move Out

Azrack made his way across the haggard ground which was now occupied with hundreds of tents, and several soldiers jumped to attention.

"At ease," Azrack said. His relaxed but official tone reassured his soldiers. He stopped in front of one soldier and took off his helmet, tucking it under his arm. "We have been assigned a secret mission to the land of Baymoor. I will give more details later, but we are to leave tonight," Azrack said.

"Tonight? But we-" Ralti started.

"I know, the King has a special task that we must perform and has entrusted it to us and only us. I know we're worn, but we must do this," Azrack said.

"What do we need and how many soldiers?" Ralti asked.

"We will need mostly traveling supplies. Baymoor is a long distance to the west and two hundred soldiers."

Ralti's eyes raised. A sense of dread hit the bottom of his stomach.

"Why such a big number? Are we going to battle again?" Ralti asked.

Ralti was young, at eighty-five rotations old, and his turquoise blue and green feathers were stained with sweat and covered with dirt. He stood as tall as Azrack but with slightly less shoulder width. He was an attractive creature, always gaining favor from the females they encountered during their travels. However, this last battle was fierce and long and took many lives on both sides. Ralti lost several close friends and soldiers and was tired of both the fighting and the loosing. It had been over two rotations since they were back in their home country, and Ralti pushed the anger in his chest into his deepest parts.

"Let's just get it done and get back home. Have the soldiers leave in small groups and meet at the falls by morning. Stagger their departure, so they are less conspicuous," Azrack said.

"Yes, Sir," Ralti said.

Ralti slapped his fist over his heart, and Azrack returned the salute. Ralti spun on his paw and turned to the men and gave orders quietly. The life Azrack once desired, he now dreaded, and his heart ached. The night would soon turn to dawn as he made his way among the sleeping soldiers. Many of them were sleeping off their drunkenness of that night's celebrations.

Azrack sank slightly as he walked back to his tent, his heart heavy and his body sore from battle. He would leave in an hour or so, giving himself enough time to gather his things and write a letter to his wife. With his helmet in the crook of his arm, he lifted the flap of his tent and squeezed into the small opening. At the foot of his bed, he pulled out a small box he kept parchment and ink in. He pushed some dirty leather bracers off the small table and took in a deep breath and scripted:

Dear Telete,

I find myself f with the pains of a broken heart, as I have to inform you I am assigned yet another secret mission. To a land far away, it will take some time before I can return. I have been dreaming of the day I can return to you and see and touch you once more.

I feel as though your face is fading from my memory and all I have left is the love in my heart I have for you. Be strong and think of me often as I never stop thinking of you!

Your forever love,

Azrack

Azrack rolled the small script up and slipped it into his satchel. He gathered his things and left his tent. Azrack skirted toward the king's tent, where he hoped to find Lahonti. The dry grass under his paws made more noise than he wished, so he half-walked-half-flew.

"Lahonti," Azrack whispered. Lahonti stirred but didn't wake. "Lahonti, wake up."

Groggily, Lahonti sat up. He jumped awake when he realized it was Azrack.

"Yes, sir. I'm sorry sir, did I oversleep? I'm so sorry sir," he blushed.

"No, no, relax, I have a message I need you to send to my wife."

"Oh yes sir, certainly sir," Azrack hesitated then gave it to Lahonti, "Sir, is everything alright? You seem troubled."

"Yes, thank you, Lahonti. You have been a good servant. I'm honored to have known you."

Azrack couldn't quite kick the feeling that this would be the last time he would see him. All night long the uneasiness kept creeping into his thoughts, making him at times feel sick and at times anxious. Azrack left quickly. He had spent too much time on this matter and put his emotions aside as best he could.

Besides, he was a soldier, born and bred. There was no choice. He was lucky to have been chosen by the royal guard early in his carrier and rose in the ranks well. His fellow soldiers not only fought for him well, but loved him. A luxury most leaders never have. He neared the plateau before the falls and fell into ranks with the selected soldiers. Most of them had had little sleep, and it showed. Azrack made his way through the gathered soldiers until he met Ralti.

"Do we have everyone?" Azrack asked.

"Over half," Ralti said.

Ralti also rose the ranks quickly. He caught Azrack's attention by exhibiting leadership qualities. Azrack took him in as his protégé and within that year made him his first in command.

"Move out," Azrack said.

"Yes, sir."

The soft light of dawn crept across the horizon, allowing small hints of light reflect the many-colored feathers of the soldiers. Bright blues, greens, reds, oranges, and purples flecked the dingy blue. Azrack leaped up as the last of the soldiers slipped into the sky.

His large flaming red and orange feathers rustled as the wind caught hold and lifted him into the air.

****

Groargoth and his small hoard moved over the forest floor. The pelting rain kept them from flying and they ran through the muddy landscape. His anger propelled him faster than usual, and his soldiers had a hard time keeping up. The muddy surface soon covered their bright feathers as they raced southward. It would take more than a day to reach on paw, and Groargoth was determined to return before Azrack started his new assignment.

The sun never broke over the clouds as night fell, and Groargoth agreed to make camp for the night. They found large pine trees with the branches hanging to the ground, and Groargoth climbed in and pawed at the years of fallen needles. The clouds broke sometime during the night, letting in meek efforts of daylight. They woke at first light and raced over the countryside, this time flying through the trees to stay hidden before the sun rose completely over the treetops.

Groargoth slowed his pace and flicked his ears back and forth. The soldiers mimicked him and moved carefully from tree to tree. They came upon a group of Kronos soldiers taking down their camp. The messenger wore a short red cape and a large satchel at his waist, and the warriors wore their swords over their dark steel-plate armor.

Groargoth pointed a toe toward a ditch, signaled for a few of his warriors to take the left side, and a few to take the right. He crept slowly hugging the ground and leaped onto the unsuspecting messenger. Groargoth flung out his talons and gripped the gryphton's neck as one of his soldiers apprehended the others.

"I have a message for Kronos," Groargoth said. The messenger nodded vigorously and wriggled under Groargoth's grip. One Kronos warrior attempted to roll out from under the soldier's grip, but he was too slow and Groargoth's soldier stuck his sword into his side. The gryphton slouched and whined. "Tell Kronos, I wish to speak to him, face to face. He can bring as many soldiers as he pleases. I offer a deal he doesn't want to miss out on," Groargoth said. The messenger scrunched his brows in confusion, but nodded. "I will wait here. He has two days."

Groargoth stepped off the gryphton and watched him scramble to his feet. Kronos' soldiers grabbed their things and darted into the woods. Groargoth found a tree to camp under as the mist of evening settled over the forest floor and waited.

"Sir, Kronos is approaching," a soldier said.

Groargoth rose to his hind paws and stood tall. Kronos and several armed warriors slipped around trees and stopped several lengths from Groargoth. Kronos rose onto his hind legs, the scar over his left eye gave him an eerie stare.

"So, I hear you have something to offer me," Kronos said.

"It would seem that my father intends on making you extinct. However, I have other plans for this nation," Groargoth said.

"Oh, you do? But you're not the king," Kronos said.

"I will be, my father is old and sick and won't last long, then I will take over his kingdom."

"So how does that benefit me?"

"You now possess land that I want. I'm sure there is something I can offer you," Groargoth said.

Groargoth remembered stories as a cub of magic so powerful it could destroy the world. It is said the artifact that evokes this magic was brought by secret travelers and hidden in that land. He had to find it if he was going to show that he could indeed lead his people with greatness. Kronos rubbed a shiny metal medallion that hung at his neck.

"I want to be the General."

Groargoth hesitated, but nodded.

"Fine."

"What land are you talking about?" Kronos asked.

"The land east of the peaks."

"I will move my forces out of the land and will make my way up through the pass. What about Azrack?"

"I will take care of that," Groargoth said with a growl in his throat, "Deal?" Groargoth asked.

Kronos hesitated.

"Deal."

They pounded their chests and Groargoth lowered onto all fours and hurried toward his lands. Kronos and his party slipped behind the mist and disappeared.

10-The Scouting Party Has Returned

The sun's early morning rays trickled over the mountains and cast dancing shadows on the sleeping gryphtons. Azrack lay with his head tucked under his front arm, his tail wrapped around him while his wings covered his body and shielded him from the night's frost. Azrack's ear twitched, and he listened to his surroundings while he slept. At first, he didn't want to admit that he'd heard anything, but the nagging in his ears wouldn't leave.

The sound came again, and this time he came to an abrupt alertness. His eyes opened, and he scoured the horizon. Ralti too woke and scanned the distance along with a few of the others. It was a dull humming noise mixed with a chomping or chewing sound.

Azrack made his way over to Ralti and Brigdon. Brigdon was quite muscular for a gryphton, and his head was a bit larger than average. He rarely said much, but what he didn't say in words he said on the battlefield.

"Ralti send out a scouting party. We need to figure out what is making this noise," Azrack said.

"Yes, sir. Brigdon, take your soldiers and make a sweep of the area," Ralti said.

"Sir," Brigdon growled.

Brigdon's copper feathers ruffled slightly and rippled down his neck and shoulders. He turned sharply, his long tan tail swished back and forth as he crept away quietly. Brigdon nudged three of his comrades awake and the four worked their way past the rest of the army. The night's frost softened and turned into dew as the sun slipped higher over the mountains, casting more rays over the trees. They carefully stepped over fallen and broken branches and ducked under moss-covered logs and climbed over large boulders.

"Shhhh, do you hear that?" Jaxton asked.

Brigdon nodded, his ears twitching. He crouched onto his hind legs and lowered his center of gravity. Jaxton followed. He had a way of understanding Brigdon when others had no clue. Brigdon's deep blue eyes scanned the trees looking both up and down for several moments, and then he crept a few more lengths toward the edge of the trees.

"What do you suppose it is?" Helios asked.

"Dunno," Brigdon replied.

Brigdon moved sideways, stepping one paw over the other until he was shaded under the last tree in a line over a mile long.

"What are those structures?" Jaxton asked.

"Dunno," Brigdon said again.

"They're ancient ruins," Helios said, crouching next to a boulder next to them.

"How do you know?" asked Jaxton.

Jaxton didn't particularly care for Helios. He was always rambling on about this or that, which made his head hurt.

"I studied them at the academy before becoming a warrior," Helios said.

"I thought those were stories for children," Jaxton said.

Jaxton flicked his purple feathered ears at another crack and more of the chomping sounds.

"It is most certainly real, and a shame that warriors are not taught in the art of the ancient lore. Not understanding what is in the past keeps us blind to the future. For example, the human mages that are now on the Ebon Hoards side," Helios said.

He was indeed intelligent for his kind, and most of the soldiers wondered why he was even accepted into the Armada, instead of spending his time in the academy for scholars.

"So, what does it say about them?" Brigdon asked.

"These are the Ruins of Basete, a once large and powerful city of the Bairr Tiornecht. A civilization deep in the earth that used its minerals to forge weapons," Helios said.

"What happened to them?" Jaxton asked.

"They were destroyed by a Necromancer and shadow magic. He left their ruins to be inhabited by the Selket."

"The what?" Pontos asked, sidling up next to Helios.

"An ancient race placed on this earth by the God of Glory to punish his children for fighting each other," Helios said.

"Puhhssh." Jaxton and Pontos scoffed.

"Come on, let's keep going," Jaxton said pushing past Helios.

Jaxton crouched onto all fours and left the protection of the trees. The others followed, except Helios, who stood seething with anger. He hated that no one listened to what he had to say. Brigdon turned back and growled under his breath, and Helios rolled his eyes but fell in behind them. They moved quickly and quietly, and at times the chomping sounds grew louder and softer. Each time they heard the noise, they felt a rumbling under their paws.

They crossed the open valley of green grass and moved strategically around the now bright sun. Small bushes were half-dead from what Helios guessed was the lack of water. *How can that be, the grass is still green and soft, but these bushes are dying?* Helios thought. The stealthy animals stopped in their tracks as a loud clacking noise echoed from around a hill that was covered with trees and shrubs. Brigdon and Jaxton crept around the west side, while Helios and Pontos went around on the east.

"What in the-" Jaxton started.

On the other side of the hill was a creature half the size of the gryphton's. The critter crawled on eight legs and its body was long and narrow, with a long-segmented tail which had a forward curve over its back. Helios determined the sound came from the arthropod sucking the moisture from the roots of the bushes. With long skinny pincers and short fangs, the insect ate the soft roots. Brigdon surveyed the area, peering out from around the small dirt mounds they were crouched behind, and found several more of the massive insects. Some scurried in and out of tunnels that they burrowed in and under the remains of the ancient civilization.

Brigdon lifted his arm and with one toe raised swirled it in the air, telling the others to wrap up and head back. As quietly as they came, they slipped back toward the trees. Once there, Brigdon halted the team and directed them, mostly with grunts and gestures, to take another sweep around the far edges of the ruins and make a complete circle.

"I wish we could stay and study these creatures," Helios said, stroking his jade-green feathers under his beak.

Jaxton rolled his eyes and followed Brigdon, first swinging wide along the last of the tree line and crouched tightly to the ground when there was no cover. Pontos chuckled at Jaxton's annoyance and went in the opposite direction and moved along the tree line until it ended. Pontos and Helios came to a cliff with a rushing river about a hundred lengths below. They flew over the crevasse, peering down, searching the bottom as they crossed.

They landed on the other side and continued working their way behind the dilapidated and fallen stones. Helios noted a peculiar mushroom on their first time around and he wanted to pick one to take back to study, but he was certain that Brigdon would not allow it. Now, however, Brigdon was not there. He spotted another one and with Pontos up ahead. He took his chances and picked it and carefully slipped the rubbery fungus into his pack.

****

"General Sir, the scouting party has returned," said a soldier standing at attention.

"Thank you. Where are they?" Azrack asked.

"They were spotted north of the tree line and will be here momentarily, sir," the young soldier reported.

"Thank you, dismissed," Azrack said.

The soldier spun on his paws and returned to his post. After several minutes Brigdon, Jaxton, and the others walked toward Azrack and Ralti. Brigdon led the group with more than his usual scowl, and Azrack's stomach plummeted to the bottom of his belly. Helios's shoulders were pushed back, showing his furless chest with rippling muscles that heaved with anticipation. Brigdon stopped in front of Azrack and turned to Helios. He took a small sidestep and allowed Helios the honor of giving their report.

"General sir, we've scouted the area and found a nest of Selket. There are hundreds, could even be thousands living underground in tunnels," he said.

"Thousands?" Azrack asked.

"I thought they were stories?" Ralti asked.

"I assure you they are not. It would do this army good be informed of their own history," Helios said.

Everyone rolled their eyes at him, yet on more than one occasion it was his knowledge of the past that kept them from harm.

"You're correct, Helios. It would do some good. That is precisely why I asked for you personally to be on this detail. You're understanding of such matters is crucial," Azrack said.

Helios relaxed slightly and glared at Jaxton, who was less concerned with the whole thing.

"They are heavily armored on the back and belly, and their tails have stingers," Pontos said.

Pontos was their weapons specialist. Even though he was smaller than many of the others, his ability to assess the opponent's weakness was a tremendous asset.

"How many soldiers will we need?" Azrack asked.

"All of them, sir. We are severely outnumbered," Pontos replied.

Azrack closed his eyes for a moment. He knew his men would fight to the death for their king, but this time none of them knew what they were up against. It didn't seem fair and all for some orb that the king wanted.

"Let's get this over with as soon as possible. I don't want to waste any time. Ralti and I will assemble a team to extract the vessel while, Brigdon, you and Helios plan for a distraction. We need to draw them out and keep them busy while we get in and get out," Azrack said.

"Yes, sir," Brigdon and Helios said, bringing their fists to their chests with a thud.

They spun on their paws in unison and left.

"Azrack, are you willing to die for this?" Ralti asked.

He knew asking was inappropriate, but Azrack always reassured him that if he felt the need to say something, he had better.

"I am," Azrack simply said.

Ralti saluted and turned on his paw and made his way to his tent. Helios promptly made his way back to his camp and stopped at his satchel and took out the mushroom. He spun the trumpet-like fungus in his paw while admiring its furry yellow-orange center. The mushroom was two of his paws tall and about one paw wide at the top. He took out his knife and slipped down the outside rubbery surface, which let out a thick clear goo.

Helios was instantly attracted to its sweet aroma, and he remembered one professor explain the hallucinogenic natures of different fungi that grew in their natural surroundings. He decided it would be wise to put small pieces of cloth in his nostrils.

"Helios, Jaxton and I were just thinking," Pontos said, walking up behind him.

Helios jumped and spun around.

"Here, you must put these in your beak," Pontos burst into a wave of rumbling laughter at the sight of his comrade with cloth shoved up his nostrils, "You will want to put these in your nose. Trust me."

"Alright, alright," Pontos said between laughs. He took the cloth and stuffed it in his nose, "Like this?"

This time Helios grinned. He cleared his throat and sliced off a small piece at the bottom of the mushroom.

"Where did you find whatever-this-is?" Pontos asked.

"I found this *mushroom* near the Selket's lair, and I have never seen one before. I brought one back to study it," Helios said.

"And, have you found anything?" Pontos asked, still trying to keep his amusement at bay.

"Ah, now that's interesting?" Helios said.

The tubular tunnel came to a point at the bottom and had small fibrous gills that encompassed the inside. He ran his talon over them, which caused them to sway back and forth.

"What?" Pontos asked.

Pontos stepped in closer to peek for himself.

"Do you see the gills? They sway back and forth when I brush against them," Helios said.

"What does that mean?" Pontos asked.

"I'm not sure, but I have never seen one do this," Helios said.

"Do you study these often?" Pontos asked.

"I have studied all that are known to us in our lands," Helios said.

Helios took the slice and cut it into smaller pieces. He grabbed a cup and poured a small amount of water from his water bag and put the piece in the cup and waited. Pontos crept closer for a glimpse inside the cup.

"Is it doing anything?" Pontos asked.

"Not yet," Helios said.

Helios took another piece and smashed it against a flat rock. The goo oozed out and as it mixed with the outer shell it turned a greenish color and started to glow.

"Oh, my! It's changing colors!" exclaimed Pontos.

"It would appear that the two chemicals, when mixed, create a sulfuric reaction, causing it to illuminate," Helios said.

He scooped the mush onto his knife and lifted it eye level.

"Amazing, I had no idea this stuff was so interesting," Pontos said.

Helios gave a small grin.

"What in the –" Jaxton asked.

Helios and Pontos were staring at the glowing ooze like a couple of cubs. Jaxton burst into laughter when they turned toward him with the small pieces of cloth sticking out of their noses. Pontos was about to respond with his newfound knowledge, but a loud bang clanged from behind them.

The three jumped and searched their surroundings, and their ears twitched back and forth. A highly seasoned soldier knocked over a pail sitting on a low flat stone near a fire. He leaped across the ground and swung his arms as though he was trying to catch something in the air.

"Here, little butterfly, come here. I won't hurt you," he said.

Another soldier that was sitting on the ground was bathing in dirt. He flipped it up and tried to catch it with his head. Another was lying on his back talking about how wonderful the water was. Jaxton turned to Helios.

"They've gone mad!"

A glint of a blade flashed in front of Helios's eyes, and he ducked in time to avoid an attack.

"Blast it all," Jaxton growled,

Jaxton pulled his blade, and the soldier stepped back and reset his position.

"Rotag, what are you doing?" Pontos asked.

"Look out," Helios said.

Helios stepped to the side and elbowed another soldier in the face to prevent him from striking Jaxton.

"Stop, everyone stop!" Jaxton yelled.

A soldier stumbled around as though he couldn't see, and one more flew in a circle chasing his tail. Before they knew it, there were three more soldiers all forming a circle around them.

"What is going on, Helios?" Pontos asked.

Pontos' voice was stuffy from the cloth in his nose. Helios shook his head and took a step back. He knocked over the cup with the piece dissolving in water.

"The mushroom... It has to be," there was only a puddle of water in the dirt, "It must have emitted a fume as it dissolved causing hallucinogenic side effects."

"Hallucinations?" Jaxton asked, blocking another blow, "So what do we do now?"

"We'll have to keep them occupied until it wears off and hope that no one gets hurt," Helios said.

"How long will that be?" Pontos asked.

"I have no idea. I guess we'll find out," Helios said.

He blocked a swing and shoved the soldier over.

"They're not very good, are they? If they fought like this in battle, we would be dead already," Pontos said.

Pontos tripped a soldier and disarmed him.

"That's the thing with hallucinations," Helios said. He ducked, letting a tankard sale over him and pegged the soldier behind him square between the eyes, "It changes the way reality is experienced in the brain."

"Shut up, Helios," Jaxton said.

Helios was about to yell at him, when Pontos asked, "Do you think the scorpions would be affected by this? After all, we are severely outnumbered."

Helios thought for a moment.

"If I remember correctly, another creature like the scorpions *are* susceptible to hallucinogenic properties. Perhaps the scorpions will be too. We don't need to kill them all, just keep them busy."

"We're gonna need more of these mushrooms," Jaxton said.

Jaxton, Pontos, and Brigdon went mushroom hunting and Helios stayed and observed the soldiers for over an hour. One by one the soldiers stumbled around blankly and had only faint recollections, as though it was a dream. Helios immediately started asking questions about how it felt and what they experienced, taking as many notes as possible as fast as he could. At one point, the soldier who'd been chasing butterflies broke down into tears with the realization that the little creatures might have been in danger.

11-And Now We Know Who The Girl Is

The aroma of cooking sausage wafted in and out of Shaz's nose as he blinked. He rubbed his eyes and sat up and finding his headache was gone, he sighed with relief. He pulled the covers off and put his feet on the cool floor. The small glass jar with the pain relief oil was sitting on the side table and he smiled. He searched around for his clothes and found the pile Serin had brought. He pulled on the tunic and trousers and was glad they were long enough in the legs. Shaz crossed the hall to the washroom and ran water through his hair and over his face and went downstairs.

"Oh, good, you're awake. How do you feel?" Mrs. Bailey asked.

Mrs. Bailey turned, waving her arms around with a spatula in one hand.

"Much better, thank you, I'm sorry to be an inconvenience," Shaz said.

Shaz smiled at her enthusiastic hand waving and shoved his hands in his pockets.

"Never you mind, it's my pleasure. But I must ask, how often do these headaches happen?"

Shaz shrugged and leaned against the doorway.

"Every so often," Shaz said.

"Do they come on after something happens?" she asked.

Mrs. Bailey slipped the cooked sausage onto a plate and set it on the table next to him.

"I never thought about it," he said.

"Sit and eat," she commanded kindly.

Shaz sat down in the little chair and tried to find a place that was comfortable for his long legs. He chuckled at the thought that Riddick would never fit in this chair. Mrs. Bailey set the table with a large plate of griddle cakes, butter, syrup, and juice.

"Help yourself and don't be shy. I made tons and I don't do leftovers," She said, rummaging in a cupboard. Shaz made himself a plate and finished everything. He hadn't realized how hungry he was and added a second helping and polished that off too. He sat back in his chair and patted his belly. "So, what are your plans today?" Mrs. Bailey asked.

She cleared some dishes and filled the washbasin with water. What Shaz wanted to do was see Serin again but thought that might come across wrong, so he made up something else.

"I need to go to the forest. I have some things to take care of," Shaz said.

"Alright, I will see you later," She mumbled from behind a pantry door.

Shaz hesitated for a moment.

"Is Serin going to be here today?"

"No, she has the day to herself. Why dear?" Mrs. Bailey asked.

"Oh, nothing, I think I fell asleep on her talking and I wanted to tell her I was sorry."

Mrs. Bailey peeked from behind the door with a curious eye.

"I'm sure she didn't mind."

He couldn't see the grin on her face, and she didn't want to be obvious, but she wanted the two of them to get to know each other well.

"Thanks, well, I'll be back later," he said.

Shaz took the stairs two at a time and put on his sword and grabbed his pack. He hurried from the house and closed the door behind him, and the city's aromas sank into his senses. He wasn't sure what bothered him most. The smell of musky damp stone or the mixture of the markets and mills mingled with the pitch of ironwork. Shaz scanned the alley and tried to make sense of all the people coming and going. A woman in one flat in the upper part of the building was hollering at the street kids that darted down a side alley and a cat screeched as they threw over the trash cans on their way by.

Shaz followed the markers he had made mental notes of and returned to the plaza he remembered where an armor shop was. The plaza was nice and big and had several kinds of shops that circled an array of stone steps and a fountain in the center. The water sprung from the ground and flowed in a tubular structure and cascaded back to the ground, and Shaz pondered on how that was even possible. He shook his head and kept moving toward the armor shop. A deli across the square had tables and chairs in patterns in front of it, and the bakers were sticking their loaves of breads on shelves in front of their shop. It differed greatly from Turob and a pain of homesickness hit his guts. Shaz grabbed the handle of the shop door and yanked, but it didn't open.

"Closed," he said.

Shaz grumbled under his breath and leaned against the cold stone wall to wait until they opened. Shaz stared into the mesmerizing effects of the waterspout until the shopkeeper switched the sign in the door's window. The shop keeper unlatched the bolt and pulled back the curtains from the little window that was hanging in the center of the heavy wood door. Shaz opened the door and went inside.

"Hello, what can I do for you today?" A jolly man said from behind the counter.

Shaz spotted the bows and arrows.

"I would like to buy a set, please," Shaz said.

"Ah yes, how about this one here?" the tall bald man said.

He reached up and pulled a bow off the hooks and handed it to Shaz. Shaz held it out straight and lined up his wrist so the bow was straight but that his forearm was out of the way of the string. He grabbed the string and pulled it back tightly.

"Ah, I see you know your bow," the shopkeeper said.

The shop keeper looked around for another for him to try.

"Yes, but this one feels a little-"

"Small," the shopkeeper interrupted.

The shopkeeper could tell that Shaz couldn't straighten his elbow enough when the string was pulled back.

"Yeah," Shaz said.

Shaz set the bow on the counter and the man pulled another off the wall and gave him the bow.

"Try this one."

Shaz again set up and pulled back the string. He let loose and pulled back a few times but shook his head. Several bows later, the shopkeeper thought for a moment.

"Still not right, hang on. I think I have just the right one."

The shopkeeper slipped around the curtain that covered the backroom and Shaz heard the man rummaging around. He returned and in his hands was a light tan bow, a little larger than the medium length bows. Shaz had seen nothing like it and took the bow and held it up and pulled the string back and forth a few times. It was perfect. He turned the weapon over and took in all the fine carved details.

"This bow's been in my shop for many rotations, I've never been able to sell it. Seems it likes you," the shopkeeper said.

An interesting sensation took Shaz off guard. It was more like a voice inside his mind that said *Remember me?*

"Who sold this to you?" Shaz asked.

"An old dark fella, I remember because he kept his hood over most of his face the whole time. Creepy kinda guy, though he didn't ask for much."

"I'll take it," Shaz said, "And the rest of the gear too."

"You bet, and since this bow's been here for so long and I didn't pay much, I will give it all to you for fifteen pence," he said.

"Sounds great," Shaz said.

He set the coins on the counter and strapped on the weapon and left the shop. The street was more crowded now, and he maneuvered around the people and fountain in the direction of the canals. The people here wore finely woven tunics in bright colors and trousers with buckles around the knees. Women wore brightly colored full skirts that swooshed as they moved, and lacy tops that covered their necks and wrists.

Shaz was not used to the busyness of big city life and a sense of awkwardness about wearing his light-colored traveling tunic, his bow and arrow on his back, a sword at his hip and traveling boots that clunked on the cobblestone streets eased into his mind. Shaz figured he has some time before meeting up with Jagwynn and decided to take a look around the next plaza which was filled with street merchants and colorful wagons that had different trinkets, pots, and clothes. A booth on the other side of the square caught his attention and the closer he came to the booth, the stronger a pit in his stomach grew and the hairs on the back of his neck stood out. His inner voice screamed at him, but his curiosity overpowered it.

His eye caught a small glass orb which hung at his eye level. The reflection of his deep blue eyes captivated his attention. The lurching feeling rose again, and he hadn't noticed the small woman standing behind the table. For a split-second, panic hit his brain, but then he saw she was just a small old woman. *I'm sure this little woman couldn't do any harm.* He thought.

'Something you like?" asked the little old woman pointing to the glass orb.

Her small beady brown eyes scrutinized his, and the prick at the back of his mind lurched into full uneasiness.

"I guess," Shaz said.

"What does it say to you?"

"Say?"

"Yes, what does it speak to you?" she asked.

The old woman's voice was raspy but elegant, and Shaz tried to shove the panic out of his mind.

"Umm."

"Look again," she said.

She touched the glass with a crooked finger and a spark shot between her finger and the orb. Panic surged, but curiosity forced his eyes to peer once again into the orb.

Many you will save, many you will kill, hope is not lost, echoed a voice in his mind.

Shaz jumped back and stared at the little woman. His pupils growing larger as he contemplated what happened. A smile formed in the corners of her lips and her long brown dress puddled on the ground. It might have fit her once in her younger years, however, time had wreaked havoc on her tiny frame. Shaz didn't know what to do. He ran his fingers through his hair and brushed it out of his face.

The woman hobbled into the tent and returned with her hand in a tight fist that almost made her tanned skin white. Shaz extended his hand, and she dropped a small object into his palm. The pain raced to his brain, telling him to drop it, but it paralyzed his hand. The harder he tried, the worse it became. Shaz closed his eyes and tried to filter the pain by focusing on anything happy.

The first thing that popped into his mind was Serin. It was her voice that was soft and soothing. It was like the same as when you return home from being away from a long time. A smile crested his lips, and the pain ceased. The realization stirred a new set of emotions for Serin, things like devotion and affection, and he wondered how she could have such an impact on him. He didn't want to, but he opened his eyes to see the small-framed woman standing in front of him. A huge grin now covered her face with her eyes all but buried by the sagging skin wrinkled by her smile.

"What is this all about?" asked Shaz.

"You are the one!" she exclaimed.

"No, I am-"

"Shazmpt," she said. She grabbed his elbow and directed him into her booth. "I must give you something."

"What is this? Who are you?" Shaz asked.

"The medallion of the black wyvern," she said.

"The what?"

"The black wyvern is the most powerful creature on this planet. Even in the cosmos, until you, that is. Most people do not remember the time of magic. It has been centuries since one has come as noble as he."

A tiny glint in her eye flashed and the hairs on the back of his neck stood out. He knew about the legends of the black wyvern, but how that applied to him he didn't, and if he played dumb, she might tell him more.

"I'm sorry, I don't know what you are talking about."

"Hush, you are stronger than you think. Now tell me, what did you think of when you soothed the medallion?" the little woman's eyes darted between his and her enthusiastic grin worsened the pit now in his guts.

"Soothe?"

"Yes, what did you think about that made the pain stop and tamed the medallion?" Shaz's mind again selected Serin. "See, there it is again," the old woman said.

She stared up at him he, being twice her height, but her spirit was bigger than he was which added to the threat level.

"Her name is Serin."

Shaz regretted saying her name as soon as it left his lips, and he wanted to slap his hand against his forehead. The woman gasped and took a step back and bumped into a small table filled with jars and bottles of different colored liquids.

"Serin Svirtari, you say?"

She gasped at the news and then opened a small wooden chest that had intricately carved patterns and symbols on the top and sides. The lid was fastened with a steel clip and hook and sealed shut, but he could tell there was a type of magic in the box. Shaz searched his mind for an explanation but came up empty. He opened his mind to the possibilities and different colors and hues surrounded the box. There had been only a few times that this had happened, and he was told it the items magical signature.

"Do you know her?" Shaz asked.

"Not exactly, ummmm…yes…hummm….it's gotta be in here somewhere?" she muttered. A sudden slam hit his mind, and he realized he hadn't said her surname. In fact, he didn't even know it. Alarm bells ripped through his being, but he couldn't leave just yet. His gut was telling him to stay a little longer. "Ah yes, here it is,"

The old woman spun on her toe and shoved a small gold medallion in his other hand. Dreading the same effects as the last one, Shaz flinched, but a cool sensation rippled over his body. It reminded him of the cool earth and warm spring breeze on the island. A soft blue and green hint of color formed around his fist. A crooked smile crept from the corners of the old woman's mouth. Shaz stood back and studied her. He wasn't sure if the pleasant little woman was about to morph into a nasty creature.

The pieces leaped out of his hands and joined with a snap, pop, and slight sizzle and a braided rope formed around the wyvern creature in the middle and the new little medallion fell into his hand. She reached for it, but he closed his fist tightly. The old woman crept close and the gnawing pit ripped through him. Her eyes were wide and fixed on his, and her scraggly old brows cinched tightly into the center of her forehead. Shaz backed out of the booth slowly placing his feet around the pots and jars of jellies and powders and reached for his sword with a firm grip around the hilt.

"What are you doing?" Shaz asked.

"The legend tells of a time when two powerful beings will come and reunite the magic to this world."

"I think you've got the wrong guy," Shaz said.

"The Velshari will be pleased you are here. They will have a great use for you," she said.

She rubbed her palms together greedily and cackled under her breath. Her beady brown eyes now almost black.

"Ah, see, I have other plans and won't be coming to your little reunion," Shaz said.

"Yes, Gavin Rhill must surely know you are here, and now we know who the girl is too."

Shaz's face suddenly went pale and his stomach lurched, and he thought he was going hurl. The sun hit his face as he stepped out from under her tent, and he used the medallion and aimed the sunlight into her eyes. The old woman screeched a wicked scream as the light burned her eyes. Small pools of blood formed at the corners of her red fleshy eye sockets. Shaz wrinkled his face in disgust and disappeared into the crowd.

Blood pumped into his veins at a fast rate, and Shaz's heartfire ignited. The strange sensation encompassed his chest and rippled through his limbs. He wasn't sure if it was the running at a quick rate or something else. He dodged in and out of the growing crowds and turned a sharp corner and darted down the passageway. His mind raced around the events and the stories he was told, and one came into his mind and he cursed. He wished he hadn't been shielded. He felt so inadequate and the fear he was going to mess up, even more, plagued his thoughts. Shaz slowed at the oncoming crowd and fought his way to the outer edges of the last city wall. The forest tree line came into view as he passed the last city gate, and he hurried into the woods.

12-Do You Believe In Magic?

The forest was cool and damp with a misty film that lingered in the air. Shaz walked quietly, taking in the details. He stepped over a fallen tree and searched the distance for Jagwynn. Jag wouldn't be welcomed in the city, so he sent her into the forest to wait for him. He figured she would be happier here, anyway. He didn't know, however, how long it would take to find her. So, he enjoyed being alone in the forest. A soft babbling brook and the familiar sounds of insect life soothed his thoughts some, but he couldn't shake the idea that he had just given Gavin Rhill Serin's name and he grew angry with himself.

He pulled his rucksack off his shoulder, slipped the bow off and put it on the ground, and then he sat and leaned against a large rock. Shaz rested his head and gazed into the treetops and again searched through the stories to see if anything would give him an idea of what to do next, but nothing stood out. He heard something in the distance but couldn't identify it at first, and then the sound came again. Shaz searched in the direction he thought the sound came from and urgency hit his chest. He leaped to his feet and grabbed his gear and ran. Shaz moved quickly over tree stumps and small bushes. Shaz recognized the snarl of an enormous cat and his heart thudded.

"Jag," he whispered.

Shaz unlatched the belt that held his bow and secured the string as he hurried around a large tree. He pulled an arrow from his quiver and slid the arrow onto the string. Shaz turned toward where the sound was coming from and fixed his eyes on a small person with their bow drawn. He shifted his sight to where they were pointing and confirmed what his gut was telling him.

"No," he whispered.

Shaz took a few more steps with his bow drawn and positioned himself where he could see the archer. He aimed at the bow of the other hunter. He didn't want to hurt them, just disarm them. Shaz was still far enough away that any normal person wouldn't even be able to see from that distance, but he wasn't sure if this new bow would shoot an arrow that far, so he crept closer. Jag hissed and lowered herself to the tree branch she was clinging to.

"Don't do it," Shaz said under his breath.

The hunter's hood covered their face, but Shaz could now tell it was a girl. *What is a girl doing out this-?* He detected the slightest movement in the girl's arm and let go of his arrow. It hit her arrow square in the middle, shattering it into pieces. The girl jumped, knocked another arrow, and spun toward Shaz. Jag rose and looked toward Shaz, then slunk into the shadows. Shaz slunk to the ground and slipped behind a tree. Shaz reached out with his mind to see if he could detect Jag and found she was already about halfway toward him.

Shaz peeked out and spotted the girl running toward him. He stepped out from the tree and kept his bow lowered in a sign of peace and looked up in time to see the large feline leap from a tree branch and land on him. Shaz fell to the ground and let the big cat lick his face.

"Yuck Jag," he laughed, wriggling out of her kisses. Shaz sensed the tightening of the girl's bow and called out, "Don't shoot, this is my pet." The girl lowered her bow. "Alright already Jag, it's good to see you too," Shaz said. He shoved her off of him and brushed off the leaves and twigs and scratched her ear. She purred loudly and rubbed her side against him and arched her back. The young woman came toward them and pulled her hood off, and his heart skipped a beat. "Serin, what are you doing out this far?"

"What am I doing? What are you doing? And what in the world just happened?" She demanded.

She stopped a few feet from him with one hand holding her bow, the other on her waist.

"I asked you first," Shaz said.

Serin gave him an intense glare, and he decided she wasn't in the mood.

"Fine, I live near here and was on my way to, well, to somewhere, when your *pet* tried to attack me," Serin said.

"What Jag? She would never attack a human. She doesn't know she's not a human. Shh, don't tell her," he replied, putting his finger to his lips with a smile.

Serin's face softened as Shaz teased the jaguar. Jagwynn gave Shaz a look as though she was saying, 'really?' and Shaz took a second look. Jagwynn yawned and moved to the shade and started licking her fur.

'Your turn, what are you doing out here?" Serin asked.

'Looking for Jagwynn, I couldn't take her into the city, so I told her I would find her out here."

'Well, this is not a safe place for her here. There are a lot of foolish game hunters in these parts, mostly prize hunters who don't know a thing about actual hunting," Serin said with a small wave.

'You seem pretty good with that bow," Shaz said.

'I guess,"

Serin shrugged.

'How long have you been shooting?" Shaz asked.

He picked up his pack and slung it over his shoulder.

"Most of my life," Serin answered.

Shaz was impressed, and even more intrigued, and Serin shifted her weight onto the other foot.

"Let's see. Hit the third knot up in that far tree over there."

"What, you don't believe me?"

"Where I come from, only a few girls can shoot an arrow well," Shaz said.

"Fine," she said.

Serin pulled an arrow from her quiver. Pulled the string and arrow straight back. Twisted her wrist just enough to keep the bow straight, but so that the string wouldn't shred the skin on her forearm. She sized up the distance, height and determined how much cross-wind there was, then let the arrow loose. It sizzled through the air, leaving a whooshing sound in its wake, and sunk deep into the third knot of the farthest tree.

"I'm impressed," he said, "You didn't even hesitate."

"Hesitate and you're dead," she said.

"Then why did you hesitate with Jag?"

Serin shook her head, lowering it slightly.

"I don't know, something about it wasn't right. Or rather, something about her did feel right. That didn't make sense," she said.

Serin unhooked the string from her bow and slipped it into its case.

"No, I understand. Hey, I wanted to tell you thank you for, well, you know," Shaz said.

He ran one hand through his hair, pulling it out of his eyes.

"You're welcome," Serin said.

Shaz needed to tell her about the crazy old lady in town to warn her, but he didn't want to sound absurd and then wasn't sure what to say.

"You might want to be extra careful," Shaz said.

"Why?" Serin scowled.

Shaz didn't want to come across as arrogant or bossy either, and wasn't sure how to explain his encounter and he had no idea how to explain the whole Gavin Rhill, and magic and world coming to an end thing.

"Well, just be careful," Shaz said.

Shaz tried to pull it off as just a suggestion, but Serin perceived his genuine concern for her and nodded. A new sensation coursed all over her body, she couldn't explain it. It was as if she understood his intentions without him even speaking. She experienced a similar vibe when she used her magic to wield water, but how would she explain making water move with your mind. He would think she was crazy for sure and she liked him, so there was no way she was going to tell him about herself.

"Where are you headed?" Shaz asked.

"I'm going to search for a plant I need for some medicine," Serin said.

"Can I help you?" Shaz asked.

Serin nodded and smiled, and Shaz's heart skipped a beat. She was beautiful, and he appreciated her fighting spirit. Shaz wanted to kiss her, but that would be moving way too fast. Plus, he had never kissed a girl before, so he didn't even know how to, but something about her made his need for her closeness increase. Serin explained what the plant looked like and where it usually grew, and they moved deeper into the forest.

"Can I ask you a question?" Serin asked.

"Sure," Shaz said.

"You said you were from far away, what did you mean?" Serin asked.

Shaz wasn't sure what to tell her. He picked through a tall clump of grass but didn't find the herb they were looking for.

"Promise you won't laugh," Shaz said.

"Why would I laugh?" Serin asked.

"Well, it might sound like a made-up story, or like I'm not telling the truth," Shaz said.

Serin gave him a perplexed expression.

"Alright, I won't laugh," Serin said.

"I come from an island called Turob in the Turbulent Reef, from a realm not like this one," Shaz said. Shaz waited for her to scoff at him, but she didn't. Instead, she nodded and Shaz could see the gears in her head chunking though the information and wondered what she was processing. "You don't think it's weird?" Shaz asked.

"No, I'm not from this realm either," Serin said.

"Really?" Shaz asked.

"The place I grew up is in another realm, separate from this one," Serin said.

"How long have you been here?" Shaz asked.

Shaz tried not to come across as eager for the connection and separated another tuft of grass.

"Not long, my father brought me here to study with Mrs. Bailey while he had some business to attend to in another realm," Serin said.

"How did you get here," Shaz asked.

Serin hesitated, but there was something different about him she trusted more than anyone else in her life.

"On a wyvern," Serin said.

Shaz stood up and turned to her with wide eyes. Serin's eyes filled with uncertainty and she bit her lip. Shaz ran his hands through his hair.

"Wow, a wyvern, what kind of wyvern?" Shaz asked.

"You don't think I'm making it up?" Serin asked.

"No, I have met one, a water wyvern," Shaz said.

Serin smiled, and her body sank with relief.

"An earth wyvern named Medrith," Serin said.

"That must be pretty neat having an earth wyvern as your companion. All I get is this big ole cat," Shaz said.

Shaz ruffled Jagwynn's fur and rubbed her ears, but Jagwynn gave him a steeling glare and Shaz almost felt her insulted emotions.

"Medrith is my father's companion, but she is a wonderful creature," Serin said.

"Do you believe in magic?" Shaz asked.

"Yes, do you?" Serin asked.

"I do," Shaz said.

"I guess we are more alike than I thought we were," Serin said.

"I like that," Shaz said.

"Me too,"

Serin smiled and pulled a wispy hair from her face. Shaz smiled and a warming sensation tickle Serin's cheeks and she looked away.

"Is this it?" Shaz asked.

Shaz pointed to a brownish-green leafy plant with black stripes across the leaves. Serin moved to where she could see the plant and nodded.

"Now we only need three more," Serin said.

"What is it used for?" Shaz asked.

"The pain medicine I used on you the other day. Mrs. Bailey said I needed to stock up on a good supply because she is concerned you might need it a lot," Serin said.

Shaz frowned.

"Why would she think that?" Shaz asked.

Serin chuckled.

"I have no idea. She mentioned it was because you get headaches frequently," Serin said.

"Yeah, I guess so," Shaz said.

"Why do you get so many?" Serin asked.

Shaz shrugged.

"I have always had them, since I was small. Grandfather said it was because of me being a war wizard,"

The words slipped out, and panic raced through his mind.

"But why would that cause you to get headaches?" Serin asked.

Shaz shrugged but was relieved she didn't appear to catch on to him being a war wizard. Jagwynn purred loudly and rubbed against Shaz's leg and then leaped into a tree and moved along the top branches until she was out of sight.

"Where is she going?" Serin asked.

"Who knows, she's such a weird cat sometimes," Shaz said.

"When did you get her," Serin asked.

"I found her as a cub when I was young and we decided we needed each other so she's been with me ever since," Shaz said.

"I bet its nice to not be alone," Serin said.

Shaz got in the impression that Serin had been on her own for a time, and his heart sank.

"Are you hungry, I brought some lunch if you would like to share it with me?" Shaz asked.

Serin was thankful for the change of subject and agreed. Serin pulled the herb and wrapped it in a cloth and stuck it in her bag, and they found a clear place to sit. The sun was high overhead and warm, and they enjoyed lunch together. Shaz shared stories of Riddick and the crew, and Serin listened. By the time they found the number of plants Serin wanted, the sun was setting, and they started heading back.

"Are you going to Mrs. Bailey's?" Shaz asked.

"No, I have something to attend to out here," Serin said.

"Can I walk you there?" Shaz asked.

"I would like that," Serin said.

The words slipped out before she could stop herself, but she again felt that she could trust him, but she didn't know why. She didn't trust many people outside her mother's people of the travelers, but he was different, and her mind raced for a reason. They causally walked through the forest and Serin lead them to the backside edge of the travelers so he wouldn't find their settlement. Not that she didn't want to take him there, she very much did, but there were very strict rules and without permission she would be in violation of the clan.

"I'll be fine from here," Serin said.

"Are you sure, I can walk you all the way," Shaz said.

"Thank you, but the people I am staying with are kind of particular to strangers and I wouldn't want to upset them," Serin said.

"Alright, but be careful," Shaz said.

A tinge of worry ate at his mind for the first time all day, and he wanted to make sure she was safe. Serin felt it too, but had no understanding for it, so she smiled. Shaz waited for her to slip passed the tree line and then headed back toward the city. Thoughts of the day with Serin rolled around his mind until the old woman and the dream from the night before crept in and his heartfire surged. Anger gripped his mind, and he was certain it was the old woman's doing, and his stupidity that he gave up Serin's name. He tried to shove it aside and think of his day with Serin, and before he knew it, he was already at Mrs. Bailey's.

He opened the door and set his pack on the floor next to the dark wood side table. The aroma of roast filled his nose, and he found Mrs. Bailey in her cooking apron.

"I'm sorry I was gone all day," he said.

Mrs. Bailey jumped and turned around, holding a carving knife in her tiny fist. Her gray hair was slightly unkempt from its usual tight bun, with a few wisps of hair hanging in her face.

"Oh, you startled me!" She said, her cheeks reddening.

"Sorry," he said, "Have you been crying?"

Mrs. Bailey held up an onion, and they laughed.

"Sit, sit, supper is almost ready," she dished him up a large slice of roast potatoes, and cooked carrot and set the plate in front of him. She dished herself and sat at the other side of the table. They ate in silence for several minutes when Mrs. Bailey sat her fork down. "I have spoken with the Dodjen, and they think you should spend some time with them."

Her chin hung slightly, and her eyes were heavy.

"You're a Dodjen?"

"Yes, an informant, like my brother, Yerild," she said.

Shaz saw her shaking hand and understood the uneasiness of her words.

"What do you think I should do?"

"Doesn't matter what I think, I don't have a choice anyway," she said as the blood under her skin boiled.

"It does to me," Shaz said. He knew she wouldn't tell him her thoughts, that's what women do, so he asked, "So when do I leave?"

"In the morning," she whispered. She shoved a piece of bread into her mouth and chewed vigorously to hide the tears that were forming. Shaz stabbed a piece of roast with his fork and rubbed it around the potatoes and gravy. "I have some business up north. I won't be back for several days and I must leave in the morning. I will leave the information for you on the counter," She said.

"Alright."

Shaz wasn't sure why this news upset Mrs. Bailey as it did, he expected that he probably would end up meeting with them at some point, but her concern left a hint of worry in his mind. Shaz offered to help clean up but she convinced him she was alright, and he turned in for the night.

13-Where's The Girl?

Shaz found the paper Mrs. Bailey had left for him next to another that looked like a shopping list, and he folded them and stuck them in his pocket and left the house. He wondered if he would see Serin again and what the Council was going to have him do. He had no idea what or who they were or what they wanted him for, but every time he thought about it, he got a sick feeling. The early morning streets had yet to become crowded, and he hurried toward the market. He wasn't sure which market it was, so he asked a gentleman which way he was to go and was relieved that it wasn't the same one he had run into the old woman. He crossed the plaza and rounded a half wall that had a set of seats on the other side.

A distant shadow crossed his peripheral vision, which left a lingering of shadowy mist across the tall buildings. The further he went, the busier the streets became and Shaz maneuvered through the people shouldering his way around merchant tables and animals. As he rounded a corner, he caught another glimpse of the shadowy figure and moved faster.

"Hey, watch where you're going," said a merchant woman.

The chase replaced by the thrill of the hunt rushed blood to his brain and gave him a quick dose of euphoria, and a familiar peace of hunting overcame him. Shaz studied the black dot and rounded a corner and slid to a halt as the alley came to a dead end.

"Blast," Shaz said. He dug his foot into the stone path and darted back. "Move out of my way," Shaz said after he bumped into a tall dark-haired man holding two sacks of potatoes, one over his shoulder and the other in a tightly gripped fist. The man's eyes narrowed tightly a deep growl rumbled under his breath. "Never mind," Shaz said, patting the mans' chest. Shaz rolled around the man and continued through the heavy throng of people.

"Shaaaaaz!" a woman bellowed.

Shaz stopped before crashing into a fruit basket.

"Shaz," Mrs. Bailey said, waving her arms, "Oh, I'm so glad I found you."

She panted as she skidded to a stop in front of him. Her face was stained with tears and dirt, and she grabbed his elbow.

"What's wrong? I thought you were gone," Shaz asked, gripping her little elbows.

"They've taken Serin, she's gone!" Mrs. Bailey coughed and put her hand on her chest, "Oh my, this body is not meant for this kind of exertion."

"What? Who? Where?!"

Shaz's heartfire blasted into full flame, and Mrs. Bailey was certain she almost saw actual flames flicker from his body. She threw out the idea, but an odor of nearly burned fabric entered her nose and she shook her head.

"The guards, they took her to the dungeons," she said.

Tears formed in the corners of her eyes.

"Why?" Shaz asked.

"I don't know. She was supposed to meet me at the house, but when she didn't, I went looking for her," She gave him Serin's torn purple cloak, "And then I found this," Mrs. Bailey said through gritted teeth.

"Are you sure it was the guards? Let's start walking," he said, grabbing her arm.

"Yes, I'm sure," she said, Mrs. Bailey's short legs struggled to keep up with his long strides, "Why would they take her? It makes no sense," she said.

She put her bent knuckle to her nose and sniffed.

"I think I know," Shaz said under his breath, his nose flaring.

"You don't think-" Mrs. Bailey started.

"Where are the dungeons?" Shaz asked.

"Why?" Mrs. Bailey asked.

"I'm going to bring her back," he said.

"No, you can't," Mrs. Bailey said, "No one makes it out of there alive," she bit her lower lip.

"Not this time," the veins on his neck stuck out, "Now, where are they?" he demanded.

Shaz stared her square in the eyes and the fierceness startled her. Mrs. Bailey rubbed the back of her neck, bit her lip, and explained how to reach the dungeons. Shaz made a mental image of her words and committed it to memory.

"We'll be back, but you need to leave town fast," Shaz said.

Mrs. Bailey nodded, but the sickening feeling she now had left a slight tint of green on her face. He started in the direction she told him, and she grabbed his arm and gave him a piece of paper.

"Don't read this until after you're out of the city," she wrapped his fist around the note, holding his hand in hers. Shaz internalized her trembling as her attention gripped him, "There are many who will tell you they are on your side, but not all of them are. Trust your instincts."

She patted his hand and scurried away briskly, her round backside bobbing as she disappeared into the crowd of people. He still didn't have a full grasp on the city streets, and it took him a few tries to navigate back to the canals. When he found the right street, he jogged until he came to the first staircase leading to the canal landings. Shaz passed two or three other boats that were beckoning to him. At the cross-section where boats could pick four different directions, he peered down each one scrutinizing the boats' operators. Four bridges down, he spotted who he thought might be Deagan and leaped up the stairs and down the other side, being careful not to run anyone over. He learned that, with all these people around, it was safer to keep a moderate pace. Shaz raised his finger as he took the next set of steps two at a time down to the landing.

"Hey Deagan, over here," Shaz said, raising his voice over the noise.

Deagan put his pay in his pocket and lifted his chin sharply.

"Hey there," he said.

"I need a ride," Shaz said, gripping Deagan's shoulder, "And a favor," he said.

Shaz leaped into Deagan's boat, and Deagan's pleasant smile shifted into a grimace.

"What kind of favor?" he asked. Deagan climbed onto the back of his boat and lifted the anchor, "Where did you say you wanted to go?"

"Go, that way," Shaz said.

He pointed toward the center of the city.

"Ooh, kay," Deagan said, propelling the little boat out into the mainstream.

"Deagan, do you know anything about the dungeons here?" Shaz asked, turning in his seat.

Deagan almost dropped his pole and fumbled to regain control.

"No, why?"

"I need to get someone out of there," Shaz said.

"Are you crazy?" Deagan said, pausing mid push, "No one makes it out of there."

He repositioned his feet, so he wouldn't lose his balance.

"So, I am told," Shaz said as he nodded, "But not this time."

"What makes you think you can do it? And who is in there that is so important you would risk your life for?" Deagan asked.

Deagan ran his hand across his slicked-down hair. Shaz wasn't sure how much he wanted to tell him yet, but if his plan worked, he would find out sooner or later, anyway.

"The girl in the purple cloak," Shaz said.

Deagan let the boat slow to a crawl, and he understood the need Shaz had.

"I do know someone who does. I'll take you to him, but no guarantees he will help."

"Fair enough," Shaz said.

A short time later, Deagan pulled into a small dock. He slung the mooring rope over a large wooden pole decorated with several varieties of bird droppings and jumped out. Shaz picked up his things and followed him.

"What part of town is this?" Shaz asked.

He saw a small man slinking out of a basket. His nose was pierced with silver rings. Several pictures were etched into his skin, causing them to be depicted by scars. Two black and gray snakes wrapped around the man's arms and neck. The creature-esque person flicked his tongue in and out rapidly while staring at him with beady black eyes. Shaz tried to keep his facial movements minimal but found it hard not to cringe.

"This is the place where the travelers and street performers practice their trades," Deagan said.

Deagan unbuttoned the top button of his shirt and loosened it around his neck.

"Do you come here often?" Shaz asked.

Deagan rubbed his arm rapidly as a voluptuously endowed woman crossed in front of them, and Shaz swatted at an imaginary bug to keep from drawing the wrong kind of attention to himself.

"Not anymore," Deagan said.

He shoved one of his fingers in his mouth and bit off the hung cuticle. A short, stalky man that barely came to Shaz's waist waddled by and kicked Shaz in the shin.

"Ouch, you little bugger. What was that for?" Shaz said.

He raised his injured leg and hoped on the other.

"Because you're a freak," the little man said.

The little man laughed and scurried away, half-hopping-half-skipping. Two women dressed in cream-colored lace dresses with several layers laughed and snickered behind lace fans. They were identical, and Shaz took a double-take in order to make sense of what his eyes were seeing. As they sauntered away, he found they shared one pair of legs. His mouth dropped open in total confusion, but shut it quickly. He turned to follow Deagan and spotted a woman dressed in black leather. She had black markings painted on her face, which circled her fierce amber eyes. Her tightly pulled hair showed the sun's reflection off its black color.

"Who is that and what is she doing?" Shaz asked.

"Oh, she's a fire weaver," Deagan answered.

"A fire weaver? What do they do?"

"Weave fire, I guess," Deagan said.

She held an arrow that was burning with orange flames. Shaz peered at her and watched her put the flame in and out of her mouth. Shaz caught up with Deagan and they continued making their way through the strange-looking people.

"You don't like it here, do you?" Shaz asked.

Shaz watched him finish chewing the nail off one of his fingers.

"Not really, and neither would you if you knew what goes on around here."

"Like what?" Shaz asked.

Deagan kept going down a long alley, and Shaz didn't push it. He kept his eyes straight forward so all the deformed and strange people couldn't disturb his senses.

"We're almost there," Deagan said as he rounded a corner. Halfway down the ally, they came to a rundown tavern, "He's in there."

He pointed to a shabby, distressed door that sat somewhat crooked on its hinges. The alley was cold and dark, with little light reflecting from a distant torch. Shaz wasn't affected by the light change as his night vision was enhanced with his magic.

"Grab my collar, shove me through the door, and demand to speak to Lucien," Deagan said.

"What? Why?" Shaz asked.

"Just do it," Deagan said.

Deagan closed his eyes and flinched as Shaz gripped his collar. Shaz kicked in the door so hard that the old wood virtually broke in half. The sudden crash echoed off the stark store wall and Shaz threw Deagan into the tavern.

"Where is Lucien?"

Several oddly dressed men sitting at the tables jumped. Three large men with rippling muscles stood slowly and scooted their chairs back.

"Why do you want to see Lucien?" one asked through gritted teeth.

"It's no concern of yours," Shaz said.

Shaz glared at the large man, but a tinge of panic hit his chest.

"Hhheee's gggoing tto kkil me iff hhe ddoesnn't ssssee him," Deagan stuttered.

"So, kill him already," said one of the other men, with a crooked grin on his face.

Laughter sounded from the other low-life scum, and the thug held out his hands for applause. Shaz had never played the bad guy before and of course, he wasn't going to kill Deagan. An old trick grandfather taught him came to mind and Shaz let go of Deagan's collar. Shaz pinched a nerve in Deagan's neck and put two fingers in strategic places along his spine. Deagan fell limp. His eyes rolled into the back of his head, and he crumpled to the floor. The room gasped with a hushed tone.

"Go get Lucien," the first man said to the other, "He's going to be ticked you killed his little brother."

The lump in Shaz's throat hit the bottom of his stomach, then lurched back up. A short man came from the back hallway with his black hair pulled back like Deagan's. The man gripped the plackets of his vest jacket as he strode into the room. He didn't want to believe the man and so with a half-smirk he gave the thug a 'I'm-going-to-give-you-a-knuckle-sandwich' look until he found the crinkled body.

"You killed my brother," Lucien said.

Lucien's face turned ashen and his knees went weak.

"He's not completely dead. But I won't bring him back until you agree to tell me everything about the dungeons."

"Not dead. What are you, some kind of freak?" Lucien said.

Lucien's pulse grew at a rapid pace under his skin, and Shaz could tell he was in full panic mode.

"Freak? Are you kidding me?" Shaz grinned sideways, "What do you call them?"

More men stood up and one stood so fiercely his chair flew back and smacked the bar.

"What do you want?" Lucien asked, his tone motionless.

"I said, I want you to tell me all about the dungeons."

"Why?" Lucien asked.

"Do you want your brother or not?"

"Fine," Lucien said.

Shaz reached down and pinched the same spot, but this time he put three fingers in different spots along his spine. Deagan's eyes shuttered and Shaz helped him stand, and Lucien's eyes nearly popped out.

"How did you do that?"

"Let's talk in the back," Shaz said.

Shaz gripped the back of Deagan's shirt and jolted him toward the back. Deagan stumbled as his body regained its strength and the nerves once again sent signals to his brain.

"What are you doing Deagan, I thought I told you to stay out of trouble," Lucien said.

"I have, I have, but this guy he-" Deagan managed.

"I need information and I don't have time for games," Shaz said, "How do I get in and how many guards?"

"I don't like you," Lucien said.

Lucien took two fingers and peeled Shaz's fist off his smooth silk vest.

"Good thing I don't care," Shaz said.

"What, or rather who, is so important to you you would risk your life to rescue?" Lucien's eyes gleamed with disdain, "Must be a woman, yes, I think so. No man would risk everything for anything less than a woman. That or money," Lucien said.

Lucien made himself comfortable in his oversized chair. His complexion was slightly paler than Deagan's and Shaz surmised it was because he didn't go out much.

"Fine, yes, it's a woman, and she means a great deal to me, enough for me to kill for," Shaz said.

Shaz gripped the hilt of the sword and began to draw it from the sheath.

"I'm not afraid of your sword," Lucien said.

Shaz read his inner energy and his body language said otherwise. Lucien scooted back and rested in his chair, trying to show his leadership to his men who were standing in the corners of the room. Shaz stood motionless, however, his blood was beginning to boil underneath, and a surge of energy rumbled in his chest as the heat of magic began to rise.

"You have five seconds to start speaking," Shaz said.

"Or what, you'll kill my brother again? Nice try but I'm not falling for that twice," Lucien said, twirling his thumbs.

"Have it your way."

Shaz raised a hand, and a surge of magic tingled in the center of his palm. A red-hot glow formed in the center and swirled around. Lucien shifted in his seat and his face drained as he focused on the swirling color.

"Alright, alright. The dungeons are a maze of tunnels under the main square. They're guarded at each opening, seven in total. One entrance is at the far end near the backside of the city. That one's the least guarded by men because of the beasts that live in the water and they'll eat anything that enters the water."

Lucien couldn't drag his eyes away from Shaz's palm, and Deagan stepped back until he hit the closed door. His mouth dropped and eyes widened, and he shoved both his hands under his armpits to keep them from shaking.

"Go, on," Shaz said.

"I have a map," Lucien said.

He broke away from the magic and fumbled in the top side drawer of the desk and produced a map. He shoved everything out of the way and laid it out, and Shaz moved to the desk. Lucien pointed to the different spots on the map.

"If you go in here, you have the best chance of getting in, but I don't know how you are going to make it out. They say once inside a force which blocks every entrance paralyzes your body, and you're stuck forever. No one has left the dungeons in centuries," Lucien said.

"The legend says the original inhabitants of this city put a magic spell, or curse on the dungeons to secure an evil necromancer, but he was too powerful and escaped. He added his own magic to the curse in hopes of trapping those who tried to lock him there," Deagan said.

Deagan had moved closer to the desk and was peeking over Shaz's shoulder. Deagan's well-colored skin was now ashen and his eyes were half glazed over. Shaz stood back and ran his hands through his hair, pulling the locks out of his face.

"Gavin Rhill," Shaz said.

"Who?" Lucien asked.

"Never mind," Drafang whispered to his mind *'the medallion is a passcode, use Shadow magic'*. Shaz studied the map again for a moment, "I'll need some help," he said.

Lucien leaped out of his chair and slapped his knuckles on the old, polished desk.

"Didn't you hear me? No one gets out," Lucien said.

"Leave that to me," Shaz said.

"How?" Lucien asked.

"Trust me."

"Alright, but you have to do something for me," Lucien said.

A greedy grin overcame his face, and Shaz wasn't surprised.

"Alright, what's that?" Shaz asked.

"Here," Lucien pointed to a room at the far end of the main corridor, "There's something in there that I want. Bring it to me," he said.

"Fine. We leave tonight," Shaz said.

Shaz folded the map and shoved it in his pocket.

"What about me?" Deagan asked.

"You stay. Put. Here," Lucien said, pointing to the floor.

"We'll need his boat," Shaz said.

Lucien shot Shaz a smoldering stare.

"Fine, but if anything happens to him, I'm blaming you."

Shaz rolled his eyes and followed Lucien back down the hall. Lucien barked orders to his men and Shaz wondered what this little man had on them that made them follow his orders.

"You'll be my lookout once inside," Shaz said.

"Inside?" Deagan said.

"Don't worry, I won't let you get stuck in the curse," Shaz said.

"Just great, we're eaten by the creatures, and he's the lookout," One of the thugs said.

"Just think, you'll go down in history as a hero," Shaz said.

The thug smiled and gazed into his future.

"Let's go," Lucien said.

Shaz gave the medallion to Deagan.

"This will let you out, so don't lose it, and I want it back," Shaz said.

Deagan nodded and shoved it into his pocket. After Lucien and his thugs lead the guards away from the door, Shaz and Deagan slipped passed the heavy gate and into the corridor. Shaz felt the magic force field a few feet from the entrance and knew it was shadow magic, and he hoped Drafang was right about the medallion. Shaz moved quickly, taking the correct turns and halls from memory. At the last hall, Shaz stood with his back against the wall and waited for the sound of sharp boots on the thick stone to pass by.

"Shhh," whispered Shaz.

He held his arm out and pushed Deagan against the wall. Deagan listened to the swoosh of the Interrogator's cloak pass by. Shaz waited until the echoes of each foot were no longer distinguishable and tiptoed from behind the large pillar. He darted across to one of several large pillars throughout the vast opening, which were used as a support system for the enormous castle above. Each column attached to a rounded vault and connected to the others creating an acoustically sound design, which muffled the cacophony that came from the torture chambers. Deagan followed behind and raced to another pillar.

"Keep your nerve, Deagan. Do not wretch," Shaz said.

Shaz ran out in front of him and stopped behind another pillar.

"I'll try not-" Deagan lurched forward and relieved his body of the once cherished stew. Shaz grimaced with the splatter, "Sorry." Deagan said, wiping his mouth with the sleeve of his shirt.

"Come on," Shaz said, "We're almost on the other side."

Deagan followed Shaz around the pillar and dashed to the next and the next. Shaz stopped short of the next room and put his back against the icy wall. It felt good on his warmed skin. Shaz rested his head against the wall and calmed his heartbeat, and Deagan shoved another finger in his mouth.

"The Interrogator wants the girl to be brought in," said a guard.

"But she hasn't even been processed yet," a deeper voice said.

"I'm not going to argue with the Interrogator, are you?" the first asked.

He screeched a chair against the gritty floor. The second guard shook his head and his eyes glossed over when he imagined what would happen if he did.

"I'll ready the 'chair' while you bring the girl," he said.

Deagan started back the other way, but Shaz grabbed the collar of his shirt and jerked him into a small alcove that was built into the wall and squeezed in after him. The heavy boots clunked down the hall and echoed into the distance as the guard disappeared.

"Shouldn't we go after him?" Deagan asked.

"No, let's wait until he brings her up. Then we snatch her and run. I'd rather only fight two guards," Shaz whispered.

"Who's there?" asked the guard in the room.

Deagan held his breath and covered his mouth as Shaz rolled out of the cubby and tiptoed against the wall to the edge of the door. He peeked one eye through the opening between the door and the wall. The guard fixed the straps on the arms and screwed in a loose spike into the back of the chair. Shaz's heart raced at the sight of the chair. *Oh my,* he thought. Small spikes were screwed into the seat, back and arms of a heavy wooden chair. Shaz crept around the door and pulled the sword from the sheath and cleared his throat. The whoosh of the blade resounded in the circular room.

"Oh, good your back," the guard said.

The guard turned, and the realization cascaded over his face.

"Who are you, how did you get out?" the guard asked.

He reached for his sword, but Shaz cut the belt that held the sheath, sending it clanging to the floor. The guard stood dumbfounded with a complete lack of intelligence in his eyes. The guard started to reach down to pick up his sword.

"I wouldn't do that if I were you," Shaz said.

Shaz lifted the point of the blade, which came within a few lengths of the man's nose. The guard's eyes crossed as he peered at the point of the blade.

"What do you want?" he asked, "Who are you?"

"I want the girl."

"What girl?" the guard asked, "There's no girl."

"The one your partner went for," Shaz said.

Shaz leaned forward and closed the last half inch.

"Oh, that girl," said the guard.

He swallowed hard and a small bead of sweat dripped off his brow and plopped onto Shaz's sword.

"Sit," Shaz said. The guard moved slowly toward his chair. "No, there."

Shaz pointed to the spiked chair behind the guard. The guard's eyes widened, and his lip quivered.

"Please," the guard said, holding his hands locked together in front of his chest, "If I sit there, I'll yell, which will only alert the other guards. Don't you want to be quiet in order to escape?"

"Fine, sit there," Shaz said.

Shaz nodded toward the other chair, and the guard moved quickly and sat down.

"Who are you?"

"It's not going to work, you know, trying to distract me," Shaz said.

Shaz took some leather straps from the spiked chair and tied the guard's wrists and feet. He took a cloth sitting on the table, half-drenched with some substance he didn't want to know about. The guard cringed as Shaz shoved it into his mouth. Shaz leaned against the recessed wall and shuddered as he thought about what went on there.

Deagan stood quietly nestled in the recessed compartment, listening. He chewed his first fingernail down to the quick and was rubbing it from the pain. Low clunks became audible as the guard returned down the hall. Deagan's heart quickened and sweat formed at his hairline. Shaz sensed his anxiousness and whispered through the hole.

"Everything will be fine. Take a deep breath."

The clunks grew louder, as did the swooshing of the cape they'd heard earlier. Shaz rose from the wall. The hairs on the back of his neck prickled, and his stomach dropped, "Oh no," he whispered, "Deagan, run, back to the boat, NOW!"

14-Your Calculations Were Correct

The sun climbed the sky and outshined the three moons. The purple haze surrounded that them, mixed with the soft blue of the sky and created a gentle blur of colors that danced as they faded. Azrack listened to his soldiers explain the cloth in the nose and found it hard not to laugh. Azrack gave permission for Helios and Pontos to begin making the hallucinogenic material and Brigdon and Jaxton to search for as many as they could find. They worked through the night and into the early morning and were filled with energy and excitement to see how their potions would work.

Azrack rehearsed the plan with his top commanders, who each barked their orders to their soldier. They slipped on their armor and cinched the straps tightly around their broad chests and strapped on their girdle and belts. They slipped their helmets on and tucked in their head feathers. With the soldiers standing in formation, Pontos took his soldiers and arranged them at the sides of the battlefield.

Brigdon and Helios' crew flew just under the treetops until they broke the edge of the trees and leaped upward. Azrack, Ralti, Nasr, and Tog slipped around the trees to the east, taking cover until they reached the edge where they crouched low and crawled across the open field. They found shelter behind dirt hills and ruins until they reached their waiting point.

Helios and Brigdon hovered high in the sky until the first un-suspecting scorpion crawled out of a tunnel. Almost in unison, they both bent at the waist and dove beak first toward the ground. They pulled in their wings, allowing a small crest of wind under them to keep them in a straight dive and plummeted to the earth. The gryphton's lifted their hind legs and released their talons.

Brigdon's claws screeched over the tough outer layer of the scorpion's shell and a loud shrill blasted the air. Brigdon's nose wrin-kled as the raw stench of blood spurted. He gripped the top shell and whipped the scorpion upside down with his muscular hind legs and released his claws, and the scorpion hit the ground. As Helios was about to grip its belly armor with his hind claws, the scorpion threw its tail backward to sting him.

The stinger hit dead center on Helios's chest but was unable to penetrate his armor. Helios jolted backward, but his razor-sharp claws ripped into the scorpion's armor. Helios felt his claws enter the soft flesh underneath and gripped tightly and jerked the armor plate off. The scorpion writhed and flailed about. With one last effort before los-ing conscientiousness, the scorpion reached up with its pincers and snapped. A loud clack sound thudded the air, but both gryphton's were hovering too high for it to reach them. Scorpions soon spilled out of the tunnels and Brigdon and Helios again dove back toward the earth and the rest of the gryphton's followed.

****

"Is the ground trembling?" Ralti asked.

He assumed it was the sound of thousands of legs from the scorpions running to the other side.

"Sounds like it, let's go," Azrack said.

Azrack slipped out from behind a dirt mound and the others followed. They crossed the clearing and stopped every few feet and listened to re-determine any changes. They quietly made their way into the tunnel and blinked a few times, to allow their eyes a chance to readjust.

"What is that smell?" Nasr asked.

All four gryphton's crinkled their noses.

"Something dead," Ralti said.

"Something awfully dead," Tog said.

"Do you hear that?" Azrack asked.

"What is it?" Ralti asked.

"Not sure, let's hurry. We need to keep going, and quickly. I'm not sure how long they will be able to hold them off," Azrack said.

They made their way down the first tunnel with help from little green glowing mushrooms that grew on the sides of the tunnel walls. The tunnel opened to a small cavern with another tunnel on the other side, but when Azrack reached the opening, he realized it was smaller than the first.

"Take your armor off. We will have to go in crawling," Azrack said.

Azrack lifted his chest-plate off and the others took theirs off and followed Azrack into the next tunnel. At times, the tunnels were small, but others were spacious and formed with four walls of stone. The glowing effects of the fungi allowed them to see the old remains of what was once a great hall. Human and Gryphton shaped shadows darkened the walls.

The tunnel exited into another vast cavern where towering pillars had been destroyed and had clashed against one another and sat in rubble. Ralti spotted an old rickety rope-bridge that they used to crawl under the pillars and across the crevasse. The bridge was narrow and swung uneasily under their weight, and they lifted their wings as much as they could to ease the swinging. The deeper they went, the colder it became. The glowing mushrooms became fewer and fewer. Ralti took out a small torch and struck a rock against another, sending small sparks onto the oil-soaked cloth.

After a few strikes, the cloth burst into flames and he picked up the torch and held it out in front. The torch was small, so there wasn't much light, but it was enough. Several times as they descended, they reached adjoining tunnels. At one point the tunnel went in circles but also sunk deeper into the ground. They figured it was a main corridor and hoped it wouldn't take long to reach the bottom. Azrack rubbed his shoulders, the bending over and crouching was taking a toll on him and anxiousness crept in the deeper they went.

"How deep do these tunnels go?" asked Nasr.

"Let's hope not much further," Ralti said, moving the torch around the tunnel.

"Do you hear that?" Tog asked.

Ralti stopped and scooted next to the wall and held the torch down near his knees, hiding the light as he listened. Azrack stopped and swung his ears around, looking for the sound. His brows scrunched to the center of his face.

"Water," Azrack said.

"Yeah, that's what it sounds like to me," Ralti held out the torch and the soft warm embers fell from the bottom, "We won't have this torch for much longer," Ralti said.

Ralti shook an ember from his foot.

"Let's keep going," Azrack said.

At the next tunnel crossing, they went toward the water and a buzz reverberated in their ears. They brought their ears down to keep out the noise.

"We're getting closer," Azrack said.

"To what, is the question?" Nasr said.

Azrack and Ralti ignored him, but they were struggling with their nerves as well. Azrack stopped abruptly as he came to the end of the tunnel.

"Now where do we go?" Ralti asked.

A cascading waterfall crashed into a sizable pool several lengths below. Azrack crawled on his belly and the others followed him and peered over the edge and searched around the gaping hole.

"Wait. What is that?" Nasr asked.

Out of the darkness on the platform below, they could barely make out the tail of an enormous scorpion. The tail moved slowly in a rhythmic pattern in conjunction with the humming, and they understood what was making the noise.

"The queen," Ralti said.

Azrack nodded and signaled for them to fly down.

****

Watching their leaders, the other soldiers repeated the same maneuvers, taking out several more scorpions. Helios hovered with his back to Brigdon's using each other as shields from the scorpions turn rotation tactics. Brigdon struck using a crosscut and sliced the small part behind the large pincers, and with a twist of his wrist, he sliced the opposite direction through the other. Helios slashed the soft joints behind the pincers and severed the deadly claws. The scorpion jerked backward as blood spurted and their claws fell to the ground. The next attacked with vigor only to have that one sliced off as well.

One scorpion slipped passed his defenses and struck him square in the chest.

"Blast," yelled Brigdon.

The scorpion's tails struck at the right height to hit the heavy steel and broke the stinger right off. A young warrior fell as a larger scorpion knocked him off balance. The scorpion slammed his claws around the soldier's leg and brought him to the ground. Out of the corner of his eye, Helios saw the soldier go down and several scorpions blasted his skin with their singers before he even hit the ground.

"Don't let them make you off balance," Helios called.

Helios leaped to the air, and Brigdon followed. The stench became so intense that they no longer smelled it. They saw only a sea of black-red legs crawling all over themselves. One by one, the gryphtons lifted into the air. It was one advantage they still had over them.

Helios flew over to the soldier but could barely make him out through of all the scorpions. It became so loud that Helios had difficulty thinking, and the scorpions' rattling overcame the sky.

"Fall back. Take them to the cliff," Brigdon called.

Brigdon waved his sword in the cliff's direction and the Armada engaged the scorpions, battling forward toward the crevasse, slicing off stingers and attacking the weak joints. A scorpion twice the size of the others came out of the main tunnel. It raised long, sleek black wings from off its back and lifted into the air.

A deep rumbling roar escalated from Brigdon's belly. He opened his mouth and let the war cry consume him. Every gryphton followed and roared, drowning out the high pitch of the scorpions' rattles. The flying scorpion made its way closer to the gryphtons, and a host of others followed it out of the tunnel. Brigdon motioned for a group of gryphtons to take to one side and another to the other side, with instructions to keep the ground crawlers busy.

"Let's take them down," Helios said with a fierce growl in his throat.

Brigdon was about to dive toward the flying creature when Pontos and his men, carrying the bombs, flew in from both sides. The gryphton army flew with long, powerful strides and gripped the clay pots. With each flap of their wings, their legs and arms moved as though they were running.

They flew in a V formation and drafted off each other. At the center of the formation, the lead gryphton bent in half and dove toward the ground. The rest split into two groups and circled around the battlefield. Staying in twos, they flanked the gryphtons that were carrying the bombs and a long line of colors streamed across the sky. The warriors dropped the pots strategically on the outside of the field, about twenty lengths apart and then into the center. Brigdon slipped a sling onto a toe and loaded it and swung it with a flick of his wrist. The scorpion reared back as the stone sunk deep into its skull. The flying scorpion fell to the ground and landed with a thud.

The gaseous poison worked wonderfully on the ground scorpions, altering their ability to receive orders with their antennae. Frenzy overcame them and they became disorganized and chaotic. The scorpions attacked the lifeless body of the winged leader and then turned on each other. Pontos and his armada swooped into the air and pulled their slings and attacked the oncoming flying bugs.

"I'm out," said Helios, watching Brigdon shoot his last stone.

"Me too."

"We're about to be outnumbered," Helios said.

Helios pointed to a wall of black coming at them. Helios swooped down toward the oncoming flying scorpions, lifted his hind legs, released his talons, and lashed out at the scorpion. The scorpion spun, almost catching Helios's wing with its pincers. Helios rolled the other way, twisted at his waist, and snagged the stinger in his paws and ripped it off.

The scorpion screeched and lunged at Helios, and he slammed the scorpions' own stinger into the soft flesh of its shoulder. Stunned, the critters' black eyes stared at Helios as its own poison paralyzed its body.

****

"I don't want to wake it up, just find the orb and let's go," Azrack said.

"What does that look like anyway?" asked Ralti.

"A gold sphere with strange markings," Azrack said.

He drew one of the symbols in the soft dirt. Azrack leaped into the air and glided to the ledge below. One at a time, they landed around the large tail and noted how much warmer it was next to the beast. The heat allowed for a plethora of glowing mushrooms to grow on the walls of the room, and an eerie green hue shone on the black and red beast. The cavern was too low for them to fly, so they had to crawl.

Their feet stuck slightly to a slime on the ground and they found it hard to walk around without making a sucking noise. A pungent odor emanated from the slime and they tried to cover their nostrils. Azrack and Tog circled around to the left as Ralti and Nasr moved around to the right. They climbed over scattered remains of columns that surrounded the enormous eight-legged body.

The scorpion's slow breaths buzzed inside their anxious chests and they were shocked by its enormous head resting on enormous pincers. Azrack pointed to the other side of the sleeping scorpion and toward three rooms. He signaled Ralti to search the one on his side, and Ralti stepped backward toward the wall. He tried to move around the pincers but stumbled on the loose ground.

Pebbles tumbled, and he threw his paws out to catch himself, and the beast stirred. Azrack and the others froze in their tracks and waited as it shifted slightly, coming within inches of Azrack and Tog. Azrack's heart pounded against his rib cage, and he held his breath. Tog sucked in his breath and threw his arms behind him and braced himself. Ralti regained his footing and made it to the entrance of the room.

Tog stayed at the entrance but peered into the room. His eyes widened, overcome by treasure. His heart beat faster as the excitement raced through his body and Azrack recognized the energy shift, but it was too late. Tog's eyes glazed over with greed. Azrack let a deep rumbling growl to warn him to back off.

Tog heard the warning but didn't respond, and Azrack knew he had but a minute to intervene. Azrack stepped inside and his eyes shifted furiously around the room. He didn't see the orb and thought it might be in one of the other rooms. Azrack slammed his shoulder into Tog's and gave him the eye of death as he walked by. Tog cowered, lowering his eyes, and squatting onto his haunches. Ralti came out of the room and shrugged. Azrack quickly leaped over a broken pile of pillars and made it to the center room. The orb was resting on a stone altar and Azrack moved toward it but stopped a few lengths away. He wondered why there was an altar in the middle of a room like this, so he searched for signs of any traps, but he couldn't find anything.

"We're going to have to move fast in case this thing is rigged," Azrack said.

Ralti agreed and signaled the others. Azrack reached for the gold orb. The shiny metal was cold on his paws and for an instant, he hesitated.

"Go on, take it," Ralti said.

Azrack gripped it tightly and darted toward the door. Ralti darted as Azrack neared him, and they veered to one side and rounded a large pillar. A strong vibe ripped through them and they stopped in mid-stride. Their chins rose until their eyes met the black eyes of the scorpion.

Ralti whipped his sword from its sheath and he swung his blade, which struck her square in the face. She reared back and screeched, and blood dripped onto the floor. Azrack and Nasr flinched under the noise but darted around Ralti back toward the waterfall. Nasr slashed the soft joint of one of the scorpion's legs, and the scorpion squealed and spun.

"Over here you scathing creature," Ralti shouted.

She spun back toward Ralti and reached for him with her massive pincer. He jumped out of the way and it slammed into a column behind him. The force sent a piece of the ceiling onto his head. The scorpion tried to stop Azrack, but he leaped over her pincer and rolled behind a pillar. Tog slipped past while she was distracted. He carried several purses of jewels around his neck, along with several silver and gold necklaces.

"Tog. What are you doing?" Ralti yelled.

Tog had an unrested grin that Ralti had never seen before. He reached the edge of the floor and jumped into the air and disappeared.

"That sorry –" Ralti started.

The scorpion attacked again, and Ralti leaped out of the way and rolled into a crouch behind the pillar. Azrack and Nasr were halfway back to the ledge when Ralti leaped over the pillar and steadied himself. Ralti ran and slipped under the beast. He swung his blade in an upward arc and sliced through the soft joint behind the armored claw. The pincer fell to the ground with a thud.

"Here's your chance, now go!" Ralti yelled.

Azrack, however, wasn't about to leave him behind. He dodged the rubble on the ground and ran straight at her mid-section. His blade sank deep into her side, sending her into a writhing fit of spasms. Ralti ran up onto one of her legs and onto her body. He threw one leg over her back and with both paws. He thrust his blade into her neck. The resistance through the joint and sinew as he cut her spine made him quiver. The scorpion's legs fell out from under her, and she sank to the ground. Ralti yanked his sword out and slid off her back.

"Well done. Now move out," Azrack said.

"What about Tog?" Ralti asked, sheathing his sword.

"He'll get his," Azrack said.

They made their way back toward the ledge but stopped just short of the edge. In the distance, they heard cries of scorpions and the clank of metal.

"Sounds like he just did," Ralti said.

"We can't go back the way we came. They're coming back in," Azrack said.

"You don't suppose we go that way?" Nasr asked, pointing to the pool of water.

"What? You don't like water?" Azrack asked.

"No, not particularly," he said, wincing at the thought of it.

"Behind the falls, is that a path?" Ralti asked.

"Yes, I spotted it earlier. I think it will lead us out of here," Azrack said.

Azrack leaped into the crashing water, followed by Ralti. Nasr took in a deep breath and jumped into the chest-deep pool. The path opened into a cavern and they struggled against the current as they made their way to the other side but found there was no way out.

"We have to turn around and go back," Ralti said.

"No, the water goes out somewhere. We have to follow it," Azrack said.

Ralti and Nasr, both fully aware it would be useless to argue, mustered their courage and followed Azrack under the water. The water drained into a rugged passageway that was small, but they were barely able to fit. They used the current to propel them into the tight space. Even though their lion side hated water, they were excellent swimmers, and they used their muscular hind legs to shove off from the edges. The passageway rounded a corner and passed under another waterfall. They gasped for air as they popped to the surface and swam to the rocky shoreline and shook their wings free of the water.

"We need to tell Helios we have the orb," Azrack said.

Their eyes followed the sheer face of the mountain.

"Looks like we're at the bottom of the cliffs," Ralti said.

"Looks like we're climbing. Unless you want to wait for your wings to dry," Azrack said.

"No way. I personally do not ever want to see another one of those scorpions," Nasr said.

They climbed over the uneven rocks and dead scorpions along the shore toward the rock face. Azrack took off a chest belt and wrapped it around the orb and hooked it to another belt and strapped it around his chest. They started up the side of the mountain, digging their claws into the earth one at a time. As they climbed, they held their wings out just enough to let the winds dry them.

Halfway up, Azrack fluttered his wings and found that they were dry. He extended them to full stretch and lifted off the wall, did a backward swan dive and shot high into the air. Ralti and Nasr followed into the deep blue sky. At the top of the cliffs, they saw the Armada hovering over the battlefield. Azrack watched the scorpions consume themselves as he met up with Brigdon and Helios.

"Seems that your calculations were correct, Helios," Azrack said.

Helios started a calculated re-enactment of the effects of the hallucinogen and explained how they could tell when the queen had died because all the scorpions fell out of the sky. Brigdon slapped him on the back with a grin and followed Azrack and the others back toward home. Helios smiled.

15-Sieze Him

Azrack stopped outside the King's tent. He sucked in a deep breath and lifted the flap and folded his wings in tightly.

"Ah, Azrack, you have returned," the King said.

The king shifted his body to prop himself against the edge of his bed.

"Sire," Azrack said.

Azrack bowed and knelt on one knee.

"Please, come. Have you the vessel?" King Ruadan asked as he fixed the sheets.

"Yes, Sire."

Azrack didn't much care for the king's temporary quarters, which was eloquently decorated for a battlefield barracks. He preferred his modest house, high in the cliffs back home. Azrack stifled the need to sneeze from the aroma coming from a gold pot with burning essences that sat on a small end table next to the king. A myriad of gold jars, bowls, vases, and trinkets of every kind surround the king with brightly colored jewels and stones that filled them to overflowing.

"You did well. Let your men rest," the King said.

The king held out his paw so that Azrack could kiss it and Azrack did, but he never cared for that tradition either.

"May we have a temporary retreat?" Azrack asked.

The king's feathers ruffled gently, and he rested on the padded headboard.

"I must attend to some business. I will know in a few days. Soon we will have the needed strength to overthrow the Kronos and Ebon Hoards," the king said.

"How, sire? With this?" Azrack gestured to the vessel.

"Yes, legend says it holds great powers."

"We are not a magical race, You're Grace, how can we use magic?"

"It can be done. I have seen it in a dream. Now, set the orb on the table and let an old gryphton rest."

Azrack bowed and obediently set the orb on the table. When he reached the door, he opened his mouth to say something but closed it instead. The brisk morning air stung his nose as he struggled with his emotions. *How is magic going to help us?* He thought and shook his head. Azrack skirted a soldier carrying a large pot of boiling water and crossed the way into the isles of tents. His shoulders sank the more he thought about his impending future.

"So, you have returned gloriously once more," Groargoth said.

Azrack turned with his shoulders toward Groargoth but didn't give him the respect of his full body at attention and rolled his eyes.

"What do you want?" Azrack asked.

"You mean, what *can* I do for you, *Sire*," Groargoth said.

"No, what do you want?" Azrack asked.

Azrack rose to his full height, which was a few lengths taller than Groargoth, and ruffled his feathers and puffed out his chest. Groargoth stretched to his full height and ruffled his feathers.

"You will obey me. I will be the new king," Groargoth said.

"That may be true, but I will never serve you Groargoth," Azrack's piercing pupils sent a shiver of fear through Groargoth, "I can smell your fear. You are no leader. You're a pathetic cub throwing a tantrum. Do not mistake anger as bravery," Azrack said.

"You will regret this, that much I do promise," Groargoth said.

Azrack puffed a snort in Groargoth's face and disappeared behind a tent. Groargoth seethed with intense anger and wanted to attack him right then, but he figured it would be more soothing to be accused of treason and hung for his crimes. Azrack tossed open the doorway of his tent and was about to slip inside for some much-wanted sleep when the talon of another gryphton tapped him on the shoulder.

"Sir," Lahonti said, bowing, "Sir, there is a very pressing matter. I must talk to you."

Azrack spun on his heel.

"Is there a problem?" Azrack asked.

"Yes, Groargoth is plot –" Lahonti caught himself.

"Go on," Azrack said.

"Lahonti, the King requires your assistance now," A soldier interrupted.

"Yes, sir," Lahonti said, "We will talk again."

Lahonti left, leaving Azrack looking out at his army. He stood tapping his talon on his helmet in his arms and the heat of the sun beat down on his bruised body. His eyes darted around the camp, taking in the soldiers who just returned and those who stayed. A tear in his heart opened as he knew what would soon be. Several moments later he turned on his paw and walked back toward his tent and fell asleep at last.

"Sir, I must talk with you," Lahonti said, peeking in through the flap of Azrack's tent.

"Can't it wait?"

"No, it may already be too late."

"Very well." Azrack crept out of his nest and ruffled his wings and crawled out of his tent. "What is it?" Azrack asked with a stifled yawn. Lahonti whispered in Azrack's ear. Azrack's eyes popped open, and he rose onto his hind legs. He searched for the king's tent and could only see the mist of evening campfires. "Where is Ralti?"

"With the others, sir."

"Send them to the falls, now, I will meet them there."

"Yes, sir."

****

"All I have wanted was the best for you, but in my old age, I fear I have made a grave error. You have not learned what I have desired for you, and I am not convinced you are qualified to lead this kingdom. You are stricken with greed and lack compassion," King Ruadan said.

"What are you saying, father?"

The king looked into his son's eyes.

"I will not be leaving the kingdom to you. Because Azrack refused the kingdom, I will hold a competition to select the next successor."

Groargoth peered into his father's eyes, trying to decipher what was just said. He couldn't wrap his brain around the words and sat silently in his anguish.

"Father, I don't know what to say. What have I done to displease you? All I have ever wanted was to please you. I have done everything you have ever asked of me."

"True, yet you only seek for your own desires and fulfillment. I love you, son, that will not change, but I can't make you someone you are not, and who you are is not a ruler of my nation."

"Then I will seek for its destruction."

Fiery anger rose in Groargoth's chest and settled in his heart. Groargoth pulled his dagger and stabbed his father in his side, and the king gasped and struggled under the pressure of Groargoth's weight. The king kicked his legs and flailed his arms, and Groargoth began to sweat. His nerves were hot and tingly as the adrenaline rushed over his body. The strength and power Groargoth felt consumed him, and he pushed even harder. Groargoth beheld his father's dying body with darkening eyes, but his mind felt alive and invigorated.

Azrack moved with eagerness through the soldiers toward the king's tent. As he rounded the last tent, he heard a commotion coming from within and raced the last several lengths. Groargoth threw open the flap and staggered out.

"My father is dead," Groargoth said.

Azrack's heart sunk into his stomach a second before his blood surged his body.

"You –" Azrack started.

"It's your fault, I had to rid him of your poison. You tried to make him give you the kingdom instead of me!" Groargoth growled. "Take him," Groargoth commanded.

The two soldiers guarding the king's tent moved toward Azrack, who stepped back.

"No, it was you. He never wanted you to be king," Azrack growled.

Azrack, however, was certain no one would believe him, or if they did, they couldn't do anything about it. It was their custom that the heirs inherited the throne unless a competition was ordered. Azrack thought carefully and knew he had but a moment to make his choice and without proof, there was nothing he could do. Groargoth would surely pin this on him and he would be put to death. The soldiers drew closer as Azrack backed away. Azrack leaped into the sky and rolled several times into the air.

"Seize him!" Groargoth yelled.

The soldiers leaped after him and chased him into the fading evening sun. Once out of sight, the soldiers, not really wanting to pursue their beloved general, backed off. Azrack dipped behind some trees and darted back the other way. He stayed low and carved around the outer edge of the camp and made his way to the falls. Azrack landed on the soft dirt just inside the cave behind the falls and shook the water from his body.

"What happened?" Ralti snapped.

"Groargoth killed the king and took control of the kingdom. The king told me he was going to give it to me, but I convinced him to hold a competition."

Azrack paced back and forth, his paws behind his back. Helios slipped through the water's edge, avoiding the full onslaught of the crashing water.

"What are you going to do?" Ralti asked.

"I have no idea," Azrack admitted.

Brigdon and Jaxton crawled down a small tunnel on the side of the cave.

"You have to leave until we can clear this up," Ralti said.

"But where will he hide, Groargoth won't stop until he finds him," Jaxton said.

"You can hide at the academy. He won't look for you there," Helios said.

"We can take that lowlife," Brigdon said.

"Yeah," they agreed.

Azrack grimaced but softened his face.

"No, I won't put you in the middle."

"But –" Helios began.

"I mean it, that's an order."

"Then what are you going to do?" Helios asked.

"We need to do recon and figure out if we can find the evidence to clear his name," Ralti said.

"This can only be between us, with Groargoth the king, the others will have no choice but to follow his commands and we can't blame them for that," Helios said.

"Where will you go?" Ralti asked.

"For now, I will hide here, but if things become too heated, I will leave and won't tell anyone where. I need to send a message to my family and get them somewhere safe," Azrack said.

"I will take care of that," Brigdon grunted.

Azrack nodded with appreciation, but his heart sank.

"I have a feeling that orb is going to be trouble. We should think about getting that out of Groargoth's paws and quickly," Azrack said.

"I have been doing some study on that, and from what I have gathered, that orb is extremely dangerous and belongs in the human realms," Helios said.

"How can you tell?" Jaxton asked.

Helios was a little surprised at his interest, but thought it might have been their discovery of the bomb together that helped soften his mind.

"To make a long story short, when researching the Ruins of Basset, I came across the part of history that told of a human sorcerer that was trying to create a portal that could be used anywhere but things went wrong when a Selket accidentally ruined the spell. It never said what happened exactly, but if there was magic and a Selket involved it can't be good," Helios said.

"I'll help you get the orb from the king," Jaxton said.

Helios nodded, and Azrack agreed.

"Alright, everyone has their orders, now let's move," Ralti said.

"Sir," everyone said.

"Stay here, I'll be back soon," Ralti said.

Azrack nodded and Ralti saluted, then left the hideout.

16-There Has To Be A Way Out

Deagan darted from his cubbyhole and raced back down the corridor. The guard's broad shoulders appeared barely before Deagan cleared the corner. The guard shook his head slightly wondering if he had seen something, then turned his attention to the girl.

"We're almost there sweetheart," he grabbed her daintily pointed chin and turned her soft oval face to his. Serin jerked away and tried to separate herself from his bearlike head, but her wrists were shackled behind her back and she couldn't push him away. She backed away but stumbled and fell into the water-stained wall, "What's the matter pretty, can't walk with those shackles on your ankles? What did you do to end up here, anyway?" his eyes wandered, and she knew what he wanted, it was written all over his face.

"Not here," said the Interrogator.

The Interrogator's raspy voice was barely audible, and Serin glared at him. The guard grabbed her chin and pulled it to his.

"I will have you," he said. Serin spit in his face and the guard pulled back and jerked her by the arm. He shoved her closer to the room while wiping his face, "Why I ought-a," he started.

"Enough, you will have plenty of time with her to do as you please later, but first, we need to find out what she knows."

Serin pulled away as a sudden dull rumbling formed in the hollow of her gut.

"Fine," the guard grumbled. The guard shoved Serin into the room first and she caught a slight glimpse of a blade from behind the door and wondered what was going on, but a calming energy eased into her chest, "Do you want to sit in there?" the guard asked, pointing to the spiked chair.

"Gregor?" the guard said.

The Interrogator stepped into the room behind the guard. He was a good foot shorter and unaware of the tied guard mumbling under the gag. Serin pulled her arm out of his grip and moved against the wall.

"Move out of the way you derp," said the Interrogator.

He shoved his way past him. Shaz stepped out from behind the door with one hand on his hip, the other holding the sword at his side.

"What do you want to know?" Shaz asked.

Serin smirked at his cocky attitude but wasn't surprised at all. She knew he had it in him somewhere and it was just a matter of time before his arrogance showed, but at this point, she didn't care, especially if it got them out of there. The men gasped, and the guard gripped his sword, but the Interrogator stopped him.

"I take it you're Shaz?"

"Yes, I am."

Serin inched her way toward the door.

"You do understand there's no way out of here," he said, his pinched face tight with certainty.

"Yeah, so I've been told, something about a curse, blah, blah, blah?" Shaz said. Serin snickered, and the guard shot her a sideways glare, "Why don't you give *me* the girl?" Shaz slid one foot behind the other in an advance parry. The guard moved his foot in acceptance of the challenge and the Interrogator rolled his eyes.

"Ah, even if you get the girl, you can't get out. Eventually, we will find you and kill you, after we torture you, of course," the Interrogator said.

Shaz assessed the situation quickly, determining that the guards would be easy, but there was a hint of magic to the Interrogator, that Shaz didn't understand and wasn't sure how hard he would be. He stepped to the side along the wall, steering clear of the trapdoor in the center of the room, and the second guard lifted his sword. Shaz took another step and with lightning speed, slammed the end of his hilt into the side of the guard's skull and the man crumbled to the ground.

"You are as good as they say," the Interrogator said.

The Interrogator slid away from the falling guard, and Shaz read the sudden jump of fear that surged across the little man's body. Shaz stepped in front of Serin and shielded her from the Interrogator and turned slightly but kept one eye on the man.

"You alright?" he asked.

"Yes, but-" she said.

Serin bit her lower lip to keep from trembling. Shaz felt her energy pulsing behind him and sensed her heart was pounding out of her chest. He didn't like that she was trembling so much.

"So, what are you going to now?" the Interrogator asked.

He reached for a ten-inch spike.

"Ah, come on now, you don't need that, you have magic," Shaz said with a crooked smile.

The Interrogator stopped and released the spike slowly. For a split-second, his face was consumed with confusion.

"What do you mean?" the man asked.

"You don't know?" Shaz asked.

"Know what?" Shaz concealed his confusion, he was certain he detected magic within the man, "What kind of magic?" The Interrogator asked.

The Interrogator gripped a pendant hanging at his navel and Shaz realized it wasn't the Interrogator with the magic, but it was the pendant he wore. The Interrogator stood tall and turned to face Shaz.

"Tell me about this magic you speak of."

"Naw, I thought you would be able to tell by now, but if you haven't figured it out, then I'm not telling you,"

"Shaz, let's get out of here. He's trying to trick you with the pendant." Serin whispered.

It was all she could do to keep from chewing her tongue off. She was freezing, and her teeth chattered. The Interrogator stood shocked. He hadn't quite understood what all of this meant, and Shaz could tell he was trying to piece the puzzle together in his mind. Shaz started to move Serin toward the door, and she pointed to the shackles on her ankles. Shaz cursed. He grabbed the pendant and yanked it off the Interrogator and kicked him square in the chest, sending him flying into the back wall. Shaz bent down and shoved his shoulder into her core and wrapped his arm around her legs just under her bottom and stood up.

Serin flopped over his shoulder, and Shaz darted out of the room. He passed through the open door and kicked it shut with a BANG. He slipped his sword into its sheath and raced down the hall. Serin saw the Interrogator rounding the corner as they reached the end of the hall with his pinched face now reddened with fury. The Interrogator ran as fast as he dared because his boots were sharp and pointed and gave him no traction at all. He slipped on the smooth stone and struggled to stay on his feet. Shaz gained distance and rounded another corner, but this time he went the opposite direction of how he and Deagan had come in.

"We need to remove these shackles," Shaz said.

Shaz took another hall that led to a small cell with a straw bed and a washbasin. He slipped into the room and closed the door and set Serin down on her bottom.

"What are you doing?" she asked.

"Don't worry, this won't hurt," Shaz said.

Shaz struck the hardened steel with the edge of his blade and the steel responded with a crack and fell off her ankles and she held out her arms and he removed the shackles from her wrists. Her soft creamy skin was now red, swollen, and raw, and she rubbed her sore wrists and ankles.

"Thank you," Serin said.

Shaz listened and quietly opened the solid wood door. They made their way back down the corridor and toward the stairs, but Shaz grabbed Serin's blouse from behind.

"Wait. I hear someone," Shaz whispered.

Serin jumped to the side of the wall and let Shaz pass her.

"Blast," Serin cursed.

Shaz took a few steps closer to the corner of the staircase.

"We'll have to go down," he said.

"Do we have to?" she asked.

Serin pushed the lump from her throat and Shaz gripped her hand, gave it a squeeze, and gave her a gentle smile. Serin tried to smile back, but she was so cold she could hardly make herself move at all. Shaz's heart sank and a burst of heat raged in his heartfire. He was angry that she had to go through this, and it was his fault. The heat rippled through his being and Serin could feel the heat in his grip. She wondered if he was using magic and caught herself hoping he was because that would mean she had met someone that was like her. Shaz moved into the stairway and Serin followed. They were halfway down the stairs when again they heard voices. They stopped and listened to the sniveling voice of the Interrogator, yap commands to guards through the echoing and musky hall.

Shaz took Serin's hand and pulled her to the other side and slipped into the wall, and with his strong arms, he pulled her into a secret alcove. Shaz realized Serin was missing half her clothes and had no shoes. He imagined his inner heat come to the surface and encompass her frame. His warmth was much needed, and she sank into his warm embrace.

"Hurry up, you numbskull," a guard said.

"Not like they can escape or nothin, so we wander around until we find them," a guard said, his voice husky and gruff.

Serin's scent was sweet to Shaz even though she was dirty from the dungeons, and he gripped her tighter. Serin leaned in and rested perfectly in the hollow of his neck and shoulder. Shaz thought back to the thoughts of her in the city and how he got the medallion and now she was in here and didn't want to let her go. For the first time in a long time, he was complete and was certain Serin was a very important person to him. Shaz wanted to stay in this moment forever, but knew they couldn't. He pulled away slightly and looked down at her, and Serin looked into his deep-blue eyes. He smiled, and she smiled in return.

"Are you alright to keep going?" Shaz whispered.

"I think so," Serin whispered.

He took in a deep breath and peeked around the corner. He signaled to Serin they were going to go down the stairs across the hall and when he felt they were clear, they slipped into the hall. They rounded the bend in the spiral staircase. Shaz stopped mid-step, an inch from a guard's sword. Shaz held out his arm, stopping Serin and cursed to himself for letting his new feelings for her cloud his senses and started to back up.

"Back up," Shaz said from the corner of his mouth.

Shaz gripped the hilt of his sword. The Honor Blade shrieked as he whipped it from its sheath and Serin ran back up the stairs as the guard gripped the hilt of his sword and twisted his wrists, bringing it up in a back rounded swing. The narrow staircase limited the movements of the long swords, and Shaz parried up the stairs a few steps to have the room to block. Shaz twisted his blade and wrapped it around the guards and locked the hilts. Shaz shoved the guard, sending him skidding down several stairs. Shaz rounded the corner with his back against the wall, and the guard regained his footing and stuck his blade out straight and lunged up at Shaz. Shaz stepped around the blade and flipped it back, sending the hilt into the side of the guard's head. The guard stumbled back, the soft light of a wall sconce flickered before his eyes as he struggled to keep his consciousness.

"Maybe he can help us find the way out of here," Serin said.

"There is no way out?" the guard sneered.

"I just have to find the grate underwater," Shaz said, irritated that Serin didn't trust him.

Serin could tell Shaz was annoyed that she didn't trust him, but she could sense the guard's nature, and he didn't want to hurt anyone.

"It's not that-"Serin started.

The guard lunged up the stairs once more and Shaz blocked with a sidestep and slapped the oncoming blade against the stone wall. The guard pulled hard and yanked it away and took a few steps back. Shaz rounded his blade over his head in a flash and brought it down toward the guard, who threw his blade out to block. The honor blade sliced straight through the other blade, and the tip fell to the floor and clanged down the stairs. The guard looked up at Shaz with terror in his eyes.

"Please, I can help. I can take you to the waterways."

"Why should I believe you?" Shaz asked.

"You shouldn't, but I am clearly not in the position to argue, and neither are you."

Serin touched Shaz's shoulder,

"I think we should trust him," Serin said.

Shaz didn't understand exactly why, but her vibes said that she was right. Shaz thought about it and peered into his eyes.

"Fine, take us to the flooded tunnels," Shaz dug his blade into the guard's back, "No funny business."

The guard nodded and moved down the stairs.

"Halt, who's there?" an old gruff voice asked.

Shaz twisted the blade against the guard's back.

"It's me, you duff head. I have the prisoners, open the gate."

"Why do you have prisoners?" said the old and feeble voice.

"It's no concern of yours."

The sparse torches in the dimly lit corridor cast long, sinister shadows on the old man's face. He fumbled for the keys and scuffled to the iron gate and Serin was saddened that his eyes had failed so much and probably because he had been in this dungeon for so long.

"Keep your knickers on, I'm a goin," he said, clinking the keys together as he shook from old age, "To the caves with ya then? You'll have time to think down there unless you freeze to death first," the old man laughed. He fumbled with the latch and slowly pulled the lock off the door. He let the gate swing free an inch or so, then opened it all the way. "Have fun down there," the old man said with a depraved cackle and a big grin on his face. Serin no longer felt bad for him and shook her head at him as she passed. Once out of earshot the guard stopped and pointed in the direction they would find the tunnels.

"Just a few more feet around this bend we will come to the shifting halls," the guard said.

"The shifting halls? I don't like the sounds of that," Serin said.

A chill ran up her spine.

"On my way in, the boat's pole got stuck in a grate in the floor of the canal. We need to swim and find the grate," Shaz said.

"I don't know of any grate," the guard said.

Shaz reached into his pocket and pulled out the map and opened the paper.

"Blast, I can't tell, it's too dark in here," Shaz said.

"Come this way, there's a lamp over here," the guard said.

Shaz positioned the map under the light and tapped his finger on a point on the paper.

"Should be around here," Shaz said.

"Ah, that's way over there," the guard pointed back in the direction they were going, "But it's too far to swim, the water is too high and there are no pockets to breathe from."

"How many floors are underwater?" Shaz asked.

"Two," the guard said, "They flooded when the city started using canals."

"Then there has to be a way out," Shaz said.

Shaz folded up the map.

"I think I can help," Serin said.

"How? Unless you can remove the water, there is no way," the guard said.

"Well, that's just it, I know how to breathe underwater," she said smiling.

Serin studied Shaz's face for any indication that he would want nothing to do with her, but instead, she found him gazing into her eyes with intrigue. The guard's face drained of color and Shaz slapped him on the shoulder.

"If we are going to work together, I think we should know your name," Shaz said.

The guard shook Shaz's hand.

"Barrick,"

"I'm Shaz and this is Serin," Shaz said.

"I'm not exactly sure what's going on here," Barrick said.

"Everything will work out Barrick, I promise, do you believe me?" Shaz asked.

"No, but what the hay, if I die today at least I won't have to be stuck in here forever," Barrick said.

17-I Couldn't Be Better

Barrick led them back to the edge of the water. Serin closed her eyes and put her hands out in front of her, one leg in front and the other in back. She swooped her hands around her and held them out, inches from each other. A small ball of pale blue light glimmered between her palms, and she pulled her hands away and made the ball bigger.

"Shaz come here," Serin said.

Shaz stepped toward her, and she placed the ball of light over his head. Instantly, the warm tingle of magic filled his lungs as he breathed in the air within the sphere. Serin did it again and placed the ball around Barrick and then herself. Shaz started into the frigid water and the cold seared through his body.

"The water is very cold. Are you going to be alright?" Shaz asked.

"I'll be fine," she said.

Serin stepped into the water and soaked in the calming and invigorating synergy. She walked down the slimy steps and plunged into the darkness. The faint light of her air bubble shone around her, allowing her to locate Shaz. She looked back and saw Barrick plunge in behind her. He gasped a few times as the cold shocked his body and he flailed around. The fear of drowning started to overcome him.

"Breathe," Serin said and pointed to her mouth.

He took in the needed breath and gave her a nervous smile. They swam to the bottom of the stairway and Shaz pointed in the direction the map led to. After several minutes in the water, the cold had muted almost all of Barrick's senses and he couldn't feel his limbs anymore. Shaz and Serin didn't seem to be bothered by it and had to help him keep up. Serin wasn't sure what to think of the tingle of energy that trickled in from her fingers and up her arms and into her chest. Thoughts she'd never had before shot into her mind with one that continued to repeat itself. '*Shape me*' it was as if the water was speaking to her in a familiar way. Shaz stopped at the end of the hall and frisked the ceiling. He came up with nothing. He searched the end wall and shrugged and swam back to the others.

"You take that wall, I'll take this one, and Serin you take that one," Shaz said, pointing to the different walls.

They felt around but found nothing, and Shaz pointed downward to search the lower level. They turned toward the stairs but found the stairs were no longer there, instead, there was a wall.

Barrick mouthed, "shifting halls," and pointed back the other way.

Serin turned, but from the corner of her eye, she noticed the water was being sucked down a small hole in the wall. Serin touched the hole, and an extra zing tickled her fingers as her hand passed a shadow that looked like the wall. She waved her arms at Shaz and Barrick, who were already swimming back the other way. She yelled until Shaz heard her faint voice from outside his bubble and turned to see her. Serin pointed to the hole and started swimming through it. Shaz signaled Barrick, who followed.

After a time, the air in the bubble became thin, and it became harder to breathe. Serin hovered in the middle of the path until Shaz and Barrick caught up to her. She swooped her arms around like before and let the magic light grow. The warmth in her chest grew with each time she cast her magic, and she understood that she was connected to the water in the same way as she was the air. After refreshing their air bubbles, Shaz breathed in and threw up his thumb to say things were good again.

Shaz was starting to swim slower, and Barrick was barely moving on his own. Shaz hovered slowly moving his arms and legs to let Barrick catch up. He peered through the darkness to search the floor for the grate. He figured that if the halls were shifting, who's to say they aren't swimming upside down. Something shiny, gold perhaps, caught his eye. He dove to the floor and picked up a gold ring that was half-buried under years of moss and slime. He removed the stringy green moss and slipped it onto his middle finger. A familiar sensation tickled his nerves as strength overcame him. *A magical ring, I wonder who dropped this here.* He took it off and handed it to Barrick, who slipped it on and smiled. At the end of the corridor, they found the grate. Shaz and Barrick, with his added new strength, managed to pry the grate open and slid it out of the way. Shaz motioned for Serin to go first, but when she got to the hole but an invisible shield stopped her.

"I can't," she said.

Shaz tested the hole and slipped right through, but he could tell it was shadow magic that created the shield which held everyone one captive. He thought for a moment and blurred his eyes until the energy of the shadow magic came into view. He gripped at the center of the shield and started to pull it apart. The shadow magic didn't want to comply, and the heavy magic stung his hands. He struggled to push out the pain, and Serin watched him labor with difficulty. She put her hand on his arm and focused on giving him some of her magic.

A blue hue of color merged off her being and wrapped around him like a blanket. Shaz could feel the added magic and with great effort peeled the shield apart enough for Serin to squeeze past. Shaz's face contorted as he struggled with the weight of the shield as Barrick tried to swim through. He made it halfway and became stuck.

Serin grabbed his arms, put her feet against the floor, and pulled as hard as she could. She tugged a few times but let go. She swirled her arms around her head quickly and the water responded immediately. The water built-up pressure behind Barrick and it wasn't long until he shot like a sizzling arrow through to the surface and into the night sky. Shaz let go of the force and swam through easily and heaved the cover back on and swam to the surface. Barrick burst the water's surface still being propelled. Deagan nearly peed his pants and squealed like a girl.

"Shhh boy," Barrick barked, splashing in the water.

Barrick grabbed onto the edge of the boat and searched for the others. Serin eased up through the water, the light blue fading from her face as she broke the surface.

"Are you alright?" Deagan asked Serin while giving Barrick a scowl.

"Yes."

Deagan pulled Serin into the boat.

"Where's Shaz?" Deagan asked.

"He's coming," she said.

Shaz popped through the water's surface.

"How in the world did you make it out?" Deagan asked.

Deagan handed a blanket to Serin and Barrick dipped under the small hull and climbed in as Shaz climbed in on the other side to equalize the boat.

"Let's move," Shaz said.

Deagan shoved away from the end of the canal. The water waved up against the wall, splashing gently and soft whooshing sounds echoed as the boat made its way from the dock. Once they moved away from the old castle wall of the dungeon, Shaz pulled out a dry cloak from his pack and wrapped it around himself.

"Sorry, I didn't expect you or I would have brought you some dry things," Deagan said to Barrick.

"I couldn't be better," Barrick said.

A huge smile covered Barrick's face, and Deagan figured it was because he too was out of the dungeon. Deagan pushed the boat quickly and meticulously, and Shaz was impressed at how well he maneuvered it. The lights of the city began to fill the space, and they could make out a few people that were out late at night.

"Back to Lucien?" Deagan asked.

Shaz grabbed at his temples and squeezed as hard as he could. The pain gripped his mind with such intensity that he wobbled.

"What's the matter?" Barrick asked.

"Blast, another headache. We need to take him somewhere safe fast and get some medicine," Serin said.

"We'll take him to my place," Barrick said, helping Shaz sit down.

Serin gave him a wary glance but decided she had no choice.

"Alright, how far is it?" she asked.

"Not far, you will be safe there, and we can help you with the medicine you need."

"Thank you," she said.

"Drop us off at the corner of Pinket and Barrow," Barrick said.

"Are you sure, we can also go to my house," Deagan said.

Serin hadn't met Deagan yet, but could tell he was honest. But his past might have consequences.

"Do you think we will be safe there," Serin asked.

Deagan questioned whether Lucien would make a scene and decided that they better not chance it and shook his head.

"Then we go to Barrick's," Serin said.

Deagan nodded, but he didn't trust Barrick either. They continued in silence until they reached the intersection. Deagan pulled the boat next to the ramp and Barrick helped Serin heave Shaz out of the boat while Deagan tied it to the landing. Barrick put Shaz's arm around his neck and gripped his waist and started down the alley. Deagan and Serin grabbed their packs and followed quickly. Barrick was remarkably quick for carrying Shaz and Deagan and Serin had to half-jog to keep up. Barrick lifted the latch of a door knocker and gave a few quick raps on the wood door. The covering over the window peeled back and the latch unlocked.

A woman opened the door wearing her nightdress, and she pulled the door open quickly. They hurried inside and she shut the door and locked the latch. Barrick set Shaz on the couch and turned in time to catch his wife, who was leaping into his arms. They laughed and cried, and Serin and Deagan were sure they hadn't seen each other in a long time.

"Deagan, do you think you can gather some supplies for me so I can make some medicine for Shaz?" Serin asked.

"Of course," Deagan said.

Serin found a paper and writing implement and made a list and gave it to Deagan, who shoved it into his pocket.

"Please hurry," Serin said.

"I'll do my best," Deagan said.

He left the house and Serin went to Shaz's side.

"How did this happen? How did you get out? Who is this? What is going on?" Barrick's wife stammered.

"It's a long story love and I will tell you all about it, but we need to help him," Barrick said.

"What happened to him?" Barrick's wife asked.

Barrick didn't actually know and looked at Serin with a blank gaze.

"He was injured during the breakout," Serin said.

The woman nodded.

"We can put them in the spare room," she said.

Barrick helped Shaz into the spare room and into the bed. Serin touched the woman's arm as she was about to follow Barrick out of the room.

"Thank you," Serin said.

"I'm Helen, buy the way, and you're welcome," Helen said.

Serin pulled the covers up around Shaz and put her hand on his forehead. A strange image came into her mind and she could tell how fast his heart was beating, that his lungs were clear of any fluids and she could see his heartfire. She had no clue what she was seeing but guessed it might be where his magic was in his body and she thought about her own. There was only one bed, and she was exhausted, so she sat in the chair next to Shaz and rested her head against the wall. A soft knock at the door stirred her drifting mind, and she opened it.

"I thought you might like a change of clothes and the washroom is across the hall for you to use," Helen said.

Serin took the items and smiled.

"Thank you. I am very sorry we have intruded like this," Serin said.

"Nonsense, you brought me my husband back from the dungeons, I owe you more than I can ever repay. They didn't tell us the soldiers couldn't leave either," Helen said.

Serin saw the flash of anger cross her eyes and understood they had been lied to and her heart sank.

"We're happy to help," Serin said.

Helen smiled and went back to her room. Serin took advantage of the washroom and washed and changed into the clothes Helen gave her. The leggings were warm and fuzzy, and the tunic was long with delicate ruffles around the bottom, giving it a dress-like appearance. The boots were warm, and she was glad to have something to cover her feet. The blisters she had gotten from the rough stone eased, and she sighed. She returned to Shaz, who was stirring. Serin sat on the bed and put her hand on his chest.

"Hold on, Shaz, Deagan has gone to get supplies. I will make some medicine as soon as he gets back," Serin said.

"Thank you," Shaz managed.

18-Oh, No, You Don't

Serin sat in the chair next to Shaz's bed and rested her head against the wall. She listened to the children outside playing a game of kickball. The curtains were closed to keep the room dark, but she had opened the window to let in some fresh air. The breeze made the little bit of daylight dance on her lap and she found herself dozing. Her lids were heavy with a lack of sleep. She slept as best she could while sitting in the chair, but that didn't offer much. Shaz stirred, and she opened her eyes and started for the jar of medicine she had used for the last three days.

"Serin," Shaz said.

Serin shook her head clear of the fog and sat on the edge of the bed.

"I'm here," Serin said.

Shaz sat up and wrapped his arms around her tightly.

"Thank you," Shaz said.

"For what?" Serin asked.

"For taking care of me and not leaving me," Shaz said.

Serin noted his energy filled with sadness, self-doubt, and frustration, and she wrapped her arms around him. Serin wondered if the shadow magic was what caused his headaches. He must have used a tremendous amount of shadow magic to cause this much pain, and the thought came that the shadow magic required a payment. Serin felt guilty, after all, she was the reason he'd done it in the first place.

"How is your head?" Serin asked.

"Much better, I think the worst it is over now," Shaz said.

"Good," Serin said.

She didn't want him to let her go but didn't want to lead him on either, especially when she didn't know what was going to happen next. She, Barrick, and Hellen had decided that none of them could stay in town and that they needed to get as far away as they could. Serin pulled away.

"How long has it been?" Shaz asked.

"Three days," Serin said.

Serin gently pushed him and he laid down and she put another dose of the concoction on his temples and under his nose.

"Where are we?" Shaz asked.

He breathed in the sweet earthy aroma.

"Barrick and Hellen's," Serin said.

"And Deagan?" Shaz asked.

"Fine, he has come every day to check on you," Serin said.

"I feel bad I got him into this mess," Shaz said.

"He's not, he talks about it all the time and how much of a hero he was," Serin smiled at the last conversation when he was telling her his story again with even more enthusiasm than the last time, then concern encompassed her delicate features.

"What is it?" Shaz asked.

Serin set the bottle on the table, and Shaz took her hand in his.

"We can't stay here. Barrick and Hellen are going to leave and go to her mother's in the grasslands, and we should leave the city too. Deagan brought a wanted poster with our descriptions. He's been pulling as many down as he finds, but they keep popping up," Serin said.

"Aye," Shaz said.

"Where are you going to go?" Serin asked.

"I guess I can try to find my family's castle and lie low there for a bit until things settle down. I'm supposed to 'report' to the Council, whoever they are, but I guess that will have to wait. What about you?" Shaz asked.

"I have some relatives in the highlands I can stay with," Serin said.

Neither of them wanted to leave each other, but they didn't know what to say either. Serin stood up and crossed the room.

"I'll let you get dressed and go find out what Barrick's plan is," Serin said.

Shaz nodded, and Serin left the room and closed the door. Shaz came down the stairs to find Barrick carrying out a large bag and Hellen with two smaller ones.

"You're awake! How do you feel?" Barrick asked.

Shaz smiled, and Barrick put the bag down and pulled him into a bearhug.

"Much better, thank you." Shaz turned to Hellen, "Thank you, mam, for opening your home to complete strangers," Shaz said.

Hellen smiled.

"It was the best decision of my life," Hellen said.

Serin came around the corner and motioned for Shaz to follow her into the kitchen. Shas found a plate of griddlecakes, cooked sausages, and warm syrup. He thought of Mrs. Bailey.

"What about Mrs. Bailey?" Shaz asked.

"Gone, Deagan has stopped by a few times but no one answers," Serin said.

Serin set her plate across from his and sat down. Shaz sat down and found the chairs were a bit larger than Mrs. Bailey's and scooted himself in.

"I guess I'll take you to your relatives and then head out from there," Shaz said.

Serin wanted to go with him, but nodded and put the last bite of griddlecakes in her mouth. Shaz could tell there was something wrong, but he didn't dare ask, after all, he was the one that caused all her troubles and figured that if she was far away from him, she would be safer.

When they were finished eating, they helped Barrick and Hellen load their wagon with the few belongings they were taking with them. Serin sucked in a deep breath and looked to the sky, and her heart pounded. She searched the cloudless atmosphere as if somehow it would give her the answers she was searching for. Her mind raced around the events of the last few days and she couldn't keep her emotions on any one string.

Serin went upstairs and packed the few things Hellen had given her and the rest of the ingredients Deagan had brought her. She put several little containers of the ointment she made into Shaz's bag knowing that he was going to need as much as possible and choked back the lump forming in her throat. She didn't want to keep them waiting, so she clasped the flap of her satchel and slung it over her shoulder and met Shaz and the others downstairs.

"Are you going to be alright?" Barrick asked.

"Aye," Shaz said.

"It was a pleasure meeting you," Serin said.

"You too, thanks for teaching me how to make that pain medicine, and bringing me back my Barrick," Hellen said.

"Of course," Serin said.

Serin gave her a hug.

"If you ever need us, you know where to find us," Hellen said.

"Thanks again," Shaz said.

Barrick pulled him into a bearhug, and Shaz grunted with the squeeze. Shaz and Serin waited until their wagon was out of sight and headed the other way. Shaz pulled the hood of the dark cloak Barrick gave him over his head, and Serin pulled hers.

"Keep your head down so we're not spotted by the guards," Shaz said.

The mid-afternoon sun was warm and Shaz wanted to take off the cloak as the sweat dripped down his back. They moved quietly around the crowded streets and tried to blend in as much as possible. Shaz and Serin entered a busy intersection when a loud CLANG echoed from around a corner. They carefully slipped passed an old man who was hobbling down a side passage and came across a pile of pots that were strewn along the cobble-paved corridor. Several people stood nearby a small café, whispering, and pointing to the mess. Shaz stepped over one of the pot's and caught a glimpse of a familiar fading hue of color in its reflection. The hairs on the back of his neck stood out and a pit in his stomach surged. He was sure there was something bad about to happen, but he had no clue what.

Serin stepped over the pots and they made it a few more lengths when a shadow overhead triggered a flash of memories. Shaz's mind raced through the events of the night when something attacked his home as a child and again when he was at the tavern. He suddenly formed the association between the creature that caused his mother's death and the blackbird-like creature in the tavern. A flash of fire filled his chest and red-hot anger ripped through him. He cursed at himself for not associating the feeling at the tavern. He would have killed that scraggly creature then.

"A sqwall," he said, his jaw clenched tight.

Shaz searched the sky, and Serin could see the anger and pain in his eyes.

"A what?"

"Never mind," Shaz said.

Shaz moved to the other side of the path and took another side passage, and Serin had to jog-run just to keep up with him.

"Where are you going? We need to turn here," Serin said.

Serin tried to get his attention, but he was focused. She recognized his intensity and knew there was something happening that she didn't understand. Shaz followed his gut and weaved through the maze-like walkways and alleys. Shaz ducked and pulled Serin to the ground as the immense black bird swooped within a few lengths above their heads.

"What in the blazes is that?" Serin asked as it soared back into the sky.

"You see it?" Shaz asked.

"Yes, why?" Serin asked.

"No one else sees it, or they would be running for cover," he said. "It must be invisible to those of non-magic," Shaz said.

"Good point. What is it?"

"It's a sqwall."

"How do you know have you've seen it before?" Serin asked.

"Yes. Come on, we're not safe here, but I don't want to alert the guards and risk getting caught again," Shaz said.

What he really wanted to do was to lure it out of the city and kill the wretched thing. His anger intensified as he thought about it, and he was going to make it pay. They didn't make it far when the large mangy black bird descended upon them again.

"Run!" Shaz said.

Shaz pointed toward the outer ring of the city. Serin darted forward, avoiding the people milling about the square and Shaz rounded a corner with precision. He leaped over bushels and barrels that were scattered over the uneven road. One poured a green liquid from the spout and another, with the lid broken off, let out a pungent odor of cabbage and vinegar. Shaz wrinkled his nose, not wanting to trudge through the cabbage.

"Serin over there," Shaz called, pointing to a small stable.

Serin tried to veer to the right but got caught in a heavy throng of people who were shoving their way up a ramp to a stone bridge. Shaz searched the sky for the sqwall and assessed his best route through the half-walls and steps of the plaza. He sped up and ran under an archway in time to reach out and grab Serin as she was shoved off the bridge on the other side and Serin darted through the doorway behind him. The sqwall rounded the city plaza with a sideways tilt and descended from the sky. The creature stretched out its long skinny wings and glided through the wind as it lowered itself into an attack distance. The bird released its small razor-sharp talons and lowered its dark-black beak.

The sharp beak pointed downward, which allowed its black beady eyes to lock onto them. Shaz drew his sword and reflected the sun into the creature's eyes, and it squawked and pulled back. Serin reached her mind out and found a nearby fountain. She imagined the water leap into the air and cover the bird, and the water obeyed. The sqwall sputtered and shrieked, jerking upward as the liquid doused its coal-black feathers, making them stick together. The creature was now flightless, and it fumbled and slammed into a wall and plopped on the ground. A loud CRACK pushed from behind them, blasting them across the stone. The sqwall transformed from the large crow-like bird to the human-like figure. The wings shifted from feathers to a cloak being held with wiry fingers. Its legs were thin and twisted sideways, and it hopped like a bird in a somewhat sideways fashion.

"Oooh," Serin said.

She wrinkled her nose in disgust at the sight of the ugly creature. Shaz expected the creature to transform, but now he understood how it did it. Shaz pointed to a doorway.

"Go that way as fast as you possibly can and don't look back. Go straight to your highlands, and never think of me again," Shaz said.

Serin looked at him stunned, but the pain and fear in his eyes was real and her heart thudded, and she nodded.

"Shaz-" Serin started.

"Go now," Shaz said.

Shaz practically lifted her off the ground and gave her a gentle but firm push. Serin's legs propelled her forward, but her heart ached, and she grabbed the edge of a large wicker basket and threw it to the ground The sqwall tried to flap his cape-like wings but tripped on the basket and went flailing to the ground with a shriek of anger. The bird regained its footing and started toward Serin. Shaz rammed his shoulder into the bird and it toppled over the half-wall behind it.

Shaz squeezed through an opening and peered down the next lane. The large hooves of a guard's horse clopped into view. The Ebassian horse-guards were large men who sat in pitch-black saddles with bright shining heavy armor that clanked and rattled as they rode.

"Blast." Shaz cursed under his breath.

Shaz slipped into a side alley that led back toward the city center, giving Serin enough time to get out of the city. Wide-eyed people scurried up against buildings as he ran by. When he reached the next corner, he stopped and checked to see if the bird took his bait. The bird was hopping through the people, knocking them over. The people scurried around in the confusion, and Shaz listened for the clopping of the horse that was fading into the distance. Shaz searched for a way out of the alley, but there were only small shops. Shaz rounded the corner and nearly smacked into the sqwall. Its blank stare sent shivers down his spine. The creature lowered its beak and raised its arms and held out its cape-like wings. It hissed and drool drip off its beak-like lips. Shaz lunged at the creature, and the cold steel of Shaz's blade sank into its chest. The creature sputtered and Shaz stepped out of its way and let it fall with a thud.

Serin ran through a dress shop and opened the backdoor and veered to the right but only made it a few lengths and came to an immediate stop. Another sqwall was standing in the center of the street, a few lengths from a guard who was sitting on his horse. She screamed. The guard and the sqwall cringed from the ringing in their ears, and the guard put his finger in his ear to soften the discomfort.

Shaz's heartfire spiked when Serin's scream echoed across the sky. The sqwall shape-shifted with a deafening crack, jolting Serin backward. She landed on her rump and struggled to catch her breath.

"Stop this at once," called the guard.

"Kill it, please, I beg you, kill it," Serin pleaded.

Serin pointed to the sqwall but all the guard saw was an empty street.

"Are you crazy?"

"NO, can't you see it?" Serin said.

Her lips tightened with anger, and she slowly stood up. The sqwall hopped a few lengths and Serin searched for a way to run.

"No, I can't see anything but an unruly girl causing trouble," the guard said.

"It's right in front of you, you idiot," Serin scrutinized the sqwall and it hissed, letting its long pink tongue flicker in the air. Serin looked up at the guard, and back at the sqwall, "I won't give in without a fight," she hissed at the sqwall, clenching her jaw tight, her hands balled in a fist.

"Hey, are you the wanted girl?" the guard asked.

The guard jabbed his heel into the side of the horse, and it jumped into a trot. Shaz peeled around the corner and found Serin and the sqwall with the guard coming toward her.

"Blast, walls all around her," Shaz cursed.

Shaz leaped over a short wall and sprinted to a horse tied to a nearby stable. Shaz leaped onto the horse and dug his heels into its side.

"Hey, that's my horse," a man yelled from a little café across the corridor.

The horse lurched out of the stable and veered to the right as Shaz yanked the lead. Shaz maneuvered around people and baskets or barrels sitting around the marketplace until he spotted Serin. He raced toward her and leaped over the small wall right in front of the sqwall. The creature jumped back and leaped into the air. Shaz held onto the horn of the saddle and leaned over the right side, and Serin raised her arm for him to grab onto. She bent her knees and thrust her legs against the ground, propelling herself up into the air. Shaz grabbed her arm and yanked her upward. She threw her leg out to catch the back of the animal and grabbed onto Shaz's waist. The horse leaped over the small wall on the other side of the corridor and jumped down the set of stairs in the middle of the plaza. The guard called after them and a bell at the top of the city guard tower sounded. They reached the last twenty lengths or so as the gates closed.

"Oh, no, you don't, not this time!" Serin yelled.

She threw out her arms and blasted the gates with a burst of air. Guards shouted and leaped away from the assailing shattered wood and they raced through the gate. Serin looked over her shoulder and saw the sqwall gaining speed on them. She sent a torrent of wind and the wind picked up the dust the horse kicked up and sent it into the sky. They heard the screeching of the frustrated sqwall in the distance as the horse raced toward the forest.

Shaz kept the horse at a steady pace for several lengths into the trees. Shaz scanned the distance as they went, and Serin could tell he was in full attack mode. She wasn't sure where he was going, but it wasn't toward her family in the highlands. She waited several more lengths until Shaz slowed the horse and his body relaxed.

"I've been thinking-" Serin said, "I think I am supposed to go with you."

"What makes you think that?" Shaz questioned.

His heart skipped a beat at her words. On one side he liked the idea that they would stay together, but on another, he didn't want to drag her into what he was going to have to do.

"Well, I don't know. It just feels like that's what I should do."

"Just feels like?" he questioned.

"If you don't want me to, then just say it," she said.

Serin's tone had a hint of anger in it, and Shaz stopped the horse and turned in the saddle.

"No, that's not what I mean. I just need you to be sure and 'just a feeling' doesn't sound really sure to me," Shaz said.

"I am sure. I want to help. Besides, you need me," Serin said.

He did need her, and he wanted her there with him.

"All right then," he said.

Serin opened her mouth, ready to blurt out her reasons, but shut it quickly. Shaz maneuvered the horse into a heavy thicket and helped Serin down. He slid off the horse and studied the forest. Jagwynn trotted out of the trees and purred loudly.

"I knew you were around," Shaz said, ruffling her head.

Serin smiled at the large cat and stroked her fur, which she replied by rubbing against her leg, knocking her off balance.

"I wish we had a map," he grumbled.

Serin reached into her pack's pocket and pulled out a piece of folded paper.

"You have a map?" Shaz asked.

"Barrick gave it to me while you were sleeping," she said.

He nodded and ran his finger over areas of the map, mumbling to himself. Serin combed her hair and pulled out the tangles the best she could and then wrapped it into a hair tie at the back of her head.

"So where are we going?" Serin asked.

"I think we should head to my family castle and see what we can find out from there, and I need to find the sheath for this sword," Shaz said.

"Why?" Serin asked.

"I'll explain on the way," Shaz said.

Shaz tried to estimate what direction they needed to go. He stood with his finger on his chin, his brows furrowed in deep thought. Serin smirked and rummaged inside the side pockets of the saddle to make herself busy. Her finger slipped across something cold and metallic. She stretched onto her tippy toes and grabbed hold of the little object and found it was a compass.

"Shaz," she called and tossed the compass to him.

He snagged the flying object out of the air.

"Oh perfect," he said. Shaz steered the little unevenly dancing needle a few times before settling on the direction of north, "We go that way," Shaz said.

Serin wasn't sure why she felt nervous, after all, she'd never felt more comfortable with anyone else before in her life, so she chalked it up to the unknown. They decided they're backsides needed a break, so they walked through the woods while Shaz explained the Sev-Rin-Ac-Lavah and how he had met Ceros in the tavern. His journey through the barrier at sea, his Grandfather, Father, Riddick and what he knew of the council. Jagwynn padded along with them and at times disappeared and then reappeared later. Serin enjoyed listening to all his stories and was glad he hadn't asked her about herself yet. She wasn't sure what she was going to tell him just yet. She was sure that at some point he would find out, but for now, she was glad to leave her history out of the current.

19-It's Time To Decide

Groargoth returned to his father's tent and began rummaging in his things. He pulled the ring of the kingdom from his father's lifeless toe and slipped it onto his. Groargoth grew angrier the more he searched and couldn't find the parchment. He was certain his father would have written a decree. Scrolls and books littered the floor as he recklessly sifted through the old king's papers. Then he spotted the old box under the corner of the bed.

He slid the lid off and pulled out the document. He took a piece of burning wood from the fire and lit the edge. Hypnotized by the fire's powers, Groargoth mused as the small flame dance and swayed. Lahonti came into the tent and saw it burning.

"Ah, good you're here. Send for Yavo, I have a mission for him," Groargoth said.

Lahonti's stomach hit the bottom of his frame and lurched up.

"The tracker?"

"Yes, you idiot, of course, the tracker. If Azrack thinks he's going to make a fool out of me, he's dead wrong."

"Last I heard, he was in the far north. It will take a few weeks for him to travel here."

"Azrack can't get far. Besides, where is he going to run? Our world is only so big."

"Sir, what about the Armada?" Lahonti asked.

"What about them?"

"You could send Ralti and Brigdon after him."

"Very well, fetch them. Oh, and from now on Lahonti, you will not advise me on anything, unless I ask."

Lahonti squatted, bowed, and left. Groargoth was in no hurry and was convinced that Yavo was the best tracker. Yavo knew this land so well that it would only be a matter of time before he found Azrack. Besides, Groargoth's spies were everywhere, and the citizens knew that if they hid Azrack, they would be put to death.

But Groargoth did know that in order to pursue him effectively, he needed to think like him. Become him. Azrack was a hunter and knew how to survive, which is why he would have Yavo do it and with Yavo after him, Groargoth would attend to what he desired most, his father's kingdom.

****

"What are Groargoth's plans?" Azrack asked.

"Groargoth has sent for Yavo and Telete," Ralti said.

"Did Brigdon get to her first?"

"I haven't heard from him yet," Ralti said.

"I see," Azrack said.

"What are you going to do?" Ralti asked.

"Have you talked to Lahonti?" Azrack asked.

"No, Groargoth won't let me near him. I think he suspects me of something, but I don't know what."

"That you are still loyal to me." Azrack said.

"Of course, I am," Ralti said.

"Yes, and that's the problem," Azrack said.

Ralti slammed his fist into the other.

"This is just ridiculous," Ralti said.

"Keep trying to talk to Lahonti and let me know," Azrack said.

Azrack slapped Ralti on the shoulder as Ralti left the cavern. Azrack sat at the back of the deep cave behind the falls watching the cascading wave's crash from above. His nerves were about shot, and he was having a hard time sitting there doing nothing. He needed to stay to see what he could learn about Groargoth, but the pit in his stomach continued to sink deeper. Ralti, Helios, Jaxton, and Pontos took turns bringing information as the time passed. Azrack's men all crawled into the tunnel and secret entrances into the cave.

"What are all of you doing here?" Azrack asked from the back of the cave.

"Azrack, it's time to decide, either get out of here or stay and fight. Groargoth called for Yavo and he's arrived. He will be on your trail in no time. His orders are not to bring you in, but to kill you," Helios said.

"There is no use in staying to fight. Groargoth is king now and has command of the army and without any proof it's hopeless. I will miss you, my friends," Azrack said.

"You're not going to stay and fight?" Pontos asked.

"There is nothing honorable in shedding innocent blood on behalf of a lie. Groargoth wants me to start a revolution against him, to prove he is the rightful leader. I won't take soldiers to their deaths to suit his purposes," Azrack said.

They understood Azrack's choice, even though they didn't like it, they supported him.

"Well then, we will delay Yavo while you get a head start," Jaxton said.

"You know how to evade Yavo?" Ralti asked.

"I taught him everything he knows," Azrack said.

"That's what scares me," Ralti said.

"But not everything *I* know," Azrack said.

Ralti sagged a little with a small sense of reassurance. Azrack nodded and slapped his fist on his chest and dismissed his men, who staggered their descent so they wouldn't be obvious. Hours into the late afternoon, Azrack emerged from the falls. The fading sun shimmered over the falling leaves of autumn. Azrack opened his wings and hovered over the ground. He sniffed the breeze for any hints of Yavo and the others. He sensed them to the east, so he climbed into the southern sky. There were only a few hours where the winds constantly change direction and he needed to reach the rocky peaks before the winds evened out. He would have to fly hard and fast to cover the long distance.

Yavo was a natural and picked up the skill of tracking almost immediately, but he also became enthralled with the taste of blood, which is why Azrack denied him from becoming his protégé. In Yavo's anger, he became the most ruthless tracker. Yavo lost all sense of right long ago and would make for a difficult escape. Azrack's wings beat against the air, propelling him farther and farther away from his family and home. The winds changed, so Azrack dove toward the ground and flew just above the tops of the trees.

He slowed to a comfortable pace as not to blow the delicate leaves off the trees. Soon the dark gray of the rigid peaks emerged. He spotted a small opening as the jagged rocks came into focus. This was the cave he used as a cub during his initiation ritual. He landed on the edge and pulled his wings in tightly and crept into the small cavern.

The cavern was secured under the overhang of a ledge and twisted around to the side, which made it look no different from the rock-face of the mountain. Azrack walked around in a circle a few times as he smelled the cave and categorized the scents he detected.

He curled up at the farthest part and wrapped his tail around him and rested on his paws. He let his eyes close but didn't let himself fall asleep completely.

****

Several long tables were arranged in the mess tent, and servants passed large plates of both cooked and raw meats to the gathered gryphton soldiers. Yavo sat near the end next to Groargoth, who was busy shoving his face with food. Yavo scrutinized each warrior and watched their body language and mannerisms for any signs of loyalty issues. He spotted immediately the top five who were still loyal to Azrack. He learned who was in command of the real army, which certainly was not Groargoth. It was clear to Yavo that in Azrack's absence, Ralti was the leader, and by the way they acted, he could tell that Ralti and the others would never tell anything about Azrack, so he moved on to studying the other soldiers.

After scrutinizing the rest of the soldiers, he determined there were one or two fair candidates. However, Yavo tired of the blabber from all the gryphton's complimenting him on his long list of achievements. He much preferred his solitary life and found his brain was about to pound from all the noise. He wanted to isolate the two soldiers to gain information, and Ralti recognized his movements and guessed what he was planning to do. Ralti watched Yavo and understood which of the soldiers he would try to tempt. He signaled for Pontos to sidle up to one and Jaxton to the other. Yavo kept his expression exempt, but a fit of irritated anger sat in his throat.

"Excuse me. I think I will be on my way now," Yavo said to Groargoth.

"Are you sure? We have plenty of drink and meat to celebrate this grand occasion," Groargoth said.

"Yes, stay, tell us of your travels," Pontos said.

The gryphton's roared with agreement and eagerness.

"I'm sorry. I have tarried too long as it is. I must go," Yavo said, trying to hold back his sarcasm.

Ralti raised his toe to Helios, who was about to start in on another round of questions.

"Let him go. He has an important task before him," Ralti said.

"Yes, yes, you're right," Groargoth stood and gripped Yavo by the forearm, grabbed the end of a leg of a steer and ripped it from its carcass and Yavo pulled his paw from Groargoth's grip. Ralti rose and gave Yavo a slight bow while swallowing the lump now in his throat. Yavo walked briskly around the drunken gryphtons and left the large tent. "Besides, we have a new General to welcome!" Groargoth said.

Ralti shot Groargoth a surprised look. Helios, Pontos, and Brigdon, too, were surprised. Groargoth stood and welcomed Kronos and several of his warriors. It fell silent as they entered the room. Kronos made his way to the head of the table next to Groargoth and sat in the General's seat. The looks of fear and surprise added to Kronos' glee, and he took a large bite of raw meat.

"I hope Azrack is long gone by now," Helios said under his breath when Ralti sat back down.

"Me too,"

Brigdon grunted and Jaxton shoved a piece of meat in Brigdon's paw before he could reach out and strangle someone. Brigdon, with his blood boiling under his skin, sat with a nastier-than-usual-scowl on his face until he couldn't take it anymore. Brigdon stood and excused himself and started after Yavo. Ralti was about to go after him when Groargoth began questioning Kronos on the best strategies for attacking the Ebon Hoards. Jaxton rose and followed Brigdon instead, and Ralti sighed before turning his attention to the new general.

20-Do You Think He Took The Bait?

Yavo stepped into the evening breeze and sucked in until his lungs were at capacity. Scents rolled around in his head for a moment before he let it back into the night chill. He wasn't concerned with the smells of soldiers and battle. He sifted through so much that he barely caught the scent he wanted. His eyes lit up, and he spun on his paws toward the falls.

He maneuvered passed the few scattered tents at the edge of camp until the landscape opened onto the trotted down grasses. He pawed at the ground and ran his beak a few inches above the dirt. The scent became stronger, and he carefully scanned the surroundings.

The scent was all too familiar and the closer he crept to the falls, the stronger it became. His mind returned to earlier exploits and training sessions with his mentor, and for a moment a slight bit of angst that Azrack was his next target hit his mind. It confused him because the accusations against Azrack were not what he knew to be his character. But who was he to say? It'd been years and creatures change. In a small way he hoped it wasn't true, but he had a job to do.

"So, this is what you have become?" Brigdon said, rising to his full height.

Yavo rose slowly and studied Brigdon's eyes.

"What do you mean by that?" Yavo asked.

"You know, you could have been his first in command."

"To do what, follow orders all day? No thanks, I much prefer taking orders from myself."

"This isn't taking orders from yourself, your taking orders from Groargoth?"

Yavo's lower lid flickered, but he kept his body still and rigid.

"I take a payday."

"So, you are going to take treasure over loyalty and honor?"

"What loyalty? Azrack has no loyalty to me. He refused me. He is nothing but a fraud," Yavo said.

"You were not ready. He wasn't about to send you into the fire without being ready."

"That's what he thought, but he is a fool," Yavo sneered.

Yavo brushed him aside, but Brigdon gripped his arm.

"You will regret this, I promise," Brigdon growled.

Yavo swallowed but puffed out his chest and ruffled his feathers. He thrust his shoulder into Brigdon's and shoved him out of his way. Brigdon let him go and watched him continue toward the falls. Helios crawled out of the shadows and nodded to Brigdon. Helios and Jaxton had taken some of Azrack's things and ran in different directions and in random patterns around the falls.

Yavo carefully walked around the falls and breathed in at each time the scent changed. He let the sensation tickle his mind as he studied each one. He determined whether it was a new or old smell based on the amount of impurities that surrounded it. Azrack wouldn't stick around for long, and he figured his men would try to throw off his scents, so he sifted out the newer scents and went with those that were older. With the oldest scent on the forefront of his mind, he lifted his wings, fluttered for a second and lifted off into the air heading north.

"Do you think he took the bait?" Pontos asked.

"Dunno," Brigdon grunted.

"Let's hope so," Helios said.

"Where did Azrack go, anyway?" Pontos asked.

"Dunno," Brigdon said.

Helios shook his head and shrugged. Pontos didn't know if they were really telling the truth. The wind pushed against Yavo as he banked in and around heavy gusts. He'd been flying now for a few hours and fought the heavy winds from the east. At one point, he almost landed because he was almost blown off course. He dipped toward the ground and backtracked, then landed quietly on a small peak overlooking a clearing. Several scratch marks gouged the soft dirt, and he searched around. He squinted and zeroed in on the slightest details.

In a nearby tree, he found a gryphtoness and her cubs and chided himself for making such a rookie mistake. He leaped into the air and flew barely above the trees to avoid the gusts when a scent crossed his mind. A skilled gryphton could determine if the gryphton was a male or female, the approximate age, and their emotions. This scent had too many things in common, and he hovered in the air as a memory of his first training session with Azrack, flashed across his mind. A lump formed in his throat. *He tricked me, that dirty-* he said to himself. The realization came that he'd missed him by a few moments, and he spun around and shot into the air. It was much easier not having to fight the wind but to use it, and he dashed across the sky.

****

Azrack lay in the alcove wondering what he was going to do. Keep running forever? It's not likely Yavo will give up and Groargoth will expect him to bring proof. He was going to have to fight Yavo and kill him Even though he was the general and served in the armed forces most of his adult life, he hated killing. It never solved any problems, only delayed them until someone or something else created a new one.

The sounds of the gusting winds crashed around the small inlet, which made him more anxious. He bent his feathers over his ears to ease the discomfort of the reverberations off the back wall. He smelled the breeze and analyzed its contents. Small particles of pollen and the heaviness from the added moisture in the air gave him a sense of the upcoming weather. Rain was coming soon and Azrack decided he would use the rain to his advantage and circle back toward Yavo in an attempt to sneak up on him.

It didn't take long before a low rumble crossed the sky and the darkening clouds rolled together, strangling any last rays of light. Azrack would have to rely on his nose now that the light was gone. He stretched his paws and crawled to the ledge, leaped off, and flew to the low-lying branches of the nearby trees. He stuck to the branches and small droplets of water drifted across the sky.

Little creatures scurried away as he invaded their homes, some even chattered loudly with displeasure until he bared his teeth at them and then they too scurried away. After about two long lengths, he leaped onto the ground, first landing on his front legs, then onto his hind legs. He dug his claws into the earth and broke a branch or two as he walked to give the impression he was landing out of exhaustion.

The rain poured out of the sky and drenched his feathers and streamed down his face. He shook briskly, partly to keep his mind clear and partly to add more scent to the surroundings. Azrack's human side normally kept him from urinating on trees, rocks, and things to mark his territory, but this time he let his lion side out and started marking the surrounding trees.

It surprised him a little at how good it was to let loose. It was hard sometimes trying to understand each part of his creation. Part eagle, part lion, and part human. On one side, he wanted to be left alone and soar in the sky whenever he wanted. On another, he wanted to be the leader of his pack and on the other, he felt the loyalty to his duties. He moved from tree to tree and circled one spot. He curled up in a ball and stared into the trees for a moment, then ran into the woods.

The rain came down so heavily it was hard to keep the water out of his eyes. There was no way he was going to get back in the sky, so he kept moving and the curvier and more disorganized the better. It was just like a game they would play as cubs, and admittedly; he was pretty good. His stomach rumbled. It had been more than a day since he ate last. Azrack thought that if he was somewhat sloppy while hunting, he could make Yavo spend more time at the scene trying to figure out the clues.

He spotted a small hole low in the trunk of a tree. He lowered his body to the ground and crept toward the hole. When he was about three lengths from it, he lowered even closer to the ground and sniffed the dirt. The rain did a good job at rinsing away most of the little critters' scents. He sidestepped the roots of the tree and slid in next to it. Azrack knew the animal would not come out on its own, especially in this weather. He flipped out his talons and slammed a paw into the tree trunk. The little animal scurried out of the hole and looked around just in time to see Azrack's talon's grip it's flesh. It squealed for a second before it fell lifeless in Azrack's fist.

21-Now Don't Do It Again

"How long do you think it will take to reach your castle?" Serin asked as she ducked under a tree.

Shaz rounded a large boulder as Jagwynn padded quietly over the thick underbrush. A gentle glistening of sweat and mist from the persistent fog formed at their hairline.

"Probably a couple more days," Shaz said.

Shaz slipped his leg over a boulder and shoved against the ground to hop over it. The ground beneath his foot sloshed out from under him and he fell backward onto a sharp edge. The rock tore his trousers and ripped the flesh on the backside of his thigh.

"Blast!" he cursed.

A sudden shot of pain hit his brain, and he slumped over and caught himself and lowered to the ground, keeping the wounded leg slightly elevated. Serin hopped a small boulder and found blood dripping from the wound and pooled in the deep brown dirt.

"Oh, my," Serin exclaimed.

"Is it bad?" Shaz asked.

His head felt light and a little dizzy. Serin inspected the wound and found that it was deep.

"Yeah, it's pretty deep, I need to wrap it and see if I can find some herbs to make a press," Serin hurried to the horse and searched her satchel but found nothing. She searched the saddlebag and found an old cloth. Serin looked around on the ground for an herb she knew would help heal open wounds, but when she couldn't find it, she returned to Shaz. "I can't find the herb. I'll just have to wrap it," Serin exclaimed and leaned over his leg, "He's going to be alright Jag," she said to Jagwynn, who pawed at the ground.

She stroked her ear and then tucked the ripped pants into themselves and away from the open skin and wrapped the cloth around his thigh. Serin collected a ball of water from the mist and swirled it around and let it dance delicately until it turned a deep blue-green. She set it carefully onto his leg. At first, it stung and Shaz hissed. Then there was heat that softened the sting and warmed his entire body. It cooled to a comfortable cold, and the pain eased. Shaz's body shuddered from the energy.

"Feel better?" Serin asked.

"Yes, thank you. It's quite amazing you can do that, you know," He propped his leg and leaned against the rock and closed his eyes. Serin situated herself on the other side. "How do you do it?" he asked.

"Umm, well, I guess I was born with it. Like you, but I learned some of what I know from the willow. I don't fully understand what I just did, thoughts just come to mind, so I do what they say,"

"Willow? You mean the tree?"

Serin blushed, saying it out loud did sound a little crazy, but it was true.

"Yes, like the tree. A form of magic that is deep in the earth. It manifested itself through the portrayal of a woman in a willow tree. She was amazing."

Shaz nodded.

"Sounds like Grandfather," Shaz said.

"You don't think it's crazy?"

"No, I don't think it's crazy," he said, opening one eye, "Tell me about her."

Serin bit her lip, but she guessed it was her turn. Serin rehearsed her meeting the willow and the little bit of magic she was taught and how she had to leave with her father and travel to this realm.

"She taught me how to wield water, to make it dance and sway, but I had to leave and didn't finish what she was trying to teach me about the water's ability to heal," Serin said with sadness in her voice.

Shaz wanted to know why that made her sad, but figured she would tell him when she was ready. He certainly knew how she felt.

"That's how you were able to throw that water on the sqwall in town? And the air bubble in the dungeon?" he asked.

"Yes, I wasn't sure it would work, but I had to try."

"Well, I am glad you did."

"Me too," Serin said.

"How does your magic take away the pain?" Shaz asked.

"I don't actually know for sure," Serin said.

Shaz nodded.

"Mine are more like images, or it just happens, and I understand its truth immediately," Shaz said.

"That's interesting. Can you walk?" Serin asked.

Shaz managed to his feet and found that he could. It was a feeble attempt at first, and Serin grabbed the reins of the horse and offered for him to ride.

"It would take too much to climb on the horse. I'll just walk a bit," he said.

Serin walked beside him for a few minutes.

"I've been thinking," Serin said.

"That's what that smell is," Shaz said. Serin elbowed him in the ribs. Shaz laughed and played along as if it hurt when she elbowed him, then winced from the pain it caused in his leg. "Go on," Shaz said.

"I wanted to ask you why you get those headaches."

"I've always had them since I was young, but it wasn't until I got my sword and Grandfather dropped his shield that they started to become so bad," he said tapping the hilt of the Honor Blade, "and they seem to be worse when I use shadow magic."

"Interesting," Serin said.

She tapped her finger on her soft pink lips.

"How so?" Shaz asked.

Serin categorized all the emotions she had detected from his last headache and how much magic he had to use and wondered how she might use *her* magic instead of the medicine.

"I think that the shadow magic requires a payment, and so it takes some of your health when you use it," Serin said.

Shaz stopped and stared at her, and she suddenly felt awkward.

"That makes perfect sense, except, when I passed through the portal it accessed my magic and then I had a headache after that, but it wasn't shadow magic then," Shaz said.

"Perhaps there is something else that's related to portals?" Serin shrugged.

"Perhaps," Shaz said.

The mist thickened, and the sun faded from the sky, which made the temperature drop. The forest noises dimmed in the evening shadows, and Serin checked Shaz's leg.

"The bleeding isn't stopping. I need to look at your leg, and we should find shelter. It's going to rain, and I would rather stay dry. I saw some large leaves back that way just a bit. We could use those to build a shelter," Serin pointed over her shoulder.

"Aye," Shaz said.

Shaz hadn't wanted to complain, but his leg was throbbing, and he was glad for the break. Serin returned with several large leaves the size of Shaz's arm and about an arm in width. Serin tossed the leaves over a fallen tree and arranged them so they would let the water run off the surface and brushed the debris from under the new shelter. Shaz hobbled over to the makeshift shelter and tried to climb under it. Serin tied the horse to the tree nearby and made sure it was out of the impending rain.

"Lay down so I can take a look," Serin said.

"It might take me some time," Shaz said.

Shaz struggled to his belly. The fibers of the cloth were now crusty and Serin decided not being able to feel the pain wasn't good because the walking made the wound ooze worse.

"I'm going to need water in order to get the wrap off the wound," Serin waved her arms around and gathered the mist into a ball of water about the size of a melon and focused on the elements that would take away his pain. The ball danced and swayed, and the familiar blue encompassed the sphere and she placed it onto his leg. Shaz sighed with the pain relief it gave and sagged into the ground. Serin waited for the crusty goo to soften to where she could pull the fabric shreds away. "I am going to start pulling the fabric off now."

She took in a deep breath and started to remove the slimy ooze.

"How does it look?" he asked, lifting his head.

A bright red mark plagued the center of his forehead.

"It looks better actually, I'm surprised. You heal fast, but it's still bleeding pretty good. Now how did you say that old man from the ship healed your chest?" she asked.

"He just waved his hands over me. He said it was because he looked with his heart and not his eyes."

A thought came to mind to imagine herself sewing the wound together with a needle and string and figured it was worth a try. Serin closed her eyes and pictured herself with a needle and thread. Serin opened her eyes and to her astonishment. She found a blue hue of mist in the shape of a needle and thread. She examined the wound and pushed the blue thread into the deepest parts of the gash. The deep red flesh started to pull together and soften to a pink color.

Shaz felt the pulling and tugging of the skin accompanied with a hot heat originating from his thigh. Serin's lips and brows pursed and puckered, as one might when thinking hard about the answer to a test. She examined her work and moved to the next layer of flesh and mended that layer with the same effort. Soft blue hues of light danced around Serin's fingers as it obeyed her instructions and the wound pulled together. The last layer pulled shut, and the wound was completely healed. A deep purple line ran about a hand's length, mostly straight but with a slight curve to it across his thigh.

"Oh, my! I did it! I used magic to sew you up!" She exclaimed.

She fell off her feet and onto her hiney and slumped with exhaustion. Shaz sat up onto his elbows and wriggled his leg and found it was pain-free.

"Yes, you most certainly did," he said.

He rolled over onto his back and was surprised that he moved easily. He bent his knees and laid on the ground. Jagwynn licked his face and lay down next to him. Serin chuckled.

"Now, don't do it again," she said.

22-You Are Not Feeding Him

Dank turf nearly sent Shaz sprawling to the ground. He caught his footing in time to avoid the fallen tree and dug his foot into the earth and shoved off. He swung on a branch at head level and dipped below the old crackling wood.

"Come back here," he shouted.

Sweat dripped down his back as he gained on the little creature. Serin leaped over a boulder and rounded the opposite direction and came straight toward Shaz. She pointed to her right and Shaz veered to his left.

"Over there," she said.

Serin skidded around a large tree trunk and Shaz darted across the wet grass and jumped over several protruding rocks and chased the rabbit-like creature into some ruins. The little varmint disappeared into a cavity of broken stone slabs and pillars.

"In here," Shaz mouthed.

Shaz motioned to Serin to move in on the right side and he would take the left. Serin saw a small gray tail sticking out on the other side of the rugged rock wall and waved to Shaz. Shaz tiptoed around the broken pillars and Serin took hold of a branch lying by her foot and mimicked to jab the creature. Serin stepped quietly over the dried leaves which were scattered over the grass-covered stone floor. The morning mist left the slabs slick, so she took slow and calculated steps. Shaz gingerly climbed into the perfect spot and nodded that he was ready and Serin leaped forward and jabbed the stick into the hole and Shaz reached for the tail.

He snatched the long fur of the little critter and tugged, pinning its hide against the inside. The stones of the wall broke free and the little creature slipped out backward. Dust and crumbled stone trickled off the varmint as he twisted his large, pointed ears back and forth. The small fur at the tip of his ears flicked forward and back as he shook his head in confusion. Shaz held his arm away from its sharp claws and was trying to hold on as it wriggled fiercely to escape.

"What is it?" Serin asked.

"I have no idea," Shaz said.

Shaz struggled to wriggle the silver and gold serpent emblem from its clutches.

"Give me my medallion," Shaz said, clenching his teeth.

"No, it's Nix's," the creature said.

The critters' voice was crackly and high pitched.

"It's not yours, it's mine."

"Nix found it," the animal said.

The rodent kicked out its long four-toed paws and Shaz jumped back and held it out further.

"Yeah, in my pack."

"No, my shiny."

"Enough," Serin said loudly.

They both stopped and looked at her, but it didn't last long. Nix twisted at the waist to release the tentacles that held him and wriggled again.

"I'm not letting you go until you give that back," Shaz said.

He held his arm out even more, dangling the creature in mid-air.

"Will you two stop?" Serin glared at Shaz as though he were acting like a child and Shaz scowled, "Now, what is your name?" she asked the little creature, paused, thought a moment, and asked, "What are you?"

"Nix, and I'm a Gray Tailix," he answered.

"Well, Nix, that is an important medallion that you took from Shaz and we need it back."

"But it's shiny," Nix said, twisting the cool metal disk in his paws while admiring its reflection in the morning light.

"I understand that, but it's essential to our mission, and we have to have it," she said in her soft and caring tone.

Nix paused, then gave the shiny to Shaz, who snatched it out of his paws and shoved it into his pocket.

"Shaz?"

"What?"

"What do you say?"

"Nothing, he took it."

"Are we twelve?" Shaz scowled and put the little creature down. "Are you alright?" Serin asked.

"He ringed my tail," Nix said.

The Gray Tailix pulled his soft and fluffy appendage into his paws and stroked the fur. Serin squatted down eye level with him.

"Yes, and I am sorry about that, let's agree though, that you won't take any more of our things and we won't hurt your tail," Serin said.

"Alright," Nix said.

Nix leaped onto Serin's neck in a hug. Serin fell back and laughed and hugged the little guy. Shaz rolled his eyes.

"He's playing you ya know," Shaz said.

"No, he's not, he's cute," Serin said.

"Fine, you'll see," Shaz said. Shaz hopped over the wall and studied the derelict structure. "What is this place?" he asked.

Serin pulled Nix from around her neck.

"Not sure, it wasn't here moments ago," Serin said.

"That's because it's magical," Nix said.

"Magical? How?" Shaz asked.

Shaz stepped around an array of scattered stones.

"It appears once a day. I have lived here my whole life and never was here before," Nix said, half-crawling-half-walking.

"When did it first appear?" Shaz asked.

Nix shrugged his thin shoulders.

"Maybe a few weeks," Nix said.

"A few weeks?" Serin asked.

"About the same time, I came through the portal," Shaz said.

"Hey check this out," Serin said.

Serin pointed to the only wall that was still standing. She stepped over a crumpled pillar and some old relics that hadn't been moved since their demise.

"What is it?" Shaz asked.

A mural on the wall depicted a man wearing black armor. His long brown hair seemed to wave in an invisible breeze. The intricate fine points showed strength and power in his brows, cheekbones, and jaw.

"This is beautiful. I wonder who he is," Serin said.

"It's Reinholt O'Connon," Shaz said.

Shaz pointed to the brass placket with engravings etched on the surface. Serin stepped close enough to scrutinize the small print.

"All I see are scribbles," Serin said.

Shaz turned to her and back to the symbols. He could read them plain as day and wondered why she couldn't.

"So, that's what my father looks like," Shaz said.

"I thought you said your father's name was Merrick," Serin asked.

"He is the father that raised me, but this is my birth father,"

Shaz said.

Serin took a few steps back so she could inspect the whole picture better and sure enough, the man in the image looked just like Shaz.

"You do look a great deal like him," Serin said.

"Is that a good thing or a bad thing?" Shaz asked.

"A very good thing," Serin said.

Shaz smiled and she blushed. Shaz ran his finger along the image of the sword that was partly drawn from a scabbard which shared his sword's markings, and he gripped the hilt of his blade. He drew out the blade and twisted it in the sunlight. Nix's eyes popped open, the polished sleekness fascinated him, and he leaped forward and Shaz shoved his boot into his stomach. Nix grabbed his belly and scurried behind Serin, putting his tail between his legs.

"He really likes shiny things, doesn't he?" Serin said, "That's not your sheath, though."

She turned her attention back to the mural and ran a finger along the image. The tiny glass shards that made up the image was sharp and bumpy.

"No, that's the other half, they need to be reunited," he said.

"The sword and the sheath? I guess that makes sense though," Serin said.

"Why is that?" Shaz asked.

Serin thought about how she felt about him.

"Well, any two things that were meant to be together would feel that way," she said.

Serin noted that on the left corner of the image, the colors in the glass didn't match the surrounding shards. Serin brushed up against him as she moved toward the discoloration and Shaz soaked in her essence, he nodded because that was the way he felt about her too.

"True," he said.

Serin tried to wriggle one of the pieces of glass. Even though it was loose, budging was not an option. She stood back and searched for something more.

"Isn't that the same as yours?" she asked.

Serin pointed to the depiction of the medallion Reinholt wore around his neck.

"Yes, but I made this one at the witch's booth. Unless-" he said.

"Unless what?"

"I don't know," he admitted.

"Look, in the center, the colors, they don't match," Serin noted.

Shaz found a broken column that was mostly flat on each side and propped it up and stood on top, balancing on the uneven surface. Now, face to face with the man, he touched the glass. An electric zing shot up his arm.

"Blast," he called shaking his hand and arm vigorously, "It shocked me."

"Let's try pushing them like buttons and see what happens," she said.

Serin put all her fingers on the stone and Shaz touched the cold exterior again, this time harnessing the electricity. He shoved the glass with his fingers and Serin pushed at the same time.

"Was something supposed to happen?" Nix asked.

"Don't know," she said.

Serin shot him an irritated frown and he sunk to the ground and folded his pointed ears over his eyes and hid.

"Try this, I'll push then you," Shaz said.

Shaz pushed again, this time the piece of glass sank into the mural and made a click. Serin pushed hers in and the lever shifted with a clack. Shaz hopped off the column, rolled the stool back from the wall, and inspected the art.

"I don't see anything," Serin said.

"If I stand back here, I might be able to find something," Shaz said, scaling the debris. Serin met him at the edge of the floor and folded her arms and searched the picture, "Ah, look, there," he said.

He pointed to a long rectangular-shaped stone just above the brass plaque. Lying on the stone was a long brass plate with more symbols etched into the soft metal. Shaz picked it up.

"What does it say?" she asked.

"Sev-Rin-Ac-Lavah: the four elements of cosmic powers, created by the sages of time to perfect the Tooatha De Danann. Divided by greed, separated, and sealed by the wise. Sev- cleaver-as Severah of Srinna Vossa, the Elder of Knowledge which bound the crypt -the *Scroll*. Rin- in relation to the powers of the ancient reed trees of Akraven, whoever holds it shall never lose a battle- the *Spear*. Ac- the base word in the dark magica of the Loig Na Tine in the volcanic mountains, the power to yield passions, appetites, and addiction- the *Cauldron*. Lavah- a rare mineral found deep in the earth of Bairr Tiornecht, used for its density for the building of indestructible weapons- the *Sword*."

"I wonder why it was left here," Serin asked.

"Aye," Shaz said.

He pulled the leather strap the fang was tied to from around his neck and inserted the end into a chiseled hole in the metal plate and tied it back around his neck. Shaz and Serin spent a few more minutes looking around, but the sun was fading, and they needed to find their camp again before it got dark. As they started back to their camp, Nix was padding next to them.

"Where do you think you're going?" Shaz asked.

Nix stood on his hind legs and his little paws were gripped together.

"I be good," he begged.

"Ah, how cute," Serin said.

"Are you kidding? I don't have the time for this," Shaz stared down at him. Nix's eyes became bigger and bigger as his ears hung lower and lower, "Fine, but stay out of my way," Shaz said.

He kicked a stone out of his way and stomped forward. Serin snickered. They found their camp and Jagwynn padded up to him from under a furry vine bush.

"Where have you been Jag, we could have used your help?" Shaz asked. Jagwynn looked at him and licked her lips then yawned and licked her paw. "Useless cat," he mumbled.

Shaz grabbed his pack and ripped open the top and shoved his hand inside and searched around.

"What are you looking for?" Serin asked.

"Anything else this little bugger stole," Shaz said.

"Nothing, just the shiny," Nix said.

Shaz shoved the pack off his lap and let it hit the ground. Serin reached into her pack and pulled out the days' old bread she didn't want and gave it to Nix.

"You are *not* feeding him," Shaz said, crinkling the map, "That's all we need."

Serin blew off his frustration with a shrug as Nix reached up and took the bread and scurried behind a tree.

23-Could This Be A Way Into Another Realm

Azrack ran around the forest, climbing up and down from tree to tree all night. The rainy season would make it a challenge to stay ahead of Yavo without being able to fly. It did, however, create a way for him to take the advantage. Azrack backtracked toward the Peaks and made a large arc, swerving in and around obstacles. He was careful not to step too hard, but enough to leave an obvious print, made another nest, and marked more trees.

The rain let up just enough for Azrack to hop-fly back toward the peaks and, being satisfied with his trails, started back to his hiding place. Azrack released his talons and jumped, holding out his wings to help extend the distance onto the rock surface and climbed to the far side of the ragged mountain. The surface of the Peaks was brittle and jagged, which caused large amounts of fragments to peel away.

The higher he climbed, the harder it became. The rocks were wet and slippery from hours of rain, which made it near impossible to grip the wind-smoothed surface. At one point, Azrack scooted around to the southern edge to avoid a large patch of moss. Azrack gripped a ledge with his beak and released and engaged his talons into the divots and pits that remained in the surface. His muscles ached as he fought against the wind and rain.

He slipped several times before he reached the first ledge he came to and crawled onto a flat surface. He took a deep breath and crawled away from the edge as far as possible. It wasn't his cave, but it would have to do for now. He wrapped his tail around him and curled into a ball with one wing lifted over his head.

A hint of uncertainty settled in the back of Azrack's mind, and he wondered if he would be out of the way here. Several hours passed and rushing winds crashed through the trees down below. He searched the horizon and found nothing but the darkened sky.

Yavo slipped between the wet foliage as he moved closer to the nest. He moved slowly and softly next to the pile of leaves and sniffed around. The large leaves sank into the ground. He crawled over the leaves carefully and turned in a circle. Yavo scanned the distance and found a set of tracks in the mud. The tracks were soft. A day or two old is all. He circled the nest as he examined the branches above, but the rain had washed away most of the scent, so he followed the tracks.

The moldy odor of the wet forest wafted around Yavo with each step. He was careful to step next to the tracks so that he wouldn't ruin the originals. After several lengths, Yavo came across the dead carcass and wondered why Azrack had left remains. He was too smart for that. Yavo pondered if what he knew about Azrack was wrong, or because of time, things changed more than he thought. Yavo studied the messy scene for several minutes and determined what the clues might lead to and continued along the path following the tracks. Yavo followed the tracks back and forth, and after several times he realized he had been played. An icy chill seeped into his bones as the temperature fell. The day would soon be over and there would be no light.

He slammed his fist on a tree and climbed to the top and opened the canopy of the tree and searched the horizon.

Yavo pulled a long skinny tube from his belt and pulled the bottom away from the top, and it elongated into a cascading circular device. He held the glass at one end to one eye and squinted the other and slowly scanned the world.

Azrack peeked from under his wing and checked the status of the clouds, and a small glint caught his eye. The slight flash flickered a few times and disappeared. It was Yavo's Seeing Eyeglass, a strange item Yavo found in the lost caves, and Azrack's heart sank.

"Blast, I forgot about that cursed thing."

Yavo couldn't see Azrack clearly, he was too far away, but he guessed the bright red blob against the dull gray and brown was him. He collapsed his magnifier and cinched it onto his belt. He shook the rain from his face and flicked his feathers. The anger and embarrassment deepened, and he huffed with a scowl. He calculated the distance and made a note of landmarks to follow, then slunk into the trees.

Azrack leaped from the ledge and skidded down the rocky surface. He lifted his wet wings just above the ground, to keep from hitting hard. He gripped the trunk of a tree and climbed to the top. Azrack carefully moved around the outer edges of the forest. He flicked his ears every few lengths and listened for sounds of oncoming movement. The pit in his stomach tightened around his guts and he was certain his innards were about to explode. He didn't fear death or even pain, but he didn't want to fail.

It was difficult to make his way in the darkness, but Azrack needed to press on. He slid his paws along the long branches and held his wings out to steady himself. Azrack pawed the thick sturdy branch, but with the next step his paw sank into a hole and he jerked backward. A nest of toe sized insects barreled out and swarmed around his head. They buzzed angrily and sprayed a stinky liquid from pointed tails on flat squat bodies.

Venom stung his eyes and burned his skin. Azrack yelped and fell from the tree limb. Before he hit the ground, he rounded his body and landed on his feet but shut his eyes tightly and rolled around in the mud, covering his body and face. Its coolness soothed his scorched feathers and fur.

A low rumble echoed from his gut as the anger grew inside. The venom of the rare Saraswati insects would take hours to dissipate. Azrack packed more mud on his face around his eyes and blinked a few times. The sting was excruciating, and his eyes filled with tears. The burning seared into his head and caused his senses to melt away. Soon he was heavy and wobbly and could hardly stand. The soft patter of rain turned into thuds and pops as the water hit the tree trunks from an angle. Wind gusts threw his body around as he stumbled forward.

Yavo sat up and twitched his ears back and forth. When he heard nothing, he sniffed the breeze to get a whiff, but he detected nothing. Azrack turned his face toward the pelting rain and blinked. The rain rushed in and out of his eyes and to his relief; the burning eased. His tight muscles relaxed as the rain melted the mud off his body, taking the venom with it. Azrack could barely see and everything was blurry, but he could make out the darkened shadows.

He continued to blink as he scooted against the ground. He needed to find shelter. The branches were the safest but, with the cold temperature, the many colorful leaves would soon fall, leaving them baron. Azrack stopped at a big dark blob and sniffed the air. It was only a rock. He wondered where the massive formation came from, since this part of the forest was filled with mostly all trees.

Halfway around, a warm breeze caught his attention, and he stopped. He crawled into the opening. The dry, warm air was refreshing on his rain-soaked frame. As the breeze surfaced from within the ground, an odor of urine and dead carcasses wafted into his nostrils. Azrack's stomach lurched. The feathers at the back of his neck wanted to lift and ruffle, giving him chills, but they couldn't.

His eyes ached, so he kept them slightly closed unless he needed to examine something. The further he went, the stronger the odor became, and he decided he didn't need to go any further. The putrid odor left an irritating image in his brain but didn't plan on finding out what was making the stench. His nerves propelled him to get out of there, but in his current condition, he would take his chances in here. It would be better than being a sitting duck for Yavo to find. So, he worked his way back toward the opening and stopped a few lengths inside. Thoughts ran around his mind of the last moon's cycle. How unusual it was that a human mage would be fighting with his kind. That the Ebon Hoards had weapons they'd never seen before. That he was in some creature's tunnel. He had never seen those insects before, only associated them with legends. He wondered what was happening in his world.

Azrack was certain that if he made it to his secret cave and gathered supplies, he could make a full circle back and reach the meeting place to find out if Ralti had any news for him. His mind wouldn't shut off and he ran through every scenario and possibilities he thought of. He decided on continuing to his secret cave in the crevasse and finally found sleep.

A strong wind whipped across Azrack and he stirred and rose to his haunches. The mid-morning air lifted slightly, and the misty rain had stopped. The dimly lit sky crested the corners of the tunnel. His eyes now itched and the burning in his skin was gone, but large red blisters hurt if he bumped them. The lingering effects of the venom made his head pound, but his vision was mostly clear.

His once beautiful feathers were now straggly, and half-melted. He slunk against the ground until he could peek out around one edge. *Yavo wouldn't be far now.* He thought. He sucked in the air around him and let the mingling of scents dance around, then took to the sky. The wind shifted directions several times before Azrack made it to the crevasse. Azrack's mind wouldn't concentrate with the stink of his singed feathers wafting around him.

The deep rip in the grounds surface sunk hundreds of lengths down. Azrack found a short squat tree surrounded by tall trees and banked a hard left and descended from the sky in a nosedive. A dark shadow covered his body as he flew into the deep. The cool air became colder the further down he went. An almost nonexistent ledge emerged several lengths in, and he landed on the edge and lunged inside the small cavern and rounded a tight corner.

With a flint and stone, he kept on a ledge he lit a torch. He wished he could take it with him, but the smoke would alert Yavo to where he was. The cavern lit up, revealing a treasure trove of gems and jewels. Shiny metals and trinkets piled in heaps around the floor. He rummaged a pile of swords and picked the one he wanted and strapped on heavy leather chest armor and gauntlets. Grabbed a sling and pouch and filled it with smooth rocks.

On the wall hung his wife's first gift to him, a silver necklace with an amber stone set in the center. If Ralti could find out if Lahonti had proof somehow, it might not be too long before he would be with her again. He slipped it on and ruffled his feathers, securing it underneath them and strapped on shin guards and wing bracers. He rubbed some Oil of The Creeping Dewberry all over his body, covering his wings with a thick layer, and stubbed out the torch. The Creeping Dewberry was a lightweight oil that repelled water and is almost impossible to find, so it was hardly ever used. Most gryphton's didn't even know about it. If it weren't for Helios, Azrack wouldn't either. Azrack kept his for the direst of circumstances.

He flew down the crevasse for a few hundred lengths and turned up toward the surface. The mid-afternoon heat squelched small patches of clouds from the sky, letting in bits of sun. He looked over the expanse of the forest toward the peaks.

He stretched out his long neck and pulled his legs in tightly to his body as he sucked in his belly. He turned his beak toward the sky and pounded his wings against the air. Azrack flew even harder and faster. He needed the speed to reach the peak he wanted, which was thousands of lengths high. He headed straight into a wall of water pouring from black clouds. The rain grew in strength, pounding against his wings.

The oil caused the rain to roll off smoothly, keeping his wings light and dry. He shot up the side of the mountain like an arrow. It was when he reached the summit that he bent at the waist and dipped back down on the other side. The rain filled a rounded bowl-like formation that sat at the top, and there was nowhere for him to land. He rounded the edge and found a perch on the other side.

He searched for a place to leave a message and in the center of a peak to the side of him; he found a crack. He lodged the note into the crack, out of the weather, and soared into the sky, back toward the crevasse.

****

Yavo leaped into the air and searched for a scent. He moved toward where the yelp the night before came from. Yavo slowed to a hover and peered into the tree struck forest floor. He found nothing at first, then he picked up a scent. He lowered himself onto a branch and prowled the branches for several lengths. Long skid marks in the mud and nicks in several trees, indicted Azrack had been there. *Not this time,* Yavo thought.

Yavo's eyes darted from mark to mark several times, trying to replay what he was seeing in his mind, but nothing added up. He leaped down and examined the marks closely, but still nothing. He jumped into the sky. A few minutes later the rain fell, grounding him again. Yavo kept a quick pace over the underbrush and leaf piles. He stopped when the flapping of wings hit his brain and his mind raced for an explanation. He quickly jumped into a tree and climbed to the highest branch. Azrack was focused on his plan and failed to see Yavo down below as he whizzed over him. A wind whiplash rippled through Yavo's feathers.

"Blast!" Yavo roared.

He leaped and jumped from branch to branch but was nowhere fast enough to keep up with Azrack. Yavo's anger grew as he tried to figure out how Azrack was flying in a downpour. He fell to the ground and ran at full speed. His heart pumped hard against his rib cage as he darted over the forest floor.

A few times Yavo leaped into the treetops, reassessing his direction was accurate. It wasn't long until he had made up the distance. The crevasse wasn't too much further, and he decided Azrack was heading there. If he could fly, and Azrack couldn't, that would be the perfect hiding place, Yavo reasoned.

Yavo reached the last few lengths of ground and slowed his pace before the sheer drop off. He trotted along the edge and sniffed out a faint remnant of odor that lingered in the air. Yavo trusted this is where Azrack rested at one point. Yavo eyed a large tree across a clearing. He stalked between large bushes, scrutinizing the area.

He lowered close to the ground and his ears twitched and shifted. Yavo spent several minutes moving a tiny length. The scent intensified and his blood pounded in his ears, and the endorphins surged to high alert. With his eyes clear and focused, he pounced into the large hole at the bottom of the tree. He landed on a spiked thorn bush. Pain receptors hit his brain, and he yelped. Yavo scurried out and blood dripped from his paws. There were several small holes and a few thorns still embedded. He gripped them with his beak and yanked. The tiny, barbed endings release its defenses into his flesh. Yavo gritted his beak and hissed.

Azrack stopped, he didn't expect Yavo to be so close. He dove quickly and landed on a branch and huddled against the main trunk. He listened for several lengths and crept along the branch toward another, when a small glimmer, several lengths to the south, caught his eye. Azrack peered through tight eyes and carefully drifted down to examine the reflective surface. The tree he was staring at seemed to sway ever so slightly, and he reached a toe out to touch it. At first, he figured it was a side effect of the venom. He wondered if his mind was playing tricks on him. A slight tingle buzzed his toe, and he jerked away. He searched around but found nothing.

Azrack couldn't quite wrap his brain around why the tree was swaying in a rippling manner and what the hint of shimmer around it could be. He remembered Yavo and was about to leap into the sky, but something drew his attention deeper. He looked again, and this time the tree was gone, and his eyes popped open. A thin dark line separated the trees and sky. Mesmerized, he crept toward it. He moved his face close and closed one eye to scrutinize it and found that it was a night sky.

An ancient story crossed his mind of a time when his realm was connected with others. *Could this be a way into another realm?* He thought of the mages and weapons. He gazed into the bright sunlight and back. His heart thudded heavily, and a tingle crept into his body. His curiosity was more than he'd ever experienced before, and he stepped closer and reached out.

This time his paw slipped into the darkness. He retrieved it and examined his paw. Seeing that nothing happened, he stepped through the thin line. The tear in the fabric of time rippled as his sizable frame entered. He swayed unsteadily as white stars whizzed past. A few more steps and the stars stopped. His body halted, and he fell forward from the slight thrust it gave him.

To his astonishment, he was standing in a different world. His senses burst with the overload of newness. Chirps, clicks, and blurps he had never heard crashed his ears. Unfamiliar smells taunted his beak. He crouched low to the ground and peered into the distance. The sun's rays were about to flood over the mountain tops in a world he knew nothing about. He breathed in slowly and carefully. The dry air tantalized his nose and gave him a refreshing awareness. Trees were dull greens and browns and blend in with the grasses and dirt.

He looked at his bright red feathers and wondered if this would be a good idea. He turned around and searched for the unofficial portal. Relieved to find the tear still there, he crept through the forest, stopping every few lengths to smell and analyze the fresh scents. His ears twitched constantly as he interpreted unfamiliar sounds. A sense of wonder and amazement filled his mind, and for a moment he forgot all about Yavo. The constant gnawing at his gut was gone and a level of peace overcame him.

He didn't dare go too far, but he needed to secure a new hiding place in case Yavo found his trail. With a quickened pace, Azrack leaped into the trees and climbed to the highest branches that would still offer cover. The treetops were thick and densely covered, which gave him an extra peace of mind. Large, feathery, leafed plants grew on branches high in the canopy.

Azrack spotted a cave made of boulders that had fallen from the top of the mountain and made his way over to it. He sniffed around and found it was clear. It was barely big enough for him to squeeze into. He preferred more space, but this would do for now. He let his eyes close and cleared his mind. A sense of safety he hadn't felt in a long time overcame him.

The sun broke over the tops of the mountains, waking Azrack from a peaceful sleep, and he slipped out of the cave. He was invigorated and yet hesitant. He didn't know where he was or what he would encounter. The dark clouds rampaging his world were now replaced with soft white puffs dancing in the sky. Warm air moved around him, but with no wind. Clicks, chirps, and buzzing echoed off the enormous mountain behind him. The three purple moons faded in the now powder blue sky.

As the morning moved on, he made note of twenty different toad-like creatures and several varieties of fungi. He imagined how excited Helios would be to sink his talons in all of them. At one point, he found several herds of steer, elk, and grazing animals. He spent the day exploring and lounging in the warm sun.

He didn't want to leave this place and return to his world where he is now a fugitive but needed to find out if Ralti was able to talk to Lahonti and see if he even had a chance to return to his family. His desire to protect his people from Groargoth was intense, but his need to save lives was deeper. If it came down to him never returning, and not to wage a needless war, it was worth it. As the sun started to fade over the edge of the horizon, he flew back to the rift.

Azrack slipped back through the rift. The tingle surged his body again and a strong sucking gripped him and pulled him the rest of the way. Stars raced by until the sudden stop at the end of the portal. The familiar early morning moisture filled his nose, and he lowered onto his haunches. The grass beneath his feet was soft and green and the breeze light and airy. He found nothing was around, so he climbed into the sky. His mind didn't grasp at first, that the leaves were in bright color, but as he moved further in, he realized it was early spring instead of autumn.

Uncertainty filled his being. He had been gone a day, but that wouldn't be enough time for the season to have changed. Carefully, Azrack made his way around the forest edge. The remnants of one of the fake nests were lost to the weather. It made little sense. He continued toward the peaks. Azrack swooped into a tall tree and crouched tightly to the trunk as he listened.

Short bursts of clinking of chain-mail armor echoed against the chest armor of gryphtons. Azrack peeked around the rough bark. Small flecks of brilliant jade-green and ruby-red flashed in and out of the trees.

Azrack slipped slightly. His hind claw gripped the bark, sending a shard into a prickly bush. The tinkling of it hitting alerted the soldiers, and they stopped and hovered above him. One of them spotted Azrack and pointed him out to the other. They circled around the full canopy until they were able to take a better look.

They confirmed with hand signals and flew away. Azrack listened carefully and heard them leave. He leaped into the air and found them heading toward the plains.

Azrack flew briskly toward the Peaks. He knew it would be a matter of time before Yavo was once again on his trail. He darted up the steep incline and landed on a perch. A small parchment swayed in the bold breeze. He opened it and read,

Azrack,

Do not return, Groargoth will kill your family if you come against him. Groargoth has made Kronos General and demoted us all. Lahonti is being protected, I can't get to him.

Ralti

Azrack's stomach sank. The sting etched at his heart, but he knew Groargoth would do it. It was over. There was no way to return.

24-What About Those *Things*

Shaz woke to the sound of hoofbeats in the distance. He listened for a time and determined they were coming fast and in their direction.

"Serin, wake up, we need to move," Shaz said.

"What's wrong?" Serin asked.

"There is a pack of… creatures headed our way, and I don't think they're friendly," Shaz said.

"How can you tell, I don't hear anything," Serin said.

She regretted the words as soon as they escaped. She didn't know what all his powers were, but she understood he had unique abilities and she trusted him, so why question him. Serin gathered her bedroll and shoved the blankets in her pack and grabbed the utensils, but when she went to put them in the saddlebag, the horse was gone. A school of glow bugs swayed in front of her. Long feather-like arms brushed against her face and arms and she giggled as they moved around her.

"What do you suppose they are?" Serin asked.

"I don't know, they're not horses, that I'm sure," he said, "It smells rancid, something evil," Shaz said.

"You can smell them too? How close are they?" Serin asked.

"We are still a good distance in front of them, but they are quick by the sounds of it."

Serin shuddered and hopped a log. She looked around and found a wave of glowing and swaying bugs. Some hung in troves and others drifted aimlessly, making a mirage of dancing colors. Serin reached out to touch one, but they glided away.

"Blast, where is the horse?" Shaz asked.

"It must have run off," Serin said.

Shaz kicked out the leftover coals and spread dirt over the fire and Serin tried to put the utensils in her bag, but they wouldn't fit.

"Come on, we need to go, now," Shaz said.

Shaz brushed the glow bugs aside and opened a path. They made their way through the other side of the wall of bugs and the night sky crippled their movements.

"I can't see a blasted thing," Shaz said.

Serin bumped against him and he stumbled forward.

"Sorry, I can't see you," Serin said.

A faint glow grew on the forest floor as a mushroom illuminated in soft hues of oranges and pinks. Shaz stuck his toe on the fungi and it glowed brighter. A small bunch of mushrooms in front of him came into view and he touched them. They began to glow and Shaz quickly started stepping on as many as he could find. The mushrooms lit up a path, and they were able to keep moving. Tree lizards floated from tree to tree on tiny blue lightning bolts, adding sporadic bursts of light, but the rumble of the hooves beating on the ground ate and his nerves.

"Isn't this amazing? I wish we didn't have to go so quickly," Serin said.

"Aye," Shaz said.

Shaz's voice was empty, and Serin was certain he wasn't thinking about how pretty things were and decided not to disrupt his engaged determination.

"It will be dawn soon, this way," Shaz said.

"But don't we need to go that way?" Serin asked.

"Yes, but we need to throw off our sent, they're getting closer,"

"Blast," Serin said.

She shifted her pack and leaped over a stump and scurried up a fallen tree that leaned on the ground. She didn't see that the log rose at first until she was a few lengths off the ground. The higher she went, the slipperier the log became. She slipped off the log and fell through the darkness but never hit the ground. Shaz heard the ripping of the old bark and spun on his heel and tore the sword from the sheath. His eyes popped out when he saw Serin was floating face down an inch from the ground. He threw his sword into the sheath and darted back to her.

"Are you alright? What are you doing?" he asked. She bent her knees and sat up. Shaz glanced up at the log and back to Serin. "Your magic stopped you from hitting the ground."

"So, it would seem. This magic stuff is pretty amazing," Serin said.

"Yeah, it is. But we've got to keep moving," Shaz said.

"I want to try something," Serin said.

She stood and held out her hands palms facing the ground and pulsed them against the forest floor. Wind pushed in and out and swirled around them. She twisted them and closed her fists around the air. Holding her palms facing Shaz, she pushed the air toward him. The air encompassed his body then settled on his feet and legs, raising him about an inch above the ground. Shaz threw out his arms to steady himself as he swayed.

"What is this?" Shaz asked.

Shaz's excitement was mixed with a dose of nervousness and surprise.

"It came to me as I laid there hovering," Serin said.

Serin began her dance again and cast the air buff onto herself. She steadied herself and soon was at ease on her feet.

"What is this supposed to do?" Shaz asked.

"What about Jag, where is she?" Serin asked.

"Here,"

Shaz pointed to a black blob and her yellow eyes popped out against the darkness. She wrapped Jagwynn in an air bubble and chuckled when the majestic cat hissed at the air.

"Well, I'm hoping it will make us as light as air so we can move faster, like the wind," Serin said.

"That would be very helpful. How does it work?" Shaz asked.

"Like this," Serin said.

Serin dug her foot into the one-inch gap and darted forward. She moved with ease and twice the speed as before, maybe even three times. Shaz jerked his head as she zoomed by. He turned on his toes, dug into the air and shot off like the wind.

"Wooo hooo," he shouted.

Serin laughed and leaped over a boulder as Shaz whizzed around it. Jagwynn even got the hang of it and was effortlessly padding alongside them. They ran farther and farther away from the beasts that were tracking them. The scents of early morning filled their noses as the sun pushed the night away behind the mountains and over the now-thinning treetops. Shaz dug his heel into the soft padded cushion of air and came to a stop. Serin stopped in time to avoid slamming into him. They had been running for at least one solid measure of time, and they hadn't even broken a sweat yet.

"Why are we stopping?" she asked.

Serin's hair whooshed into her face.

"I need to figure out where we are and where we need to go," he said. He pulled out the compass and map, "This way."

"What about those *things*?" Serin asked.

"Oh, we are long gone. This air magic has given us quite the advantage. How long does this last anyway?" Shaz said.

Shaz sank onto the ground and Serin's toes touched first and she landed with a soft bump.

"I guess that's how long," Serin said.

"Let's go on foot from here. We're just about out of the forest now. I think. Jag, we'll meet up with you on the other side."

Shaz started walking and Jagwynn slipped into the fading shadows.

"We need supplies," Serin said.

"And we need to keep a low profile," Shaz said.

Serin nodded.

"I hope whatever it was, doesn't follow us passed the villages," Shaz hadn't thought of that.

"Me too," he said.

"Me too," Nix said.

He popped his head out of Serin's satchel.

"You can't be serious!" Shaz exclaimed.

Nix slunk into the pack with his eyes peeking out. Serin chuckled and patted Shaz on the arm. They walked out from the last line of trees and into tall grasses that surrounded the southern forest border. The gentle smell of the fresh ginger flower and lilacs mixed with the tall grass, sweetened their noses as the long stems swayed on the breeze. Soft hues of greens and blues now slipped into warm oranges as the true blaze of sunrise rose above the last vestiges of night. The warmth of the new sun felt good on Serin's skin. The refreshing rays danced from the large yellow disk climbing over the horizon, and the dew moistened their clothes.

"Look, smoke," Serin said.

Fires in a village began popping up around the edges. The aroma of cooking food mixed with animal dung and fresh-cut hay filled the air the closer they came to the village. A small child and a woman stood on the other side of a hut, pulling down the wash left overnight to dry. The woman gazed a moment, then hushed the child. The woman, across the road in the next hut, just stared.

"Friendly huh?" Shaz said.

"I don't think they like strangers," Serin said.

The woman huffed and returned to her mixing bowl.

"It's not that they don't like strangers," A man said from behind them.

Serin jumped out of her skin, and Shaz reached for his sword.

"No need for that, I didn't mean to alarm you," he said, holding out a hand for Shaz to shake. "I'm Orand Kianzad, I have been waiting for you Shaz, Serin."

Orand nodded as if to say, 'you are Shaz and Serin correct'. His olive complexion and his deep-set eyes were friendly. He was trim and fairly built.

"How do you know us?" Serin asked.

She folded her arms across her chest.

"I'm old friends with Yerild. He sent word that something was amiss when he returned to find Mrs. Bailey distraught over your being taken to the dungeons. I see you are well, I will send her word," Orand said.

"And Yerild?" Shaz asked.

"Doing fine, doing fine, returned your friends to the island," Orand said.

Shaz took in a deep breath and exhaled.

"Good," Shaz said.

Serin fidgeted at her belt. It made her uneasy that he knew who they were. Who else out there knew?

"Come, I have food and supplies," Orand said.

Shaz and Serin were surprised at how briskly he walked as they traveled down the road. The people shifted from wary to friendly, and some even waved. Serin decided they were waving at Orand. The sun rose several inches into the sky, expelling any last mist or dew from the land. They passed a few huts and crossed a small bridge over a babbling brook.

"This way," Orand said.

Orand's hut was off the main road by several lengths, and when they reached the edge of the dirt pathway Shaz leaned over to Serin.

"Trust no one," Shaz whispered.

Serin looked at him with surprise and curiosity. She thought she was the one with trust issues. On the inside sat a small table next to a small window where little light from the west sun had yet to show the warm colors. A bed just big enough for two covered the other side of the room where a small child was sleeping.

"This is Shaz and Serin," Orand said to his wife.

She was pretty with no face paints or jewels like the women in Ebassia. Her long chestnut-brown hair was softly rolled into a bun and small wisps hung at her temples, framing delicate green eyes and pink cheeks.

"Hello," she said with a smile.

"Nice to meet you," they said, almost at the same time. Serin picked up an intricately woven blanket, "This is beautiful, did you make it?" She was trying to hide the sudden feelings of uncertainty.

"Yes, do you like it?"

"I do," Serin said.

"You must be hungry?" Orand said.

"Yes, thank you," Shaz said.

"My name is Siva, my husband here doesn't appear to do niceties," she said, catching him licking some berry jam from his fingers.

"Oh, yes, sorry dear," he wiped his fingers on his trousers, "Sit, eat, and then we will get to business."

The soft but hot morning mush felt good in their stomachs next to the cold, refreshing milk. Orand cleared his throat.

"So, what is the plan?"

"Plan?" Shaz asked, wiping his mouth.

"Aren't you searching for the medallion?" Orand asked.

Shaz sat back in his chair and studied the man.

"I'm not sure I have the information you are seeking?" Shaz said.

"Oh, yes, of course, I should never have asked about your delicate mission. It's just that we never get any excitement around here and I just can't help the intrigue," Orand said.

Serin watched the childlike gleam in his eyes nearly overload his face.

"Tell us what you know. It could be useful to us," Serin said.

"Well, I was told that you are on a quest to search out the medallion of Broma, to access the gateway to the mithril caves deep within the Bairr Mountains. The legend that says, 'In order to enter the mountain city one must hold the two serpents'."

Orand's mouth nearly drooled with the words. Serin smiled at his enthusiasm.

"Nonsense, I keep telling Orand that he's ridiculous to believe his cousin's silly tales," Siva said.

Siva gave him a sideways glare and took a few dishes to the sink. Shaz decided he was not a threat and retrieved the medallion and set the shiny metal on the table in front of Orand.

"You have it already? But-" he asked, then slapped his forehead, "Of course you would have it, I didn't mean-"

"It's alright. Tell me more about this legend," Shaz said.

Siva stood over Orand's shoulder gawking at the medallion.

"I thought it was a legend. Stories to tell children when they were bad," Siva said.

She wiped her hands on her apron.

"Well," Orand said, ignoring his wife, "the legend says that the sages of ancient times held these medallions to open and close portals with which they could travel to other lands. Lands where magical creatures and mystic beings lived."

Orand motioned for permission to pick it up, and Shaz nodded. Orand turned the medallion around in his fingers and admired the fine details. A trance-like glaze overcame him, and they could tell he was living a dream.

"The Shadow World, being one of them, to which bad children are sent and never come back," Siva said.

Shaz raised an eyebrow at hearing the shadow world. Siva gave a penetrating gaze into the back of Orand's head and then at her sleeping child. Serin guessed that had become a source of contention between them and smiled gently.

"The Shadow World, huh?" Shaz asked.

"But I guess it's not just a legend now, is it?" Siva said.

Her voice trailed off with a trickle of fear.

"It doesn't work that way, right Shaz," Serin said.

Shaz looked at Serin with confusion, but quickly understood her attempt at comforting Siva.

"No, it doesn't," Shaz shrugged.

He had no idea what to tell her.

"The Sun Goddess protects the children, no one less than an adult can enter with or without a medallion, so the children are safe," Serin said.

Shaz was impressed with her instant lie, but he understood it was for a good reason. Siva nodded with appreciation and returned to the sink.

"Why would these sages travel to other lands?" Shaz asked.

"No one knows why. Some say for power and gain over humans. Others say it's to keep the creatures from coming here. Some say to hide the most powerful objects from evil," Orand said.

"The Sev-Rin-Ac-Lavah," Shaz said under his breath. He tapped his finger on his lips.

"The what?" Orand asked.

"Oh, nothing," he said.

"More like all of the above," Serin said.

Shaz nodded and picked up the medallion. The tickle of magic embraced his skin as he slipped it back in his pocket. Orand's eyes widened at the new possibilities, and Serin instantly realized what she said and frowned. Shaz chuckled.

"So, now that you have the medallion, what are you doing next?" Orand asked.

Serin was about to say something, but stopped, remembering what Shaz said on the way in and that she probably had already said too much and reached for a piece of bread and put it in her mouth instead.

"We need supplies and horses. We have a long way to travel," Shaz said.

"Yes, of course," Orand stood and bumped the chair but caught the back before it tipped over, "I'll take you to where you can find supplies."

Orand kissed his wife and opened the little door and slipped out. Serin thanked her, but before she reached the door, Siva stopped her.

"Is that actually true about the Sun Goddess?" Siva asked.

"Yes, the children are safe," Serin said.

She wasn't exactly lying. A warm tickle in the center of her being gave her the impression there was truth to it, but she didn't have exact knowledge, but she hoped so. Siva nodded and pulled a small jar from her pocket.

"Here, you might need this."

She slipped the small jar into Serin's hand.

"What is it?"

"Mrs. Bailey's ointment."

"Oh, thank you."

"You are meant for him and he is meant for you," Siva said in a whisper.

Serin studied Siva's warm expression.

"Why do you say that?" Serin asked.

Serin watched Shaz as he talked with Orand.

"You have a *very* unique element of energy about the two of you. I can see it," Siva said.

"Is it that obvious?"

Serin bit her lip.

"Only to those who have truly loved before," Siva said.

Serin blushed and patted Siva's hand that was resting on her arm, then left the house. The several stops they made took a good part of the morning. Serin sat on a stone wall at the edge of the stable yard while Shaz bought the horses. Apple trees decorated the fields and children scattered about ran and played in dirt paths while men tended flocks and fields. She grew up in a village similar to this one and remembered the times she would travel with her father through the portal. The distant memories were fading, and her heart ached for her father.

"I think that about covers it," Shaz said, returning from the stable.

"Do you think you have to have a medallion to pass through a portal?" Serin asked.

"Aye, why?" Shaz asked.

"I never saw my father with one and we passed through them a few times," Serin said.

"Hmmm, maybe the wyvern is a type of passkey," Shaz said.

"That would make sense," Serin said.

"You alright?" Shaz asked.

"Yes, why?" Serin asked.

"You seem preoccupied with something," Shaz said.

"Oh, nothing really, just trying to organize memories and what I thought were dreams and stories and what all," Serin said.

"I know how you feel. You ready, I think they're done saddling the horses. I know it's not your air spell, but with all the people around we'll have to settle," Shaz said.

"What, you don't think I can't buff horses?" Serin asked.

Shaz looked at her with wide eyes, and she gave him her sly grin.

"Really? Don't tease me," Shaz said.

Serin chuckled. They made their way to the stable and Shaz exchanged coins for the horses and they walked them to Orand's house.

"Where are you headed now," Orand asked.

"We are going to search for the sheath for the Honor Blade," Shaz said.

Orand leaned in and lowered his voice.

"Can I ask where you found the medallion of Broma?" Orand asked.

"An old witch had it," Shaz said.

Orand's eyes widened with the childlike glee, and Shaz slapped his shoulder.

"Seriously, if there's anything I can do for you, just ask, anytime."

A little red-haired boy about the age of eight scurried out of the house and wrapped his arms around his father's leg.

"Actually, there is something," Serin pulled the sleeping Nix from her satchel, "I need someone that can take care of Nix here, while I am gone. Can you do that for me?" she asked.

The boy looked up, and Orand nodded.

"You bet."

Nix looked up sleepily, and when he saw the boy, he hugged him, knocking him over. They laughed, grabbed the reins, and left the village the opposite way they came.

25-Remember You Started It

Shaz and Serin traveled a fair distance from the village when Jagwynn caught up to them. Serin cast her wind-walk on the horses while Shaz steadied them and then buffed Jag. It took a few minutes of training the horses to run with the magic, but soon the horses eased into the new speed and raced across the land. Shaz determined that with the current speed they were able to travel, it would only take a few days to reach his castle. They quickly came over a grassy ridge and found plumes of smoke that came from several chimneys of a small town. They slowed their horses, but the air magic was making their walking speed more like a trot. Shaz started around the outskirts of the town and found an angry mob forming in the town's square.

"I wonder what's going on?" Shaz asked.

"That can't be good," Serin said.

"Let's go check it out," Shaz said.

"Maybe we shouldn't interfere," Serin said, reaching for Shaz's elbow.

"Why not?" Shaz asked.

He looked at her with surprise. She was usually the one that wanted to help people.

"We're outsiders, and I don't know that they will take kindly to us butting into their business," Serin said.

Jagwynn pawed the ground and hissed.

"We'll be careful, but I think Jagwynn agrees," Shaz said.

"Alright, but let's go in quietly and check it out first," Serin said.

Shaz and Serin slowed to a trot and rounded the backside of the town where they could see the situation. A woman was tied to a pole with her hands behind her back and her hair was stringy and covered her face. She was wearing clothes that had been torn and soiled and she was barely able to stand. A rotund man with big rosy cheeks climbed the steps to the woman and slapped her. Shaz and Serin jumped as the sound rippled across the air. Shaz's heartfire lit and he started to get off the horse.

"What are you going to do?" Serin asked.

"I have no idea, but what's the point of being a war wizard if I have to stand idly by, while these people torture each other?" He leaped off his horse. Serin jumped off her horse and ran in front of him.

"I agree, but if we are exposed, we'll all be in danger. Not only us but everyone,"

"What do you want me to do? Let them hurt each other?" Shaz said.

"No, but I don't know what to do. They seem very angry and I don't know if we are making more trouble for ourselves," Serin said.

"Aye, but I have to do something. How can I save the world if I can't save one person?" Shaz said.

"You bring up a good point, just, be careful," Serin said.

Shaz nodded and walked into the crowd with one hand on his sword while the other pushed the angry mob out of his way.

Jagwynn's stealthy swagger startled the townspeople as she followed behind him. Shaz stopped in the center of the crowd and searched for any magic users. Shaz's nerves quickly became frazzled as the crowd rumbled with shouts and jeers. Another man climbed the steps and slapped the woman. Serin hurried around the platform and found the woman's left eye was swollen shut. Blood dripped from her lip and her wrists were raw and swollen and tears ran down her cheeks as she stood with her head drooped.

Shaz slammed his shoulder in the back of a man knocking him off balance and stopped in front of the man who was coming down the stairs. The man stopped and glared at Shaz and started toward him. Shaz didn't move, and the man took a swing. Shaz stepped to the side and let the man's momentum carry him and slammed his elbow into the back of the man's head. The middle-aged man fell to the ground and rolled, hugging his head. The crowd quieted and Serin climbed the stairs to the woman. People didn't know what was going on and quietly whispered amongst themselves. Shaz took the stairs two at a time and lifted the woman's chin.

"She's hurt really bad Shaz, she won't make it much longer," Serin said.

Shaz spun around and scanned the people. Looks of fear, anger, and contempt covered their faces and Shaz wondered what the woman had done. Serin closed her eyes and imagined the healing element of her water magic rise from her chest and ease down her arms. She touched the woman's arms and sent the magic into her body. The woman stopped trembling and her breathing steadied.

"Let her go!" Shaz yelled.

"Who are you and why should we listen to you?" asked a woman in the front row.

Shaz's blood boiled, and he had had enough. His anger now reached its max. Maybe he was just tired of all the running, dodging, not having a hot meal, and traveling to his inevitable doom. He slapped his hands together. A thunderous crack echoed over the village and rumbled into the distance. The crowd ducked and fell silent with wide eyes and trembled.

"What has this woman done?" Shaz yelled.

"She brought the serpent upon us," A woman called out.

He opened his mouth when a calming voice came from his left. Serin stood on the platform next to him.

"If we can stop this beast, will you let this woman go and never resort to this nonsense again?" she asked.

Serin's long, brown, wavy hair gently fell to just above her waist. Her bright green eyes twinkled in the setting sun. The confused crowd murmured to one another and a man in the front row called out.

"You think you can kill that serpent? You're a woman!"

The crowd broke into laughter. Shaz combed his hair out of his face and jumped down from the platform.

"Jag, stay here," Shaz said, pointing to the feet of the bound woman.

Jagwynn leaped onto the platform and hissed at the people. She circled the woman and sat her large rump on the ground and bared her teeth at anyone who dared look at her.

"Shaz, what are you doing exactly?" Serin asked when they got to the horses.

"I don't know yet."

"Well, I'm coming with you."

"No, you are not. You are staying here."

"Oh yes, I am. You can't tell me what I can and can't do."

"Serin, don't start with me, I am not in the mood."

He brushed past, and toward his horse as his face reddened with anger and frustration.

"I can see that, but neither am I. You need my help and you know it. Besides, you don't have a choice. I am going!"

Shaz threw up his arms.

"AAAAHHH! You are so stubborn," Shaz said.

"Yes, and just stubborn enough to put up with you," Serin shouted back.

He stared at her blankly as she slammed the leather strap of her pack here and there and climbed onto her horse. Shaz mounted his horse and started out at a fast gallop. Serin kicked her horse and followed him. He did know better than to argue with her. She *was* just as stubborn as he was, and right now, she *was* all he had. They rode toward the mountains until the sun fell behind them.

"Let's make camp over there," Serin said.

Serin pointed to a small grove of trees to the west. They veered toward the marker and Shaz halted his horse and slipped out of the saddle onto the soft damp ground and stretched with a large yawn. It had been awhile since they slept in a bed and the exhaustion wore on them. Shaz un-cinched the center billet strap and ring and flopped the stirrup strap over the saddle. He gripped the horn opposite the cantle and hoisted the saddle off the horse and rested it on a nearby branch. Serin too unsaddled her horse then dug into her pack for food.

"Blast!" she slammed the cover back over her pack and kicked the ground, "We have no supplies!"

"I'll find something, just start a fire," he grumbled.

"Fine, I would like a large bird, one of the red ones," Serin said.

She put her finger up as though she were hailing a servant at one of the fancy eateries in Ebassia.

"Ha ha, sure. Your order coming right up."

Shaz grabbed his bow and gave her a mock bow, then slipped into the trees. Serin found as much dry wood as she could and put it in a pile. She took out her flint and stone and flicked the flames on the kindling. A small flame bit at the dried twigs, and she blew gently until the flame grew. She put on a few bigger twigs and started looking for some larger logs. She stepped over a tiny trickle of water, rushing its tiny self as fast as it could over a large leaf and down a tiny stream bed.

Serin wished she could take a bath. She didn't care about having to sleep on the ground again it was a bath she wanted. She was always energized after spending time in the water. Serin found a few good-sized logs and was carrying them back to her little fire when Shaz came into the firelight. She didn't want to be obvious, but she loved looking at his handsome face. Every day her feelings grew for him, although he was stubborn and arrogant and a bit obsessive, well, a lot obsessive. Shaz was also kind, and strong both mentally and physically. He was willing to fight for others when they couldn't fight for themselves. He was determined to do the right thing, and she admired his charisma.

"Here you are...a red one," Shaz said.

Shaz set the bird in front of her.

"Wow, you're awesome," Serin said.

Serin turned as she noticed the heat sitting under her cheeks and began plucking the feathers. Shaz flopped down on the ground and propped himself against his pack. He put his hands behind his head and gazed into the sky. The small opening in the tops of the trees made him miss his little island, Ebassia wasn't horrible, but it wasn't his home.

Serin was about to ask him about his plans, but found him deep in thought. Serin wondered what he was thinking about and caught a glimpse of his deep blue eyes, which she found profoundly inviting. There was something more to them, something she couldn't explain. She had seen handsome men before, but Shaz held a certain attraction that was different.

He never gave her reason to think he was different than he was or hide his true character from her. Serin wasn't sure what to make of the growing impressions she was getting. It was almost like she could tell what his intentions were, even before he did anything. Serin was starting to understand his different emotions and the chaotic nature of his multiple magics. The more time they spent together, the stronger her perceptions became and because of that, the more she trusted him. It was the deepest magics that was what bothered her. She felt sorry that he had to carry such a burden on his own.

A crackling brought her from her thoughts, and she checked the cooking bird. She pulled it off the skewer and pulled out her knife she kept on her thigh and cut sections of the meat off the bird.

"Shaz, would like some supper?" Serin asked.

"Huh? Oh yes, of course, I am starved," Shaz said.

Serin handed him the plate and found a spot on a log next to the fire. The hot food brought comfort to their stomachs, and the fire was warm. Shaz realized he had spaced off and Serin had cooked the meal. He appreciated her being there. It was nice not to be alone. "Thank you, I'm sorry I spaced helping, I'm a total derp," Shaz said.

Serin smiled, it was nice that he didn't expect her to do things like that. He usually was good at working with. It was one thing they didn't have to argue about.

"So, Mr. Smarty, what *is* your plan for getting this serpent, thing?" Serin asked.

She set her plate on the ground and took a big draw from her water bag.

"I was thinking I would stand at the top of the highest rock and yell and see if it comes out of the sky to eat me," Shaz said.

Shaz flipped his hair with a smile. Serin blurted a guffaw and Shaz smiled even bigger.

"You are a derp," Serin said.

"Thank you, I try," Shaz said.

"I'm not sure they will want to eat all that cockiness," Serin said.

"What?" Shaz asked.

Shaz gave her a 'why wouldn't they want to eat all this amazing' look and fiend mock disappointment. Serin chuckled.

"But seriously," Serin said.

Shaz appreciated her ability to get things done. She was tough and spirited and, so far, could hold her own. He didn't have to help her with just about anything. An attractive feature in his eyes, for sure.

"You're right, while hunting for your red bird," he gave a little wink, "I came across tracks next to a stream. I think we need to follow them they may lead us to the creature."

"How far it is?" she asked.

"Not far, and the tracks were fresh."

"What kind of tracks were they?" Serin asked.

"That's the weird thing. They looked like a large cat's, like Jag, but had deep gouges like you might see from a bird," Shaz said.

"Humm, interesting. I suppose though, if the ruins by Nix barely showed up, then maybe random portals are showing up too," Serin said.

Shaz sat up and stared at her. Serin's cheeks warmed, and she wasn't sure what she had just said.

"I bet you're right, which means we might have some big problems," Shaz said.

"Like what?"

"Those creatures from the other night, and this serpent thing, and who knows what else," Shaz said.

Serin cringed and tried to shove the lump in her throat back down.

"Sounds like fun, maybe," Serin said.

Shaz chuckled.

"I'm not sure I would call it fun, but I suppose. Let's get some sleep, tomorrow might be a very interesting day," Shaz said.

"Remember, you started it," Serin said.

Shaz chuckled.

"Alright, you got me there,"

They pulled out their bedrolls and arranged the fire for the night and fell asleep. Mostly. The night lasted much longer than either of them wanted, and Shaz decided to get up early and make breakfast since Serin did supper. He started the fire and began warming the bird from last night and filled their water bags from the tiny stream nearby. Serin woke and rolled up her bedding and stood by the fire.

"Which direction are we headed?" Serin asked.

Shaz pointed, and Serin nodded. A shriek came from the top of the rocky hillside outside the cover of the trees.

"I guess that's our cue," Serin said.

"Let's start moving," Shaz said.

Serin whispered into the air and with a sweep of her hand sent a gush of wind around camp, eliminating signs they had been there.

"We can't take the horses into the woods the thickets are too heavy. If we go around the outskirts, we can get there faster, but we will have to leave the horses and go in on foot the rest of the way," Shaz said.

They saddled their horses and started out around the edges of trees. They found a place to leave the horses and tied them up and started out on foot. The terrain was rocky and heavily wooded, and they found it hard to make good time. They were about to the creek when they heard the screeching again, more like felt it in their bones.

Shaz touched the ground to feel if he could sense any movement, but he couldn't. Shaz led Serin to the place he'd found the night before and scrutinized the forest for clues. Serin stopped and tilted her head, listening for anything unusual. A pungent odor of fresh blood filled Shaz's nose as he breathed in deeply. The side of his lip peeled with disgust and a rock formed in his stomach. He felt the discomfort of not knowing what he was up against, and he slipped in and around trees and tall shrubs. The babbling of water got louder as they crept along the upper banks of what was once a large river.

"Did you hear that?" Shaz asked.

"Yeah, but what was it?"

"I don't know, so be careful," Shaz said.

He slid onto his belly and crawled to the ledge.

"I don't see anything," she said.

"Me either, but can you smell that?" Shaz asked.

"No, smell what?" she said.

"Not sure."

"Look, over there," Serin said, pointing toward a rocky ridge.

"Oh, my!" Shaz said.

Its razor-sharp black beak was tearing the limbs off a mountain goat and feeding fiercely as though it hadn't eaten for weeks. The sun magnified its copper color, and it radiated a gold hue around it as though it were on fire. It stood like a man while its long lion-like tail swayed behind its immense body as the feather-like tufts danced behind it. Sharp talons on its part-lion paws gripped the goat's flesh, and the talons on its paw-like feet dug into the ground to steady itself.

"Is that a human, bird, or a lion?" Serin asked.

"Looks like all three, it does explain the prints," Shaz said.

It stood on its hind legs, searched its surroundings, then went back to eating.

"If we sneak a little closer, we might be able to place a few arrows into its neck," Shaz said.

Serin put out her arm in front of his chest as he rounded the backside of the tree.

"What?" he whispered.

"Two more over there," Serin whispered.

He nodded and whispered.

"I'm going up."

Shaz crept around the boulder several lengths. Light on his toes, he ran toward the boulder and shoved off, using his momentum to carry him upward. Serin flicked her hand and sent a small tuft of air under him. He nearly flew over the branch but caught it and gave her thumbs up after centering himself on the limb. Serin lifted herself off the ground with an air spell. When she reached the height she wanted, she pulled out her bow and arrow and stood ready. Shaz drew his bow, strung it, and pulled out an arrow. He pointed to the neck just above his collarbone to tell Serin where to aim. She pulled back the arrow making the string taut and took in a deep breath.

"On three," Shaz whispered.

Serin steadied her nerves as the forest greens and tans disappeared from her view, and all she saw was the gentle heaving of the gryphton's feathers.

"Three," Shaz said slightly above a whisper.

Their arrows whizzed through the air and the copper beast reared backward at the sudden sense of pain as its body became paralyzed. Shaz scooted back on the branch into the cover of the shadows. Serin dropped to the ground and slipped behind the boulder. The beast managed an ear-piercing screech and alerted the others, who dropped their carcasses and leaped into the air. Bright-green and ruby-red feathers sent radiating glints of color as they moved. They carried swords and wore leather armor on their human-like chests, forearms, and lion-like shins.

The green one landed in front of the copper one and searched the surroundings. The copper-colored gryphton grabbed at his throat and struggled to stay standing. The bright-green gryphton grabbed the arrows and broke them from his comrade's neck and crushed them in his grip. An odd sensation rippled through Shaz's nose and into his brain, and he found he understood their fear. Serin held her breath, and the creature scrutinized the bank of the riverbed above him. Serin squatted but pulled another arrow. The stone in Shaz's stomach turned to a lump in his throat, and he pulled another arrow and took a few steps out onto the limb. Serin slipped out around the boulder just enough to find her mark and waited for Shaz to give her the cue.

He whistled a soft bird call, and they each let go of another arrow. Shaz's arrow penetrated the leather and settled deep into the copper gryphton's heart, and Serin's sunk into the soft flesh just under the breastplate of his leather armor. He fell backward and hit the ground with a thump against the hollow rocks. The other gryphtons flared out their massive wings and leaped into the air. They frantically searched the direction the arrows came from and the red one moved closer to the bank.

26-It's About Time You Found Me

A strong odor wafted into the air as the two gryphton soldiers flew over the remnants of the last battle with the Ebon Hoards. Heaps of smoldering remains plagued the landscape. The soldier's guts twisted as they internalized the broken and shattered long blades, shields, and battering rams protruding from the ground. It has been a fierce battle, one in which they were successful in driving the Ebon Hoards back into their own lands, for now.

A soft breeze eased the stench as they crossed the last few lengths, and the soldiers slowed under the waning pressures of fatigue. Last they had heard, Yavo was making his way around the outskirts interrogating residents of the King's lands. They were close and pushed hard just to keep to the sky. Small prides that scattered the open grasses roared angrily as they crossed.

One soldier pointed to a landing, and they banked a hard right. In the distance, they heard a commotion and quickly made their way through the last undercurrent. Yavo drug an elderly gryphton from his cave and his family roared and snipped at him.

"You will tell me where he is, or else," Yavo growled.

"Sir, he's in the forest," one soldier interrupted.

Yavo gripped the neck of the old gryphton.

"What?" Yavo asked.

"Azrack, we saw him on our way to the secret-"

The second gryphton elbowed him in the ribs.

"Toward the gorge," the second said.

"When?"

"We came straight here, no stopping," the soldier said.

Yavo's eyelid twitched with anger, and he squeezed even harder as the old gryphton gripped his paw to release him. The old gryphton opened one talon and sliced the top of Yavo's paw. Yavo growled in pain and jerked away, and the gryphton fell to the ground. Yavo searched their eyes and found them to be telling the truth.

"Well, then, I best go hunting."

Yavo's eerie swagger and ruffling of his feathers was a signal that he is not to be trifled with. A trickle of blood dripped from the back of his paw before he leaped to the sky. Yavo's chest exhilarated with renewed energy and he flew through the night. Yavo ran through the last several moons and tried to piece the puzzle together. He spent many days following each trail only to find they overlapped, and the trails went in circles. He thought of every exercise Azrack taught him and retraced his paths and scrutinized the finest of details.

Every trail and non-trail he found went back and forth all over the countryside, and for what seemed like forever, he had covered every inch of the land. As fall turned to winter, Yavo slowed his search, having to wait until the snow melted, he took up his search into the lands to interrogate prides. He even took it as a chance to settle a few scores. He left his mark on the land and frightened the creatures that lived there.

One night in the late winter he was in an old rundown eatery when a mysterious gryphton approached him. The gryphton wore an unusual cloak and ornate jeweled necklaces. He asked him if he was interested in a mission for a very wealthy payment. But Yavo became obsessed with finding Azrack he dismissed him. Before the gryphton left, he spoke in Yavo's ear and told him a powerful necromancer could use his unique talents, but Yavo was to tunnel visioned to think more of it and once the snow melted enough, he returned and again and retraced all the trails.

Yavo prided himself on his even temperament, but the last few moons pushed him to his max on more than one occasion. Prides began guessing as to why he would be searching amongst them. Soon rumors surfaced Azrack had outsmarted Yavo, and the storytellers told stories of Azrack having extraordinary powers to the young ones. They said Yavo was losing his mind and couldn't hunt a ribbard. They said he'd gone deaf and blind with furry and was begging for food. As the rumors spread, they became less afraid of Yavo and some even laughed at him. This drove Yavo to greater depths of fury, and he felt at times he couldn't make sense in his own head. He found himself having several conversations with trees or rocks and cursed Azrack even more.

There was no logical explanation. He shook his mind clear and dismissed it all. He needed to focus now. A small part of his mind wouldn't let go, however, of the thought that Azrack must have some extraordinary powers. A snap up ahead alerted his senses, and he stopped and quickly lowered to the ground and hunched under a thicket. He listened but heard nothing more. He hadn't realized the darkness creep into existence and searched for a large thicket and slunk underneath.

Yavo's heart raced as the taste of revenge sank into his senses. But the one thing that kept coming back was how Azrack was able to fly in the rain. No matter how many gryphtons he interrogated, he couldn't find anyone who knew the answer. That and where could he have gone. His mind wrestled between sleep and awake until the sun gave a hint of light to the sky and he shook off the debris of the thicket and leaped into the early morning. Yavo weaved in and out of the currents and narrowed his vision for anything that was similar to

Azrack's fire red-orange feathers. A hint of scent crossed his senses, and he nosedived into the tree canopy.

Yavo crept along the large branches and scoured his surroundings. He leaped from the tree and kept low to the ground and searched for clues. He spotted marks on the bank of a river that wasn't there before. Yavo prowled around the area, sniffing for information. He studied the other side of the bank and found tracks there too. Angry he didn't see them before his nerves shook inside his body.

He flew across the empty riverbed, half-flying-half-crawling, and followed the trail. The edge of the river was nestled in next to a steep embankment which had suffered a heavy rockslide, and he lost the trail and slammed his paws on the ground. He chided himself to get a grip, but the energy that surged into his bosom was almost more than he could take, and he breathed heavily. His eyelids sagged under his blurry black eyes and Yavo ran his paws over his face. He stared into the distance with a chaotic and fierce emotion and recalculated his steps. The trails he followed, the marks he found, the scents he examined. Still, nothing seemed to measure up.

"He's toying with me," he hissed.

Yavo went back to the river and leaped over to the other side. He moved slower, making sure he didn't miss anything. He gazed into the treetops for signs that Azrack used the canopy. Several lengths down, he discovered another set of tracks and he leaped across and followed them up the side of the gorge. A thought came to him as he recounted the soldier's message. *Where were they going? To a secret what? What is out here that Groargoth would want? After I catch Azrack, I will be sure to find out.* He shook his head clear of the extra thoughts and doubled his efforts.

The wind whipped over the top of the ridge with intensity and an ear screeching pulse broke his concentration. Yavo struggled against the gusts and leaped onto a branch and climbed a few more lengths until he was in the upper layers of the tree. Yavo pulled out his looking glass and stuck one eye on the glass and closed the other. A bright red form emerged from the corner and he aimed and twisted the levers and Azrack came into focus. He slammed the magnifier shut and tried to fly, but the wind was too strong. He dropped to the ground and started out at a fast pace.

Azrack's emotions were all over the place. Sadness, anger, regrets, and frustration rippled his body in confused patterns. A sharp sting in his jaw jarred him from his misery. Yavo shot out from the trees and landed his fist on Azrack's jaw. For a second, Azrack didn't know what hit him. Yavo's hunter-green and brown feathers whizzed past him. Azrack banked hard left as Yavo twisted and bent at the waist. Yavo whipped his blade from its sheath and swung with an upward thrust toward Azrack, who threw out his hind legs. With one he smacked Yavo's paw and with the other caught Yavo on the side of the head. Yavo almost dropped his sword, but regained control. Azrack pulled his sword and hovered a few lengths away.

"It's about time you found me," Azrack said.

Yavo's lower lid flinched, and a growl escaped his throat. Yavo tightened his grip and lifted his arm. He swung downward as he lunged toward Azrack. Azrack pulled in his wings and lowered, twisting like a siphon. Yavo fell into thin air and spun back around. Azrack opened his wings, catching the undertow and pulled away.

"I've waited too long for this," Yavo growled.

"You never were good at waiting. I knew it would somehow drive you mad."

"Mad, mad, you think me mad? I'm not mad, I'm furious."

"And delusional," Azrack said.

"I've had enough."

Yavo lunged again, his blade out straight. Azrack engaged his sword with Yavo's. He twisted his wrist and rolled his paw around Yavo's. Azrack yanked his sword, but Yavo kept a tight grip on his own blade. Yavo brought up his elbow and smacked Azrack in the side of the head. Azrack released his talons and struck Yavo on the side of the face, pulling his talons through his flesh.

Yavo pulled back and roared with pain. Bright red blood gushed from the long gouges. Azrack lifted his hind legs and shoved Yavo with fierceness, flinging Yavo into the air. Yavo rolled uncontrollably for several lengths, and Azrack pulled his sling and loaded a rock. He flung it toward Yavo, but at the last second the sling snagged on his belt and the rock soared over Yavo's head.

Yavo laughed and flew back toward Azrack. Azrack swerved sideways and came in from behind. He sliced at Yavo's wing, but Yavo pulled it in and dropped a length. Azrack reset as Yavo rolled upward and hovered.

"What makes you think you can defeat me?" Azrack asked.

"Because I'm better than you," Yavo sneered.

"You may be strong and quick, but you are not stable. You have always let greed and self-gloating be in your way of truly becoming what you could have," Azrack said.

"What are you saying? That I'm weak?" Yavo sneered.

"Yes, and weak-minded."

The words stung Yavo's heart. A wave of uncontrollable anger surged to the surface, and Yavo's face turned red with fury. His chest heaved heavily as he contemplated his next move. Yavo moved toward Azrack, his beak fixed on Azrack's jugular. Yavo could see the vein pulsing, he could hear the blood beating and he could taste it. Azrack saw the discord in his face and knew he had lost it. There was nothing worse than an unstable combatant, they might do just about anything and Azrack's guts twisted. Yavo lunged at Azrack but jewked at the last second, and Azrack caught Yavo's fist with his back. The pain hit his brain, but not before he twisted.

The motion carried him through, and he snagged Yavo by the neck. Azrack wrapped around Yavo and pulled his forearm around his neck and gripped his paw with his other paw and squeezed as tightly as he could. Yavo struggled to breathe and squirmed frantically under Azrack's chokehold. Yavo managed to pull his dagger and tried to relax even though his brain was screaming for air. Azrack loosened his hold to evaluate if Yavo was incapacitated and Yavo stabbed a dagger into Azrack's side. Azrack roared with pain but didn't let go. He squeezed tightly around his neck but couldn't muster the strength to snap any bones.

Yavo squirmed and Azrack pulled his blade as Yavo rolled out of his grip. Azrack lashed out, and the blade slashed Yavo's wing tendon. Yavo roared and staggered and swayed and sank from the sky. Azrack gripped his side and winced from the pain. He pulled his paw away and examined the dark red blood. Azrack gritted his beak and dove after Yavo. Yavo pulled his wing in and was holding it when Azrack landed.

"Give up Yavo, it's over," Azrack said.

"I will never give up," Yavo snarled.

"Then I have no choice," Azrack said.

Azrack lunged and sank his blade into Yavo's heart. They toppled to the ground and Azrack waited until his life force left his body. Azrack's heart both sank and rejoiced, but that didn't change the way things had worked out. Azrack pulled his blade and wiped the blood on a patch of grass and returned it to its sheath. He knew the time was now and pulled a cloth from his pack and shoved it over his wound and tied it on as best he could and then headed to the rift.

27-That Last One Got Away

Shaz rested against the tree and searched the sky between the thinning canopy. Serin made her way back and Shaz jumped down.

"Now what?" she asked.

"Maybe it's time I stand on the highest point and yell and see if they come out and eat me," Shaz said.

"Yeah, let's give it a try, I mean you are kind of rough around the edges, could take a minute to chew you up," Serin said.

Shaz chuckled.

"Well, we do need to reach higher ground and away from here," Shaz said.

Serin nodded, and they started toward the peak they could now see on the other side of the bank. The sun kept coming in and out of view as the clouds floated over and they tried to hurry across the exposed riverbed. Shaz studied the atmosphere, and when he didn't see the creatures, he and Serin dashed across the uneven surface. A whoosh of air rippled over the top of their heads. Shaz threw himself over Serin, and one of the flying beasts slashed Shaz's back. Shaz yelled as the pain surged through his being, and Serin shuddered at the sting of his pain and flinched.

Shaz turned to see the second creature coming and ripped the blade from its sheath in time to slash through the animal's thigh. The beast pulled back and rolled in the air and returned to a higher atmosphere.

"Hurry," Shaz said.

Serin dashed across the last few lengths and under a large overhang near the first dead beast. Shaz hurried in partial-backward step and watched the sky. He darted into the cove and Serin pulled back the torn leather jerkin.

"Shaz, these are really deep," Serin said.

"Can you at least reduce the pain?" Shaz asked.

Shaz gritted his teeth to keep his body from falling into shock.

"I'm going to try something," Serin said.

"Anything," Shaz said.

Serin closed her eyes and pictured her magic in the center of her being grow. She twisted her body and waved her arms and called the energy into her hands and placed them on his skin. The pain instantly ceased, and he sagged with relief. Shaz moved to check the perimeter, but Serin held him back.

"Hang on, I'll try to do this really fast," Serin said.

Serin called more magic into her fingers, and the threads danced around the wounds and pulled the skin together. Serin scanned the wounds as she kept her fingers working quickly and the gashes sealed shut.

"That was fast," Shaz said.

"I guess I just needed to do it once first to figure out what to do," Serin said.

"I'm the luckiest man alive," Shaz said.

Serin smiled at his compliment but kept on topic.

"What are we going to do?"

"I don't think going up is the better option, we need to find a way to ground them," Shaz said.

"The riverbed is too uneven," Serin said.

"Aye, I think we can make it around this formation and into the trees," Shaz said.

"Alright," Serin said.

"When we're in the trees, can you make the wind blow chaotic so that they have to land?" Shaz asked.

"I can try," she said.

"If we can keep them from flying, then I can take them out." Shaz said.

"But there are two of them!" Serin said.

"We don't have much choice."

"I can help," she said.

"No, you need to stay undercover and protected. I can't fight them and keep you safe at the same time. Plus, I need you to keep them out of the sky," Shaz said.

"Alright," she said.

They checked for clearance and then hurried around the edge of the rock formation and ran into the trees behind it. Shaz pointed out the bright-red feathered animal, and Serin nodded. Serin lifted her arms halfway and closed her eyes tightly. She cleared her mind and focused on the surrounding air. She pulled at the invisible force with her thoughts and sent her magic into the air. The tops of the trees swayed back-and-forth rustling leaves about. Shaz made his way to the edge of the trees. Serin raised her arms higher and placed one foot behind her. She bent her knees, dipped toward the ground, and threw her arms up and a gust of wind crashed over the trees, sending leaves and debris whipping around the air. Serin dug in deeper and the wind gusts became strong enough to blow the flying creature's around.

Shaz opened and closed his grip around the hilt of the sword as he waited until they touched the ground. The green bird-like human pulled his wings tightly and scaled several nearby rocks. A dark cloud moved in front of the sun, casting a cool shadow over the land, and Shaz shot out with the moving shadow. He used the adrenaline and closed the gap by about twenty lengths before the animal's sharp eyesight saw him. The animal reached for his sword but fumbled it in his grip.

Shaz leaped off a small rock and flew into the air and twisted and thrust the tip of the blade in a downward strike and into the green enemy's neck. His eyes met the bird's black eyes that were wide with fear and pain. Shaz felt the resistance against the blade cutting the bone as the spinal cord severed before piercing the lungs. A sensation of power came over Shaz, a feeling that he liked, powerful and strong, the feeling of control. A hint of guilt that he enjoyed killing the beast sat at the back of his mind and yanked his sword out as he continued through the twist. He came full circle and landed and ran through the motion to a stop. The creature's knees buckled, and it fell face down on the ground. The ruby-red creature charged at him, and Shaz spun on his toes. Wind whipped around, throwing Shaz's hair around in his face, and he tried to keep his locks from whipping his skin. The bird-man-lion raised his sword and ran with long, powerful strides.

Shaz lifted his blade in an upward strike, nicking the creature's shoulder as he leaped out of the way and fell into a somersault and came to his feet. The beast grimaced but threw his body weight toward Shaz, who sidestepped the punch and slammed the butt of the hilt into the side of the beast's skull. The hit threw the animal off balance and it tried to open its wings and Shaz circled around the back. It spun on its heels and blocked Shaz's thrust with a counterstrike. Shaz slipped on some loose stones and tumbled to the ground, but rolled to the side and came to his feet, half-crouched.

The animal returned the strike and seeing he missed, stood up and squared his shoulders. Shaz stepped over a fallen tree trunk as they circled each other. The beast lashed out in an upward strike, and Shaz blocked and countered with a side strike. His blade sliced across the beast's hip. The winds decreased and Shaz feared Serin wouldn't last much longer. He stepped into an upward thrust, slashed the leather armor and cut deep into the beast's skin.

Blood and splintered feathers flew into the wind as the beast fell backward. Shaz tried to stab him straight into the heart, but the beast lifted his legs and kicked Shaz in the chest. Shaz soared through the air and slammed into a tree. Serin fell to her knees, and the wind died to a gentle breeze. Shaz scurried to his feet holding his chest and gasping for air while he reached for his blade. Before he could grip it tightly, the animal leaped into the air and feebly flew away.

"Blast," Shaz cursed and hurried to Serin.

Serin knelt on her knees and gripped her shoulder.

"I'm sorry, I just couldn't keep going," Serin said.

Tears slipped out without her permission, and she struggled to stifle the pain in her arm.

"Why the tears? You did magnificently," he said. Bright red blood trickled between her fingers, "Blast, you're hurt," Shaz said. He slipped the sword into his sheath and gripped her arm to give more pressure, "We need to get you back to the horses and bandage this," Shaz said.

"Give me a second," Serin said.

Serin rested a minute and tried to heal herself, but her attempt was weak.

"What's wrong?" Shaz asked.

"I'm so thirsty," Serin said.

"Of course," Shaz said.

Shaz helped Serin back to the riverbed, where he had seen a small trickle running at the side of the main depression.

"The last one got away," she said.

"That thing won't make it far it's wounded pretty bad," Shaz said.

They got to the trickling spring and Serin removed her bloody hand from her skin and felt the peel against the wound and she winced and bit her lip. Shaz wiped the blood and studied the wound.

"How did this happen? Something ripped your skin."

"A branch or something, from the wind I guess," she said.

He helped Serin with a drink and Shaz dripped water over her arm to clean the blood and Serin soaked in the energy the water gave her. Serin relaxed as the water brought relief to the pain and she focused on the skin mending and with each time Shaz dripped water over the wound she healed a little more. The clouds Serin called didn't seem to want to leave, and a rumble crossed the sky.

"The horses aren't far, let's hurry before we get rained on," Shaz helped Serin to her feet, "Wait, I'll be right back."

"Where are you going?" Serin asked.

"Getting proof."

Serin shivered and made her way to the horses. Storm clouds continued to darken the sky as they returned to the village. The sky opened and rain pelted the dusty road as they entered the small town.

"You don't think I caused the rain, do you?" Serin asked.

"I have no idea, maybe, can you do that?" Shaz said and asked at the same time.

Serin chuckled and wiped the water from her face.

"Where are all the people?" Serin asked.

The village was quiet, and an uneasy sensation settled in Serin's gut. A low muffling of voices came as they rounded the corner of one of the meager buildings on the inner side of the town. Shaz halted his horse and climbed off and untied the animal's head from the saddle.

"They're back," called a villager.

Villagers let Shaz through but muttered amongst themselves.

"This is what was killing your flocks. Not this woman," Shaz said, holding it up. Jagwynn hissed at the dead creature.

"What is it?" a woman called.

"A gryphton," an old man said.

Shaz peered at a ragged man standing near the edge of the gathered people.

"Untie her," Shaz demanded.

"How do we know she won't bring more?" a man from the center of the crowd asked.

Shaz wasn't sure what to do with that. He was certain she was not a magical being, but how could he prove to them without causing more panic.

"Prove to me she did," Shaz countered.

The crowd discussed what they were going to come up with and Serin hurried to the woman and tried to untie the knots, but they were so tight, and she couldn't undo them. Serin pulled her knife and started cutting through the thick rope.

"Shaz, I need to move her somewhere safe. She's not going to make it," Serin said.

"Well, what is your answer? What proof do you have that she or anyone summoned these creatures?" Shaz called.

He waved his hand around the crowd, pointing to different people to come forward. No one did. "Alright, this matter is closed, and this woman is exonerated of any crimes against her. Do you all agree?" Shaz said.

The crowd hesitantly agreed, and Shaz went to help Serin.

"So how do you explain the creatures, where did it come from, are there more, what do we do?" the man in the center asked.

"I can't answer that, but if you put together a group of your strongest and most skilled fighters and make a plan on what you can do to protect yourself and work together, you outnumber them and you can fight back, but I don't think you will have any more issues," Shaz said.

The crowd cheered and started mingling with each other, discussing new ideas, and Shaz and Serin helped the woman off the platform. Shaz turned to the wrinkled and leather-like face of the old man.

"How do you know what this is?"

The old man's crinkled finger bent back and forth.

"I have seen them before," he whispered, "Come, we will talk. My daughter will tend to the woman," he said to Serin, "Bring your cat," he hobbled away and invited them into his house on the edge of the square. "Please sit, Reanne, come help this young woman," he said.

The mostly unfurnished room was dark and held little attraction. The walls made of old pine timbers had a thatched roof that needed mending, and gentle drips fell from a hole in the center of the room as the rain increased.

"My name is Liang, you can call me Liang," Liang said.

"My name is Shaz, and this is Serin," Shaz said.

"What brings you this way?" Liang asked.

"We're just passing through," Shaz said.

Liang poured some hot tea and Shaz wasn't sure how much was going to end up in the cup and how much would be on the floor. A gently aged woman came from the other room of the small three-room house. A small table sat in the center of the adjacent room with two chairs nestled under it.

"Oh, dear," Reanne said. Shaz and Serin were holding up the woman, "Bring her here," She took Shaz's place and she and Serin went into the kitchen.

"How do you know about the *gryphton*?" Shaz asked.

"You certainly get right to the point, don't you," Liang said.

"I'm sorry Liang, I do wish I could stay and enjoy your village, but things are in need of my attention," Shaz said.

"Why must you be the one to handle this?" Liang asked.

Shaz didn't really want to play twenty questions, but he understood that the man was probably bored and lonely and decided it wouldn't hurt to take a few minutes. Serin and Reanne helped the woman into a bed and when Rianne went for water, Serin sent a burst of her healing magic into her. The woman's breathing evened out and the color in her skin returned. Rianne returned with a bowl of water and a washcloth.

Serin dipped the cloth and imagined her energy mix with the water and a gentle blue hue deepened the water. Serin wrung out the cloth and dabbed the dried blood on the woman's eyebrow and cheekbones. With each dab, the skin underneath eased in redness and Serin was confident the woman would heal quickly. Shaz sat in the chair adjacent to the rocking chair and Jagwynn nuzzled his leg. The old man sat in his thatched rocking chair.

"I'm really not sure how to answer that. I guess I have a duty to the people of this area," Shaz said.

"Why do you say that?" Liang asked.

"I am the heir to the Reinholt Castle that isn't far from here," Shaz said.

Liang sat up in his chair and stared at Shaz. Shaz squirmed in his seat and ran his hand along Jag's neck and side. Her soft purring softened his nerves, but the weird tug at his core made him uneasy.

"You are the heir to the Reinholt Castle?" Liang asked.

"You know of it?" Shaz asked.

"Ah, the legends, yes, but how would you be related, if you don't mind me asking?" Liang said.

Shaz studied the man for a moment and was confident he was not a threat.

"I am the son of Reinholt," Shaz said.

"That would make you-"

"Three hundred rotations old, yes," Shaz said. Liang sat back in his chair and rested his head. "May I ask, how you know about the gryphton?" Shaz asked.

"I have met one. He called himself a gryphton, and he's not from this world. He lives deep in the shifting woods," Liang said.

Liang used his tiptoe to ease the chair back and forth.

"The shifting woods?" Shaz asked.

"Deep in the forest is a place unlike any other. Trees move tending to the needs of the earth."

"How did you escape?" Shaz asked.

"Escape?" the old man chuckled, "No, need to escape. We talked, and he pointed me in the right direction to find my way back home when I was lost,"

"You mean he didn't attack," Shaz asked.

"No, he was quite friendly. I tried to tell the villagers that the creature taking their flocks was a gryphton, but they think I'm a crazy old man," he sipped his tea, "Maybe I am, but maybe now they will believe me, but maybe I don't care," he smiled with only a few white teeth left but it was kind and sincere.

Shaz tapped his chin in thought and the fang tingled his skin.

"How do I find him?" Shaz asked.

"The gryphton?"

"Yes," Shaz said.

"Why?"

"I just need to talk to him. Can you tell me how to find him?"

"I have a map around here somewhere," Liang said as he struggled out of his chair. He wobbled over to a small chest and fiddled around, then pulled out an old map. "Ah here," he held the faded and torn map in his shaking hands. "Now, keep in mind this is an old map and like I said, the trees don't stick to one place. In fact, I suppose this belongs to you now," Liang said.

"Why would it belong to me?" Shaz asked.

"Because as a young man, I found this while exploring around the deserted Reinholt Castle," Liang said.

Shaz smiled at the adventures he was sure many people had with his deserted house. Liang handed him the map. Shaz studied the old paper for a moment.

"Is this red x where he is?" Shaz asked.

"Oh, no, that is where I buried my treasure," Liang said.

Liang struggled his fragile frame back into his chair. Shaz's brows twitched, and he scrunched his face. He wasn't sure if the old man was teasing or not. Serin came out from the kitchen with a relieved smile, and Shaz nodded.

"You can stay the night here," the man said, "Besides, I would like to hear all about your travels."

"Unfortunately, we really need to keep moving," Shaz said.

"The weather is not getting any better, and the sun has already set," Serin said.

Shaz looked outside and found that the sun was setting into late evening and agreed. Reanne came in the front-room with some extra bedding and Shaz and Serin made up a bedroll and Shaz went out to fetch the horses. He didn't have the time, but he felt bad that this old mas was living in such poor conditions. He promised himself that when he found his castle, if there was a treasury there like most castles were rumored to have, he would send aid to this man and his family. The rain drizzled into a bucket that made a plinking sound, and Shaz found it hard to sleep. He dreamed of all kinds of things, one of which was the blasted tinking to stop and the roof to be fixed.

The smell of warm morning potage wafted into their senses, and Shaz and Serin woke. Shaz moved the bucket out of the way and found that there were no drips. He looked up and there was no hole either. His mind engaged in a rapid finding of explanations and decided on he must have used magic while sleeping to fix it. Shaz smiled and took the bucket outside to dump the water that was still in it. The sun broke through the last bit of dingy clouds and a certain zing of renewed energy soaked into his lungs.

28-Not Another One

Shaz knew it wouldn't be much longer and they wouldn't be able to see anything. The deeper they went into the forest, the more their surroundings shifted from the bright green trees, shrubs, and grasses to gray hues of green and tan with an ever-increasing mist that seemed to sit on the forest floor. Shaz rounded a large tree trunk and spotted a makeshift shelter. It was made of the ginormous bush leaves that were strung across a broken Waslick tree.

One side of the trunk was propped up on an old half rotting stump and a huge rock that had been moved into place on the other. The moist earth had been moved and scuffed, leaving a deep trench where it had been dragged or pushed. Shaz wondered what would have the strength to move the rock and analyzed whether it would be safe to use it.

"Let's stop here," Shaz said.

Serin nodded and climbed off her horse and pulled the saddle off and set it on a log. She took the bit out of the horses' mouth and set it on the saddle. Shaz dismounted and unsaddled his horse too and then stretched his back by arching it and swinging with his hands gripped together in a wide circle, then side to side. He examined the details of the shelter and noted a depression in the center. He concluded it might have been the gryphton Liang had talked about and scouted out the area a bit. Shaz hopped a fallen tree and disappeared into the woods. Serin pulled out some dried meat and unwrapped it and broke it into bite-sized pieces. The constant mist made her hair hang softly around her face and was now a cold that was sinking fast into her being. She pulled out her long heavy wool cloak and wrapped it around her and pulled the hood over her head to keep in as much heat as possible.

Serin examined the structure and found that it was quite roomy considering it was makeshift and not meant to be permanent. She too wondered if it had belonged to the gryphton at some point. She found herself thinking about Shaz again. It was all she seemed to think about lately, and it was making her crazy. *Maybe I should just tell him how I feel, then it will be out in the open and I can think about other things, but if I did, it would make things weird for sure. He has enough to worry about. I wish he would tell me what he was thinking more, I could help. Does he think he has to do this on his own? Men are so complicated.*

"I think we'll be safe here tonight," Shaz said.

Serin jumped, her pale skin turned paler, and she bumped her head on the top log. Shaz laughed but coughed into his elbow.

"It's not funny," Serin said.

She slugged him in the arm as he rounded the end of the long pole sticking out the end of the shelter. Shaz turned into the punch, knowing that she wouldn't hit him that hard and flexed his bicep.

"Yeah, it kinda was," Shaz strode to the horses that nibbled on the tall grass, "I'm starving, you?"

Serin glowered at him while he piled some branches together and pulled out a bit of dry kindling from his pack. He struck his knife against the stone and sent a spark into the tinder, and a small flame burst into life. Serin shivered in the evening's coolness, even with her wool cloak over her light-pink traveling tunic and skirt over leggings. She snugged the cloak and scooted a log near the fire and sat with her legs to the side and rubbed her arms. Jagwynn crawled up against her offering her body heat and Serin smiled and rubbed her ear. They sat and listened to the quiet night. The crackling of the fire made the perfect backdrop for the tiny specs in the sky to pop out through the small opening in the trees' tight canopy high above them which shielded most of the night sky. The night drifted on and Shaz found his mind settle more than usual and wondered if it was being outside and away from people. It's not that he didn't like people, but he found that the amount of energy he expended keeping an eye out everywhere he went and searching for other magic elements drained him faster. He relaxed into the soft ground and fell asleep.

The horses suddenly reared on their haunches and lurched, darting away. Shaz and Serin jumped awake, and Shaz yanked the sword from the sheath and leaped to his feet. Jagwynn scurried toward a tree. A crackling came from a branch high above them as if it were about to give way to something heavy perched on it. An enormous creature sat on the branch. Its lion-like hind legs were bent and sat under its body, and its lion's tail wrapped around the tree trunk. Its head was that of a huge bird of prey with a razor-sharp black beak and deep brown eyes staring down at them.

The brightly colored feathers started with a deep red at his head and flawlessly transitioned to orange and then to yellow as the feathers tapered off at its neck, exposing a bare human-like chest and arms that had sharp talons extruding from a lion's paw. It clawed the branch it sat on, posing a stress on the timber. The fang Shaz wore around his neck stung more than usual, and he thought about his conversation with Liang. Jagwynn hissed and arched her back, and Shaz reassured her.

"Not another one?" Serin said.

Serin moved to where her bow was lying.

"Another one?" the gryphton asked.

"Yes, another one, we have already killed two of you and injured a third," Serin said.

"Are you the one the old man spoke of?" Shaz asked.

Shaz's neck muscles tightened while his fingers shifted slightly on the hilt of his sword.

"You have seen my kind before? What old man?" the gryphton asked, his face contorted in confusion.

"The man in the village, he said he met you once," Shaz said.

"My kind, have no knowledge of this world."

"There were three of them. They were attacking the flocks of the villagers," Shaz said.

"A scouting party," he rubbed his chin with the back of his paw. The gryphton lunged out of the tree, landing softly in front of Shaz. "What do you know of me?" the gryphton asked.

"Stay back. Don't make me kill you too," Shaz said.

"Don't be silly human, I prefer steer, but will settle with mountain elk," Azrack said, licking his beak just thinking about it, "I am very hungry, but you don't fit my tastes."

"Well, that's nice to know," Serin said.

The persistent tingle of the fang against his chest acknowledged to Shaz that he could trust him.

"I'm Shaz and this is Serin. We were told that you lived in this forest. Why would there be scouts here," Shaz said, sheathing his sword.

"And you are?" Serin asked with a bit of annoyance in her tone.

"Azrack, tell me, did the scouts say anything to you?" Azrack asked.

He pawed at the ground with his talons that dug easily into the soft dirt.

"No, we were busy trying to kill each other," Shaz paused, "Why?"

"Groargoth," Azrack said.

"I take it, they are looking for you?" Shaz asked.

"So, it would seem," he growled.

"Why?" Serin asked.

"It's none of your concern," Azrack growled, spinning on her.

"Don't you *dare* growl at me," Serin snarled.

Serin stomped her foot and slapped her hands on her hips and gave him the stare of death. Azrack pulled back with his eyes wide.

"A feisty one, this one," Azrack said.

"You have no idea," Shaz mumbled.

"What?" She hissed.

"Remind me to stay on her side," Azrack said.

The pink in her cheeks grew under her pale skin.

"Serin, what's the matter, we're on your side," Shaz said.

Serin stormed off into the trees. Shaz was about to go after her, but Jagwynn padded after her and Shaz was sure she was in good paws and let her go and turned back to Azrack.

"So, what is going on? Why are you here? Why are there scouts here? Where do you come from?" Shaz asked.

Azrack paced back and forth a few more times, then sat down.

"I don't want to talk about it."

"I don't care if you don't want to talk about it. Your 'kind' has caused havoc and I need to know why," Shaz declared sternly.

"Fine," Azrack paused, then continued, "Groargoth is the king of my nation, a wicked gryphton. He killed his father. Blamed me and cast me out and apparently is now after this world too."

"What does he want?"

"Gold, silver, jewels, usually, but I wouldn't put anything past him," a sudden memory came to the forefront of his mind, "Blast," Azrack cursed, "We must get the orb."

"Orb?" Shaz asked.

"Before my king's death, he sent me on a mission to retrieve a vessel that held special powers. The king believed it had magic that would help him defeat the Ebon Hoards who used mages to battle with them."

"Gavin Rhill," Shaz muttered,

"What?"

"Nothing, where is it?"

"Groargoth has it," Azrack said.

Azrack slammed his fist into the earth.

"Hmm," Shaz paced, "How do we get it? Is it not common to have mages fight in your world?"

"No, we are a prideful race and don't need humans to solve our problems. And *we* don't, *I* will," Azrack said.

"But you'll need help."

Azrack lowered his eyes with shame.

"No, this is my fault I must do it," Azrack said.

"How is this your fault?" Shaz asked.

"They have been searching for me for many rotations. They must have finally found the rift," Azrack said.

"The rift?" Shaz raised one eyebrow.

"Yes, after I fled, there was nowhere to hide. I kept to the outer parts of our kingdom and found a tear in the shield of time. I discovered it led me here," Azrack looked around the forest he'd come to love, "to your world. I managed to keep out of sight of humans, well, except Liang."

"The old man? Why keep out of sight of humans?" Shaz asked.

"During one of my earlier visits through the rift, I explored, and upon returning to meet Ralti for news, I witnessed a great massacre of my fellow warriors. I determined humans were not ready for our kind, but I had nowhere else to go. I found this place and have had no trouble here," he paused then said, "Until you two."

"Where is your world?"

Shaz tapped his finger on his lip, ignoring the jab. Something didn't fit, though he couldn't figure out what.

"I am from the Northlands, on the other side of the Tarumite Mountains. From a time, separate from this one," Azrack replied.

"Just like the island," Shaz said, pacing.

"You are from another time also?" Azrack asked.

"Yes," Shaz said, then asked, "How do we find the rift?"

"I told you, I will go. It is my duty, and my men are still loyal to me. If I can send a message to Ralti, I can take over the army and stop Groargoth," Azrack said gruffly.

"What are you going to do to stop him?" Shaz asked.

"Whatever it takes."

"We have to destroy the orb," Shaz said.

"Why, what is it anyway?"

Shaz remembered the stories Grandfather used to tell and wondered if it was one of the objects Gavin Rhill used to store the powers he removed from creatures.

"Nothing good, that's for sure," Shaz said.

"That's comforting," Azrack said.

"I wonder where Serin is, we should be going. I better go after her,"

"Maybe she wants to be alone. She seemed pretty upset," Azrack said, "She'll be fine. There is nothing in these woods except mist."

****

Serin found she had no idea where she was, and being even more frustrated, picked up a stone and threw it as hard as she could into the misty dusk. She was even more upset that she lost her temper and for no reason. As the time went on, she had felt more and more aggravated but couldn't explain why. The rock bounced off something hard, sending a returning ping instead of a thunk from hitting dirt. She carefully climbed over, under, and around the trees, rocks, and debris. She saw a tall stone statue that sat in the middle of several hand-carved stones which stood several lengths tall. The statue was preserved well and there appeared to be nothing broken, however; it was covered in spongy moss from years of constant moisture.

"What in the world?" Serin asked Jag, who whined.

A line of markings was carved into the long rectangle box-like stones that were set in organized placements around the statue. The statue was a woman with long hair who wore a delicately carved braided headpiece and flowing gown. The same symbols on the stones were etched into a belt that hung delicately over her hips. The face had fine features, but it was the marks on her skin that struck Serin's curiosity the most. One of the statue's hands stuck out to the side while the other grasped at a pendant hanging from her neck. The marks in her skin showed a fine twirling and spinning effect.

They moved up her hands and partially uncovered arms, then resumed at her low-cut collar and onto her lower neck. Serin also saw them on her bare feet. Serin was perplexed at the expression on the statue's face. It was almost as if the statue had been turned to stone in the middle of speaking to someone. Serin rarely feared most things, but this time she had a pang of angst standing in a place she didn't know, and she wrestled with her comfort. Serin's eye stopped at one symbol she recognized from Shaz's sword and felt it with her finger. A heavy weight of sleep overcome her, as if she had just evoked a spell of some kind without knowing it.

She couldn't help herself and slid in next to a stone box and fell asleep. Serin woke and found herself standing next to the statue. It encompassed the surrounding area in a weird radiating force that shielded her from the world she came from. Serin found Jagwynn sitting on the other side of the force and she wondered why she had a grin on her face, as if a jaguar could smile.

A slight glowing red shimmer danced around the force and Serin's brain was screaming to run, but her heart was at total peace. She walked around the circular stone platform and noticed the spots where pillars once stood. As she walked around one of the boxes, a face hovered at the top barely inside and her heart skipped a beat. She turned to the statue in the center and the woman's eyes, now deep green, blinked and stared at her. Serin gasped to hold in the automatic scream she wanted to let out.

The woman's features softened, and a fleshy tone overcame the gray hardness of the stone. Serin's heart raced, and she wanted to run, but her body was frozen in place. The statue moved her head slowly, then her arms, and then her entire body was released from its permanent prison.

"What is your name, child?" the woman asked.

"I'm Serin Svirtari," Serin said before she realized she probably shouldn't.

The statue studied her deeply, then knelt on one knee and bowed to her.

"My queen, I am so sorry for your loss. I loved your mother deeply she was my best friend."

"What, wait, what? Queen? You knew my mother? How, where? I have so many questions. Who are you?" Serin managed.

The woman looked around, trying to find an explanation in her mind that wouldn't take too long to tell.

"I am Lady Fortuna from the water and sky Wyvern Nations," Lady Fortuna said, her voice gently echoing off the stone.

"What are you doing here, why are you here, who are these people?" Serin asked.

"I am the High Priestess of the Wyverns. Gavin Rhill entombed me here to keep me and my wyverns from taking him into exile. This is a portal, and these are my high court protectors," she said, "We have been here for hundreds of rotations."

"I'm not sure I understand what is going on here," Serin admitted.

"There is no time my Queen, you are the single heir to the crystal city, Srinna Vossa, and you must return and bring magic back to the world. Together with your Tooatha De Dannon, you must reach the crystal catacombs and find the secret entrance that will take you into the city. There you must take possession of it and become Queen. I will summon the wyverns, but you must search out the black wyvern and find your wyvern companion. You must bond to your Tooatha De Dannon in order to complete the circle," She said.

"My Tooatha De Dannon? What are you talking about?" Serin asked.

"The man you travel with, he is your Tooatha De Dannon."

"You mean Shaz the war wizard," Serin said.

Lady Fortuna gasped.

"The war wizard, you must under no circumstance leave him, you are his elemental mage, you *must* remain with him. He cannot die. You together are the key to stopping Gavin Rhill. You are now the new High Priestess and you have great power to heal and call on the wind to help you. You must strengthen your powers, for you will need them. Here, I will give you this." the woman lowered her pendant over Serin's head and let is gently fall between her breasts. She raised her finger and touched Serin's temple with the point of her first finger. A sharp prick etched into the softness of her flesh and Serin flinched. A hot sting moved over her body and into her limbs but subsided, leaving a numb prickling sensation, "My court is now yours. Even though they are in stone, they will help you in your journey. Now return to your Tooatha De Dannon. Waste no time, you must hurry. My queen, be careful! Gavin Rhill is sly and evil, and he will stop at nothing to get what he wants."

"I don't understand."

"Go, quickly!" her voice became agitated, her tone filled with fear and urgency. "There is no time to explain, only trust him. Gavin Rhill has secrets everywhere. People I trusted betrayed me. You must succeed!" the voice faded.

The image of the woman became the flat stone once more, and the stone crumbled. Serin jumped back as the statue shattered and fell to the ground, leaving only a heap of broken stone. Serin stood slightly slouched, partly from the numbness of her body but also from what she'd seen.

"Wake up, Serin, you have to wake up!" she told herself, slapping her cheeks and shaking her head.

The misty hues of the people faded back into darkness, and she hoped she would wake up any moment. She sucked in a deep breath and the frosty night sank into her lungs, but it didn't help. She sat down on a stone while the images of the woman and the people flowed through her mind. The same words in her mind as before, over and over.

****

Shaz heard a flapping and whooshing sound coming from overhead. He crept out from under the shelter. Several trees he hadn't seen before stood along the edge of the clearing. He wondered if it was the mist that hid them or if they'd wandered here. The whooshing deepened as it moved closer and the treetops swished back and forth as Azrack's stunning red feathers emerged from the branches. Leaves and small debris fell to the ground and Azrack landed softly, almost soundlessly. In his muscular arms, he held Serin's body.

"What have you done?" Shaz yelled as he gripped his sword.

The muscles in his neck pulsed heavily, and he gritted his teeth.

"I found her like this, in the forest. Why did you let her out of your sight?" Azrack asked, his voice strict with his own anger.

"I didn't- you said to let her be," Shaz said.

"She's breathing and I don't believe she is harmed. Very cold, but not hurt," Azrack said coarsely.

"Set her down here," Shaz said.

Azrack moved with a slight bouncy swagger, and he set her down. Her breathing was steady and Shaz could feel her pulse. He sensed a force around her and recognized it as magic. His mind raced through everything he had learned about magic, but nothing rang a bell.

"She means a lot to you, doesn't she?" Azrack asked.

"Huh? What, her, well-yes actually,"

"Ah, I see, that kind," Azrack said.

A minuscule smile crested the corners of his beak. Shaz blushed slightly and grabbed his blankets from the ground and wrapped them around her. Jagwynn came into camp and Shaz gave her a mysterious eye. Serin stirred and sat up bleary-eyed.

"What's going on?" Serin asked.

"Are you alright?" Shaz asked.

"What happened? How did I get back here?" Serin asked.

"I don't know, you tell me. Azrack found you and brought you back," Shaz said.

"I-" Serin paused and thought about how absurd it sounded and said, "I'm sorry I went so far," Jagwynn licked her face, "Yuck Jag."

Shaz chuckled, he knew how slobbery her kisses were.

"Hungry?" he asked. He gave her a small, wrapped package. She nodded and took it from him. "But we need to keep going, we are getting closer and I can feel the beasts not far off."

"From before?" Serin asked.

Shaz nodded, and Serin stuffed a big bite of food in her mouth.

"Meet back here when you have the orb," Shaz said to Azrack, who grunted and leaped into the morning sky.

"Where are the horses?" Serin asked.

"Blast," Shaz said.

Shaz whistled, and they picked up the saddles and followed their tracks. They finally found them several lengths away and quickly saddled them and started back toward where he believed the castle was.

29-I Can't Believe That Actually Worked

'It must be here somewhere," he said, running his hand along the rough stone wall.

The long wall ran along the east side of the old, deserted castle. Bright emerald-shaded grass shimmered as the soft misty rain fell from gray skies. A low rumble echoed against the mountain ranges to the east and west. Their hair hung straggly around their round faces from the hours in the damp air.

"What?" a small-framed man asked from behind the other.

He tried to reach around to inspect what the other was doing.

"The door. Get away Ladtwig, I am going to find it," he said, pushing his brother back.

"What door Turkill?" Ladtwig said.

Ladtwig sniffed while wiping his nose on his sleeve.

"The invisible door," Turkill said.

"But if it's invisible, how are you going to find it?" Ladtwig asked.

"I just will."

"But how can you, it's invisible?"

"Yes Ladtwig, I know that's what I said, the invisible door," Turkill said.

"Yeah, but invisible means you can't see it," Ladtwig scratched his chin.

"Well, maybe you can't see it, but I can," Turkill said.

Turkill kept his fingers on the rough, hand-carved stone wall.

"But how can you, you can't see something that isn't there?"

"What are you babbling about?" Turkill asked.

"The invisible door," Ladtwig said.

"What invisible door?"

"The one you are looking for," Ladtwig said.

"Oh yes, that one, I can't find it, it's invisible," Turkill said.

Shaz stared down from his horse at the two little men. He couldn't help but snicker under his breath, but Serin found the little men irritating and was losing patience. The notion of an invisible door perplexed Shaz until Serin elbowed him.

"Excuse me, is this the Reinholt castle?" Shaz asked.

Turkill and Ladtwig jumped, spun on their heels, and thrust themselves against the wall.

"Who are you?" demanded Turkill.

"Who are you?" Shaz asked with a smirk.

Ladtwig studied Shaz, then Serin, and then back to Shaz.

"I'm Serin, this is Shaz, and Jagwynn, and we are searching for the Reinholt Castle. We believe this is it, do you know for sure?"

Serin's beautiful voice gently carried over the bristling of the nearby branches. Jagwynn came up next to Shaz's horse, and the men jumped and held onto each other.

"She won't eat you. She might nibble a little though," Shaz said.

"Shaz, don't tease," Serin said.

The men looked between Shaz and Serin. Serin smiled at them, reassuring them he was teasing.

"I'm Ladtwig and this is my brother Turkill," Ladtwig said, bursting out.

"Shhh, are you daft? You don't just go giving out our names to complete strangers, you numbskull," Turkill said and covered his brother's mouth.

"Nice to meet you, Ladtwig, Turkill," Serin said.

She elbowed Shaz in the arm for not addressing them politely.

"Uh, oh yes, nice to meet you," Shaz stammered, trying to hide his laughter.

Their smitten expressions humored him. It happened every time men first meet Serin. Shaz knew of her beauty, both inside and out. It was hard to keep his growing feelings for her from confusing things.

"Well, then," Turkill said addressing Serin, "yes this is the Reinholt Castle but there's no way in. The door is invisible."

"No door, you say?" Shaz said.

Shaz and Serin had noticed as they rode over the hill that the peaks of the rooftop spires towered over a rundown roof and the remaining building was in total disrepair. The wall stood over ten feet tall and unlike the castle itself was in impeccable shape.

"I am sure there is a door here somewhere," Serin said.

"We have been over every inch of this wall and there is no door, that's why they call it an invisible door," Ladtwig said as he mimicked Shaz.

Serin blurted out a loud laughter, covered her mouth quickly, her eyes wide.

"Thanks," Shaz said.

Shaz dismounted and moved toward the little men, who took a few steps to the side. As Minca, the taller one, Turkill, came to just above Shaz's waist and Ladtwig was a few inches shorter. Serin dismounted and followed Shaz.

"So how do you suppose we get in with no door?" Shaz asked.

Serin shrugged.

"What do we do? We have to get in," Serin stated as she gazed at the towering wall above them.

"I could try to throw you and you can grab the top and climb up," Shaz said, stepping backward.

"What? No thank you," Serin said.

"We could throw one of them then," Shaz said. The brothers scowled at Shaz, took a step back, and resumed their catfight. "What you're small, I could throw you all the way up there and you can-"

"Can what? Fall to our death on the other side, no thank you," said Turkill.

"Thank you, brother," Ladtwig said, a sigh of relief in his voice.

"Your welcome, brother," Turkill said.

"Oh, so now you're not mad at each other," Shaz asked.

"Of course not," they said at the same time, looking at each other then back at Shaz.

The Minca stepped back with wide eyes as Jagwynn walked right next to them, and a small bead of sweat dripped from Turkill's face. Something caught Shaz's attention, and he maneuvered around the skinny little men and over to the wall. Several large bushes covered sections of the wall. Low rumbles echoed on the other side of the mountains as a storm steadily moved toward them. Serin followed Shaz, and as she passed Ladtwig and Turkill, she brushed up against Turkill's bare arm. Turkill went beet red under his chestnut-brown skin. Ladtwig laughed and teased his older brother. Serin ignored them and Shaz snickered.

"You have some admirers," Shaz said.

"Yes, so it would seem. Did you see that?" Serin said.

"Aye, but I am not sure what it was," Shaz said.

He pushed back the branches of a bush. The brothers began arguing over who was going to have the girl, barely lifting their arms while flicking their hands at each other. Shaz took several steps back from the wall to assess the distance and noticed a silvery glow that seeped from between the individual stones. The tendrils formed the shape of a door.

"Serin, over here. There, do you see it?"

"Yes, but it wasn't there moments ago, was it?"

"No, it just formed."

Shaz walked to the door and a large, nearly invisible handle appeared. He gripped it and gave a heave. The door budged slightly, releasing a small puff of dust. Ladtwig and Turkill were confused that he was trying to heave open a stone wall and broke into laughter. Shaz pulled again, and the door creaked open slowly. The stone wall materialized into a door which opened into a courtyard. The Minca clutched each other and shook. The horses whinnied and became restless.

"That's odd," Serin said.

"We better be careful," Shaz said.

Shaz stepped through the open doorway and scanned the area, and he determined it was a side gate to the complex. Several small pathways sunk into the overgrown weeds and grasses and ruined stone carvings of what appeared to have been people and different kinds of creatures scattered the courtyard. Shaz configured a route to take and noted the possible escape routes and hiding places. Serin was drawn to the heaviness of the weeds and overgrown plants. It felt like they'd been placed under a heavy burden. The sadness in the air was palpable as the clouds above sifted and swayed around the castle spires but didn't move on.

"This place is very sad," Serin said.

She lifted a wilting yellow rose. Shaz touched a ruined statue.

"Aye, and I sense a great deal of magic here," Shaz said.

"What kind of magic, exactly?" Serin asked.

She let the little flower droop again.

"Not shadow magic if that's what you're worried about."

"Magic, what do you mean, magic?" called Ladtwig from the other side of the doorway.

Turkill was holding him back, checking for booby traps and possible danger.

"They just walked through the door, you dim bat, and they aren't hurt," Ladtwig said.

"Yes, but they are not Minca, we don't just go in anywhere ya know," Turkill said.

"Nonsense, you're just superstitious," Ladtwig said.

"Remember what Murleck said about doors?" Turkill said.

Ladtwig stopped dead in his tracks and a small bead of sweat appeared on his forehead. He gulped heavily and slowly stepped back and took a deep breath. Turkill squared his shoulders.

"I'll go first," Turkill said.

"No, you can't, what if you're turned to stone?"

"Then you will know you are safe, do you want the treasure or not?" Turkill said.

Ladtwig let go of his brother's cloak.

"Ok, then hurry up," Ladtwig said.

"Oh, so now the treasure is more important than me, is it?" Turkill asked.

"Oh, come on, what do you want from me. First, you say I can't go through the door without being turned to stone and then you say you will and then you ask me if I want the treasure and then you say that I am just thinking of myself, make up your mind," Ladtwig said, throwing up his arms in exasperation.

Turkill thought for a moment, then with a large grin.

"You're right I'll go through the door," Turkill said.

"Fine, but what if you are turned to stone?"

Turkill gave Ladtwig a sideways glare and Ladtwig burst into laughter.

Shaz and Serin watched the two little men. Serin with her hands on her hips and a slight scowl and Shaz grinned with his hands in his pockets.

"You find this funny?" she asked.

"What, they're funny," he replied, chuckling as he flinched from her hardly-any-effort smack.

"We don't have time for this, remember?"

"Oh, come on, it's been a long time since anything good has happened and this is funny," Turkill and Ladtwig blankly looked about. Shaz couldn't help it and burst into a loud chuckle. Serin huffed, spun on one foot and started along the old broken pavers. Ladtwig and Turkill shrugged and continued to argue about going through the doorway. "You have to admit, they are funny," he said, as he caught up with her, "I see that," he said.

"Ok, fine, but we don't have time for this."

"It's good to see you smile, even if it's half of a smile," Shaz said.

Serin couldn't help to smile at him. He was right it had been a while since she felt happy, and she admitted they are funny little men. She still didn't know why she was grumpier than usual and tried to keep her mind from racing down that road. Shaz gave her a one-armed squeeze and went back to being serious.

"Now that we are here at the-" read the header stone on top of the heavy wooden doors to the entrance far across the courtyard, "Reinholt Castle." Shaz read.

Shaz rubbed his face. The years were not good for the castle. Several holes of different sizes had eroded into the walls. Many towers of varying sizes decorated the landscape along with several partially ruined sculptures. Remnants of extensive gardens scattered the court-yards.

"What is it?" Serin asked.

"The name of this castle is the 'Reinholt Castle,'" he said.

Shaz pointed to the door, but Serin could hardly make out any letters, let alone any words.

"How can you see that far?"

"It's part of my unique abilities," Shaz said.

He smiled his charming grin and Serin waved off his flirtation, but inside he was certain he was inadequate and a little angry that he was the one the universe picked to travel this horrible path.

"This makes this your home," she said.

"Yep, I guess so. Welcome to my piece of junk castle," Shaz said.

Serin turned to find his emotions were all over the place, but she didn't blame him. The Minca stopped arguing instantly when they heard Serin declare it was his castle. They ran through the doorway together without even thinking. Once on the other side, they stopped, looked at each other, and laughed at themselves and how dumb they both were.

"It's not all bad," Serin offered.

"Maybe after some good housekeeping it might be a great hole in the ground," Shaz said.

Serin smiled softly and put her hand on his shoulder. She guessed how he might internalize things. He knew little about his parents and his past, and now to find nothing left of them was sure to leave a bigger hole.

"This is your castle?" Ladtwig asked.

"It would appear to be that way," Shaz replied.

"I'm sure it was once a wonderful place," Serin said.

"Let's go inside and find what we came for and then leave," Shaz said.

A tiny movement, on a wooden arch that led to another walkway around the inner castle wall, caught Serin's eye and she took a second look, but the movement was gone. They reached the heavy wooden door and based on the dirt that filled the corners halfway up, the edges hadn't been opened for quite a long time. Small knotty holes eroded to the size of Shaz's fists, one being eye-level let him peek inside the door. The corridor was dark and there was more debris and shattered stone.

"It's too dark to make anything out," Shaz stepped back, "Here help me," he said, reaching for the solid iron ring handles.

"Let me, my lady," Turkill said, bowing at the waist.

"No, let me," Ladtwig said, butting Turkill out of the way.

"I'm stronger than you," Turkill said, shoving his brother out of the way, "And taller, besides a Lady shouldn't have to do a man's job," he said, as he winked at Serin and glared at Shaz.

Serin was in disbelief, and Shaz smirked. He remembered the first time he tried to do the same and got an ear full. Serin is a small woman but hardly weak and certainly not one to sit down and let men be in charge.

"Very well, go right ahead," she said, bowing in return, and stepped aside.

Shaz's mouth dropped open in surprise. He was sure she was going to unleash her enthusiastic speech on the roles of men and women. Turkill and Ladtwig grabbed hold of the handle and heaved and pull. Several minutes later and dripping with sweat the two little men released the handle and stood back panting.

"Are you done?" Shaz asked with half a smirk.

He towered above them, but he gave them credit for their tenacity.

"Uh-huh," they said.

Defeated, they stepped away and crouched over their knees as though they had just run miles. Shaz grabbed the handle confidently and jerked. His body recoiled as the gate sat encased tightly in its immovable prison. Shocked, Shaz scowled and grabbed the handle with both hands and jerked again with still no movement. He stood back confused and examined the door and heaved again. Several heaves later, the door hadn't budged. Shaz released the ring and a sharp crack sounded as it hit the steel plate it was mounted to. Shaz's hair was disheveled and his skin glowed pink from exertion. The Minca burst into laughter. Jagwynn continued to groom herself, and Serin watched in total amusement with her arms folded.

"It won't budge," Shaz said.

"I can see that," Serin said.

"We could take your horse and tie it up to the latch and have it pull the door open," Ladtwig said between blurps and sputters of laughter.

"No, I don't think that would work, but it was a good idea," Shaz said.

He was impressed by his quick thinking.

"Now what?" Serin asked.

"Magic, I think, but I have no idea how," Shaz said.

"Magic!" Ladtwig and Turkill said.

They started to run back toward the outer wall.

"Stop," Shaz called.

They froze, not wanting to make anyone use magic on them.

"We are not going to use magic on you," Serin said gently, "On the door."

Turkill turned around slowly. He saw them standing motionless and relaxed slightly.

"Have you ever seen magic?" Shaz asked.

"Nnno," Ladtwig said shakily.

"Then why are you so afraid of it."

"The curse," they said while shuddering.

"What curse?" Serin asked.

"It doesn't matter, there is no curse, but if you must, go ahead and leave," Shaz said.

Shaz returned to the large, locked entryway. He rubbed his chin, closed his eyes, and pictured the lock opening, but his mind went blank, completely blank. He stared at the lock again to give himself a mental picture and again nothing.

"Blast, it's not working," Shaz said.

Shaz slammed his fist into the wood and small splinters fell off the door, leaving slight remnants of letters.

"Serin, look,"

Shaz pointed to the door and Serin slid in next to him.

"Letters?" she asked, "What does it say, can you read it?"

"No, there's not enough of the letters to make anything out," Shaz said.

He stood back to examine the door.

"Maybe, it's just a sign that says leave your shoes at the door in order to enter," Ladtwig said.

Ladtwig burst into laughter, knocking himself off balance as Turkill blurted out a hearty guffaw. Serin gave him a disapproving frown and was about to chide him on his not-so-funny sense of humor.

"Hmmm?" Shaz said.

"You're not seriously contemplating this, are you?" Serin said.

"Well, what do you suppose? Besides, my feet are killing me," Shaz said.

He found a broken column and pulled his worn boots from his feet, revealing sweaty socks. Serin scrunched up her nose as the pungent odor wafted her direction. Ladtwig and Turkill began another bout of uncontrollable laughter and could hardly stay standing. Shaz stretched his legs a bit and wriggled his toes, finding amusement in Serin's distress. She was vigorously waving in front of her face to expel the fumes from her flared nostrils. He strode to the door set on making a joke when the latch clicked with a heavy thud. A sudden silence commanded the air as each looked from one another to the door and back.

"I can't believe that actually worked," Serin said.

"No, kidding!" said Turkill.

"I knew it," Ladtwig said, blowing on his clenched knuckles and rubbing them on his shirt in a polishing fashion.

"No, you didn't," Turkill said.

"Did too."

Shaz gripped the handle and tugged and the heavy door swung with ease, letting out a small burst of dusty breath.

30-Oh My Head

The inside was dark and gloomy. A thick weight sat in the air and seemed to push against the ground.

"It feels like a lot of sorrow happened here," Serin said.

She touched the wall as she entered.

"I wonder," Shaz said.

He picked up a once shiny helmet, now faded and rusty. He rolled it around and inspected the details and set it back on a large stone-shelf carved into the wall of the entryway.

"Are you coming?" Serin asked.

The Minca shook their heads and took a step backward. Shaz walked into the large, cavernous hall.

"There might be poisonous toads out there," Shaz said.

The Minca darted through the open door and rushed next to Serin, each picking a side. A grand stone staircase that once circled the outer walls of the room and led to the second level was now piled in heaps and resembled small tinker blocks a child would play with. Shaz stopped in the center of the room and examined how he was going to make it up the broken staircase. Serin stepped over a broken pillar and stopped next to Shaz, leaving the Minca huddling together.

"Poisonous toads?" Serin asked, out of the side of her mouth.

"Ya never know," Shaz said, "I need to reach the top."

He pointed to the upper deck of the staircase.

"Why?" asked Turkill.

"That's where the treasure is," Ladtwig whispered.

Ladtwig elbowed his brother in the ribs and shushed him, then gave him a secret signal of 'that's where we need to go too'. Turkill's eyes brightened as his brows reached his pure black hair, which was slicked back in a ponytail on the top of his head. The two nonchalantly scooted around the room, looking for another way up. Serin caught their secret signal but dismissed it. Shaz stepped over the crumbled stone at the bottom and climbed the uneven remains.

He scaled a short column on his way to another that had been blasted with something powerful. Shards struck the wall behind it so fiercely, and some were still embedded in the two-foot-thick bricks. With both hands, Shaz gripped the top of the pillar. His fingers slipped on the ruble that remained on the top. He wiped off a small section he could reach and gripped the edge, flexed his biceps, and with one foot on the column and the other against the wall, he pulled himself into a crouched position on the uneven surface.

"It's too far to jump," Serin said.

"I can do it," Shaz said.

He wiped his palms on his trousers and leaped to the next column. He gently swayed back and forth and jumped to a large shard protruding out of the wall and caught the edge with his hands. Serin threw her hand over her mouth and gasped. Shaz pulled himself onto the ledge and searched for the next move. A small shard stuck out above his head and he found a pole sticking out of the wall about six lengths up and to the left. It once held a series of chandeliers but had been thrust into the wall at great speed and shattered. The splinters had rotted at the intersection of the pole and the wall.

"There's got to be another way, I'm going to go around back to see?" Serin said.

Serin made her way around the debris and out of the main hall with Jag right behind her. The Minca on the other side of the room were having a hand war to see who was going to lift the other up onto a broken ledge, about six lengths up. Shaz jumped and grabbed the small handle and swung high, propelling himself to the next step that sat suspended on one pillar. He barely caught the edge and lifted his body with his fingers, which were white, and his muscles bulged under the stress.

With his chin barely above the stone, he bent his knees and dug his toes into the column. He struggled to crawl on top and steadied himself and took in a deep breath. Shaz rocked back and forth on his feet and lowered his center of gravity and swung his arms up and jumped, throwing his feet out to swing his body around the pole. He caught the wood snugly, but the splintered wood pierced his flesh. His momentum carried him around the pole, and he flipped up and landed in the center of his belly. Sweat dripped down the sides of his face, framing the anguished pain in his eyes from his ripped-up skin. He rested on his stomach and elbows and inspected the slivers covering his palms. Bright red blood seeped from the damaged skin and he gritted his teeth and steadied himself.

Shaz estimated the next leap would be easier if he were standing on the pole. He grunted with the exertion and pushed against the pole and lifted his body. Shaz wedged a foot between him and the pole, and with one leg still hanging; he balanced his three limbs on the pole. He gripped tightly while his thigh and core muscles flexed to create balance and lifted himself, so he was standing on the top side of the pole. Holding his arms out straight, he set the other foot down and tightened his core muscles and squeezed his buttocks to keep from teetering on the uneven surface.

If I can make it to that set of stairs, he thought. The old staircase was suspended on two remaining columns in the center of where the original stairs used to be, which was about four lengths above him. He wiped the blood off his hands, but that didn't stop them from bleeding. He worried the blood would make his hands slippery and he might not get a firm grip. Shaz sucked in and steadied his breathing. He tried to block the pain from his mind and determined he was going to have to use more energy to propel him far enough so that he would land in the center. He bent his knees, squatted, swung his arms back, and lunged toward the wall. Shaz stuck one leg out and shoved hard against the wall and twisted at the waist. The rebound off the wall propelled him to the solitary stairs, and he skidded to a stop before he ran off the other side. Serin returned defeated and searched for Shaz. Her stomach lurched out of her body when she found him so high.

"Be care-" Serin silenced herself. She knew how she would feel if it were her. Serin shoved her hands under her armpits and bit her lip to keep from saying anything. She knew Shaz was more than average, but it didn't stop her stomach from churning with uneasiness. But her eyes were glued to him. "You're almost there," Serin called instead.

For the first time since he started climbing, he looked down. Serin was about half the size she usually was, and the Minca, even though they had now made their way onto the ledge, resembled small children crawling on the ground. Adrenaline surged in his body as his skin heated up and his nerves tingled. The blood flowing through his body raced oxygen to his brain, giving him a heightened alertness. *Just one more gap to cross,* he thought. He clenched his fists, but it made them sting even more. He flung them open and shook them instead, but nothing helped.

Calculating the distance and rise of the final landing, he doubted he would be able to jump that far. There were no more rock shards or broken poles to use. *Well, I've come this far why not try,* he reasoned? *You're crazy, you're going to get yourself killed,* he argued. A surge of energy rose from his gut and filled his chest, and a certain kind of confidence filled his mind that hadn't before. He moved to the edge and bent his back leg as though he were at the starting line of a race and ran toward the wall.

"Is he insane?" Serin said.

Serin covered her face but peeked between her fingers. With his next step, he leaned his body back and shifted onto the wall. At first, it felt like he was going to fall, but then a suction drew him to the wall. As he reached the last short distance, he rotated his head and shoulders toward the landing. Shaz shoved off with his last step and leaped toward the landing. The vibrations of running, however, shook the decrepit stone, sending it crumbling to the ground. He was certain now that he wasn't going to make it. Serin's arms shot out like lightning and air engulfed him, throwing him over the chasm. The added force sent him somersaulting to a halt. He slammed into the adjacent wall with his legs straight up on the wall and his back on the floor. He gripped his head and tried to keep his brain from rattling around inside his skull.

"Oh, my head," he moaned.

"Are you alright?" Serin shouted.

"If you call getting my brains scrambled, then yes," Shaz called.

Shaz crumpled off the wall and pushed himself into a sitting position.

"There is no way I'm doing that to make it up there, just so you know," she yelled.

"Me either," Turkill yelled.

"Or me," called Ladtwig.

Shaz waited till the ceiling stopped spinning and stood up shakily. At the edge, he looked down.

"I'll look around and see if I can find some rope or something," Shaz said.

He disappeared behind a tall arched entryway, and a few minutes later, Shaz returned with some rope. He tied the rope around a remaining rail-post and tugged as best he could with his now poorly wrapped hands and kicked the rest over the edge. Serin hurried to the rope and hopped onto the swinging tendril. She wrapped her leg in the rope and crawled like a caterpillar. She made it to the top in no time. The adrenaline receded, leaving Shaz's pain receptors at full capacity. He gritted his teeth and helped her over the edge. Serin grabbed his hands and un-wrapped his feeble attempt.

"You could have died," Serin said angrily.

Shaz felt bad, but wished she trusted him more. He wanted to say something but figured nothing he could say would change anything. Serin took one of the cloths and dabbed the blood. His fingers were like raw sausages and his palms were purple and red with pockets of dark pink puffiness. She gathered water molecules from the air and set the ball of water on his wounds and washed the blood away so she could determine how many slivers there were.

"You're lucky, only a few big ones, it's mostly heat-burn. This might hurt," Serin said.

"Can't you use your magic and make the pain go away?"

"I could but I'm mad at you for scaring the tar out of me," Serin said.

"I'm sorry, I didn't mean to scare you, but you need to trust me if we're going to do this together," Shaz said, lifting her chin so her eyes met his, "Alright?"

Serin's brow softened.

"Alright."

"You have to admit that was pretty cool," Shaz said with a smile.

"I guess," Serin admitted.

Serin rested her palms over his, and her skin was cool. Her lips parted. She took in a deep breath and whispered the words that came naturally to her mind. She felt a certain power within her that was getting stronger, and a soft azure-blue glow shimmered as she began her healing magic. Shaz shivered at its tingle and heard a pop and then another.

"Thank you," Shaz said softly.

The warmth of the healing magic masked the pain, and he sighed. Serin wrapped the cloth around his hands again. Serin's head swayed, and she sat next to the wall.

"Are you alright?" Shaz asked.

"Yes, my head is just a little wobbly," Serin said.

"Just rest a minute," Shaz said.

"Thanks."

She rested her head on her arm that was crossed over her raised knees. Turkill popped up over the edge with a huge grin of achievement. It turned immediately to a scowl when he found her sitting against the wall.

"What did you do?" He growled, searching for Shaz.

Turkill lifted himself onto the edge with his arm and with his legs tight against the rope, heaved his body over the edge. He rolled onto the deck and marched over to Serin. He glared at Shaz the whole way, who rolled his eyes and went back through the doorway.

"I'm fine, just a little dizzy," Serin said. She was pale but alive with new strength and she wondered why this time using her magic was acting this way and the other times it didn't, "Where's Ladtwig?" she asked.

"Right here," he said.

Ladtwig's head popped up over the ledge, and Serin smiled. Serin gasped when she found a soft violet mark etched under the skin of each palm. It started as a dot and grew into the pedal of a vine-like flower. Soft vines wove around each other and wrapped around her hands. They grew longer, swirling and twisting in delicate details, and she shoved them under her knees to hide them. They reminded her of the marks on the woman in the stone statue.

"You alright?" Turkill asked.

"Yes, I'm feeling much better," the realization of her new tattoos shoved the hazy mist from her mind, "Let's help Shaz," she said, getting to her feet and catching up to Shaz, "It's a lot bigger in hear than it looks from the outside," Serin said.

The room opened to another large room. There was a large fire pit carved into the center of the floor with remnants of chairs and cushions, once used to bask by the fire, scattered around. The mid-day sun illuminated a faint brightness down two long open hallways which stretched the length of the room with six doors on each side that lead to what they presumed were sleeping quarters. Arched pillars held up the vaulted ceiling, some of which had been destroyed, leaving pockets of light.

Shaz peaked around a shattered door and found nothing but broken furniture. Ladtwig and Turkill made their way into the chamber, and Shaz and the Minca both assessed potential escape routes and likely dangers. Serin occupied herself with the details of a half-ruined drape still clinging to the rafters.

"What is this place?" Turkill asked.

Shaz and Serin shrugged.

All the way down the halls they looked in each room but found nothing interesting.

"Now what?" Serin asked when they met at the other end.

"I don't know, I really thought something would be here," Shaz said.

"Ouch!" Serin said and slapped her neck.

She pulled out a tiny stick that was like a dart and held it in between her fingers and inspected the minuscule thing.

"Is that a-" Shaz started, Turkill and Ladtwig hollered too. They were hopping up and down rubbing their arms and legs, "What is going on?" Shaz asked.

Serin yelped again, this time pulling a dart from her arm and another from her thigh. Shaz stood as the three of them swatted and grappled as though they were being attacked by a swarm of mosquitoes. Ladtwig opened his mouth to shout when a tiny dart embedded into his tongue and Turkill spun in circles, warding off the onslaught of tiny projectiles. Serin rubbed her skin.

"What... is...this?" she asked, pointing to where the first dart hit her.

"You're not going to like it," Shaz said. Serin's frantic look surprised Shaz, "It's alright, it's just a huge orange lump on your neck."

He didn't want to tell her about the one in the center of her forehead between her eyes, making her look like a three-eyed creature. With disbelief, she looked down at her arms and legs. Tiny bumps formed into large boils of different colors. She was consumed with disgust and fear until she saw Ladtwig. It was hard not to laugh. He was frantically yanking tiny darts from his lips and face. His tongue slipped out of his mouth and he couldn't put it back in. Drool slipped from the corner of his lips and his mumblings rang as he tried to explain to Turkill that he couldn't feel his lips. With distorted motions and gestures, he frantically explained that his tongue was also numb. Turkill was too busy hopping on one foot, rubbing his big toe that stuck out of the hole in his shoe. He tripped on a silver goblet and tumbled into the fire pit, coming to a halt as his head smacked the soot-filled bottom. Groaning, he laid down and stared into the sky.

"Why weren't you hit with any darts? Where are they coming from?" Serin asked, then remembered the movement outside in the courtyard.

"Yah, whry doth ihehh hanf?" Ladtwig mumbled.

"Dunno," Shaz said.

A tiny movement crossed his vision.

"There," Serin said, scratching her boils, "That's what I saw outside."

She scratched her forehead, finding that there was one right in the center of her face.

"You saw something outside, and you didn't tell me?" Shaz asked.

"I wasn't sure I had, but now I am," Serin fired back.

Turkill untangled himself from the debris in the pit while Ladtwig stared blankly, panting, and drooling like a dog. Tiny figures ran along the wood beams along the top parts of the remaining walls and door casings. They scaled the heights running one by one, like ants. The tiny soldiers leaped onto a large wood chandelier that was still hanging from the center vault. They floated through the air and landed silently and formed in ranks and encircled the rounded beams.

"They're tiny soldiers," Shaz said.

"I barely see anything moving," she said.

Serin covered her face with her arm to cover the boils. A female draped in tiny orange and yellow feathers drifted out from behind the soldiers and floated down softly and hovered, her feather-like dress flowing.

"Welcome Master Shaz," the tiny voice sang.

She was barely the size of his thumb, but her head was large for her size and she had bright green eyes with soft wavy blonde hair and pale rose-colored skin.

"Who are you?" he asked.

"Don't you remember me? I sang you to sleep when you were a baby and played with you as you grew."

"No, I'm sorry I don't," Shaz admitted.

"Never mind, you were young, and it has been many, many rotations since then," she sang.

"How many exactly?" Shaz asked.

"Three hundred and ten," the tiny woman sang.

"I still can't believe how time is so different, I had just had my twenty-third celebration," Shaz said.

"Yes, we have waited for such a long time for your return, protecting your home from those who would take your inheritance."

"You knew where I was? Inheritance?" Shaz asked.

"Treasure?" Turkill asked, now alert.

"Turkill," Serin said sharply.

"Who are you?" Shaz asked.

"I am the Whispmother of the Inugami," The Whispmother said.

The Whispmother raised her arm to signal an attack.

"No, no, they're with me," Shaz said.

The Whispmother lowered her arm.

"You have returned, yes?" she asked.

"Yes, and no, we can't stay, but I hope to return soon," Shaz said.

"Your father left you something, come I will show you."

"My father?" Shaz asked, looking at Serin hopefully.

31-How Bad Do You Hate Him

The night slipped seamlessly into morning as Azrack dipped back into the thick tree coverage and landed on a branch high in the treetops. The sky blended into the trees, causing a mirror-like reflection against the surface. He leaped out and landed on the ground. Azrack walked carefully and twisted his ears back and forth, listening. He scanned the distance and made his way to the barrier. He stepped into the middle of the tree and peeked enough to see to the other side. Azrack moved slowly and examined around the tear. He determined he was safe and crossed the energy field back into his world.

Azrack walked for about a length before he could take to the sky and found the trees had less color than they once did, and the earth was dry and crackly under the pads of his paws. He tried to stick to the trees with bright red and orange leaves to stay concealed, and when he felt it was safe; he soared into the sky. The coolness of the autumn sky felt good on his face. It was much dryer here, which was a pleasant change. Over a hundred Ebassia rotations had passed since he'd been this far into the land he loved, and he wasn't sure how much time had passed here. A torrent of emotions rages through his being and he struggled to keep his mind clear.

The further in he flew, the worse it became, and his heart sank. The once bright and vibrant colors were now dingy and dreary. Rivers barely trickled, and the landscape was void of roaming elk, steer, and buffalo. Dwellings once inhabited by healthy packs no longer existed. The anger he repressed so many rotations ago now opened the floodgates into a state of rage. It wasn't just him that was affected, but his entire world. How could he have been so selfish and stupid? How could he have thought that things would be fine?

He dipped in and around the falls that were once gushing with water and found hardly a trickle dripped off the jagged rocks. His heart plummeted into his stomach when he saw his home. Groargoth had destroyed it. He set down softly on the ledge and bent onto all fours and crawled into the small opening. The scent of ash wafted heavily throughout the cavern, even after all this time.

"It's not pretty, is it?" Lahonti said.

Azrack turned sharply.

"What are you doing here?"

"I don't know, I just had a feeling I needed to come."

"When did this happen?" Azrack asked.

The muscles in Azrack's neck flexed and his feathers ruffled as he breathed short, powerful breaths.

"There was nothing you could have done. I didn't want you to-" Lahonti said, "I'm sorry. I should have told you."

"No, you're right. There was nothing I could have done. Besides, it's not your fault, it's mine," Azrack paused, "What happened?"

"Groargoth destroyed everything and took your whole family prisoners. They are still alive, but they are servants in his court," Lahonti said quietly.

"And my men?" Azrack asked with a broken voice.

"Helios is at the Guardian Feather Academy in hiding. Brigdon is in prison for striking Groargoth and has been for a very long time,"

Azrack snickered and waved Lahonti to continue.

"Ralti and Jaxton are still in the Armada under Kronos, the new general."

"My armor, did they take that too?"

"No, I was able to sneak that and your weapons out. I have hidden them," Lahonti said.

"Good, I will need them," Azrack said.

"What are you going to do?"

"Kill him."

"Azrack I have to tell you, Groargoth has united with the Kronos and the Ebon Hoards," Lahonti said.

Azrack looked at him with glossy eyes, and Lahonti sank low to the ground.

"I understand," Azrack said.

"Here, take this," Lahonti said.

Lahonti slipped the gold ring he found off his toe and gave it to Azrack.

"What's this?" Azrack asked.

"It has given me good luck. I figure you're going to need it more than me."

"Lahonti, you have been a good friend. Thank you," Azrack said.

"Sire," Lahonti said, bowing.

"I'm not the king," Azrack said.

"But you should be."

Azrack kicked the debris in front of him and pushed his way past Lahonti.

"Send word to Ralti to meet at the falls tomorrow at sunset."

"Where are you going?"

"To fetch Helios," Azrack said.

A renewed sense of strength, fueled by emotions Azrack hadn't felt in a long time, sustained his long flight. He would have to fly high through the heavy clouds that shielded the mountain tops. These clouds were not the usual fluffy clouds that drifted across the sky. Legend says the mages used magic to shield the school from the Velshari. Whether or not it was true, didn't matter, all he knew was that they were different and hard to fly through and he struggled to break the barrier. Azrack inched upward, hoping that at any second he would break the other side. With one last stoke, he soared into the icy blue sky above. Azrack searched for the main building and set down on a light stone pathway.

"May I help you?" asked a pale-yellow and orange feathered gryphton, his eyes bright and welcoming.

"I must speak with Helios, my name is Azrack," he said.

"Azrack, you say," he said carefully.

Azrack scrunched his brows and scrutinized the old gryphton.

"Yes, is there a problem?"

"You tell me?" he said.

He slipped his paws into the large armholes in his hooded robe.

"I don't have time for these games. Will you send for him or do I have to go find him myself?" Azrack said.

"Helios did say you would act like this. He has been sent for and will be here shortly. Come, walk with me, I fear there is something troubling."

Azrack walked with him down a long path that circled several buildings.

"Who is the head monk here?" Azrack asked.

"That would be Mazark. Do you wish an audience?" the gryphton asked.

"Yes, I think so," Azrack said.

"Very well."

Helios darted from the sky and landed right next to Azrack. Azrack slammed his fist against his chest in a salute. Helios returned with the same.

"I can't believe you're back. What's wrong?" Helios asked.

"What makes you think there is anything wrong?" Azrack asked.

"Are you kidding, you wouldn't come all this way for an afternoon of tea," Helios said.

Azrack gave Helios the condensed version.

"So, it's true then," Helios said.

"What's true?"

"The legend, I was just studying it, in fact. The boy, Shaz you say is his name?"

"Yes, and he travels with a girl, Serin," Azrack said.

"She is an elemental?" Helios asked.

Azrack gave Helios one of those 'you're-an-expert-on-magic-now' looks, and Helios chuckled.

"I don't know." Azrack said.

"Mazark will see you now," the monk said, motioning his arm toward an open door.

They had walked to the center and were now in front of the main study. Several skylights allowed for light to rest strategically on different desks and shelves.

"Azrack, I am honored you have come. What can I do for you?" the grand monk said.

Azrack took his paw.

"I'm afraid I bring sorrowful news," Azrack said.

"The legend is true, Your Grace," Helios said.

The grand master half-sat-half-stood against the desk and rested his paws in his lap.

"I see. What do you plan on doing?" the grand master asked.

"We have to secure the orb from Groargoth and give it to the boy," Azrack said.

"Groargoth has the orb?" the grand monk asked as his brows lifted and his voice broke.

"It was our last mission before-" Azrack trailed off.

"King Ruadan sent for it," Helios said, watching the pain crest Azrack's face.

"I see," the grand monk said.

"May I ask how you know about all this?" Azrack asked.

"It has been our duty for centuries to study the history of our world and make a full account of its happenings. We have known about the legend for quite some time," the grand master said.

"Why didn't you tell anyone?" Azrack asked.

"Who would listen?" Helios asked.

"You're right," Azrack said.

"What about the Necromancer?" Helios asked.

"I'm not aware of that, Shaz mentioned he knows him, but I don't know what presence he has," Azrack said.

Helios rubbed his chin and walked in a half circle.

"Helios, I need you to help me find the orb. We have to get Brigdon out of prison and gather the armies." Azrack said.

"Of course, when do we leave?"

"Now, with your permission, Your Grace," Azrack said.

"Of course," the grand monk said.

"Let me get my things," Helios said.

"Thank you, I will have to rely on you more now than ever, my friend," Azrack said.

Helios nodded and hurried out of the room.

****

"Wait," Helios said as he grabbed Azrack's shoulder, "Things have changed since king Ruadan."

"How?"

"Political prisoners are kept in the fortress keep along with the treasure," Helios said.

"Perfect, then we free Brigdon and the orb at the same time," Azrack said.

"It's not that easy, it's heavily guarded. More so than before." Helios said.

"That's why we need Ralti," Azrack said.

"Need me for what?" Ralti said as he landed on the rocky surface.

"It's about time you show up," Azrack smiled.

"Yeah, I was keeping myself out of prison while someone I know was gallivanting around without a care," Ralti said.

"Gallivanting? I like to gallivant," Jaxton said, landing behind Ralti.

"No gallivanting for you," Azrack said.

Jaxton opened his mouth in mock sarcasm. Pontos plummeted to the ground and landed softly next to Helios. Azrack gripped them all in a tight squeeze and slapped shoulders.

"Good to see you, my friends," Azrack said with a lump in his throat.

"Same," they replied.

"All right enough of the male bonding?" Helios said.

"We need to free Brigdon and get the orb," Azrack said.

"That blasted thing again?" Ralti said and sighed.

"Yes, but this time, we are going to get rid of it for good," Azrack said.

Helios filled them in on the events and explained the legend of the boy. Ralti, Pontos, and Jaxton listened carefully, reacting with spurts of shock and surprise, and finishing with anger.

"What will it take to breach the keep?" Azrack asked.

"Won't be hard, it's the getting out that will be the task. Kronos is in charge of the keep," Ralti said.

"Yeah, and you thought he was ruthless before," Jaxton said.

"All right, so what do you suggest?" Azrack asked.

"How bad do you hate him?" Ralti asked.

"Why?" Azrack asked.

"You're going to hate him pretty good when you hear what he's done to your family," Ralti said.

"I know, Lahonti told me, I'll rip his throat out," Azrack growled.

"Good, because we need you to bring your can of whoop-ass if we are going to pull this off. I'm tired of all this ridiculousness. It's time we got our kingdom back," Ralti said.

32-Because You Have Returned

The tiny woman hovered over to the blank wall at the end of the room and held her palms out. Dust fell from a stone header that wasn't there seconds ago, and a large door emerged from the stone. She threw her arms out, and the door parted down the center, retreating into the stone wall. A spacious room brightened with crystal chandeliers that glistened in the sunlight from the skylights high in the ceiling. A gorgeous gold-spun comforter covered the length of a majestic deep-red-wood bedframe that sat in the center of the room, and the scent of fresh roses filled their noses.

Serin ran her finger along the thin table at the side of the entrance. Not a single speck of dust was on any surface. Even though it had been nearly three-hundred rotations since anyone lived there. Turkill and Ladtwig gaped in disbelief, standing paralyzed by the beauty and sparkle throughout the room. A long sofa sat at the front of the room and faced the bed, and large gold and silver vases filled with fresh flowers in bloom sat on side tables. Large-scale paintings hung on the walls depicting delicate scenes of landscapes they'd never seen.

Serin stared at her reflection in front of a large silver framed mirror. Displeased, she picked at the boils on her skin. She noticed a soft lavender mark at her temple where the High Priestess had touched her. It was the same as the delicate swirls on her hands. She wondered how long it had been there and why Shaz said nothing about it. She looked at the mark and an insecurity she didn't understand sank into her chest. *Would people think I'm ugly now? Will they be frightened of me?* She thought. Shaz picked up a small wooden picture frame with delicately carved vines surrounding two figures.

"Your parents," the Whispmother sung in his ear.

Shaz studied it for a moment and sat it back on the table's glass surface.

"This is amazing," Serin said.

"Aye, it is. What happened here?" Shaz asked.

"It was destroyed by the Velshari. Your father died protecting you and your mother, but only you escaped with the Dodjen. His dying breath was commanding us to protect this place until you returned," Serin put a soft hand on his arm as she listened to the sad news. "And this," she continued, floating over to another large door.

An armoire cracked open, and the door slid to one side. On the inside hung the black armor that his father wore in the mural in the woods.

"Where is the sheath?" Shaz asked, touching the empty metal hooks.

"Taken by the Dodjen for protection, one was taken with you, the other I know not," the Whispmother answered.

"Bairr Tiornecht," he guessed.

"Ah, yes, that would make sense," the Whispmother said.

"Why is that?" he asked.

"Because that is its place of origin, and if it is to be destroyed, it must be done with both pieces and the tools that created it."

"I have to destroy them all in their places of creation too?" he muttered.

"Yes, or bind them together as one," the Whispmother sang.

"Bind them together?" Serin asked.

"Yes, and become like the Gods," the Whispmother said.

"What will happen if I do that?" Shaz asked, his brows raised.

"You will draw the powers of the universe and become as the creator of this world. None can overpower you, but you must decide what kind of God you will become."

"What kinds are there?"

"Aren't you supposed to destroy them," Serin asked.

"That's what Ceros said, but how do I know if that is what is really supposed to happen? I don't even know or trust for that matter, this Dodjen organization," he said.

"There are many gods, but you are either Good and serve the Light or Evil and serve the Shadow," the Whispmother said.

"Can't a God be both Good and Evil?"

"I should think so, but what would be the point? If one is good, he does good, and if one is evil, he does evil."

Shaz didn't want to believe it was one or the other. *What about me, I am both, so what does that make me*? His reflection in the shiny black armor stared back at him. The only thing he saw was all the uncertainty of himself. Coins clinked and jingled as Ladtwig and Turkill tried to make their escape. Some hit the floor and rolled to a stop on the smooth polished floor.

"What are you two doing?" Serin snapped.

"Hurry!" Turkill said.

Ladtwig held up his clothes from falling off with the weight of silver and gold coins.

"Stop right there," shouted the Whispmother.

Her voice was loud and sharp, and she signaled her army to attack.

"No, they're alright, they won't make it far, plus I can share," Shaz said.

"You little rascals," Serin chided. Their cheeks reddened sheepishly and slowly let down their clothes. "Put it back, *all* of it!" Serin demanded, pointing her arm outstretched.

Hanging their heads low, they slunk back over to the chest at the head of the bed and dumped the coins. It took a moment for them to put it all back, and Serin tapped her foot on the floor with a tat-tat-tat. Shaz laughed and sat in a tall winged-back chair covered in cream velvet fabric that sat next to the sofa. Ladtwig slowly turned from the chest and with big eyes he peered at Shaz.

"I'm starving." Ladtwig said.

Most of the numbness in his mouth had worn off, and Ladtwig bent over his arm in a highly distressed fashion.

"Me too," Turkill said.

"I'm kind of hungry too," Serin said, "But we don't have much left."

"Do not fret," the Whispmother said, "We will return to the dining room where food will be ready," she said floating toward the door.

Shaz and Serin shared confused glances.

"How, the castle is in ruins, and there are no stairs," Shaz asked.

"Come."

Shaz rose, and they all left the room. To their amazement, the castle was now in impeccable shape. Where he had run on the wall, jumped and leaped to the top were now smooth stone steps. Complete with a deep-blue rug caressing each step all the way to the bottom. The stone walls reflected the light of three large chandeliers that were now hanging in the vast entrance room. Large silver vases with fresh flowers decorated tables around the room. The floor that was once filled with stone rubble, and debris was now clean with a brand-new shine.

"How did you do this?" Shaz asked.

"Because you have returned, we are allowed to rebuild the castle," said the Whispmother.

"I can't stay," Shaz said.

"We will continue to keep the Senate Sanctum Secure. Your father's protection spell is now complete."

"Senate Sanctum? My father's protection spell?"

Serin ran her finger along the crystal railing as they walked down the stairs. Jagwynn swaggered up the stairs and met them halfway.

"Your parents were part of an organization that held Senate meetings here for the Teorran Travelers, an unknown group within the Dodjen," she said floating next to him. "Your father gave me all his magic to keep you safe from the Jaduuk who hunted you."

"Jaduuk?" Serin asked.

"Four-legged beasts that hunt like wolves in packs that were brought from the underworld by the necromancer to be his foot soldiers. Most have returned to the underworld, but we have felt them near the castle from time to time, searching for you, I'm sure," the Whispmother said.

"They must have been what I heard in the forest," Shaz said.

"What are they exactly?" Serin asked.

Her imagination took her to something awful.

"I suppose they won't be far behind," the Whispmother said.

Shaz and Serin grimaced. She led them to the dining room where they found beautiful tables and chairs finely decorated with bright golds, blues, and soft cream colors. The soft colors and sparkling crystals everywhere from vases to lighting fixtures brought a welcoming warmth to the room. They didn't have torches or flames in them, and Serin wondered how they illuminated the light.

"Please sit," the Whispmother said.

Shaz sat on one side while Serin and the Minca sat on the other. Ladtwig and Turkill climbed into the chairs. The table's surface was even with their necks. Food, plates, goblets, and silver utensils

appeared on the table. The aroma of cooked meat and steamed vegetables wafted from the center.

"This is magic," Turkill said, smacking Ladtwig's hand as he
reached for the drumstick of the golden-brown roasted turkey sitting
in front of him.

Ladtwig argued back, smacking Turkill's hand away from his
and stuck his tongue out.

"So, I'm starving, it's been moons since we have eaten this
good, and I'm tired of dried bread."

Ladtwig gripped the juicy bone and ripped it from the body
with a sucking sound. Turkill crossed his arms and huffed. Ladtwig
took a big bite and tore the meat off the leg. Turkill licked his lips in
eagerness and gave in to the rather large grumbling in his stomach.
Shaz and Serin filled their plates with biscuits, gravy's, vegetables, and
roasted meats. Shaz popped a bite of a stuffed mushroom into his
mouth.

"We have much to discuss Master Shaz when you are finished,
we will meet in the parlor," the Whispmother said.

She floated above them and left the room.

"This really tastes good," Shaz said.

"Yeah, it does," Serin agreed.

The Minca agreed vigorously and shoved more food into their
mouths. Serin sipped sparkling cider from her goblet.

"What do you suppose the Whispmother needs to talk about?"
Serin asked.

"Not sure, I guess things about the castle. I wonder if this castle
has an armory," Shaz asked.

"Armory, for what?" Serin asked.

"Weapons, those things that are chasing us won't give up.
They'll just keep coming until they find us, and I don't want to be un-
prepared."

Serin shivered and thought about the night they woke to the sounds of hooves beating against the ground. Shaz said that it wasn't horses, but more like a beast that stood on hind legs. Either way, she didn't want to ever meet them, however; she was certain it would happen, eventually. Several minutes later, Serin finished and took the soft silk napkin and dabbed at the corners of her mouth.

"Turkill, Ladtwig, why don't you make yourselves busy while Serin and I talk with the Whispmother," Shaz said.

He scooted his chair in.

"Why can't we come?" Ladtwig asked.

"Because you numskull, it's about magic," Turkill interrupted.

"Fine. But I'm not a numskull, you are." Ladtwig said.

He shoved another piece of food into his already-half-full mouth and gave Turkill a steely glare. Serin tucked in her chair. The brothers ensued another argument over who was more of a numskull and why.

"I can't believe they can eat so much," she said as she met Shaz at the end of the table.

"I heard that," Turkill called.

Shaz and Serin chuckled and left the room. They crossed the entryway, chose the first hall on the left, and went down a wide-open corridor. Several large hand-painted pictures protected by intricately carved frames hung from top to bottom. The faces that peered back at them showed similar features. They were obviously the family members from long ago. The end of the hall opened into another large room. Several chairs and small desks lined the rounded walls, all facing the center of the room. The room had tall walls that vaulted at the ceiling with several arches and a few windows toward the upper part.

"What is this room for?" Serin asked.

"Maybe the Senate room," Shaz said.

They continued through the castle and found another room.

"I guess we found the armory," she said.

They wandered around the vast room admiring the weapons of superior craftsmanship that rested in cradles on the walls and in isles of the room.

"This one would be perfect for you," Shaz said, holding out a deep-blue bow, "it's a Whisperwood," Shaz said, tapping the engraved sign under the hooks it sat on. Seeing her perplexed stare, he said, "It just felt like you."

Serin took the bow, her finger brushing against his, which caused his energy to ripple through her body. She faced the other way and twisted her wrist back and forth in order to cover her growing need for him. She now understood his full intentions and occasionally his next thoughts. *Why does he make me feel this way, what feeling is this anyway?* She thought. Love was a part of it, but there was something different, more like a need.

"Yes, I like the bow, and I like the name too," Serin said.

Shaz rummaged around for some leather straps and tethers to strap it on her back and helped her secure it comfortably, and she smiled at him.

"What about you?" she asked, as he fastened the last buckle.

"I have my sword and bow already, but I stocked up on some short blades and a couple daggers."

He patted his body where he hid them under his clothes, and she figured he must have done it while she was wandering the other side of the room. Shaz gave her a few daggers to pick from, and she tied one on her other thigh and tucked one into the small of her back.

"I guess we need to find the parlor still. I wonder if the Whispmother knows where we are?" Serin asked.

"She does, we've had little escorts following us since we left the dining room," he said.

"Where?"

"They're pretty good at blending in, but I can sense them and every once in a while, I see one."

33-They Are Record Keepers

They left the room and climbed the stairs. A few more halls and they came to the parlor. It was a square room with chairs and sofas surrounding a stately fireplace on one wall. The Whispmother hovered at the front of the fireplace and welcomed them to the room.

' We have much to discuss, please sit," the Whispmother said.

Serin eased the bow off her back and sat on a soft orange chair. Shaz tossed one leg on the other and propped his ankle onto his knee and sat back on the sofa. Jagwynn curled up next to the fireplace and rested on her paws.

"So, what do you want to discuss?" he asked.

"Is the Senate going to resume its meetings?" she asked.

"I was not instructed on this matter. Tell me about the Senate," he said.

"Our world began with the God of Glory, who desired to be mortal for a time. He gave up his deity and dwelt on Edenocht, creating a fair maiden whom he took to wife. She bore three sons and a daughter. When the God's time was up to live on Edenocht, he left the first-born son later known as the Tooatha De Danann, as the leader.

The other two were angry saying they were cheated out of their inheritance. Their mother tried in vain to get them to get along, but they separated from each other, each going their own ways. The daughter remained to care for the aging mother, and when the mother died, she was lifted up as the Sun Goddess. The brothers never returned," she paused.

"Go on," he said.

"The Tooatha De Danann being in favor of the father was a race of supernaturally gifted people who lived in the North Country of the world. They made it their priority to study occult lore and sorcery, druidic arts, witchcraft, and magical skill. Eventually, they became the sages of the elements. Four cities were dedicated to these studies, Srinna Vossa in the sky, Akraven on land, Loig Na Tine in the volcanic mountains, and Bairr Tiornecht deep in the earth." Shaz felt for the tablet under his shirt as she said this. "Ah, you already know," she said.

"Yes, we found this in the ruins in the forest, and Grandfather taught me all this as a youth," he said, pulling out the gold plate.

"Another Senate Sanctum," the Whispmother said.

"Why did it just appear when I came through the Teorran of Time barrier?"

"All of them returned to their original existence."

"How many are there?"

"Twelve."

Whistling in astonishment, he shifted in his seat.

"Then you know each city's legacy," the Whispmother stated.

"Yes, from Srinna Vossa came the 'Binding of the Crypt' scroll which defies death. The earth city created the spear which no battle was ever won against the man who held it. From the Volcano, came the 'Cauldron of the Gods', no company ever went away from unsatisfied, but it usurps power over them for its payment of total satisfaction. The city in the mountains brought the 'Honor Blade', a sword which no-one ever escaped. Once it was drawn from its deadly sheath, no one could resist it," Shaz paraphrased.

"Correct, and the Velshari?" she asked.

"An over-zealous group of elemental mages that became greedy and fell under the control of Gavin Rhill."

"Gavin Rhill found a way to travel back and forth from the underworld and found powerful shadow magic this world had never seen. With it he overthrew Ar-ti-bus, the first ruler of the Velshari, by casting him into a prison within the underworld," the Whispmother said.

"What about the daughter?" Serin asked, "What happened to her?"

"It is unknown what happened to her. Her mother, The Sun Goddess, was angry and formed a secret organization of Tooatha De Danann calling them 'Agents of Light' or the Dodjen. It was their purpose to supervise the Velshari, to know what the Shadow was up to. It was under the rule of Ar-ti-bus that the Velshari began stirring up the hearts of the Tooatha De Danann to go to war against the descendants of the second son who were the Fir Bolg. They were the most hostile and become a ravaged race. Though they had much gold, precious metal, and land. The leader of the Tooatha De Danann, at the time, was weak-minded and under the advice of his trusted adviser, Ar-ti-bus, he feared they would not be strong enough to go against the Fir. So, he sent Ar-ti-bus to make arrangements to marry the daughter of the ruler of the Bair Tiornecht, or the second privileged of the Gods, to unite forces to take over the Fir Bolg."

"What happened?" Serin asked.

"The union was made, and the Tooatha De Danann and the Bair took fleets to the land of the Fir Bolg, to take it by force. The leader of the Tooatha De, however, was convinced that his own men would retreat after seeing how strong and powerful the Fir Bolg had become. So, he commanded to have all their own ships burned once they made port. The Fir Bolg was highly superstitious and believed the Tooatha De had come in on mists of the sea because of all the smoke. This created fear, confusing them, which gave the Tooatha De the advantage and they were able to defeat them."

"That's the same story Grandfather told," Shaz said.

"It's no story, this is our history," the Whispmother said sharply, "After the great and terrible battle, the Fir Bolg surrendered and entered a pact agreeing that they would never go to battle against the Tooatha De Danann and would forever be subject to them. This wasn't enough for Ar-ti-bus who convinced the Tooatha De to force the Fir to give up their supernatural abilities and be subject to being completely mortal, like their mother who GOG made of the earth."

"Where is the Fir Bolg now?" Serin asked.

"They are the human race, they were forced out of the Northlands and settled in the middle part of our world, here in this realm and a few others," she said, motioning to the world around her.

"That makes sense," Shaz said.

"There's more," the Whispmother said.

"More?" Serin asked.

Serin had never heard of this till now, and her mind raced around where she came from.

"The God of Glory returned after his affairs were finished to find what his sons had done and cursed the land with all kinds of wild creatures with varying powers or abilities to overpower the sons. The sons, however, withstood them and after another war, the creatures and the sons made alliances in order to stop the bloodshed and have peace," the Whispmother sagged slightly, sitting lower in the air than before. "That is when the Realms were created, to give each race a chance to live within their dominion without strife. Yet, this did not keep the Velshari from tainting the minds of the people and evil continued to creep into their hearts. The Teorran Travelers moved through the time realms, keeping things in order and securing ancient artifacts."

Two little soldiers floated down from the wood moldings near the ceiling and held the Whispmother's arms to keep her floating.

"We can finish later," Serin said, concerned for the Whispmother.

"Almost finished," she said thanking her guards, and Shaz wondered if she was required to share this information for some reason, "Upon his return GOG, seeing the destruction from his family, made a prophecy. He would send a boy-child to bring balance back to the world. He would possess all powers needed to correct the imbalance that greed and evil have wreaked on this world." A knot formed in Shaz's stomach as he knew what she was about to say. He rested his elbows on his knees with his chin sitting in his palms. Serin looked between the Whispmother and Shaz. "That boy-child is you, Shaz," the Whispmother said.

"I know, but how can I save this world from Gavin Rhill, who clearly understands a great deal more than me?" Shaz blurted.

It was on his mind and had been for some time. Serin sympathized with him and the Whispmother. With a slight swish of her finger, she sent a gentle surge of air to hold the tiny queen up. The Whispmother was surprised.

"I'm sorry, was I not supposed to do that?" Serin asked.

"You are an elemental of air?"

Serin nodded hesitantly.

"And water and healing. You should see her healing magic," Shaz interjected excitedly.

"Of course. Why didn't I see that?" the Whispmother said.

"See what?" Serin asked.

"Yes, the lost heir," the Whispmother said.

"What are you talking about?" Serin asked.

"That is why you have been chosen to be bonded and complete the circle, to unite against Gavin Rhill," the Whispmother said.

"What do you mean, lost heir?" Serin asked.

"What does that do? What is this bonding?" Shaz asked.

"A process which completes the cycle of magic and allows both parties to complete their training. You will find the information you seek in the Crystal Catacombs and there you will complete the bonding," the Whispmother said.

"Where is the Crystal Catacombs?" Shaz asked.

"In the realm of the Bair Tiornecht Mountains," the Whispmother said. "I have extended myself too much. I must rest, we can talk more tomorrow," the Whispmother said, motioning to her guards to escort her to her quarters.

They floated over to the parlor door and disappeared into the lights shining in from nearby windows. Shaz stood up and started to the door, and Serin picked up her bow and followed him out of the parlor. Serin's thoughts raced through her interaction with Lady Fortuna, and she remembered she told her she needed to bond to Shaz too. She didn't think too much of it then, but now a new emotion stirred in her chest. A feeling of longing, as though something was missing from her being. Her mind kept running through the fact that the Whispmother didn't answer her question about the lost heir, but a kind of truth sat in her soul that she already knew she was the lost heir she spoke of. Shaz and Serin spent the rest of the afternoon exploring the castle in near silence as they digested the information. Turkill and Ladtwig wondered about in their own exploration, but they weren't as quiet as Shaz and Serin.

Serin took a walk around the courtyard and found the yellow flower from that morning. The flower was bright and standing tall, and she smiled. The castle grounds had been released from whatever force was on it before, and the grass was bright and green, and the flowers and plants grew with vigor. The statues had been rebuilt, and Serin wondered about the details and the creatures. She found one that looked like Azrack and she smiled. She found a half wall of polished stone at the top of a terrace on the west side and lifted herself onto the top. Her legs swung slightly, and she made a note of the way the three purple moons eased into the sky. Shaz walked toward her with his hands in his pockets and the riveting reds and oranges of the sunset captured behind him.

"See, I told you it just needed a little housekeeping," Shaz said.

Serin smiled.

"You have a magnificent home," Serin said.

Shaz could hear the hint of jealousy, but not because of its size and beauty, but because of being his. She had told him she traveled with her father a lot as a child, but when she got older, she would stay with relatives in the highlands for months at a time. As travelers, however, they would move around as well, so she never had a solid place she called home.

"The Whispmother has made up bedchambers for everyone. When you're ready, I'll show you which one is yours," Shaz said.

"Alright," Serin said.

Shaz leaned against the wall next to Serin and his arm brushed against hers. The sun crept a little lower behind the rolling hills and Serin yawned.

"Things are going to get crazy and I don't know how things will work out, so before I don't have another chance, I need to tell you something," Shaz said.

"Alright," Serin said.

Shaz moved, so that he was standing in front of her, and he scooted in close. Serin's heart raced, and she looked into his eyes. Shaz's heartfire surged, and Serin shivered with the wave of warm heat that came from his body. Shaz put his hand on the side of her face and she closed her eyes. She wanted this moment so much, but if she let her love for him get in the way of him doing what he needs to, then she could never live with herself. Serin pulled away and lowered his hand.

"Shaz, I want this, believe me, but I don't think this is a good idea and I'm afraid if this were to get in the way," Serin said.

"It' won't," Shaz said.

"You can't guarantee that," Serin said.

"Serin-" Shaz started.

Serin pushed him away and hopped off the wall and went into the castle. Shaz put his hands in his pockets and leaned against the wall. He was certain that their love would be a good thing, and he was glad she wanted him, but he understood she needed to come to that realization on her own time and exhaled a deep breath.

****

Shaz woke with a start and sweat dripped down his bare chest. The pelting rain beat against the tall window in his room. He searched the large room and found that nothing was there, nothing but the coals crackling in the fireplace and the bedside table. He pulled off the covers and rested his feet on the cold floor, rubbed his eyes, and pulled the disheveled mess of hair out of his face.

It was just a dream, he said to himself. He knew he was trying to convince himself, but it didn't help. He was certain it wasn't just a dream and the hairs on the back of his neck prickled sending shivers down his spine. He moved to a polished table across the room and watched out the window. Jagwynn stirred by the fire but didn't wake. The darkness covered the hills and mountains. It wasn't until a bolt of lightning struck that the sky illuminated the land's features. Shaz listened to the rhythm of the rain that came in waves as the winds thrust it around the sky and hit into the stone walls and glass. His body ached from the wear of the night terror and the image of the shadow man from his dream stuck in his mind.

He pulled a shirt out of the tall armoire and slipped the soft silk on and opened the door into the dimly lit hall. His bare feet were silent on the polished stone, but his trousers bushed in the silent night. He scaled the long-rounded staircase and into the kitchen for a drink of water. He finished the entire glass and set it on the glossy counter and leaned against it. His mind raced with the images and he struggled to make sense of all the commotion. Dreams never made sense anyway, but now with the mix of magic and foretelling, he was even more confused.

He tried to pay attention and commit to memory the things that stood out. Like the shadow man's left eye that peaked out from under the hood. It was black but had a reflective quality and Shaz could see his reflection, and Serin's, even though she wasn't there. A long, dimly lit tunnel, and the fire weaver from the travelers. The thing that bothered him the most, however, was the deep pit in his stomach that was always there when these dreams came. The dream world seemed to intensify its strength, as though something was trying to overcome him when he wasn't able to fight back. He was sure that the hair on the back of his neck and the pit in his stomach was how he experienced his shadow magic but couldn't figure out which part of the dreams were dreams and which parts were shadow magic manifesting somehow.

When he thought he had made enough mental notes, he tried going back to bed. At the bottom of the stairs, a thought from the back of his mind emerged. There was nothing or no one in the impressive entrance hall. The hairs on his neck prickled, but he didn't have the dread in his stomach and guessed it meant something else.

He entered the dim walkway. At the end he went left, obeying the instructions in his ears. He rounded a few more corners and ended at a set of downward stairs. The wood railing was warm on his skin, unlike the cold stone. The aroma of mint and musk filled his nose, and his mind whirled around what could have been memories. At the bottom, the carved walls faded into the eroded effects of a stone cavern. It wasn't particularly large, but enough that he could stand comfortably. At the far side, a flat wall sat surrounded by the uneven chiseled rock.

"That's odd," he said, breaking the silence.

"It's an earth portal," an old and weak voice came from behind him. Shaz jumped and wished for his sword. An old man walked with a slight hobble toward him, "Can you find the face in the rock?" he asked.

"Aye," Shaz said.

He couldn't help but stare at the old man.

"It has been a long time. You don't remember me, do you?"

"No, I'm sorry, but you look just like Grandfather."

The old man chuckled.

"Mathieu is my brother. My name is Inelius." Shaz felt a tingle of magic in his touch as they shook hands. "You have grown strong. Mathieu has done well," Inelius said, "This earth portal is activated with magic. The energy the portal emits is so subtle that only those with magic, who have trained themselves to recognize them, can find them."

"Where did you come from, you weren't here earlier, were you?" Shaz asked.

"No, the Whispmother informed me of your return and I only now arrived," Inelius said.

"From where?" Shaz asked.

"We shall get to that at a later time, but first, the earth portal," Inelius said.

Shaz followed his slow frame toward the end of the cave and noted a handful of symbols.

"What are these for?" Shaz asked, pointing to symbols that surrounded the face.

"I don't see anything?"

Inelius leaned into the drab-gray of the rock.

"Symbols, like the ones I found in the cave back home," Shaz said.

He put his first finger on the stone and traced one.

"Ancient symbols?" Inelius said, "I have never known anyone to have seen them, you are the first. Can you read them?" he asked.

"Aye, but it doesn't make much sense," Shaz said.

"Each portal is different and has a different protocol to activate them," Inelius said, "You must figure it out for yourself, that is what tells the portal who you are."

"They're alive?"

"Oh, yes, you see, they are record keepers. Commissioned by the Gods to document history and relay truths to those who worthily seek it."

"So, they tell you information?" Shaz asked.

"Think of it this way, energy is information, it's a conscience. When energy is present, there is conscience. A kind of intelligence that is different from our own."

"How do you know when you are at an earth portal?" Shaz asked.

"You sense something change in your body. Like a sensation in your hands or a tingling. Perhaps you will observe different colors surround an object or rock formation. Earth portals exist within the realm they are in, and there is always something unusual about the surroundings that you must be in tune with." Inelius said.

"How do you use one?"

"You must first clear your mind, then create an energy ball that you can connect with the energy of the portal," Inelius said, tapping his withered finger on his wrinkled temple.

"How do you do that?"

"Like this," Inelius held one hand at his chest with his palm facing down and the other at his pelvis with that palm facing up. He rotated his hands, swapping their positions with each other back and forth as though there was an invisible ball in between them. "By rotating your hands, you take the energy from your core and channel it into this energy ball. Once you have enough energy to offer, you let it go, sending it toward the portal," Inelius gently shoved the ball outward, letting the glistening purple glowing ball hover toward the wall. "You must open your imagination. A faculty that is open to possibilities. You are not making things up, but if you don't have a good imagination when a piece of information comes to you. You will dismiss it as impossible and doubt. This is the hardest part, even for powerful magic users like you," Inelius said.

Shaz mimicked Inelius and rolled his palms around an invisible ball. He focused on the feeling the magic made inside his body and imagined the magic coming from his core and filter into the ball. He let his imagination take over him and open his mind to possibilities. *What do I have to lose? Nothing's the same, anyway.* His logical, critical mind reasoned.

Inelius stood with excitement as the brilliant colors flowed from Shaz's body into a dancing sphere.

"Is there something wrong?" Shaz asked.

Inelius coughed to clear his voice.

"No, nothing wrong, but everything right. Do you feel the energy, that is your magic?" Inelius tried to control his excitement.

"What do you mean?"

"Magic is energy, its conscience, intelligence, alive," Inelius paused, "Now, just let it go," Inelius said, "Oh, wait, but first, you must always gain permission to interact with an earth portal, or any portal for that matter."

"How many portals are there?"

"No one knows. Some are dormant, but most are in a state of being active. Earth portals are not for traveling through time and space and take you to another realm or place. They offer information, enlightenment, and instruction. You don't know what they have to offer until you interact with them and some of them have to be called upon by those who protect them," Inelius said.

"Like the stories that Grandfather used to tell," Shaz said.

"They aren't stories, dear boy."

Inelius said, slipping his hands into the armholes of his light blue robe. His white under-robe blended in with his pale aged-skin.

"Yeah, I know that now," Shaz said, a hint of dread in his voice. "May I?" he asked the portal.

A small breeze flowed over his body. Even though they were under the castle and there were no windows or doors to the outside. Inelius reassured him and he released the energy like Inelius did. Shaz's colorful magical-ball hovered for a moment and then merged into the stone. The stone-like eyes squinted and fluttered before opening wide.

"How may I assist you, Shazmpt?" it asked.

The voice was deep and almost rumbled in his chest.

"What earth portal is this?" Shaz asked.

"I am the portal of the portals. I teach how to use the time portals. I see that you have your medallion already," Shaz nodded, "Good, let's begin."

Illuminated images flowed into Shaz's mind from the rugged rock-face. Images in different forms: a mirror image from a river flowing under a stone bridge in the forest forming a perfect circle, the high-pointed arch high in a dark sky, oval stones set between pillars and many more. The images changed from the different portals to showing how to use them. Showing pictures of objects that act as keys and how they work in the portals. Symbols faded in and out, telling Shaz that each symbol had a meaning and did different things. His mind filled with new understanding.

After several minutes, the images faded away. The collar of his blue silk shirt was now damp from sweat and was cold on his skin. His hair flipped back as a breeze blew past him. Shaz faced Inelius and was about to speak. Inelius stirred from his trance-like state, and stopped him before he could say anything,

"What is said is only for the one who seeks it." Inelius said.

34-Not That Thing Again

The gryphton's keep was buried deep inside the Tarumite Mountains, which was an exceptionally tall and rugged formation that encompassed the majority of the southern part of the realm. The king's fortress was almost like a mini-city inside, with vast caverns and dwellings. Azrack and the crew crept along a ridge to the top and left of the main entrance and huddled behind the jagged peaks which grew out of the rock-face in random patterns. Azrack lowered to the ground tightly, and Helios pulled out a map of the structure.

"This is the first print of the fortress after it was built, and I believe there are access points that aren't used anymore and maybe even forgotten about that we can use," Helios said.

"Where did you get that?" Azrack asked.

"The academy," Helios said.

"Why would the academy have a map of the Fortress?" Jaxton asked.

"The academy has many things," Helios said with a hint of irritation.

Jaxton put his paw on Helios' shoulder to reassure him he trusted Helios completely, and Helios nodded. Helios ran his talon across the map and tapped it at the location it indicated would be the keep. Helios showed the others the location and gave them a minute to study the map. They discussed quietly how the best way would be to maneuver the structure and settled on a plan. Azrack refreshed his memory on the king's quarters, as it had been many years since he was there last.

Azrack rolled his talon around in the air and the gryphton's started their executions. They climbed up and around several peaks until they found the opening that was on the map. Helios smiled and Jaxton slapped him on the back. The opening was sealed with an iron grate that allowed for the air to escape, but nothing could get in. Jaxton pulled out a thick iron rod and shoved it under the grate.

He gripped the rod and heaved, but the grate didn't budge. Jaxton pulled out a bottle of orange goo and dripped a few drops onto the bolts that were driven into the rock.

"What is that?" Pontos asked.

"This is an acid made from the base chemical reaction of the rotting placid-rose and elk guts," Jaxton said.

"You have been spending time with Helios, haven't you," Pontos said.

Helios beamed, and the two chuckled. The acid sizzled and popped when it hit the iron. They waited a few minutes and Jaxton tried again. The grate groaned and then the bolt popped and the grate broke free. Jaxton and Pontos heaved the grate out of the way enough for them to squeeze through.

"You be careful," Jaxton said.

"You just keep the guards from getting in the main gate," Helios said.

Jaxton nodded to Helios, and the others dropped into the air shaft. Azrack lowered himself to the bottom of the short shaft and checked the surroundings. It was clear and dimly lit. He rolled out of the shaft and hovered close to the cavern's ceiling. The others followed and split up. Ralti, Pontos, and Helios would go after Kronos and then find Brigdon and break him out, then find the orb while Azrack took care of Groargoth. Azrack veered to the side where the common areas of the fortress would be and lowered to the ground and pulled his wings in tight. A pit in his stomach lurched when there were no other gryphton's around.

When King Ruadan was in the fortress, he had many political leaders and government officers that used these commons as their personal retreat, but it was bare and had an element of death, or deathly-like sorrow and Azrack swallowed the lump in his throat.

****

Ralti dropped to the ground and scooted against the wall and peeked around the corner. The hall was empty, and he waved to others behind him. Ralti started down the hall and rounded the corners he recalled from the map. The corridors were long and empty, and they wondered where everyone was. Ralti turned the last corner and started at a quick pace toward the keep. Helios and Pontos followed into an enormous cavern that was once the reception hall for political meetings.

"It's too quiet, and I don't see the usual guards," Ralti said.

"Where are they?" Jaxton asked.

"I don't know, Kronos thinks he runs things now," Ralti said.

"I do run things now, with you no longer the first in command," Kronos said. They spun on their heels and inspected the mangy and unkempt General. "I see you brought some friends with you," waving to the side, he continued, "So did I."

Several heavily armed soldiers appeared from the dim corners of the room.

"Great, just great. I just polished my talons and now I have to scuff them up on your shiny armor," Pontos said.

Helios snickered, and Kronos signaled for his henchmen to attack. One thug parried forward, bringing his sword up in an arc. Ralti sidestepped and slammed his fist into the soldier's side. Helios swung his battle-ax up across his body, blocking a forward thrust from another soldier. Helios rotated his wrist and stepped toward him and threw out his paw and jerked the sword from his opponent's grip. The startled gryphton spun out of the way and elbowed Helios in the ribs. Pontos lifted off the ground and whipped his sling backward and flung a polished stone. It smacked the thug's armor with such speed that it shifted him back several feet and dented the metal.

Ralti ducked away from a forward strike and came up under the opponent's chin with his fist, jolting him up and backward. Ralti scooted around him with the intent of engaging Kronos. Helios felt the slam hit his ribs and recoiled sharply, throwing up his ax to block his body. Helios took a few steps back, and the henchman advanced. Helios lifted his ax and spun it around the soldier's battle-ax and slammed his fist into the soldier's ribs. The crack of the soldier's bones breaking pleased Helios and he brought his ax down, slamming the edge into the soldier's chest plate. The soldier recoiled and fell backward.

The dampness of the mildew-drenched walls wafted across the cave as Ralti threw a gryphton against it. Pontos reloaded his sling and let loose another stone, this time smacking into the center of the gryphton's forehead. It lodged into the skull, knocking the soldier dead to the ground. Ralti's brain hit the panic button as a blade lodged into his side just below his chest armor. Ralti hit his knees as the pain seared through his body. Helios spun just in time to throw his ax into the assailing blade, blocking it from hitting Ralti a second time. Ralti spun on his knee behind the protection of Helios and stood, bringing his blade up and over his shoulder, slicing the shoulder of the gryphton who struck him.

The thug retreated as his arm lost the ability to carry his blade. Blood hit the ground, mixing with the odor of the musky dirt. Pontos was about to load another stone when a gryphton, who'd come from an adjacent tunnel, slammed a stone of his own into his back. The impact knocked him into a stalactite. Blood dripped from his temple as he hit against the sharp edges. Ralti spun on his knee again and swiped his leg under the legs of another gryphton, sending the soldier falling to the ground. Ralti flipped his blade and sunk it into the fallen gryphton.

****

Jaxton flew back over the peaks and rounded the main turret. He scrutinized the inside and found that there were no guards and wondered why. He slipped through the open bay and found the hatch had also been sealed shut. Jaxton searched the distance and found that the guards had taken up residence in the common grounds and were half drunk and half asleep. He wasn't sure why, but assumed it might be because Groargoth and Kronos were overconfident that no one would try to overtake the keep. Jaxton searched for a route to the main gate and leaped off the turret. He dipped behind a sizable pillar and landed near the gate and pulled his royal-purple feathered wings tightly to his back. Jaxton gripped his sword and sniffed the surrounding air. He didn't detect anyone near, so he slid along the edge of the now finely carved stone walls. The grand entrance was a sizable façade with majestic, solid wood doors in the center that opened into the fortress. A bit of worry sat at the back of Jaxton's mind because he has never seen the fortress so unprotected. The sun had set beneath the horizon and small lanterns and fires crept into existence.

Jaxton made his way to the latch at the main door and he lifted the lever and pulled against the iron handled. The door didn't open, so he pulled out his glass jar and drizzled the orange goo into the center of the locked handle. The metal sizzled and popped, and he tried the latch again. The door partially opened, but he realized the other side of the door also had a lock. He repeated the process on the other latch and then opened the door a tiny crack. He wasn't supposed to open it completely, just enough to make it so they could make their escape if needed.

Jaxton put the jar away and closed the gate and flew back up to the turret and hid inside the arched crenulations.

****

Ralti stepped back with his raised elbow and slammed it into the eye of another soldier. He flipped his sword backward and palmed the hilt of his blade, and with both paws. He shoved the blade in the small separation of his chest plate and girdle. The soldier fell with a thud. Pontos spun around and peered through the one eye that still opened. Hovering a few lengths higher than the others, he lifted his hind legs and released his talons in time to sink them into the thigh of an oncoming soldier. The combatant roared with pain as the sharpness sliced his muscle. Pontos gripped his blade and attempted to pull it from its sheath, but the soldier sliced his belt, causing it to fall to the ground. Ralti rounded a stalagmite, crossed his body with his blade, and engaged a gryphton. The clank of metal on metal sounded in the cavernous room. First, a forward jab blocked with a sideways step, a kick to the chest and a crash against the rocks.

"We're about to be outnumbered, Helios," Ralti said, catching a glimpse of an adjacent hallway.

"Now," Helios said.

They all shoved a cloth into their nostrils and took out the masks Helios had given them and strapped them around their beaks. Kronos and the others blurted out with laughter. Helios reached into a pouch and pulled out a little glass jar.

"You may think you are stronger than us, but we are smarter," He said with a glint in his eye.

Helios threw the jar at the paws of the oncoming soldiers, shattering it into pieces. The gaseous fumes of the mushroom evaporated into the air. Kronos glanced around and when he saw nothing happen, he threw up his blade. Ralti blocked, sliced, blocked, parried, sideways strike, block. Pontos engaged two new soldiers first blocking then striking, then spun in the air and sliced the flesh of one and elbowed the other. Helios ducked, sliced, sidestepped, and ducked again. It would only take a moment until the effects of the hallucinogen would take over. Helios spent many hours perfecting his poison and was eagerly watching for results.

Ralti shook his head clear of the fog from a blow Kronos gave. He gripped one of Kronos's wrists while the other engaged his blade and slammed his forehead into Kronos's. Kronos stumbled back as the hit took his senses. Ralti slammed his fist into Kronos' throat, knocking the air from his lungs. He brought the hilt of his blade up and thrust it against Kronos' temple, and Kronos crumpled to the ground. Ralti pulled his blade down through the flesh of Kronos' neck. A soldier coming from the adjacent tunnel saw the mask Helios, and the others were wearing and dropped his sword. He started toward the others, frantically trying to escape. Others soon too dropped their swords and scrambled past the oncoming gryphtons.

"Why are they running away?" Pontos asked.

"I isolated the components of the mushroom that evoke fear and heightened it, then mixed it back in with the hallucinogenic effects. When they see our masks, they think they see something they can't explain," Helios said.

Ralti smiled, slapped Helios on the back and ran off down the hall toward the keep.

"Good to have you back," Pontos said.

Helios smiled, it was a long time, and it did feel good, even with a broken rib and bruised and bleeding.

Ralti ran around the corner and came to a skidding stop. Brigdon looked up through swollen and beaten eyes.

"It's about time you got here," Brigdon grunted.

Ralti looked for the keys to open the shackles.

"I thought you were just a political prisoner," Ralti said, spotting the key on the table across the room.

"I was, until the rumor that Azrack was back started. Is it true?" Brigdon asked.

"Yes, he's back."

Ralti snagged the keys and darted back to Brigdon. He unlatched the shackles and Brigdon's arms fell.

"Can you walk?"

Ralti helped him stand.

"I'm fine," Brigdon said. He shook the fog from his mind and rubbed his swollen wrists, "Never felt better."

"Where's the treasure keep?" Ralti asked.

"Why?"

"Because, we have to secure the Orb," Ralti said.

"Not that thing again," Brigdon said.

Ralti laughed, "That's what I said."

Brigdon grimaced through his black eye.

"This way."

35-It Wasn't Here Before Was It?

The next morning Shaz woke to the pelting of the rain on his window and tried to roll over and go back to sleep, but the dull ache at the back of his head ripped through his brain and the pain throbbed against his skull. He closed his eyes tight and tried to focus on anything but the pain and the only thing he could do was grip his head and squeeze. Serin sat up in her bed and rubbed her temple and laid back down. She rolled over and tried to go back to sleep, but a gnawing ache in the back of her head increased.

She climbed out of bed and grabbed her nightdress overcoat and threw it on as she hurried from the spacious room. The castle was cool from the night's chill, and her feet were cold on the stone as she hurried across the hall. She tapped on Shaz's door, but he didn't answer, so she pulled the latch. The door opened, and she peeked in and found Shaz curled up in the bed. She was certain now that the irritations she was experiencing was the pain Shaz was experiencing. She hurried to the side of the bed and sat down.

"Shaz, let me help you," Serin said.

Shaz rolled over but couldn't let go of his head or open his eyes. Serin put her hands on his hands at the sides of his head and breathed in a deeply. She focused her energy to relive the pain in his head and the azure-blue force seeped into his skin and the relief encompassed his frame. Shaz sighed as the headache subsided, but his body still trembled with the nerves.

"What happened, did you use shadow magic for something?" Serin asked.

Her voice was soft but full of worry, and Shaz blinked. He found he could open his eyes, and he shook his head.

"I had a dream, or rather a nightmare, but this time it was worse than any others before," Shaz said.

Serin thought about it and wondered if her weird dream had anything to do with his. She pushed the thoughts away and closed her eyes and put her hand on his chest and studied his heartbeat. Shaz put his hand on hers and smiled as her brows scrunch with her thoughts.

"Well, your heart is beating normal and your heat is about the same, so I think you are alright," Serin said.

Shaz looked at her with surprise.

"You can tell how hot I am?" Shaz asked.

"Mmhm, and I can sense your magics and how they get along or not get along," Serin said.

"Humm, interesting, what kinds of magic do you sense?" Shaz asked.

"All of them, but the shadow magic is what I keep a tight watch on, that and your heartfire," Serin said.

"Heartfire?" Shaz asked.

"Well, I don't know if that's what its really called, but that's what it looks like when I heal you," Serin said.

"I like it," Shaz said.

Shaz wanted to find out what the core of her magic looked like, but thought maybe it should wait. Serin pulled her hand off his bare chest and he let her hand go. Serin got up and pulled the robe snugly.

"What are the plans for today?" Serin asked.

"I would like to do some study in the library and I'm hoping Inelius will be able to help," Shaz said.

"Inelius? Who is that?" Serin asked.

"Grandfather's brother, apparently," Shaz said.

"Here at the castle?" Serin asked.

"I'll fill you in over breakfast?" Shaz half-asked-half-stated. Serin nodded and started for the door. "Thank you," Shaz said.

"You're welcome," Serin said.

Serin closed the door behind her, and she returned to her room and dressed for the day. The rain against the window had died to a slow drizzle, and she gazed into the wet landscape. She put her boots on and her cloak and wrapped a belt around it. Serin hated the way the cloaks were always so baggy and drapey, and she wondered how anyone was supposed to do anything in them. She met Shaz in the kitchen and the Whispmother had a pot of warm morning mush on the table and some fresh fruit. Ladtwig and Turkill were just finishing and headed to the game room where they were especially interested in the war games.

Shaz filled her in on the earth portal, and Inelius and Serin asked about his dream. He tried to explain it but, like all dreams, they were random at best. Serin seemed to understand, however, and she wondered how much of her own dream was part of his. They finished and made their way to the library. The library was a vast room with two balconies and a level below ground. The smell of leather and paper filled Shaz's nose, and he made a funny face. In the center of the room were isles and isles of shelves. Shaz had never seen so many books in one place. The room was decorated with tall silver and crystal vases. Some with flowers arranged in them and others had marbles of illuminated glass.

Shaz spotted Inelius sitting in a soft overstuffed leather chair and resting against the tall back. He avoided a large globe sitting in the center of the room, but ran his finger on the hand-painted surface. The old man stirred in his chair and opened one eye.

"Ah, you're here, and who is this?" Inelius asked.

"This is Serin," Shaz said.

"Nice to meet you Serin, where do you come from?" Inelius asked.

"Umm," Serin looked at Shaz.

"She's kind of from all over the place," Shaz said.

"What is your surname?" Inelius asked.

"Svirtari, my father is Jerim Svirtari," Serin said.

Inelius' eyes widened, and he smiled an old man's gentle grin, which made Serin's nerves settle. She did, however, wonder why he seemed to know something they didn't and seemed he wasn't going to tell them either.

"Inelius, do you know where I would find some information on portals," Shaz asked.

"Ah yes," Inelius climbed out of his chair. Shaz shoved his hands into his pockets as Inelius rummaged around a desk and Serin evaluated a small golden trinket that was sitting on a side table, "Ah, here it is," he said, "This is a *Time* Portal map. It shows you were the Time Portals are in each realm."

Shaz took the paper and unfolded it. Small spheres rose from the surface and hovered over different areas of the map. Bright glittering hues of gemstones contrasted the earth-tones of the planet and indicated the locations of each realm.

"These are the same symbols the Earth Portal taught me last night," Shaz said, pointing to the sides.

"Yes, that's right, and since you can't take the earth portal with you, this map will help you."

"Thanks," Shaz said.

Shaz wondered what he was going to do with all these maps he now had. Inelius nodded and sank back into his overstuffed chair and fell asleep. Shaz chuckled and Serin smiled and they left the library. They rounded the corner from the library and noticed a door that hadn't been there when they came down that hall earlier. The door was larger than the rest and very heavy. Shaz tugged on the handle and it opened slowly. As they walked into the dark room, sconces around the walls lit by themselves. It was as if the room knew they were there. The walls curved around in a rounded pattern and large window-like frames circled the room. The domed ceiling reflected more symbols carved into the stone, along with depictions of stars and planets. Shaz walked around the room, studying the symbols on the sides of the oval doorway.

"What is this place? It wasn't here before, was it?" Serin asked.

"I'm guessing it's the portal room, and now that I have permission and the understanding of using them, it became visible," Shaz said.

"That makes sense, so, each of these frames is a portal to another time and place?" Serin asked.

"One does not travel through time, but that time is measured at a different rate in each realm," Inelius said.

With a gentle smile, he entered the room. Shaz was used to him there one minute and gone the next, Grandfather did that his whole life, but it bothered Serin.

"Does every portal look different?" Serin asked, "I mean from the other side?"

"This is the place where all portals come to the same location. Each opposite portal has its own environment, so yes, each portal would look different," Inelius said, walking to the center of the room.

A light flashed across one of the frames, causing them all to jump.

"What was that?" Shaz asked.

He quickly made his way to the frame.

"Or rather, who?" Inelius said.

"What do you mean, who?" Shaz asked.

"A portal doesn't just activate itself, dear boy," Inelius said. "Remember, it's the lack of imagination that keeps a person limited from the possibilities."

Shaz tried to open his mind but found it more difficult than before. There was so much stuff running through his mind. *If I had a box for each worry, I could organize all the chaos*, he thought. A bolt of lightning crossed the sky and illuminated some of the symbols.

"What's happening?" Serin asked.

"I must find the book of time," Inelius said.

"The what?" Shaz asked.

"A very large book about the portals," Inelius said.

Shaz thought he saw something in the blackness of the frame. The hairs on the back of his neck stood out as a pit formed in his stomach.

"Blast, shadow magic," he mumbled.

"What did you say?" Serin asked.

"Nothing."

Open me, came a whisper. Shaz couldn't see anything in the portal, *Open me, I won't hurt you*. It came again. *I have much to show you, open me*. Shaz's heart began to beat stronger, and the pit grew. The tingle of energy inside his core came to life and rippled into his limbs. Serin noted his heartfire surge and sensed the shadow increase too. *Both magics?* Shaz questioned, *We don't care what magic uses us, we only want to serve*. The voice came again. Something felt very wrong, but also right. *Look at the possibilities*, the whisper said, growing louder.

The frame popped to life with dazzling colors that glimmered. Serin jumped. Shaz raised his hand toward the light.

"Shaz, I don't think you should do that," Serin said, taking a step closer to him.

"There is something drawing me in," Shaz said.

"We don't know where it goes and Inelius isn't here," She said, her tone soft but filled with panic.

The pit in her stomach felt as though it was going to consume her entire body any minute, and she could tell Shaz was falling into some kind of trance. She touched Shaz's shoulder a second before Shaz touched the energy wall of the portal. The energy of the portal sucked them into it and threw them through time and into a realm unknown.

****

"Ah, so the rumor is true," Groargoth said.

His tortured black eyes pierced Azrack's with a maddening leer.

"What rumors?" Azrack asked as he gripped his sword.

"Was it not just yesterday you were a hero? The one everyone loved, worshiped?" Groargoth asked. A low growl rumbled deep in his throat, "I remember watching you cut down twenty men in the blink of an eye and for what, to run away, to escape. What a coward," Groargoth said his voice deep and raspy.

Azrack flinched at the words. He was right he had been a coward. A real soldier would have stayed and faced his accusers. Azrack sidestepped around a small bench.

"I'm here now," Azrack said, with a low deep growl.

"And what do you suppose that means to me? You think you can just come in here and take what wasn't yours, to begin with?" Groargoth said.

Groargoth threw contents of his goblet on the small fire, making it hiss and sizzle.

"Not mine to begin with?" Azrack asked.

"You know what I'm talking about, the fact that my inheritance was given to you. I was going to be left with the scraps," Groargoth growled. He circled Azrack, looking for signs of weakness. Groargoth was delirious with revenge, which made him an unpredictable foe. "You don't have what it takes, you think me evil, but you're the one that was going to steal everything from me," Groargoth said, his tongue slipping in and out of his beak.

"Oh, you see, I do, and now that King Ruadan is gone there is nothing keeping me from killing you," Azrack growled.

He pulled his blade from its sheath. Groargoth picked up his battle-ax from the table with a crooked smile.

"I have been waiting a long time to do this," Groargoth admitted.

With both paws on his battle-ax, Groargoth lifted his arms high and brought the heavy blade down. Azrack sidestepped and caught the ax in the center of his blade and locked the blade against the ax, twisted his wrist and threw his arm out. Groargoth allowed the staff to spin in his paw and at the last second, he gripped the staff and the sword slid off. Groargoth took a step back, rotating the ax behind him and over his head. He lunged toward Azrack with a full swing and twisted at the waist for added momentum. Azrack ducked, sidestepped, and twisted his paw with his talons released, and jabbed at Groargoth's side, slicing his flesh. Groargoth gripped the staff of his ax as the pain thrust his brain deeper into the frenzy he suffered.

Azrack threw the table out of his way as he circled. Dishes clattered to the floor and echoed throughout the large room. Groargoth swung his ax around and whipped it toward Azrack, who slid under Groargoth's ax and stepped out of the way. Groargoth's eyes widened with a hint of fear, and he lowered his arm and spun the ax's tip upward as he stepped back. Groargoth stepped forward and flicked his wrist upward, slicing Azrack on the chest barely below his neck. Azrack roared as he stepped back. Azrack attempted another strike, which Groargoth blocked.

"I tire with this nonsense, I thought you were ruthless, you're nothing but a whimpering cub," Groargoth said.

He faked an advance and stepped to the side as Azrack stumbled. Groargoth whipped his ax around him, coming up in a diagonal slice. Azrack dodged, spinning around with the momentum. Azrack threw out his blade in time to catch Groargoth's ax in the crook and yanked it out of his paws. It skidded across the ground, coming to rest on the other side of the cave. Groargoth growled and lowered himself to the ground. He readied himself to pounce.

Azrack leaned down onto all fours and circled Groargoth. Groargoth leaped at Azrack, who leaped toward Groargoth. Azrack gripped around Groargoth's neck, unleashing his talons, and thrust his beak into Groargoth's neck. Groargoth squirmed and thrust his beak into Azrack's neck. They reared onto their hind legs and pushed against each other. Black and red feathers went flying. Groargoth moved Azrack across the floor until he was pinned against the wall. Azrack rolled out from under his grip.

Groargoth landed on his front legs and circled quickly. Azrack reached up with a paw and struck Groargoth on the side of the head, knocking him to the ground. He pounced onto Groargoth and pinned him. Azrack growled and reached for Groargoth's neck when Groargoth folded up his hind legs and launched Azrack across the room.

Azrack smacked up against a jagged stalagmite. He roared as a jagged edge pierced the side of his back and he fell to the ground. Groargoth pawed and paced back and forth.

"The mighty Azrack has fallen after all. What would your men say about you now? Watching you fight like a cub," Groargoth said.

Azrack tried to get up, but the rock shard was lodged in his side. Azrack reached out slowly as Groargoth paced. He gripped a broken shard of rock and slid it next to him. Groargoth reared on his hind legs and leaped toward Azrack. Azrack gripped the shard tightly as Groargoth's beak came in for the kill strike. Azrack pulled the shard up and stabbed it into Groargoth's heart. Groargoth stopped and looked down at the jagged rock protruding from his chest and staggered backward. The sudden loss of his heart beating caused a lack of oxygen and he became disoriented and fell backward with a thud.

Inelius returned to the room and found it empty. The portal swayed gently from the rippling effect it gave after items went through it.

"Oh, blast," Inelius muttered.

He set the heavy book on a table and hobbled out of the room. As quickly as he could, he made his way to where Jagwynn was sunbathing in the great hall.

"Miss Jagwynn dear, you must find the Minca and take the sword to Shaz. Hurry now you know the way."

Jagwynn leaped to her feet and lunged up the staircase. A moment later she trotted down the stairs with the sword in her mouth and the Minca scurrying down behind.

"What is the trouble?" Turkill asked.

"Shaz and Serin have slipped through a portal."

The Minca gasped and Turkill rubbed the back of his neck.

"What are we going to do?" Turkill asked.

"Jagwynn will take you to where he is. You must go quickly."

"What? Ride on her back?" Ladtwig asked.

Turkill smiled big. His heart leaped at the idea of getting to ride the massive cat. Jagwynn rolled her eyes as if to say *Oh, brother, I have to put up with them.* She lowered to the floor and Turkill jumped on.

"Hurry up," Turkill grumbled.

"Fine," Ladtwig groaned.

"Make haste, there is no time," Inelius said.

"Where are we going?" Ladtwig asked.

"Jagwynn knows the way, she is his spirit companion sent by the Sun Goddess," Inelius said.

"How do you-"

Jagwynn lunged forward, causing the Minca to nearly fall off. Turkill reached down and grabbed their packs, sitting by the open door as she ran out of the castle.

36-You Don't Have Power Over Me

Small torches around the room gave little light to the vast cavern. Jagged rock walls surrounded a well-smoothed platform on which sat the sacrificial altar. Serin blinked, and the fogginess faded from her mind. Serin lifted her head, but it weighed so much she could hardly move. The ceiling of the cavern was filled with stalagmites and some of them dripped murky water that was seeping from the earth above them. Serin managed to flop her head to the side and found a small, thin woman bent over a cauldron. Serin could only see the back of her, but her scraggly hair alerted Serins reflexed, and she pulled against the restraints. The bands were so tight that they bit through her skin, and tears seeped from her eyes as she struggled with the pain.

Panic raced through her body and she tried to move but found she was bound to the icy surface. Her mind quickly took in as many details of the room and she understood she was bound to an altar. Her heart raced and her endorphins surged as the realization came that she was the sacrifice. The witch turned around and crossed the ragged floor. Serin tried to turn her head to the other side and gagged as the rancid scent of the Velshari witch's foul breath stung her nose as she stood over her.

"Welcome to my lair," the Velshari witch said, "I'm glad you could join me."

"Did I have a choice?"

"Now, now, don't be that way. It saddens me you think me to be so evil."

The skin around one of her eyes was burned, leaving the eye covered with a dark circle of crusty skin and Serin knew it was the witch Shaz told her about. Her heart was beating so hard against her ribs that she wondered if the witch could hear it.

"Except, you are," Serin said and spat in her face.

The Velshari witch wiped her face.

"Nasty girl, it's a good thing I'm going to suck all the magic out of you, you don't deserve it."

"Oh, and you do?"

"Silence," the witch said, her voice raised and sharp, "I've had enough of this."

"And what's 'this' you're talking about?" Serin said.

"Ah, so you want to play that little game, do you? Well, I can tell you it's not going to do you any good. As much as I love a good riddle, I have more important things at hand."

"Like stealing magic from innocent beings," Serin said.

The witch picked up a long skinny pick and dipped it into a cauldron which was sitting over a small fire. The pick turned from a shiny silver to deep orange and then blood-red. Steam wafted from the tip as she waved the pick in the air. She spoke words Serin didn't understand. Serin gritted her teeth and yanked against the restraints again.

"That's right elemental, you're too weak for this kind of magic, and I'm the only person who can use it," the witch said.

"If you call yourself a person."

Serin closed her eyes and thought of Shaz, but she didn't know where he was. She didn't know what happened after flying through the portal and feared he'd been killed, and now it was her turn. Her pulsating heart beating in her chest caused her stomach to churn with nerves.

"Do what you must," she said, sagging into the cold rock of the stone slab.

"Ah, now that's more like it."

The witch took the pick and mumbled as she hovered the tip over Serin's wrist and moved up her arm to her armpit. The pain was so unbearable that Serin's voice lurched from her body with an ear-piercing scream. Her body tightened and her back arched off the cold stone. The witch slid the pick as not to touch the skin. The dark magic it held sucked out Serin's magic. She placed the tip into the bowl sitting on the cold stone and a steady stream of blue liquid splashed into the bowl.

The small reprieve left Serin gasping for air and her chest heaved heavily as she tried to gain her breath back. Tears fell freely from her eyes and her hair and clothes were now soaked with sweat. The witch began again and Serin's body writhed in the pain. Pieces of her soul were being taken from her and each time it left a dark gaping hole inside her chest. For the first time in her life, she wanted to die.

****

The cavern was dark and damp with an eerie silence. Shaz sat with his back to the cold rock wall. He was drained of energy and his wrists were bound behind his back. His head hung over his bent knees and total darkness surrounded him. A hint of iron from the depths of the mountain left a bitter sting in his mouth. He had been in this cell for what seemed like days, hungry and cold. *How did I end up here? What happened? All I remember is soaring through the portal and crashing to the ground and couldn't use my magic to open it back up. After trying a few times everything went dark and I woke up here*, he thought over and over as if replaying it in his mind would give the answer.

The tingle of magic he now was accustomed to had disappeared and was replaced with magic which stung like prickly thorns. The darkness overpowered his thoughts and his head ached more than ever before. Scattered and mixed up, he tried to shake his head several times to clear it, but the darkness kept coming. *I can't do anything more.* Shaz pulled against the bands, but the harder he pulled the tighter they cinched.

I have failed, there's nothing left for me, I've let everyone down, Serin, Jagwynn, the Minca, the council, the world. It's not fair, asking this of me in the first place, I'm just a regular guy, a selfish one too, I give up; he thought. In the corner of his mind, he heard something but couldn't quite place it. Shaz shoved the thoughts from his mind and sat up as straight as he could and shook his sweat-soaked medium-length hair out of his face. He peered into the distance as if he could see into the darkness and searched his mind, and the sound became as loud as though it were right behind him. Screams of pain and terror were coming from another cavern.

"Serin!" Shaz shouted.

Shaz's anger surged through his body, and he shuddered with fear. Genuine fear crept into his mind. He struggled against the bands for several lengths and nearly fell over with exhaustion. He leaned on the cold stone as tears ran down his face. Shadows floated around the darkness and his heart sank with a wave of despair. As he sat listening to the screams of agony, he realized they were echoing around him.

She's behind me. The thought came out of the darkness as if someone turned on the lights and a surge of energy shot to his limbs and he jumped to his feet.

A dot of light shined through a tiny hole and he moved closer and closer till his nose touched the cold surface of the rock wall. He peered through the tiny hole and bits of Serin, lying on a smoothly carved altar in the center of a cavernous room, came into view. He could barely make out her wrists and ankles bound at each corner with cords and the Velshari witch, in her blood-red robe, stood bent over a book. A large bowl sat on the rock platform between Serin's feet and had a blue liquid in it. Long thin cut-like marks sank into Serin's arms.

"Oh no, no, no, no!" he said, slamming his forehead into the wall. "Blast that hurt."

Her skin as pale as it was made her soft purple markings that now covered most of her arms, a deeper shade of violet. Shaz noticed an opalescent string of glittering light coming from a large oval shape which stood on another pillar opposite of the book with a reflection of a man.

"Gavin Rhill," he cursed.

The witch was doing Gavin Rhill's dirty work. The more he tried to find his way out of the darkness, the angrier he became. His heart beat faster, and his muscles tightened. Sweat dripped down his back, but the angrier he became, the less dark it became. He closed his eyes and searched into his heart, and he found pure fury burst from his bosom. He had spent too much time thinking, and it was time to just feel, and right now he was seething.

"Bonds release!" he commanded.

The bonds obeyed and fell from his wrists. He searched his mind for a way out and at the edges of the darkness was a fuzzy blur. He reached out and touched the blackness, and it shuddered as if it was a shroud of magic. Shaz gripped the fuzzy darkness like he had in the dungeons and shoved the darkness away, and a small tunnel appeared. He reached for the sword, but it wasn't there, and he cursed himself for not putting it on that morning. Not having the sword would put him at a sizable disadvantage, and he reeled through as many ideas as he could.

"You don't need the sword, use your shadow magic," came the voice of Drafang.

Shaz nodded and slipped effortlessly into the tunnel, crawling for several lengths. The light grew until he moved closer to the end. The witch moved to Serin's legs. She was patient and careful, sliding the pick from her inner thigh to her ankle and collected as much magic as the pick would hold. Serin screamed, but her body was growing so weak that she could barely move. The witch put the magic in the bowl. As he rounded the corner of the tunnel, the witch was moving the pick to Serin's navel.

Shaz shot out of the tunnel and into the cavern with lightning speed. He leaped toward the witch, thrusting his hand toward the pick, and sent a blast of magic and knocked it from her crinkled hand. The witch jumped back coming out of a trance and saw Shaz hurl himself toward her and knocked her to the ground. Anger that now encompassed his body gave him the desire to kill, and he rolled to a crouched position. The witch pulled herself up and Shaz reached with his magic toward the altar and untied the ropes, then sent a burst of magic at the witch, sending her sprawling backward into the rock-wall. The witch yelped with pain as she slammed into the jagged rock-face and fall to the ground. The witch pulled herself up as if something else was making her move and her eyes were void of color.

"So, your magic does work here," the witch said.

Her voice was shaky but eerie, and it left a bitter taste in the back of his mind. Shaz leaped out of the way as she shot a burst of sizzling magic over his head and blasted the rocks behind him. Serin's head wobbled and swayed, and the pain erased most of her senses. Serin blinked a few times and thought she saw Shaz coming toward her.

Shaz started running to her, but he didn't make it as the witch plunged, a dagger slicing his shoulder. Shaz winced with pain, and he dove behind a pillar. As he bumped up against the pillar, the mirror fell to the ground and rolled across the floor, ending up propped against the wall. The witch lunged, but Shaz sent another wave of magic which hit the craggy witch and lifted off her feet and flipped head over heels twice before slamming into the wall.

"Shaz, over here," yelled Turkill.

Turkill hobbled into the opening of a passageway next to Shaz, pulling the Honor Blade behind him. Blood dripped from his lip and landed on his stained tunic. He slid the sword to the front so Shaz could see it and Shaz hurried over to him.

"What happened to you?" Shaz asked.

"Never mind," he scowled, wincing one eye with the other eye swollen shut, "take this,"

Shaz sensed the buzzing of energy surging toward them and threw Turkill out of the way and somersaulted from the oncoming blast.

"Get her out of here, she needs water!" Shaz yelled to Turkill.

"I've got her, you take care of that nasty-"

The witch's stinging magic caught Turkill square in the chest, thrusting him backward and smacked him into the sharply broken stone wall. Turkill rubbed his aching head and found his fingers were covered in blood.

"Blast," Turkill cursed.

Turkill staggered to his feet and hid behind the large mirror. Shaz gripped the sword and rounded the outer edge toward the witch. A shiny medallion caught his eye, and he reached out with his magic to inspect its abilities. The piece of jewelry was like that of the Interrogators, but not the same as his medallion he now wore as a belt buckle. His report came back with the information that the necklace was a type of portal key, but it had limited access. *That's how the portal opened here, and that's what she was up to in the city.*

"Why this portal?" Shaz asked.

"You see, *my* special gift is the power to see flashes of one's future. In Ebassia I saw the rift and the mirror and knew I needed to find it. I followed the clues you gave me," the sting of responsibility ripped into his chest. He deflected a sizzling hot energy bolt, "That's how I knew who Serin was. I know who all your Dodjen friends are, and as soon as I take Serin's and your magic, I'll move on to them. Nothing can stop me," the witch said.

Shaz's lip peeled as he caught a glimpse of the singed skin around her eye.

"No, I don't think you will," Shaz said.

Shaz circled the spilled blood-oil and the gold dish sat half-empty on the ground. The witch laughed a hearty cackle.

"I already have."

"Come on, we need to get you out of here," Turkill whispered to Serin.

"You boast of your magic, yet you are nothing compared to me," the witch said.

The witch's eyes flash toward the mirror.

"You mean Gavin Rhill's magic? You need that amulet and mirror, but I don't," Shaz said.

"Ha, you think that the training you received from that washed up pathetic grandfather of yours is enough to defeat me?" she said.

"You know what the funny thing about this is?"

"What?" she asked.

"You can't win without this," Shaz spun his blade and struck the chalice.

"No!"

The gold bowl shattered into pieces, and a puff of magic dissipated into the air. Shaz twisted the blade over his head and blocked the witch's next blast of magic, which rebounded around the room.

Serin was barely able to see, and her body wouldn't respond to her brain. Turkill tried with all his might to move her, but she was too big for him. He tried shaking her. Then he remembered the water bag in his satchel outside the door. He slipped down from the altar and ran around the outer edge of the room, back toward the tunnel.

Shaz checked to see how Turkill was managing and found that Serin's lifeless body was still on the altar. His heartfire surged with heat and his body was never so invigorated, he'd fought so long to keep his anger under control, but now he didn't care. The witch grabbed the jewel around her neck and held it out. Dark purple and green shadow magic burst from the necklace. Shaz leaped out of the way and the bolt of magic split open a tall stone column behind him, shattering it into pieces. A sharp fragment lodged itself deep into Shaz's flesh and he cried out and fell to his knees.

He cast a shield over himself before the rest of the column toppled onto him. Shaz gripped the fragment and yanked it out and blood gushed from the wound and he put his hand on his side. He imagined the heat of fire in his hand and a wave of heat sizzled and burned the flesh which seared it shut and stopped the bleeding. Shaz yelled out as the red-hot pain shot through his torso. His frame quivered with the stifling pain and sweat-soaked his tunic.

Turkill returned to the tunnel with a water bag and pointed at Serin. Shaz struggled to his feet and moved toward the mirror against the wall, and the witch hobbled toward Shaz.

"Well, you are persistent, I'll give you that, but you won't last much longer," she said.

Turkill waited another moment and darted across the room. The man in the mirror noticed the Minca warrior and shouted, but only the witch could hear it and she turned on Turkill, sending a burst of air that knocked out several of the small candle flames. Shaz shoved his arm against the cave wall and propelled himself toward Turkill.

Shaz bent his elbow and grabbed the surrounding air with his empty hand. The air pulled against the witch like a cord bound to her back and the harder Shaz squeezed, the harder it pulled against her. Turkill leaned back and slid on his knees under the witch's blade a second before her dagger would have sliced his neck. The fury of the wind yanked her backward and threw her to the ground.

Red-hot pain wreaked havoc on Turkill's bare skin as he slid against the surface of the stone floor until his momentum carried him back to his feet. Shaz thrust the witch into the wall, slamming her against the rock. She fell lifeless to the floor and Shaz ran to help Turkill, who was trying to make Serin drink water, but she was too weak and nearly unconscious. Shaz lifted the water bag and poured the water on her face and down her body. Steam rose from her skin as the water evaporated.

"Blast, we need more water," Shaz said.

Serin stirred and opened her eyes.

"Shaz," she whispered and feebly pointed behind him.

Shaz spun around, threw his sword up and rebounded another surge of energy.

"You will not win. I have shadow magic at my disposal," the witch said between her now broken teeth.

"No, you're the one who won't win. It's not your magic, Gavin Rhill has possessed you."

"Serin, you must get up, I can't carry you," Turkill said.

"I-I-" Serin tried.

Her entire body felt like it was on fire and there was no feeling in her arms or legs. Turkill grabbed one arm and one leg and pulled. It took several tries to wriggle her body to the edge, but he finally maneuvered her to the ground. Once on the ground, Turkill grabbed her wrists and heaved her across the floor. The witch sent a steady stream of magic toward Shaz. His brows pulled in as he focused his strength and lifted his arms to shield himself from her magic attack, and his neck muscles pulsed as he held off the witch's constant blast. His side ached deeply, and he jerked at a twinge in his back. Shaz released his hold and let his sword swing downward. Shaz parried forward and brought his sword upward in a swooping motion. The witch leaped away and it surprised Shaz at how limber she was and how much she was enduring and decided it had to be Gavin Rhill's possession of her.

Sweat dripped onto the floor and Turkill gritted his teeth and grunted with each heave. He was halfway across the floor when a shiver ran down his spine as the man in the mirror stared at him. Turkill set Serin down and ran with a limp toward the mirror. He grabbed a fragment of stone and slammed it into the glass, shattering the retched image. The glass went in every direction, crashing and tinkling to the ground. A loud pop echoed throughout the cavern as the portal-like connection vanished. Turkill dashed back to Serin and heaved her a few more steps until a tap on the shoulder made his body seize.

Images of something evil crossed his mind, but instead the big bright eyes of his little brother beamed back at him. Dried blood crested Ladtwig's eyebrow, and his oversized clothes were torn and shredded. Ladtwig took one of Serin's arms and Turkill grinned back. The two heaved and pulled her toward the passageway.

"Gavin Rhill will destroy you, even if I don't," the witch said.

Her crazed look sent chills through Shaz's body.

"Maybe, but it won't be easy," Shaz said.

Shaz wondered if now that the mirror was broken, she would know how to use the pendant. The witch held out the pendant using Shaz's name in a spell. Shaz's head about exploded as the shadow magic forced its way into his mind. Shaz dropped his sword and fell to his knees in agony. The pain was so intense he didn't know if he was dead or dying. The pounding grew stronger as a voice made its way past the haze of fear and pain. Within a few seconds, a man's voice became clear.

"Give up Shaz, you have no choice, I own you now," Gavin Rhill said.

"No, you don't, no one owns me, but me,"

"There's no use fighting, you can't overpower the shadow."

Shaz felt as though an ice pick had propelled itself into his skull. It was so hard to think of anything but pain. Shaz lost his strength and melted onto the ground, and he fought to search his mind for a way out.

Then, Shaz heard a second voice, *Shaz you are the only one that can harness its power, that's why I have chosen you to overcome and control the shadow that is in your heart. It is you and you alone that can achieve this heavy burden;* he recognized it from a dream and understood now that in order to harness the shadow magic. He needed to let it become him. Not for greed or power over others, but because he loved them. He thought of Serin, who loved all people even before she met them. She always gave them the benefit of the doubt. *That's it, mercy, that's the key,* he thought.

Shaz filled his mind with images of his friends. Serin, Turkill, Ladtwig, Azrack, his father, Grandfather and even the townspeople. The pain lessened, and the voice came again.

"What do you think you are doing?" Gavin Rhill growled.

"Here's the thing Gavin, you can only control those who allow you to," Shaz got to his feet and reached for his sword. "I choose to accept my shadow magic as a part of me. Because of the love I have for my friends and my people, I will use my shadow magic to destroy you," Shaz said.

"You will never succeed, now *bow* before *me,* I *command* you."

"You don't have *power* over me," Shaz yelled.

Shaz shoved Gavin out of his mind and locked it down, creating a barrier, and rubbed his eyes. The witch, still under Gavin Rhill's control, rose up. Shaz stepped forward and closed the gap. With mercy in his heart instead of anger, he thrust his sword into the witch's heart and the witch stopped and gasped. Gavin Rhill shouted an agonized cry, which died off quickly as the witches' body fell lifeless. Shaz waited until there was no more movement and he couldn't sense her life force and then withdrew his blade and her body crumpled to the floor. Shaz yanked the amulet off her body and tucked it into his tunic.

He half-hobbled-half-ran across the cave, and when he reached the tunnel, he extinguished the last of the flames still burning around the room. He started down the passage but stopped.

"Chada'rrha narata noshari, tay're nar'rah chari so'ametay narro," Shaz said.

A wall formed and magically sealed the access shut. Shaz's head ached and his side was sore and tender, and he struggled down the passageway. A dim light cast by the glowing minerals in veins along the walls and ceiling, allowed him to make his way out.

37-Now What Do We Do With It

Shaz managed to shove more of the pain from his mind and focus on the surrounding energy. He had no idea where he was or how the Minca got there. He stopped at an intersection of stone-carved passageways and reached out with his mind. A faint image came into view of a creature that resembled Azrack, and he wondered if he was in his realm. He followed the images down one corridor and the images became stronger.

He could now tell that there were a handful of the gryphtons and was sure he was at least in his realm. Shaz passed a small cave that was adjacent to the hall he was in and heard a noise come from behind him. He shoved off the wall with one foot and darted back the other way and skidded to a stop before the tunnel opened into a small cavern. A ripple in a small body of water brushed against the smooth edge and Shaz scanned the room. His senses detected Serin was in there, so he started into the cave.

"Shh, you fool. You're going to expose us," Turkill whispered.

"I am not. If you remember, I'm the smart one," Ladtwig said.

"No, you're not."

"Yes, I am. Plus I saved your butt." Ladtwig said.

"No, you didn't."

Shaz chuckled as he came around the edge and saw Turkill and Ladtwig sitting in the water, each holding one of Serin's arms as she floated.

"You two at it again?"

Turkill and Ladtwig jumped.

"Oh, it's just you," Turkill grunted.

"Are you happy to see us?" Ladtwig said, beaming.

Shaz ruffled his hair.

"I sure am."

Shaz squatted down and checked Sein's pulse.

"She's weak. We almost didn't make it in time," Turkill said.

"Stay here and be quiet. There's something I need to do. I'll be back soon," Shaz said.

Shaz made his way through the passageways toward the images in his mind and heard voices coming from a room up ahead. He moved to the wall and pulled the sword that was now secured to his hip and leg and crept along the wall. He stopped at the doorway and listened.

"Now what do we do with it?" Brigdon asked.

"We give it to the boy," Ralti said.

"What boy?"

Ralti's ears twitched as Shaz's footsteps in the hall came closer and he turned toward the opening. Shaz came around the corner slowly with his blade drawn.

"That one," Ralti said, holding out the orb.

Shaz eyes shifted from the two very large gryphtons in the room then around the edges, taking in the details of the treasure trove of gems and precious metals.

"I take it you're with Azrack?" Shaz asked.

"At least he's a smart one," Brigdon said.

Ralti shot him a glare, which Brigdon returned with a 'what' look.

"Are you going to take this thing or not?" Ralti asked.

Shaz sheathed his sword.

"What am I supposed to do with it?" Shaz asked.

"What, I thought you said he would know what to do with it?" Brigdon said.

"No, I said we needed to give it to him. After that it's out of our paws," Ralti said.

Shaz took the orb from Ralti, who skirted out of the way. The orb was the size of one of the large green melons from back home and just as heavy. Shaz searched the orb, rolling it around as he looked for anything that might tell him what he was supposed to do with it.

"Where's Azrack?" Shaz asked.

"Opening a can of whoop-ass on Groargoth, I hope," Ralti said with a glint in his eye.

"A can of what?" Shaz asked.

"Never mind, we gotta get out of here," Ralti said.

"Right behind you," Brigdon said.

The gryphton's hurried out of the room. *What am I going to do with this*, Shaz thought? *It's too big to carry around, and I have no idea how to destroy it. I wish it were smaller, then I could put it in my pocket and figure it out later.* The sphere came alive and a sizzling tingle of energy radiated from the orb. It shrunk to the size of a walnut and rested in Shaz's palm. He found a necklace with a locket and slipped it inside, latched it shut and slipped it over his neck. Shaz hurried back to Serin and the Minca.

"How is she?" Shaz asked as he rounded the large boulder.

"Much better," Serin said, getting to her feet.

Shaz pulled her into a tight embrace, and Serin buried her face in his chest.

"I'm so glad you're alright. I totally screwed up," Shaz said into her neck.

"Ya, you kinda did," Serin paused, "Turkill said you totally kicked but," Serin said into his chest.

Shaz laughed.

"I guess, but he's the one that kicked but. Turkill, how did you find us, anyway?" Shaz asked.

"Jagwynn brought us through the rift."

Shaz cocked his chin sideways as he thought about how she knew where it was.

"I'll explain later," Turkill said.

"Come on, we need to find Azrack," Shaz said.

Shaz took Serin's hand, and they hurried out of the cavern and along several tunnels before stopping at an intersection with several passageways exiting in all directions.

"Where do we go?" Serin asked.

Shaz shrugged and looked around.

"Follow me," Ladtwig said.

Ladtwig scurried across the cavern at an angle toward a doorway on the other side.

"How do you know?" Shaz asked.

"We got lost trying to find you," Turkill said, running after Ladtwig.

"Where is Jag?" Serin asked.

"Chasing birds," Turkill shouted over his shoulder.

****

"Where's Azrack?" Helios asked.

Helios' voice was plugged and stuffy with the bits of cloth still in his nose.

"You know that is the best sight I have seen in rotations," Ralti said, slapping Helios on the shoulder.

They burst into laughter as Helios gazed around at his comrades with a blank stare.

"I'm here," Azrack said.

Azrack came from a tunnel on the other side of the room and hobbled into the cavern.

"You look like-" Brigdon started.

"Don't say it," Azrack said, "I feel like a million gems." Azrack cocked his head and twitched his ear, "Ah, it's good to see you two," Azrack said, giving Serin a wink as they came from an adjacent tunnel.

"Who are *these* two?" Helios asked, motioning to the Minca.

"This is Turkill and Ladtwig," Serin said.

"And this?" Helios asked.

Jagwynn strode across the floor, licking her lips.

"Jagwynn," Shaz said.

"Ah, I see you had a *fowl* lunch," Azrack nodded to her and winked, "Do you have the orb?" Azrack asked Shaz.

Shaz nodded.

"Then let's move out," Ralti said.

Helios agreed to carry the Minca so he could study them as they made their way back to the surface. The last tunnel opened into a giant cavern with a crystal-clear lake. The minerals from the mountain reacted to the salty water and made it glow brighter the deeper the lake went. Water dripped from stalactites feeding the lake and sent small ripples across the glass-like surface. Along two sides of the cave were buildings carved into the rock-face, which extended deep into the mountain.

"Sire,"

Lahonti knelt on one knee, his head bowed, and his arms lifted. In his paws sat the scroll.

"What's this?" Azrack asked.

Lahonti rose and turned to address the growing crowd.

"On our sacred throne sat a gryphton who despised all things good. You have seen him flaunt our ancient laws and corrupt our customs. Each and every one of you, who serve in our noble regiment, has been forced to watch in silence as he brought foreign troops to the soil of our ancestors. You have been forced to watch as he threw away your victories. The past cannot be rewritten, but we can write the future today."

Ladtwig and Turkill scurried behind Shaz and Serin as the crowd broke into a deafening throng of roars and shrieks from the birds of prey. Jaxton, who was standing in the front of the crowd, knelt on one knee and the others followed. Lahonti read from the scroll the proclamation King Ruadan left the night he died. He gave the scroll to Azrack and knelt again with Ralti, Helios, Brigdon, Jaxton, and Pontos.

38-Let's Party!

The emotions erupting in Azrack's chest nearly overpowered him, and sounds of gentle music played behind the heavy wood doors.

"You ready?" Azrack asked.

Azrack turned and looked at Ralti, Pontos, and Jaxton, who gave him a nod. He turned to the other side and looked at Helios and Brigdon, who also nodded. Azrack stepped forward as the doors opened. The Isles of gryphton warriors stood at attention along with political leaders and scholars. In the stadium seats were the gryphton's of his kingdom. Wonderful chandeliers hung from the rock ceiling and cast glimmering rays of light from the white glow-stones. Swags of fine satins reflected the light while candled sconces lit the edges of the enormous cave. Azrack was taken back by its beauty. He tried to calm his nerves and focused his attention on Shaz and Serin, who stood at the opposite side next to Inelius and Mazark of the academy.

Lahonti stepped aside and revealed Telete, and Azrack's knees went weak. Ralti and Brigdon gripped his elbows to steady him. She smiled at him, and her beauty he had started to forget surged through his being. He hadn't seen her in rotations, and he ached to hold her once again. His heart thudded in his chest so hard he struggled to find air, and the lump in his throat was now the size of a melon. Shaz winked and looked down at the Minca and Jag standing next to him. The Minca appeared smaller than usual compared to the enormous room full of creatures that towered over all of them. Serin was pleased she was finally able to make Ladtwig wear dress clothes that fit him, but he wriggled and pulled at the fittings.

Ladtwig's favorite articles had been ripped and shredded and draped off his small body, so he had little choice, but he was not pleased. Azrack's eyes met with his men, and then each row of soldiers bent to one knee and bowed. The gryphton Armada stood and turned in perfect unison. Mazark motioned to Telete to join Azrack on the stairs. Her beautiful soft flowing lavender feathers flowed in the breeze as she rushed to him with her delicate swagger. Azrack wrapped her up in the embrace of a century, and the gryphton nation roared and shrieked with joy and salutes. Serin couldn't keep the tears from seeping out of her eyes, and her heart swelled for their reunion. Shaz too, found it hard to keep the lump in his throat from overcoming him.

Mazark waited for the reunion to ease, and he motioned for them to take their place in front of him. Azrack held out his paw and Telete put hers on his and they took the last few steps and knelt, letting the green velvet cape fall over his shoulders and brush the floor. Ralti and the others also knelt on one knee.

"As in ancient times we have gathered here to swear in our rightful king," Mazark winked at Telete, "and queen, and unite our kingdom with Edenocht," Mazark, the head monk said into the silence.

Shaz and Serin exchanged smiles, and Azrack nodded to Shaz and Serin. The monk lifted the elaborately decorated crowns from a satin pillow which sat on a stone pillar in the center of the platform.

"Behold your King and Queen," he set the King's crown on Azrack's head, and then the Queen's crown on Telete's.

The crowd erupted into a thunderous roar and Azrack rose and faced his people, then roared back to them. Azrack wore the medallion Shaz took from the witch. That way it wouldn't fall into the wrong hands again, along with ceremonial gems and jewelry once used in their old customs.

Azrack lifted his paw to quiet the crowd and allowed for the echoes to die off.

"I Azrack do solemnly swear myself to this kingdom, to guide and protect this nation from the evils that would scourge us," Azrack held out his paw and said, "I swear our solemn allegiance with the people of Edenocht as long as it is in alignment with the Dodjen, and always to my friends Shaz, Serin, Turkill, and Ladtwig."

Azrack took gold and silver medals and pinned the uniforms of his men.

"Behold the King's council."

Ralti, Helios, Brigdon, Jaxton, and Pontos bowed to Azrack, Shaz and Serin and then the gryphtons. Shaz, Inelius and the Minca bowed while Serin curtsied. Shouts and roars filled the room, and Azrack signaled for the music to begin.

"Let's party!" Ladtwig said.

Everyone burst into laughter as the music filled the room. Ladtwig scurried in and around the legs of the gryphton's toward the food table and jumped up to see what was on the tables.

"Having trouble friend?" Helios asked.

"I can't see what's up there," Ladtwig said between jumps.

"You won't like anything on this table, yours is over there," Helios said and pointed to a regular sized table.

"Thanks."

"I spent a great deal, searching out what types of foods to prepare," Helios said, but Ladtwig was long gone.

Helios laughed and picked up some raw fish rolled around the cooked remains of a Ribbard. Shaz grabbed Serin's hand and lead her to the dance floor. He wrapped his arm around her and held her tight for a moment. She looked into his eyes and smiled, and he moved her around the floor, not taking his eyes off hers.

"Are you sure they will be able to pull this off?" Mazark asked Inelius.

"Of course, why?"

"Because if their feelings get in the way, they won't be able to what is necessary," Mazark said.

"Let's hope that won't happen then."

Shaz and Serin danced in the center of the room as other gryphton pairs danced in unison around them in a circle. Turkill was having an unevenly matched arm wrestle with a gryphton cub across the room and Ladtwig, who found the table, was stuffing his face with cheese and piling a plate full of everything he could fit on it.

"So how does it feel to be the official kingdom scholar?" Ralti asked Helios.

"Good. How about you, General? And your first in command?" Helios asked.

They laughed at Brigdon who banged on his puffed-out chest showing off to several of the gryphtoness' in the corner of the room.

Azrack and Telete sat on their respective thrones holding paws and admired the wonderful festivities.

"I'm glad your back. I have missed you so much," Telete said.

"I will never leave you again," Azrack said as he gave her paw a squeeze.

****

"Are you ready?" Shaz asked.

He peeked around the door, which was half-open.

"Just about," Serin said.

She cinched the strap and flipped the top of her satchel and blew out the candle.

"Ralti and Brigdon will take us to the rift, and Azrack is waiting in the council room. He wants to talk to us before we go," Shaz said.

Serin nodded and slipped through the door. Turkill and Ladtwig came out of the kitchen arguing as usual over how much food Ladtwig talked the cook out of. They caught up with Shaz and Serin.

"We must keep this portal secure," Inelius said to Azrack.

"Yes, Helios is well informed in the nature of the portals. He has performed the needed security measures,"

"Very good," Inelius said. Shaz and the others entered the room, "Oh good, you're here,"

"Are you sure you will be able to close the rift?" Azrack asked.

"I'm sure," Shaz said.

"What about your head?" Inelius asked.

Shaz winked at Serin and nodded.

"Good there too," Shaz said.

"And us, don't forget us," Ladtwig said with half a mouth full.

Everyone laughed at Turkill who scowled at his brother who ignored him.

"Ralti and Brigdon are waiting outside," Azrack said.

He crouched down on his haunches and held his paw out to Shaz, who shook his large paw as best he could. Serin leaned in and kissed his cheek.

"Let's go," Shaz said.

The four friends left the room, leaving Azrack and Inelius next to the portal.

"You'll see them again," Inelius said.

"I hope so," Azrack said.

****

"Do we have to wear these?" Brigdon asked, fiddling with the harness.

"Yes, now stop fiddling your acting like a youngling," Ralti said.

Ralti and Brigdon were near the entrance when Shaz and Serin came out into the bright sunlight.

"At your service," Ralti said as he lowered himself onto his front paws, "Climb on."

"Are you sure?" Shaz asked.

"It's our pleasure," Ralti said.

"Not mine," Brigdon grumbled under his breath.

Ralti elbowed him, and Brigdon lowered himself onto all fours.

"Well, can I at least carry the pretty one?" Brigdon asked.

Serin stretched onto her tippy toes and kissed Brigdon's cheek and Brigdon smiled and Serin climbed onto his back. Shaz patted Brigdon's shoulder who nodded then climbed onto Ralti.

"What about us?" Turkill asked in a huff. Ralti pointed to a basket with straps. "I'm not riding in that," Turkill huffed.

"Where's the cat?" Ralti asked.

"She's already gone, on her way back through the rift," Shaz said.

Ladtwig jumped with glee and hopped into the basket.

"Then stay here," Ladtwig said to Turkill.

Turkill huffed again and climbed into the basket. Ralti lifted off and grabbed the straps of the basket. The Minca held onto the edges as it shifted and lifted off the ground and the gryphton's flew into the morning sun. Ladtwig hollered as the wind blew in his hair and stood at the front of the basket and looked out over the mountain peaks. Turkill sat inside and gripped the edges tightly. A forest that stretched for hours soon replaced the high mountains and after a full day of flying, they located the marks Azrack gave them and descended. Ralti lowered the basket to the ground and let go of the straps. Brigdon landed behind Ralti, and Shaz and Serin climbed down.

"Thank you. I know it's not your way to let humans ride you," Shaz said.

"We are a prideful race, but we are also driven by honor," Ralti said.

Ralti stretched his toes as Brigdon stretched his back.

"Thank you," Serin said.

Brigdon bowed and whispered, "The honor is mine."

Shaz searched for the rift and at first, all he saw were more trees and rocks, until he realized one of the rocks was actually behind him.

"It's a mirror image," he said.

"The barrier?" Serin asked.

"Yeah look," he said, pointing to the rocks.

"Wow, that's pretty nifty," Ladtwig said, looking back and forth.

Turkill's brown complexion was tainted with a hint of green as he climbed out of the basket and puked behind a rock.

"I don't see it?" Serin said.

"Over there," Ralti said, pointing to his right.

"I do," Shaz said.

He set his pack down and stepped toward what appeared to be a broken reflection and touched the gel-like illumination.

"It's strong," Shaz said.

"Can you close it?" Ralti asked.

"Yes, but it's going to be difficult and I'm going to need your help, Serin," he said.

"We best get to it. Turkill you ready yet?" Serin asked.

Turkill came out from around the rock.

"Are we staying on land?" Turkill asked. Serin smiled and nodded. He reached into the basket and grabbed his pack. "Then let's go."

Ladtwig grabbed his overstuffed pack and tried to throw it over his shoulder, but it pulled him over, so he dragged it in the dirt.

"Why don't you leave half that here?" Serin asked.

"Because I am not about to starve," he said.

"I can't believe how much you can eat and be so small," she said.

The Minca stepped through the rift with Serin behind them.

"Until we see you again," Shaz said to the Gryphton warriors.

"Until then," they said together.

The time shift was like the one on the sea, and they watched the evening sky pass by and then turn to night. Stars whipped passed as they stood still, and a hefty burst of air blew past them, making them unsteady. The wind stopped and the early morning sun capped the familiar mountains. The breaking rays gave enough light for them to see the rift on the other side.

"This is going to take some time," Shaz said.

"I'll make a sweep of the area and be back," Turkill said.

"I'm not looking forward to this," Shaz said quietly to Serin.

"I know, but I'm here," she said.

Shaz took in a deep breath and concentrated all his efforts on the feeling his magic and the shadow magic gave him. His new understanding of how to use shadow magic gave him the command of it, but what he didn't know, however, was if it would still expect payment. He was tiring of the headaches it caused and was glad that Serin could heal his body from its payment. Serin drew from the elements of the water and air. A bright white light grew until it was big enough to surround Shaz. She let it drift toward him, and Shaz felt the added protection in his mind and chest and sent his energy into his hands.

He gripped the edges of the torn fabric of time and pulled. The tug the fabric made strained his muscles, and his breathing increased as the pressure pulled against him. He dug his feet into the ground and felt Ladtwig pushing against one leg, and a moment later Turkill gripped his other leg. Shaz felt the warmth come from the love of his friends and his heart swelled. The heat of its power stifled the pain the shadow was trying to inflict, and he was able to focus his thoughts on the fabric and pulled with all his might. The wall of magic inched closer but was resisting.

Serin sensed Shaz's muscles getting tired, and she pulled more energy from the elements and released another cast of magic. Shaz felt the energy and the fresh surge of power. *You can use the elements too,* the words came into his mind. He extended his mind into the forest around him and pulled from its energy. A course thudding-like vibration eased over the landscape and sank into the barrier. The rift responded and moved together slowly. A vision flashed across Shaz's mind as the surrounding energy flooded his senses. With the last few inches near, Shaz struggled to keep his thoughts on the rift and not the vision. It disturbed him as he watched a young boy incinerate a flight of gryphton's. He thought back to Azrack's story in the forest and something nudged at his understanding, but he didn't know why.

"Shaz concentrate, your almost there," Serin said.

Shaz refocused and imagined the fabric binding itself together. A gush of wind escaped the last few inches before it locked shut. Turkill and Ladtwig tumbled as Shaz fell to the ground, breathing heavily. Serin lowered her arms and rested on a large rock.

"You did it," Serin said.

Shaz looked up and with sweat dripping down his face.

"No, we did it."

"So now to the Mountains of Bair?" Serin asked.

Shaz nodded and picked up his pack.

"We're coming too," Turkill said.

"I wouldn't have it any other way," Shaz said.

To Be Continued…

www.ingramcontent.com/pod-product-compliance
Lightning Source LLC
Chambersburg PA
CBHW071740110726
47908CB00006B/1643